Readers are buzzing about *White Hot Kiss*!

"Jennifer L. Armentrout is a master of weaving rich contemporary realism with magic and mayhem. Her characters will grab hold of your heart and refuse to let go. Every page left me wanting more."
—*New York Times* bestselling author Brigid Kemmerer

"I know I spend a portion of any review of [Armentrout's] books raving about how epic she is, but really, I've yet to read something written by her that wasn't awesome and this is no exception."
—Tabitha, *Bows & Bullets Reviews*

"I have so many feelings right now... How does Jennifer L. Armentrout do this to me every single time? Gargoyles, demons, aliens, humans, it doesn't matter what she writes about. She has this knack for making me fall in love with her stories and her characters. Completely."
—Sheri, *Tangled Up In Books*

"So far I have to say the Dark Elements series is my favorite! *White Hot Kiss* is a phenomenal start to a spectacular dark and lush series!"
—*Enchanting Reviews*

"*White Hot Kiss* was one of my most anticipated reads of the year... and the wait to read it was killing me, so I was very happy it arrived on release day and had to speed through my current read so I could get to this one. And. It. Was. Awesome."
—Jessica S.

"I am obsessed—utterly obsessed with Ms. Armentrout's books... Like Sarah J. Maas, Ms. Armentrout is a master."
—Diana, The Book Nerd

Available by Jennifer L. Armentrout

The Dark Elements series

WHITE HOT KISS
STONE COLD TOUCH
EVERY LAST BREATH

A Dark Elements ebook novella

BITTER SWEET LOVE

For a complete list of titles by Jennifer L. Armentrout,
please visit jenniferlarmentrout.com.

#1 *NEW YORK TIMES* BESTSELLING AUTHOR

JENNIFER L. ARMENTROUT

WHITE HOT KISS

The DARK ELEMENTS

CANARY STREET PRESS

CANARY
STREET
PRESS™

Recycling programs
for this product may
not exist in your area.

ISBN-13: 978-1-335-01252-4

White Hot Kiss

First published as White Hot Kiss in 2014. This edition published in 2024.

For questions and comments about the quality of this book, please contact us at CustomerService@Harlequin.com.

TM is a trademark of Harlequin Enterprises ULC.

Canary Street Press
22 Adelaide St. West, 41st Floor
Toronto, Ontario M5H 4E3, Canada
CanaryStPress.com

Printed in U.S.A.

WHITE HOT KISS

The DARK ELEMENTS

1

THERE WAS A DEMON IN MCDONALD'S.

And it had a powerful hunger for Big Macs.

Most days, I loved my after-school job. Tagging the soul-less and the damned usually gave me a mad case of the warm fuzzies. I'd even given myself a quota out of boredom, but to-night was different.

I had a paper to outline for AP English.

"Are you gonna eat those fries?" Sam asked as he grabbed a handful off my tray. His curly brown hair fell over his wire-frame glasses. "Thanks."

"Just don't take her sweet tea." Stacey slapped Sam's arm and several fries fell to the floor. "You'll lose your entire arm."

I stopped tapping my foot, but kept my eye on the interloper. I don't know what it was with demons and the Golden Arches, but man, they loved the place. "Ha-ha."

"Who do you keep staring at, Layla?" Stacey twisted in the booth, looking around the crowded fast-food joint. "Is it a hot guy? If so, you better— *Oh.* Wow. Who goes out in public dressed like that?"

"What?" Sam turned, too. "Aw, come on, Stacey. Who cares? Not everyone wears knockoff Prada like you."

To them, the demon looked like a harmless middle-aged woman with really bad fashion sense. Her dull brown hair was pinned up with one of those old-school purple butterfly clips. She wore velvet green track pants paired with pink sneakers, but it was her sweater that was epic. Someone had knitted a basset hound on the front, its big, sappy eyes made of brown yarn.

But despite her drab appearance, the lady wasn't human.

Not that I had a lot of room to talk.

She was a Poser demon. Her astronomical appetite was what gave away the breed. Posers could eat a small nation's worth of food in one sitting.

Posers might look and act human, but I knew this one could snap the head off the person in the booth next to her with little effort. Her inhuman strength wasn't the threat, though. It was the Poser's teeth and infectious saliva that were the real danger.

They were biters.

One little nip and the demonic version of rabies was passed to the human. Totally incurable, and within three days, the Poser's chew toy would resemble something straight out of a George Romero flick, cannibalistic tendencies included.

Obviously, Posers were a real problem unless you considered a zombie apocalypse fun times. Only good thing was that Posers were rare, and every time one bit somebody, its life span was shortened. They usually had about seven good bites in them before they went poof. Sort of like a bee and its stinger but dumber.

Posers could look like anything they wanted. Why this one was rocking an outfit like that was beyond me.

Stacey made a face as the Poser moved on to her third burger. She wasn't aware of us watching her. Posers weren't known for their keen powers of observation, especially when preoccupied with secret-sauce awesomeness.

"That's disgusting." Stacey turned back around.

"I think the sweater is hot." Sam grinned around another mouthful of my fries. "Hey, Layla, do you think Zayne would let me interview him for the school paper?"

My brows rose. "Why do you want to interview him?"

He gave me a knowing look. "To ask what's it like to be a Warden in D.C., hunting down the bad guys and bringing them to justice and all that jazz."

Stacey giggled. "You make the Wardens sound like superheroes."

Sam shrugged bony shoulders. "Well, they kind of are. I mean, come on, you've seen them."

"They're not superheroes," I said, falling into the standard speech I'd been giving ever since the Wardens went public ten years ago. After the skyrocketing increase in crime that had nothing to do with the economic downturn the world faced, but was more like a signal from Hell saying they no longer wanted to play by the rules, the Alphas had ordered the Wardens to come out of the shadows. To humans, Wardens had come out of their stone shells. After all, the gargoyles adorning many churches and buildings had been carved to resemble a Warden in his true skin. Sort of.

There were too many demons topside for the Wardens to continue to operate without exposure. "They're people. Just like you, but—"

"I know." Sam held up his hands. "Look, you know I'm not like those fanatics who think they're evil or something stupid like that. I just think it's cool and it would be a great piece in the paper. So what do you think? Would Zayne go for it?"

I shifted uncomfortably. Living with the Wardens often made me one of two things: a back door to gain access to them, or a freak. Because everyone, including my two closest friends, believed I was just like them. Human. "I don't know, Sam. I don't think any form of press makes them comfortable."

He looked crestfallen. "Will you ask him at least?"

"Sure." I fiddled with my straw. "But don't hold your breath."

Sam leaned against the hard seat back, satisfied. "So guess what?"

"What?" Stacey sighed, exchanging a woeful look with me. "What random piece of knowledge are you going to wow us with?"

"Did you know you can freeze a banana until it's so hard you can actually nail something with it?"

I lowered my sweet tea. "How do you know these things?"

Sam finished off my fries. "I just do."

"He spends his entire life on the computer." Stacey pushed thick black bangs off her face. I don't know why she didn't cut them. She was always messing with them. "Probably searches for random crap for the fun of it."

"That's exactly what I do when I'm at home." Sam rolled up his napkin. "I search for little-known facts. That's how cool I am." He threw the napkin at Stacey's face.

"I stand corrected," Stacey said unabashedly. "It's porn you spend all night searching."

The hollows of Sam's cheeks turned bright red as he straightened his glasses. "Whatever. Are you guys ready? We've got some outlining to do for English."

Stacey groaned. "I can't believe Mr. Leto wouldn't let us do our classics report on *Twilight*. It *is* a classic."

I laughed, momentarily forgetting about the job I had to do. "*Twilight* is not a classic, Stacey."

"Edward is definitely a classic in my book." She pulled a hair tie out of her pocket, tugging her shoulder-length hair up. "And *Twilight* is way more interesting than *All Quiet on the Western Front*."

Sam shook his head. "I can't believe you just used *Twilight* and *All Quiet on the Western Front* in the same sentence."

Ignoring him, her gaze bounced from my face to my food. "Layla, you haven't even touched your burger."

Maybe somehow I'd instinctively known I was going to need a reason to stick around. I sucked in a sigh. "You guys go ahead. I'll meet up with you in a few minutes."

"For real?" Sam stood.

"Yep." I picked up my burger. "I'll be down in a few."

Stacey eyed me suspiciously. "You're not going to bail on us like you always do?"

I flushed with guilt. I'd lost count of how many times I'd had to ditch them. "No. I swear. I'm just going to eat my food and I'll be right there."

"Come on." Sam wrapped an arm around Stacey's shoulders, steering her toward the trash can. "Layla would've been done eating by now if you hadn't talked to her the entire time."

"Oh, blame it on me." Stacey dumped her trash, sending me a wave as they headed out.

I set the burger back down, watching Lady Poser impatiently. Pieces of bun and meat fell out of her mouth, splattering on the brown tray. My appetite was effectively slaughtered within seconds. Not that it really mattered. Food only eased the ache gnawing at my insides, never stopping it.

Lady Poser finally completed her feast of fatness, and I grabbed my bag as she ambled out the door. She plowed straight into an elderly man, knocking him right over as he tried to come in. Wow. This one was a real gem.

Her cackle could be heard inside the noisy restaurant, sounding as thin as paper. Luckily, some dude helped the man up as he shook his fist at the retreating demon.

Sighing, I dumped my food and followed her out into the late-September breeze.

Different shades of souls were everywhere, humming around bodies like an electrical field. Traces of pale pink and robin's-egg blue trailed behind a couple walking hand in hand. They had innocent souls—but not pure.

All humans had a soul—an essence—good or bad, but demons weren't rocking any such thing. Since *most* demons topside looked human at first glance, the lack of soul around them made my job of finding and tagging them easy. Besides the soulless factor, the only difference between them and humans was the odd way their eyes reflected light like a cat's.

Lady Poser shuffled down the street, limping slightly. Out in the natural light, she didn't look well. She'd probably already bit a few humans, which meant she needed to be tagged and dealt with ASAP.

A flyer on a green lamppost caught my attention. A fierce scowl and sense of protectiveness filled me as I read the thing. Warning. Wardens Aren't God's Children. Repent Now. The End Is Nigh.

Underneath the words was a crudely drawn picture of what I assumed was a rabid coyote mixed with a chupacabra.

"Sponsored by the Church of God's Children," I muttered, rolling my eyes.

Nice. I hated fanatics.

A diner down the block had the flyers plastered across its windows and a sign proclaiming they refused to serve Wardens.

Anger spread through me like an out-of-control wildfire. These idiots had no idea of all that the Wardens sacrificed for them. I drew in a deep breath, letting it out slowly. I needed to focus on my Poser instead of silently stomping my mental feet on my pretend soapbox.

Lady Poser turned a corner and glanced over her shoulder, her glassy eyes drifting over me, dismissing me outright. The demon in her didn't sense anything abnormal about me.

The demon inside of *me* was in a hurry to get this over with.

Especially after my cell went off, vibrating against my thigh. Probably Stacey wondering where in the Hell I was. I just wanted to be done with this and go back to being normal for the rest of the evening. Without thinking, I reached up and pulled on the chain around my neck. The old ring dangling off the silver rope felt hot and heavy in my hand.

As I passed a group of kids around my age, their gazes moved over me, stopped and then swung right back. Of course they stared. Everyone did.

My hair was long. Big deal there, but it was such a pale blond that it looked nearly white. I hated when people stared. It made me feel like an albino. But it was my eyes that really caught people's attention. They were a light gray, almost leached of color.

Zayne said I looked like the long-lost sister of the elf in *Lord of the Rings*. *That* was a huge confidence booster. Sigh.

Dusk had begun to settle in the nation's capital as I rounded Rhode Island Avenue and came to a complete stop. Everything and everyone around me disappeared in an instant. There, in the soft flicker of the street lamps, I saw the soul.

It looked as if someone had dipped a brush into red paint and then flicked it over a soft black canvas. This guy had a bad soul. He wasn't under the influence of a demon, but was just plain old evil all on his own. The dull ache in my gut flared to life. People pushed past me, casting annoyed looks in my direction. A few even muttered. I didn't care. I didn't even care about their soft pink souls, a color I usually found so pretty.

I finally focused on the figure behind the soul—an older man dressed in a generic business suit and tie, briefcase handle clutched in a meaty hand. Nothing to run from, nothing to be frightened of, but I knew different.

He'd sinned *big-time*.

My legs moved forward even as my brain screamed at me to stop, to turn around, even to call Zayne. Just hearing his voice would make me stop. Would stop me from doing what every cell in my body demanded I do—doing what was *almost* natural to me.

The man turned slightly, his eyes drifting over my face, down my body. His soul swirled crazy fast, becoming more red than black. He was old enough to be my father and that was gross, really gross.

He smiled at me, smiled in a way that should've sent me running in the other direction. I needed to go in that direction, too, because no matter how rotten this man was—no matter how many girls out there would hand me a gold medal for taking him out—Abbot had raised me to deny the demon inside. He'd raised me to be a Warden, to act like a Warden.

But Abbot wasn't here.

I met the man's stare, held it and felt my lips curve into a smile. My heart raced, my skin tingled and flushed. I wanted his soul—so bad my skin wanted to peel itself off my bones. It felt like waiting for a kiss, when your lips were moments away from joining, those breathless seconds of anticipation. But I'd never been kissed before.

All I had was *this*.

This man's soul called to me like a siren's song. It sickened me to be so tempted by the evil in his spirit, but a dark soul was as good as a pure one.

He smiled as he eyed me, his knuckles blanching around the handle of the briefcase. And that smile made me think of all the horrible things he could have done to earn the swirling void around him.

An elbow dug into my lower back. The tiny speck of pain was nothing compared to the exquisite anticipation. Just a few more steps and his soul would be so close—*right there*. I knew the first taste would spark the sweetest fire imaginable—a high for which there was no equivalent. It wouldn't last very long, but the brief moments of pure ecstasy lingered as a potent allure.

His lips wouldn't even need to touch mine. Just an inch or so, and I'd taste his soul—never take it all. Taking his soul would kill him and that was evil, and I wasn't—

This was evil.

I jerked back, breaking eye contact. Pain exploded in my stomach, shooting through my limbs. Turning away from the man was like denying my lungs of oxygen. My skin burned and my throat felt raw as I forced one leg in front of the other. It was a struggle to keep walking, to not think about the man and to find the Poser again, but when I finally spotted her, I let out the breath I was holding. Focusing on the demon at least served as a distraction.

I followed her into a narrow alley between a dollar store and a check-cashing place. All I needed to do was touch her, which I should've done back in McDonald's. I stopped halfway, looked around and then cursed.

The alley was empty.

Black garbage bags lined mold-covered brick walls. Dumpsters overflowed with more trash and creatures scurried along the gravel. I shuddered, eyeing the bags warily. Most likely rats, but other things hid in shadows—things that were worse than rats.

And a Hell of a lot creepier.

I walked farther in, scanning the darkening passage as I absently twisted the necklace between my fingers. I wished I'd had the foresight to pack a flashlight in my schoolbag, but that would've made too much sense. Instead I'd put a new tube of lip gloss and baggie full of cookies in there this morning. Real helpful stuff.

Sudden unease trickled down my spine. I dropped the ring, letting it bounce off my shirt. Something wasn't right. I slipped my hand into the front pocket of my jeans, pulling out my beat-up cell as I turned around.

The Poser stood a few feet away. When she smiled, the wrinkles in her face cracked her skin. Thin slivers of lettuce hung from her yellow teeth. I took a breath and immediately wished I hadn't. She smelled of sulfur and rotting flesh.

The Poser cocked her head to the side, eyes narrowing. No demon could sense me, because I didn't have enough demonic blood flowing in my veins for them to pick it up, but she was looking at me like she was truly *seeing* what I hid inside.

Her gaze dropped to my chest and then her eyes flicked up, meeting mine. I let out a startled gasp. Her washed-out blue irises began to churn like a whirlpool around pupils that retracted into a thin point.

Crap on a cracker. This lady was so not a Poser.

Her form rippled and then scrambled, like a TV trying to digitally piece back together an image. The gray hair and banana clip disappeared. Creased skin smoothed out and turned the color of wax. The body stretched and expanded. The track pants and horrible sweater disappeared and were replaced by leather pants and a broad, muscular chest. The eyes were oval-shaped and churned like an endless sea—no pupils. The nose was flat, really just two holes above a wide, cruel mouth.

Double crap on a cracker the size of my butt.

It was a Seeker demon. I'd only ever seen one in the old books Abbot kept in his study. Seekers were like the Indiana Joneses of the demon world, able to locate and retrieve just about anything their handler sent them after. Unlike Indy, though, Seekers were mean and aggressive.

The Seeker smiled, revealing a mouth full of wicked-sharp teeth. "Gotcha."

Gotcha? Got what? *Me?*

He lurched toward me and I darted to the side, fear spiking so fast my palms dotted with sweat as I touched his arm. Bursts of neon light shimmered around the Seeker's body, making him nothing but a pink blur. He didn't react to the tag. They never did. Only the Wardens could see the mark I left behind.

The Seeker grasped a handful of my hair, wrenching my head to the side as he grabbed for the front of my shirt. My cell slipped from my hand, smacking on the ground. A stinging sensation shot down my neck, over my shoulders.

Panic flooded like a dam had burst open, but instinct propelled me into action. All the evenings I'd spent training with Zayne kicked in. Tagging demons could get hairy every once in a while, and while I didn't have ninja-stealth skills, there was no way in holy Hell I was going down without a fight.

Rearing back, I brought my leg up and planted my knee right where it counted. Thank God demons were anatomically correct. The Seeker grunted and jerked back, ripping out several strands of hair. Red hot pins and needles burned across my scalp.

Unlike other Wardens, I couldn't shed my human skin and kick major behind, but hair-pulling flipped my bitch switch like no one's business.

Agony exploded along my knuckles as the Seeker's head jerked to the side when my closed fist hit him in the jaw. It wasn't a girlie hit. Zayne would be so proud.

Slowly, the demon turned his head back to me. "I liked that. Do it again."

My eyes popped wide.

It rushed me, and I knew I was going to die. I'd be ripped apart by a demon or worse yet, pulled through one of the many portals hidden throughout the city and taken *downstairs*. When people inexplicably disappeared into thin air, it was usually because they had a new zip code. Something like 666, and death would be a blessing compared to that kind of trip. I braced myself for impact.

"Enough."

Both of us froze in response to the deep, unfamiliar voice oozing authority. The Seeker responded first, stepping to the side. Turning around, I saw *him*.

The newcomer stood well over six feet, as tall as any Warden. His hair was dark, the color of obsidian, and it reflected blue in the dim light. Lazy locks slipped over his forehead and curled just below his ears. Brows arched over golden eyes and his cheekbones were broad and high. He was attractive. Very attractive. Mind-bendingly beautiful, actually, but the sardonic twist to his full lips chilled his beauty. The black T-shirt stretched across his chest and flat stomach. A huge tattoo of a snake curled around his forearm, the tail disappearing under his sleeve and the diamond-shaped head rested on the top of his hand. He looked my age. Total crush material—if it wasn't for the fact that he had no soul.

I stumbled a step back. What was worse than one demon? Two demons. My knees shook so bad I thought I might face-plant in the alley. A tagging had never gone this horribly wrong before. I was so screwed it wasn't even funny.

"You should not intervene in this," the Seeker demon said, and his hands curled into fists.

The new guy stepped forward noiselessly. "And you should kiss my ass. How about that?"

Uh…

The Seeker grew very still, his breathing heavy. Tension became a fourth entity in the alley. I took another step back, hoping to make a clean getaway. These two were so obviously not on the same page with one another and I did not want to get caught in the middle of this. When two demons went at it, they were known to bring down entire buildings. Faulty foundations or poor roofing? Yeah, right. More like an epic demon death match.

Two steps to the right and I could—

The boy's gaze slammed into me. I sucked in air, staggered by the intensity of his gaze. The strap of my bag fell from my limp fingers. His eyes lowered, thick lashes fanning his cheeks. A small smile pulled at his lips, and when he spoke, his voice was soft, yet deep and powerful. "What a predicament you've gotten yourself into."

I didn't know what breed of demon he was, but by the way

he stood there like he'd created the word *power,* I figured he wasn't a lower demon like the Seeker or a Poser. Oh, no, he was most likely an Upper Level demon—a Duke or Infernal Ruler. Only the Wardens dealt with them, and that usually ended in a bloody mess.

My heart threw itself against my rib cage. I needed to get out of here and fast. No way was I going toe-to-toe with an Upper Level demon. My measly skills would earn me a butt kicking to remember. And the Seeker demon was growing angrier by the second, clenching and unclenching his meaty fists. Things were about to blow and blow bad.

Grabbing my book bag, I held it in front of me like the lamest shield ever. Then again, there wasn't a thing in this world besides a Warden that could stop an Upper Level demon.

"Wait," he said. "Don't run off yet."

"Don't think about coming any closer," I warned.

"I wouldn't think of doing anything you didn't want me to do."

Ignoring whatever that meant, I continued to edge around the Seeker demon and toward the mouth of the alley that seemed so incredibly far away.

"You're running anyway." The Upper Level demon sighed. "Even after I asked you not to, and I think I was really nice about it." He glanced at the Seeker, frowning. "Wasn't I nice?"

The Seeker growled. "I mean no offense, but I don't care how nice you are. You're interrupting my job, you tool."

I stumbled over the insult. Besides the fact that the Seeker was speaking to an Upper Level demon like that, it was such a...*human* thing to say.

"You know what they say," the other demon countered. "Sticks and stones may break your bones, but I'm going to demolish you."

Screw this. If I got back on the main street, I could lose both of them. They couldn't attack in front of the humans—

rules and all. Well, if these two were going to play by the rules, which seemed doubtful. I whipped around, dashing toward the opening of the alley.

I didn't make it very far.

The Seeker hit me like a freaking NFL linebacker, knocking me against a Dumpster. Black spots darkened my vision. Something squeaky and furry dropped on my head. Shrieking like a banshee, I reached up and grabbed hold of the squirming body. Little claws tangled in my hair. Two seconds from stroking out, I yanked the rat out of my hair and tossed it onto the garbage bags. It squeaked as it bounced, then darted into a crack in the wall.

With a low snarl, the Upper Level demon appeared behind the Seeker, grabbing him by the throat. A second later, he had the Seeker dangling several feet off the ground. "Now, *that* wasn't very nice," he said in a low, ominous voice.

Spinning around, he tossed the Seeker like a beanbag. The Seeker slammed into the opposite wall, hitting the ground on his knees. The Upper Level demon raised his arm…and the snake tattoo lifted off his skin, breaking apart into a million black dots. They floated into the air between him and the Seeker, hung for a second, then dropped to the ground. The dots oozed together, forming a thick black mass.

No—not a mass, but a huge freaking snake at least ten feet long and as wide as I was. I sprang to my feet, ignoring the wave of dizziness.

The thing spun toward me, rising halfway up. Its eyes burned an unholy red.

A scream caught in my throat.

"Don't be scared of Bambi," the demon said. "She's only curious and maybe a little bit hungry."

The thing was named *Bambi?*

Oh, my God, the thing stared at me like it wanted to eat me.

The…the giant snake didn't try to make me his snack pack.

When it swung back toward the Seeker, I nearly fell over from relief. But then it shot across the small space, rising until its monstrous head hovered over the petrified lesser demon. The snake opened its mouth, revealing two fangs the size of my hand and, past them, a yawning black hole.

"Okay," the demon murmured, smirking. "Maybe she's a lot hungry."

I took that as my cue to book it out of the alley.

"Wait!" yelled the demon, and when I didn't stop but ran faster than I ever had before, his curse echoed in my head.

I crossed the avenues bordering Dupont Circle, passing the shop I'd planned on joining Stacey and Sam at. Only when I reached the spot where Morris, our chauffeur and about a dozen other things, would pick me up did I stop to breathe.

The gently hued souls thrummed around me, but I didn't pay attention to them. Numb to my core, I sat on a bench by the curb. I felt wrong, off. What the Hell had just happened? All I'd wanted to do was outline *All Quiet on the Western Front* tonight. Not almost devour a soul, nearly get killed, meet my very first Upper Level demon or watch a tattoo turn into an anaconda for chrissake.

I glanced down at my empty hand.

Or lose my phone.

Crap.

MORRIS DIDN'T TALK ON THE way to the house on Dunmore Lane. No big surprise there. Morris never spoke. Maybe it was the stuff he saw going on inside our house that left him speechless. I really didn't know.

Fidgety to the tenth degree from sitting on the bench for about an hour waiting on Morris, I bounced my foot on the dashboard the whole way home. It was only four miles, but four miles in D.C. equaled a billion miles elsewhere. The only part of the trip that went fast was the private stretch of road leading up to Abbot's monster of a home.

With four stories, countless guest rooms and even an indoor pool, it was more like a hotel than a home. It really was a compound—a place where the unmarried male Wardens in the clan lived and operated like command central. As we drew closer, I blinked and let out a muttered curse that earned me a disapproving look from Morris.

Six stone gargoyles that hadn't been there this morning were perched on the edge of our rooftop. Visitors. Great.

I pulled my feet down from the dashboard and grabbed

my bag off the floor. Even with their wings folded in and faces turned down, the hunched shapes were a formidable sight against the starry night.

In their resting form, Wardens were nearly indestructible. Fire couldn't harm them. Chisels and hammers couldn't breach their shell. People had tried every form of weapon since the Wardens went public. So had the demons since, well, forever, but Wardens were only weak when they looked human.

The moment the car drifted to a stop in front of the sprawling porch, I jumped out and tore up the steps, skidding to a halt in front of the door. In the upper-left corner of the porch, a small camera shifted to where I stood. The light blinked red. Somewhere in the massive rooms and tunnels under the mansion, Geoff was in the control room and behind the camera. No doubt getting a kick out of making me wait.

I stuck out my tongue.

The light turned green a second later.

Rolling my eyes when I heard the door unlocking, I opened it and dropped my bag in the foyer. Immediately, I started toward the stairs. After a second thought, I swiveled around and raced toward the kitchen. Finding the room blissfully empty, I dug out a roll of sugar-cookie dough from the fridge. I broke off a chunk and then headed upstairs. The house was cemetery quiet. At this time of the day, most would be in the training facility underground or had already left to hunt.

All except Zayne. For as long as I could remember, Zayne had never left to hunt without seeing me first.

I took the steps three at a time, munching on the dough. Wiping my sticky fingers across my denim skirt, I nudged his door open with my hip and froze. I seriously needed to learn how to knock.

I saw his pearly-white, luminous glow first—a pure soul. Different from a human soul, a Warden's essence was pure, a product of what they were. Very few humans retained a pure soul once they started exercising the whole thing called free will. Due to the taint of the demonic blood I carried, I knew I didn't have a pure soul. I wasn't sure I had a soul at all. I could never see mine.

Sometimes...sometimes I didn't think I belonged with them—with Zayne.

A sense of shame curled low in my stomach, but before it could spread like noxious fumes, Zayne's soul faded, and I wasn't really thinking about anything.

Fresh out of the shower, Zayne tugged a plain black T-shirt on over his head. Not quick enough that I missed a tantalizing glimpse of abs. Rigorous training kept his body chiseled and rock hard. I dragged my gaze up when the stretch of skin disappeared. Damp sandy hair clung to his neck and sculpted cheeks. His features would be too perfect if it weren't for those watered-down blue eyes all Wardens had.

I shuffled to the edge of his bed and sat. I shouldn't think of Zayne the way I did. He was the closest thing I had to a brother. His father, Abbot, had raised us together and Zayne looked at me like the little sister he somehow ended up saddled with.

"What's up, Layla-bug?" he asked.

Part of me loved it when he used my childhood nickname. The other part—the part that wasn't a little girl anymore— loathed it. I peeked at him through my lashes. He was fully clothed now. What a shame. "Who's on the roof?"

He sat beside me. "A few travelers from out of town needed a place to rest. Abbot offered them beds, but they preferred the roof. They didn't—" He stopped suddenly, leaning forward, grabbing my leg. "Why are your knees scuffed up?"

My brain sort of shorted out the moment his hand touched my bare leg. A hot flush stole over my cheeks, spreading way, way down. I gazed at his high cheekbones and those lips—oh, God, those lips were perfect. A thousand fantasies blossomed.

All of them involved him, me and the ability to kiss him without sucking out his soul.

"Layla, what did you get into tonight?" He dropped my leg.

I shook my head, dispelling those hopeless dreams. "Um... well, nothing."

Zayne moved closer, staring at me as if he could see through my lies. He had an uncanny ability to do so. But if I told him everything, like the Upper Level demon part, they'd never let me leave the house alone. I liked my freedom. It was about the only thing I had.

I sighed. "I thought I was following a Poser."

"And you weren't?"

"Nope." I wished he'd touch my leg again. "It turned out to be a Seeker pretending to be a Poser."

Amazing how quickly he went from superhot guy to all serious-faced Warden. "What do you mean the Seeker was pretending?"

I forced a casual shrug. "I really don't know. I saw it in McDonald's. It had the appetite of a Poser and behaved like one, so I followed it. Turned out it wasn't a Poser, but I tagged him."

"That doesn't make sense." His brow pinched, a common expression whenever he was turning over something in his head. "Seeker demons are errand boys, or they're summoned by some idiot to find something stupid like frog eyes or the blood of a bald eagle for a spell that will inevitably backfire. Pretending to be a Poser is not typical."

I remembered what the Seeker had said. *Gotcha.* As if it had been looking for me. I knew I needed to tell Zayne that, but his father was already overbearing when it came to where I went and who I was with. And Zayne was pretty much required to tell his father everything since Abbot was the head of the D.C. clan of Wardens. Besides, I had to have misheard the Seeker, and demons rarely had a reason for doing weird or unexpected things. They were demons. Explanation enough.

"Are you okay?" Zayne asked.

"Yeah, I'm fine." I paused. "I did lose my phone, though."

He laughed, and oh man, I loved the sound of his laugh. Deep. Rich. "Jesus, Layla, how many does that make so far this year?"

"Five." I stared at his heavily stocked bookcases, sighing. "Abbot isn't going to get me another one. He thinks I lose them on purpose. I don't. They just...unfriend me."

Zayne laughed again, nudging me with his denim-clad knee. "How many did you tag tonight?"

I thought about the few hours after school, before I met up with Stacey and Sam. "Nine. Two were Posers and the rest were Fiends, with the exception of the Seeker." Which Zayne would probably never find since there was a good chance Bambi had eaten it.

Zayne gave a low whistle. "Nice. I'll have a busy night."

And that was what Wardens did. Generation after generation, they'd been keeping the demon population in check since long before they went public. I was only seven when it happened, so I didn't remember how the public responded. I'm sure the big reveal included a whole lot of freaking out. Oddly enough, I moved in with them around the same time.

The Alphas, the angelic guys who ran the show, understood that there needed to be good and bad in the world—the Law of Balance. But something happened ten years ago. Demons began pouring through the portals by the buttload, creating chaos as they wreaked havoc on everything they came in contact with. Possession of humans became a huge problem, and things spiraled out of control at that point. Hell's lovelies no longer wanted to stay in the shadows and the Alphas couldn't have mankind knowing that demons were real. Abbot once told me it had to do with free will and faith. Man needed to believe in God without knowing Hell truly existed. Willing to do anything to keep mankind in the dark about the demons, the Alphas had issued their mandate. Seemed like a big risk and that humans would eventually add one plus one and get demons, but what did I know?

Only a select few humans knew the truth. Besides Morris, there were some within the police departments, the government and surely military personnel around the world who knew demons existed. Those humans had their own reasons for keeping the general populace in the dark, reasons that had nothing to do with faith. The world would descend into chaos if humans knew demons were ordering their morning coffee right alongside them.

But that was the way it worked. Wardens helped the police departments with capturing criminals, and some of those criminals hunted down were demons, who may have had a get-out-of-jail-free card, but who went straight back to Hell and did not pass Go. If the demons ever exposed themselves to the world, the Alphas would destroy all the demons that were topside, including my happy half-demon butt.

"Things are getting kind of crazy," he said, mostly to himself. "There's a Hell of a lot more Poser activity. Some of the Wardens in different districts have even run into Hellions."

My eyes popped. "Hellions?"

As Zayne nodded, an image of the overgrown, beastly things formed in my thoughts. Hellions weren't supposed to be topside. They were like cracked-out mutant apes and pit bulls rolled into one.

Zayne bent at the waist, rummaging under his bed. Strands of hair fell forward, obscuring his face. I could openly gawk now. Zayne was only four years older than me, but being a Warden, he was a lot more mature than most human guys his age. I knew everything about him, except what he *really* looked like.

That was the thing about gargoyles. The skin they wore during the day wasn't who they were. For the millionth time, I wondered about Zayne's real appearance. His human skin was hotness, but unlike the others he never allowed me to see his true form.

And since I was only half-Warden, I couldn't shift like a normal one could. I was permanently stuck in human form, irrevocably flawed. Wardens typically didn't do well with flaws. If it wasn't for my unique ability to see souls and tag those who lacked them, I'd be pretty damn useless in the big scheme of things.

Zayne sat up, a lump of stuffed fur in his hand. "Look who I found. You left him in here a couple of nights ago."

"Mr. Snotty!" I grabbed the raggedy teddy bear, grinning. "I was wondering where he was."

His lips curved into a smile. "I can't believe you still have that bear."

I flopped onto my back, clutching Mr. Snotty to my chest. "You gave him to me."

"That was a long time ago."

"He's my favorite stuffed animal."

"He's your *only* stuffed animal." Zayne stretched out beside me, staring up at the ceiling. "You came home earlier than I expected. I thought you were studying with your friends?"

I gave a lopsided shrug.

Zayne tapped his fingers along his stomach. "That's strange. You're normally whining to have a later curfew, but it's not even nine yet."

I bit my lip. "So? I told you what happened."

"So, I know you're not telling me everything." Something in the way he said that made me turn my head toward him. "Why would you lie to me?"

Our faces were close, but not close enough that it would become dangerous. And Zayne trusted me, believed I was more Warden than demon. I thought about the snake…and the boy who really wasn't a boy but a high-ranking demon.

I shuddered.

Zayne reached across the tiny space between us, placing his

hand atop mine. My heart missed a beat. "Tell me the truth, Layla-bug."

I could easily recall the first time he'd called me that.

It was the night they'd brought me to this house. At seven years old, I'd been terrified of the winged creatures with jagged teeth and red eyes that had taken me from the foster home. The moment they had set me down in the foyer of this very home, I'd torn through the house and tucked myself into a tiny ball in the back of the first closet I'd found. Hours later, Zayne had coaxed me out of my hidey-hole, holding a pristine teddy bear and calling me Layla-bug. Even at eleven, he'd seemed larger than life to me, and from that moment on I'd been attached to his hip. Something the older Wardens relished giving him a hard time about.

"Layla?" he murmured, tightening his hold on my hand.

Words tumbled out. "Do you think I'm evil?"

His brows furrowed. "Why would you ask that?"

I stared at him pointedly. "Zayne, I'm half-demon—"

"You are a Warden, Layla."

"And you always say that, but it's not the truth. I'm more like a...like a mule."

"A mule?" he repeated slowly, brows furrowing.

"Yeah, a mule. You know, half horse, half donkey—"

"I know what a mule is, Layla. And I really hope you're not comparing yourself to one."

I didn't say anything, because I was. Like a mule, I was a strange hybrid—half demon and half Warden. And because of that, I would never be mated with another Warden. Even demons, if they knew what I was, wouldn't claim me. So, yeah, I thought the comparison was accurate.

Zayne sighed. "Just because your mother was what she was doesn't make you a bad person, and it sure as Hell doesn't make you a mule."

Turning my head, I resumed staring into space. The fan spun dizzily, creating odd shadows across the ceiling. A demonic mother I'd never met and a father I didn't remember. And Stacey thought her single-parent household was messed up. I reached down, toying nervously with the ring.

"You know that, right?" Zayne continued earnestly. "You know you're not an evil person, Layla. You're a good, smart and—" He stopped, sitting up and hovering over me like a guardian angel. "You…you didn't take a soul tonight? Layla, if you did you need to tell me right now. We'll figure something out. I'd never let my father know, but you have to tell me."

Of course Abbot could never know if I did something like that—not even by accident. As much as he cared for me, he'd still turn me out. Taking a soul was forbidden for a ton of moral reasons.

"No. I didn't take a soul."

He stared at me and then his shoulders squared. "Don't scare me like that, Layla-bug."

I suddenly wanted to hold Mr. Snotty closer. "I'm sorry."

Zayne reached down, prying my hand off the bear. "You've made mistakes, but you've learned from them. You're not evil. That's what you need to remember. And what's in the past is in the past."

I worried my lower lip, thinking of those "mistakes." There'd been more than one. The earliest incident had been what brought the Wardens to the foster home. I'd accidentally taken a soul from one of the caregivers—not all of it, but enough that the woman had to be hospitalized. Somehow the Wardens had learned about it through their connections and had tracked me down.

To this day, I didn't understand why Abbot had kept me. Demons were a matter of black-and-white to the Wardens. There was no such thing as a good or innocent demon. Being part demon meant I should've fallen under the old "the only good demon is a dead demon" adage, but for some reason, I'd been different to them.

You know why, whispered an ugly voice in my head, and I closed my eyes. My ability to see souls and the lack thereof, a product of my demonic blood, was a valuable tool in the battle against evil, but Wardens could sense demons when they got close enough to them. Without me, their job would be harder, but not impossible.

At least that was what I told myself.

Zayne turned my hand over, sliding his fingers between mine. "You've been in the cookie dough again. Did you save any for me this time?"

True love meant sharing odd food cravings. I so believed that. I opened my eyes. "There's half a pack left."

He smiled, easing back down on his side this time, keeping his hand wrapped around mine. Hair fell across his cheek. I wanted to brush it off his face, but didn't have the nerve. "I'll get you a new phone tomorrow," he said finally.

I beamed at him like he was my own personal cell-phone manufacturer. "Please get me a touch-screen one this time. Everyone at school has one."

Zayne arched a brow. "You'd destroy that in a matter of seconds. You need one of those giant satellite phones."

"That'll make me real cool." I wrinkled my nose as I glanced at the wall clock. He'd need to be leaving soon. "I guess I should go study or something."

Golden-hued skin crinkled as he smiled. "Don't go yet."

Nothing in this world could stop the warmth building in my chest. I glanced at the bedside clock once more. He had a few more hours before he left to hunt the demons I'd tagged earlier. Grateful, I rolled onto my side. Mr. Snotty lay between us.

He untangled his fingers from mine and plucked up a few strands of my hair. "Your hair is always in knots. Do you even know how to use a brush?"

I smacked his hand away, shuddering at the reminder of the rat. "Yes, I know how to use a brush, you ass."

Zayne chuckled, returning to my knotted hair. "Language, Layla, language."

I quieted down as he gently pulled a few of the tangles out. This touching-my-hair thing was new and I didn't mind. He held the pale strands between us, eyes narrowed in concentration. "I need a haircut," I murmured after a few moments.

"No." He draped my hair back over my shoulder. "It's... beautiful long. And it suits you."

My heart practically exploded into mush. "Do you want to hear about school today?"

His gaze brightened. All the Wardens except me had been homeschooled, and most of Zayne's college classes had been online. He listened as I told him about the paper I'd gotten a B on, the fight in the cafeteria between two girls over a boy and how Stacey accidentally locked herself *in* the guidance counselor's office after school.

"Oh. I almost forgot." I paused, yawning obnoxiously. "Sam wants to interview you for the school paper. Something about you being a Warden."

Zayne grimaced. "I don't know about that. We aren't allowed to give interviews. The Alphas would see that as being prideful."

"I know. I told him not to hold his breath."

"Good. Father would flip out if he thought I was talking to the press."

I giggled. "Sam's not the press, but I gotcha."

He kept me up for a little while longer, asking question after question. Against my will, my eyes fell shut. He'd be long gone before I woke up; out hunting demons. Maybe even a few Upper Level ones. Maybe even the demon boy with the snake named Bambi.

Bleary-eyed, I dug out my bio book. I had three seconds to myself before a soft green soul edged into my line of vision. I lifted my head, inhaling deeply. I liked to be around innocent souls. They were pretty average and not as tempting as—

A fist slammed into my arm. "You didn't come to our study group, Layla!"

I stumbled to the side, catching myself on the locker door. "Jeez, Stacey, that's going to bruise."

"You left us hanging. Again."

Slamming my locker door shut, I faced my best friend. Stacey had some oomph behind her punches. "Sorry. I had to run home. Something came up."

"Something always comes up." She glared at me. "It's ridiculous. Do you know I had to sit and listen to Sam talk about how many people he killed on *Assassin's Creed* for an entire hour?"

I shoved my books into my bag, laughing. "That sucks."

"Yeah, it did." She ripped a hair tie off her wrist and pulled her hair into a short ponytail. "But I forgive you."

Stacey always forgave me for being late or not showing up. I really didn't understand why. I could be a terrible friend at times, and it wasn't like Stacey wasn't popular. She had a lot of other friends, but ever since freshman year, she'd seemed to like me.

We stepped into the throng of students. The mingled scents of perfume and body odor turned my stomach. My senses were slightly heightened. Nothing super extraordinary like a full-blooded demon or Warden, but unfortunately, I could smell what most humans couldn't. "I'm really sorry about last night. I didn't even get to study for our bio exam."

She stared at me, her almond-shaped eyes narrowing. "You still look half-asleep."

"I was so bored in homeroom that I dozed off and almost slid out of my chair." I glanced at a group of jocks slouched near the empty trophy case. Our football team sucked. Their souls were a rainbow of soft blues. "Mr. Brown yelled at me."

She snickered. "Mr. Brown yells at everyone. So you didn't study at all?"

Pink souls surrounding a group of giggling sophomores caught my attention. "What?"

Letting out a long-suffering sigh, she said, "Biology—as in the science of life? We're on our way to class. We have an exam."

I tore my gaze from the pretty trails, frowning. "Oh. Duh. No, like I said, I didn't study at all."

Stacey switched her books to her other arm. "I hate you. You didn't crack a book and you'll probably still get an A." She brushed her bangs out of her eyes, shaking her head. "So not fair."

"I don't know. Mrs. Cleo gave me a B on the last exam and I really have no clue what's on this one." I frowned, realizing how true that was. "Man, I really should have studied last night."

"You still have Sam's notes?" She grabbed my arm, steering me out of the path of another student. I caught the tail end of a deep pink soul blurred with streaks of red. "Wow, he is so checking you out."

"Huh?" I looked at Stacey. "Who?"

She glanced over her shoulder as she pulled me closer. "The guy you almost plowed into—Gareth Richmond. He's still checking you out. No!" she hissed into my ear. "Don't look. That's too obvious."

I fought the natural urge to turn around.

Stacey giggled. "Actually, he's checking out your butt." She let go of my arm, straightening. "It is a nice butt."

"Thanks," I murmured, my gaze following the powder-blue soul surrounding a guy ahead of us.

"Gareth checking out your butt is a good thing," Stacey continued. "His dad owns half of downtown and his parties are freaking awesome."

I turned into the narrow corridor leading to bio. "I think you're just imagining things."

She shook her head. "Don't act clueless. You're cute—way hotter than that hobag over there."

My gaze went straight to where Stacey pointed. A faint purple aura surrounded Eva Hasher. Meaning she was a few more mean-girl moves away from slipping into questionable soul status. My throat suddenly constricted. The darker or purer the soul was, the stronger the allure.

The really, really bad and the really, really good were the most appealing, which made Eva very interesting to me, but eating the soul belonging to the most popular girl in school would be way uncool.

Eva leaned against a locker, surrounded by what Stacey referred to as the bitch pack.

Eva flipped Stacey off with one perfectly painted blue nail and then glanced at me. "Oh, look! It's the gargoyle whore."

Her pack of mindless followers laughed.

I rolled my eyes. "Ouch. New one."

Stacey returned the gesture with both hands. "What a stupid bitch."

"It's whatever." I shrugged. Being called a whore by Eva while knowing the status of her soul was too ironic to get mad over.

"You know she and Gareth broke up, right?"

"They did?" I couldn't keep up with those two.

Stacey nodded. "Yep. He cropped her out of all his pictures on Facebook. Really crappy cropping job, too, because you can see her arm or leg in half of them. Anyway, you should go out with him just to piss her off."

"How did checking out my butt end up with me going out with a guy who doesn't even know my name?"

"Oh, I'm sure he knows your name—and probably your bra size, too." She stepped around me, pushing through the door to bio. "Yes, there are sixth graders taller than you. But guys like that. They want to pick you up and put you in their pockets. Take care of you."

I brushed past her, smirking. "That's the stupidest thing you've ever said."

She followed me to our seats at the back of the classroom. "You're like this little doll with those big gray eyes and pouty lips."

I shot her a scathing glare as I dropped into my seat. Most days I looked like a creepy anime character. "Are you coming on to me or something?"

Stacey grinned evilly. "I'd go gay for you."

Digging out Sam's notes, I snorted. "I wouldn't go gay for you. Eva Hasher? Maybe."

She gasped, clutching the front of her shirt. "That stung. Anyway, I texted you at least a dozen times last night and you didn't respond once."

"Sorry. I lost my phone." I flipped a page, wondering what language Sam had scribbled this crap in. "Zayne is supposed to get me a new one today. I'm hoping it's a touch screen like yours."

This time Stacey sighed. "God, can Abbot adopt me, too? Seriously. I want a superhot adopted brother. Instead I have a whiny, craps-himself brother. I so want a Zayne."

I tried to ignore the red-hot jolt of possessiveness darting through my veins. "Zayne's not my brother."

"Thank God for that. Otherwise you'd be plagued with incestuous feelings all the time and that's just gross."

"I don't think of Zayne that way!"

She laughed. "What man-parts-loving female in this world doesn't think of Zayne that way? I can barely keep myself breathing when I see him. All the guys in school have squishy waists. I can tell Zayne doesn't. He's the awesome sauce with extra sauce."

That he was, and he so didn't have a squishy waist, but I tuned Stacey out at that point. I really did need to cram for this test and I also didn't want my fantasies involving Zayne to occupy my mind right now. Especially after I'd woken up this morning, carefully tucked under the covers. The bed had smelled like him: sandalwood and crisp linen.

"Oh, sweet baby Jesus in a manger," Stacey murmured.

I clenched my jaw, cupping my hands over my ears.

She jabbed me in the side with her elbow. At this rate I'd be covered in bruises before lunchtime. "Our bio class just got a billion times more interesting. And hotter, lots and lots hotter. Holy mother, I want to have his babies. Not now of course, but definitely later. But I'd like to start practicing soon."

The cell wall is a thick and rigid layer covering the plasma something, something plant cells...

Stacey stiffened all of a sudden. "Oh, my God, he's coming—"

Composed of fat and sugar—

Something slender and shiny fell from who knew where, landing in the middle of Sam's notes. Blinking tightly, it took me a couple of seconds to recognize the faded and half-peeled *Teenage Mutant Ninja Turtles* sticker covering the back of the silver cell phone.

My heart slammed against my ribs. Gripping the edges of the notebook, I slowly lifted my gaze. Unnaturally beautiful golden eyes met mine.

"You forgot this last night."

3

HE COULDN'T BE HERE.

But he was, and I couldn't look away. Suddenly I wished I could sketch, because my fingers itched to draw the lines of his face, to try to capture the exact slant of the bottom lip that was fuller than the top. Not exactly a helpful line of thinking.

The demon smiled. "You ran off so fast I didn't get a chance to give it to you."

My heart stopped beating. This wasn't happening. An Upper Level demon didn't return missing cell phones and he sure as Hell didn't go to school. I had to be hallucinating.

"You little secret-keeping elf," Stacey whispered in my ear. "*This* is why you didn't show up for our study group last night?"

His gaze had a hypnotic, paralyzing effect. Or I was just that stupid. I could feel Stacey practically coming out of her skin beside me.

He leaned down, placing his palms on my desk, smelling of something sweet and musky. "I've been thinking about you all night."

Stacey sounded like she'd choked.

The door to our classroom swung open and Mrs. Cleo shuffled in, her plump arms filled with papers. "All right, everyone in their seats."

Still smiling, the demon straightened and turned. He sat down in the desk directly in front of us. Not even a second passed before he rocked the chair back on two legs, hovering there and completely at ease.

"What the frick, Layla?" Stacey gripped my arm. "Where did you pick him up last night, somewhere between the Big Mac and fries? And why didn't I get an order of him?"

Stacey's fingers continued to dig into my arm, but I was utterly dumbstruck.

Mrs. Cleo cradled the exams to her chest like they were a newborn infant. "It's quiet time. Everyone face the front of— Oh, we have a new student." She picked up a small pink sheet, frowning as she looked up at demon boy. "Well, the exam won't count toward your grade, but it should give me an idea of where you're at."

"Layla," Stacey whispered. "The look on your face is starting to freak me out. Are you okay?"

Mrs. Cleo dropped the exams on our desks, snapping her fingers. "No talking. Test time, Ms. Shaw and Ms. Boyd."

The questions on the paper blurred. I couldn't do this—sit here and take an exam with a freaking demon sitting in front of me.

"I don't feel good," I whispered to Stacey.

"I can tell."

Without another word, I gathered up my stuff. My legs shook as I stood and hurried to the front of the class. Mrs. Cleo glanced up as I flew past her, my cell slippery in my hand.

"Ms. Shaw, where do you think you're going?" she called out, rising to her feet. "You can't just leave class in the middle of an exam! Ms. Shaw—"

The door slammed shut, silencing whatever else she said. I

didn't know where I was going, but I knew I had to call Zayne—maybe even Abbot. The gray lockers lining the halls blurred. I pushed open the door to the girls' bathroom, and the lingering scent of cigarettes and disinfectant washed over me. The graffiti on the walls looked completely unintelligible.

Flipping open the phone, I caught a glimpse of my eyes in the mirror. They were bigger than normal, taking up my whole face. My stomach tumbled as I thumbed through my contacts.

The door to the bathroom creaked open.

I swung around, but no one stood there. Slowly, the door inched closed with a soft clink. A shiver danced over my skin. My finger trembled as I pressed down on Zayne's name. There was a chance he'd still be awake and not completely encased in stone at the moment. A small, unlikely—

Demon boy was suddenly standing in front of me. He folded his hand over mine, snapping the phone shut. A startled shriek escaped me.

His lips pursed. "Now who are you calling?"

My pulse raced at breakneck speed. "How...how did you do that?"

"Do what? Leave class so easily?" He leaned down as if he was about to share a secret. "I can be very persuasive. It's a gift of mine."

I knew Upper Level demons held powers of persuasion. Some could just whisper two or three words to a person, and whatever the demon wanted, the human would do. But that was also against the rules—free will and all.

"I don't care about the class thing. You were freaking invisible!"

"I know. Pretty cool, huh?" He pried the cell out of my hands. Didn't take much since my fingers felt boneless. He looked around the bathroom, dark brows raised. "It's only one of many talents." Casting a look over his shoulder at me, he winked. "And I do have many talents."

I inched around the sink, toward the door. "And I really don't care about your many talents."

"Stay still." He kicked open a stall with the toe of his black boot as he kept an eye on me. "We need to chat, you and I. And that door isn't opening for anyone but me."

"Wait! What are you doing? Don't—"

My cell flew through the air, landing in the toilet. He faced me, shrugging. "Sorry. I was hoping the phone could be a white flag of friendship, but I can't have you calling those creatures of yours."

"That's my cell phone, you son of a—"

"It's not your cell phone anymore." He grinned playfully. "Now it belongs to the sewer department."

I backed away from him, successfully cornering myself between the sink and the gray cement wall, where a heart had been carved under a small window. "Don't come near me."

"Or what? Remember how far you got fighting the Seeker last night? You won't get even that far with me."

I opened my mouth to—I don't know—scream, but he shot forward, clamping his hand over my lips. Running on instinct, I slammed my balled fists into his stomach. He grabbed my wrist with his free hand and pressed against me, trapping my other arm between my softer stomach and his much, much harder one. I tried to wriggle away, but he held me in place.

"I'm not going to hurt you." His breath stirred the hair around my temple. "I just want to talk."

I bit his hand.

He let out a low hiss, wrapping his hand around my throat. He pressed his fingers in, forcing my head back. "Biting can be a lot of fun, but only when it's appropriate. And that wasn't appropriate."

I wrestled an arm free and gripped his. "I'm going to do worse to you than biting if you don't let go of me."

The demon blinked and then laughed. "I might be interested in seeing what more you can do. Pleasure. Pain. Kind of the same thing, but we don't have time for that right now."

I drew in a deep breath, trying to calm my pounding heart. My gaze darted to the door. The reality of the situation sank in. I'd escaped the Seeker demon and this one last night, only to die in the bathroom of my high school. Life was freaking cruel.

There was no place for me to go. Any movement I made brought us closer together and we were already way too close. The word leaked out of my mouth. "Please…"

"Okay. Okay." To my surprise, his voice dropped, became soothing as his grip relaxed. "I scared you. Maybe I should have picked a better way of showing up, but the look on your face was priceless. If you knew my name, would that make you feel better?"

"Not really."

He smirked. "You can call me Roth."

Nope. Knowing his name didn't make me feel better.

"And I'll call you Layla." His head shifted, sending several locks of black hair forward. "I know what you can do. So let's cut the crap, Layla. You know what I am and I know what you are."

"You have the wrong person." I dug my nails into his arm. It had to hurt, but it didn't even faze him.

Roth looked up to the ceiling, sighing. "You're half-demon, Layla. You can see souls. That's why you were in that alley last night."

I opened my mouth to lie again, but what was the point? Taking a deep breath, I struggled to keep my voice even. "What do you want?"

He tipped his head to the side. "Right this moment? I want to understand how you've let the Wardens brainwash you into hunting your own kind. How you can work for them."

"They haven't brainwashed me!" I pushed against his stomach. He didn't budge. And wow, his stomach was so not squishy, either. It was ridiculously hard and trim. And I was sort of feeling him up. I jerked my hands back. "I'm nothing like you. I am a Warden—"

"You are *half* Warden and *half* demon. What you're doing is—is sacrilegious," he announced with a look of disgust.

I scoffed. "Coming from you, a demon? That's almost funny."

"And what do you think you are? Just because you choose to ignore your demon blood doesn't change its existence." He leaned in so close his nose brushed mine as his hand cupped my chin, forcing me to maintain eye contact. "Don't you ever wonder why the Wardens didn't kill you? You're part demon. So why did they keep you? Perhaps it's because your ability to see souls is valuable to them? Or something else?"

My eyes narrowed as anger replaced the fear. "They don't use me. They're my family."

"Family?" It was his turn to scoff. "You obviously can't shift or you would've done so last night."

Heat burned my face. Jeez, even a demon knew I was defective.

"Whatever Warden blood you have in you isn't as strong as your demon side. *We* are your family—your kind."

Hearing that was putting voice to my own personal version of Hell. I knocked his hand away. "No."

"Really? I think you're lying. Seeing souls isn't the only thing you can do, is it? The last one who could?" he whispered, catching my chin again with the tips of his slender fingers. "She could do much more than that. Let's just say she'd get a very unique hankering."

I started to shake. "Who are you talking about?"

Roth smiled like the cat that ate an entire roomful of canaries and had moved on to the parrots. "I know what you wanted before you went into that alley."

The floor seemed to roll under my feet. "I don't know what you mean."

"You don't? I was following you."

"Oh, so you're a demon *and* a stalker?" I swallowed hard. "Because that's not creepy or anything."

He laughed softly. "Deflection doesn't work on demons."

"Then I guess I'll just have to try biting again."

Something flared in his golden eyes, brightening them. "You wanna try?" He leaned in again, his lips brushing the curve of my cheek. "Let me suggest more appropriate places. I have this piercing—"

"Stop!" I jerked my head to the side. "Now I can add *pervert* to *stalker* and *demon*."

"I have no objection to any of those titles." One side of his mouth curved up as he pulled back a little. "You wanted that man's soul—the one you saw on the street? I'd be willing to bet a whole circle in Hell it's all you ever want—ever think about sometimes."

I did need it. Sometimes I shook just thinking about how a soul would feel slipping down my throat, and talking about it made it worse. Even now, when there were no souls near me, I could feel the pull—the need to cave to the urge. Like a junkie after a fix. My muscles cramped in warning. I pushed against his chest. "No. I don't want that."

"The one before you never denied what she was." His voice then took on that soft, teasing quality again. "Do you know anything about her—about your heritage, Layla?" he said, and then his arm slipped around my waist, fitting my body against his. "Do you know anything about what you are?"

"Do you know anything about personal space?" I snapped.

"No." He smirked, and then his eyes seemed to turn luminous. "But I do know that you really don't mind me in your personal space."

"Keep trying to convince yourself of that." I sucked in a breath, forcing myself to meet his stare. "Being this close to you makes me want to shave off layers of my skin."

Roth laughed softly. His head tipped down and suddenly our lips were inches apart. If he had a soul, he'd be entering dangerous territory. "I don't need to do any convincing. I'm a demon."

"Duh," I murmured, my gaze now fixed on his mouth.

"Then you know that demons can smell human emotions."

They could. I'd missed out on that ability, though. I could smell burnt food a mile away, as helpful as that was.

The corners of his lips tipped higher. "Fear has a sharp, bitter scent. I can smell that on you. Anger is like a chili pepper—it's hot and it burns. And I can smell that, too." Roth paused, and somehow, he was even *closer*. So close that when he spoke next, his lips brushed the corner of mine. "Ah, yes...and then there's attraction. Sweet, tangy and heavy—it's my favorite of them all. And guess what?"

I strained back against the wall. "You *do not* smell that on me, buddy."

He reclaimed the distance with little effort. "That's the funny thing about denial. It makes for a really bad weapon. You can say you're not attracted to me all you want and maybe you don't even know it yet, but I know differently."

My mouth dropped open. "You need to get your demon nose looked at, then, because it's seriously broken."

Roth leaned back, tapping a long finger on the tip of my nose. "This has never lied before." But he did step away. Though the smug grin remained on his face like his lips had been made for it, his next words were laced with seriousness. "You need to stop tagging."

Grateful for the breathing room, I let out a ragged breath and clutched the edges of the sink. Now it made sense—this Upper Level demon showing interest in me. "What? Have I tagged too many of your friends?"

One dark brow arched. "I frankly don't care how many demons you tag or how many the Wardens send back to Hell. As you can see, your glow-in-the-dark touch doesn't work on me."

I frowned as I eyed him. Crap. He was right. And I hadn't even noticed it until now. Nice.

"It doesn't work on any Upper Level demon. We're just too cool for that." Roth folded muscular arms across his chest. "But back to the whole tagging thing. You need to stop."

I barked out a short laugh. "Yeah, and why in the world would I do that?"

A bored look crept across his striking features. "I could give you one good reason. The Seeker last night was looking for you."

My mouth opened, because I'd been preparing another dismissive laugh, but the sound caught in my throat. Fear was back, and rightfully so. Had I heard the demon correctly?

A keen light reflected in his eyes. "Hell is looking for you, Layla. And they've found you. Don't go out tagging."

My heart pumped painfully as I stared at him. "You're lying."

He laughed under his breath. "Let me ask you a question. Did you just have a birthday? Turn seventeen recently? Say, within the past couple of days?"

I could only stare at him. My birthday had been just three days ago, on Saturday. I'd gone out to dinner with Stacey and Sam. Zayne even joined us. During dessert, Stacey had tried to get Zayne to tie a cherry stem with his tongue.

The smirk was back. "And yesterday was the first day you tagged since then, right? Hmm…and a Seeker finds you. Interesting."

"I don't see the connection," I managed. "You're probably lying, anyway. You're a demon! You expect me to believe anything you're saying?"

"And you're a demon. No—don't interrupt me with your denial. You're a demon, Layla."

"Half," I muttered.

His eyes narrowed. "You have no reason to think I'm not telling you the truth. I also have a thousand reasons to lie to you, but the whole tagging thing? I'm not kidding. It's not safe."

The bell rang, startling me. I stared at him, wishing Hell would open up and welcome him back with open arms.

Roth glanced at the door, frowning. He turned back to me, lips curving into a strange smile. "I mean it. Don't tag after school." He pivoted around. At the door, he stopped and looked over his shoulder. His eyes met mine. "By the way, I wouldn't tell your *family* about me. I'm afraid you'd find out just how much they really do care for you."

My brain was having a hard time processing Roth's sudden appearance. Telling me that I was attracted to him? Ordering me to stop tagging? Who in the Hell did he think he was? First off, he was a demon—*a hot demon*—but ew. There was no reason for me to believe anything he said. Second, he wasn't just any demon, but an Upper Level one. Double the reason not to trust him.

He might have been right when he said I didn't know a lot about my heritage, but I knew my demons. Hundreds of years ago, there'd been a race of them that could pluck up a soul just by touching a human. They'd been called the Lilin, and they'd been wiped off the planet by the Wardens. Sure, there were still succubi and incubi who fed off the energy of humans, but in this day and age, the ability to completely take a soul was rare. Abilities and traits in the demon world were hereditary, just like in the human world.

The first stirring of unease I'd felt upon hearing Roth's words tripled.

If the other demon he'd mentioned, "the one before me," was my mom and she was still alive… I couldn't even finish that thought without my chest squeezing. Because even though mommy dearest was a demon, the fact that she hadn't wanted me still hurt. The only good that could come out of discovering who she was would be learning what kind of demon she was, and who knew if that would actually be a good thing.

At lunch, I managed to convince Stacey that faking sick had been my last-minute solution to getting out of the bio exam. She bombarded me with questions, wanting to know how I'd met Roth.

"Met who?" Sam asked, shrugging off his backpack and sitting down next to us.

"No one," I muttered.

"Whatever. Layla ditched us last night so she could shack up with this superhot new guy." Stacey pointed her square slice of pizza at me. "You dirty ho. I'm so envious."

"Layla hooked up with someone?" Sam laughed as he popped open his soda. "Was it a Warden? Wow."

Pulled back into the present, I frowned. "No. It wasn't a Warden. And what the Hell is that supposed to mean?"

Sam shrugged. "I don't know. I just can't picture you hooking up with anyone." He took his glasses off, using his shirt to rub them clean. "And I assumed he was a Warden or something. Who else gets Stacey all crazy?"

Stacey took a bite of her pizza. "He was...wow."

"Hold on a sec. Why can't you picture me hooking up with anyone?" I sat back in the chair. I had this ridiculous urge to prove I was hookup material.

Sam shifted uncomfortably. "It's not that people wouldn't want to hook up with you.... It's that, well, you know..."

"No. I don't know. Please elaborate, Samuel."

Stacey sighed, taking pity on him. "What Sam is trying to say is that we can't picture you hooking up with anyone because you don't really pay attention to guys that way."

I started to disagree, because I totally paid attention to guys. But I was always on the sidelines, which probably made me seem uninterested. The truth was I was so interested. It was just that I couldn't have a relationship with anyone who had a soul, and that really limited the whole dating pool.

"I hate you both," I grumbled, attacking my pizza with a vengeance.

"All right, as much as I love talking about hot guys, can we change the subject?" Sam poked his slice around the plate, watching Stacey from under his lashes. "Guess what I learned last night."

"That the number of hours you play video games per day equals the number of more years you'll be a virgin?" she asked.

"Ha. No. Did you guys know that Mel Blanc—the guy who voiced Bugs Bunny—was allergic to carrots?"

We stared at him.

His cheeks flushed. "What? It's true and it's also ironic. I mean, Bugs Bunny ran around all the time with a damn carrot in his hand."

"You are such a fountain of random knowledge," Stacey murmured, somewhat awestruck. "Where do you keep it all?"

Sam ran a hand through his hair. "In my brain. You have one, too, I think."

The two kept up the bickering, and after lunch, I spent the rest of the day expecting Roth to pop up and snap my neck, but I didn't see him at all. I could only hope he'd gotten run over or something.

After the last class of the day, I shoved my books into my locker and hurried outside. Don't tag? Ha. I was going to be a tagging maniac.

I was just going to be a little more careful about it.

Paying close attention to the demons I spotted as I wandered the D.C. streets, I waited until I was absolutely positive the suckers weren't going to whip around and morph into waxy, soulless Seekers. In other words, I was being a total stalker. Within an hour, I'd already bagged a Poser and three Fiends.

Fiends were the most common demon topside and they always appeared to be young. Although no less dangerous than Posers or Seekers, they were more into creating mayhem wherever they went than fighting. Their abilities were a smorgasbord of messed-up-ness. Some were little pyro-heads, able to create fires with a snap of their fingers. Others were into mechanical things. Well, they were into breaking down mechanical things, which they could do with just a touch. I could usually find them loitering near construction sites or power grids.

I lit them up, every single one I came across, knowing full well the Wardens would find them later that night. Sometimes, but not often, I wondered if it was unfair that the demons had no clue that after I "accidentally" knocked into them, they had a bull's-eye on them. But it didn't stop me.

Demons were evil, no matter how normal they might look.

I just didn't know what category I fell into.

Tagging three more Fiends by five, I decided it was time to call it a night and found a pay phone. Morris answered with his normal silence, and I asked him to pick me up. He hit the keypad twice, signaling a yes. My totals for the evening weren't astronomical, but I felt good about them, and as I waited at my usual bench, relief eased the muscles in my neck. Nothing out of the ordinary had happened. The tagging had been run-of-the-mill.

Since no one tried to play grabby with my head, it proved that Roth was full of it. Now I just needed to figure out what to do about the punk demon. From the moment I'd first begun tagging, I'd been ordered never to interact with Upper Level demons and required to report any possible sighting. Roth was the first one I'd ever seen.

But if I told Abbot about Roth, he would pull me out of school.

I couldn't have that. School was my only real link to normalcy. High school was Hell on Earth for most, but I loved it. I could pretend to be normal there. And I refused to let a demon—or even Abbot himself—take that from me.

As I waited for Morris, I wished my cell phone wasn't floating somewhere in the sewers. Damn Roth. Without my cell, I couldn't even play solitaire. Instead all I could do was people watch, and I'd been doing that since I left school.

Sighing, I sat on my bench and kicked my feet out. I ignored the looks I was getting from an old lady sitting on the other side.

The first tingle that danced along the nape of my neck didn't really raise any warnings, but as the sensation increased, so did the feeling of restlessness. Twisting around, I scanned the crowd of people hurrying down the sidewalk. A pretty parade of souls hummed along, but in the mix, standing back under the alcove of a thrift store, was a void where no color shone through.

I sat up straight and turned around so quickly that the old lady gasped. I caught a glimpse of a dark suit, pale skin and hair that seemed to stand straight up. It was definitely a demon, but not Roth. The height and width of the man was larger, but there was a flash of golden eyes.

An Upper Level demon.

My heart rate tripled and then a horn blew, causing me to jump. I looked away for only a second, long enough to see that Morris had arrived, but by the time I turned back to where the demon had been standing, he was gone.

I actually waited for Morris to park the car before I jumped out this time. As we entered the kitchen through the garage, I heard childish giggles and shrieks.

Curious, I turned back to Morris. "Did we turn into a daycare center since this morning?"

Morris slunk past me, smiling.

"Wait. Is Jasmine here with the twins?"

He nodded, which was the best answer I'd get from him.

A big smile pulled at my lips. I forgot about the mess that had been today. Jasmine lived in New York with her mate, and since she'd had the twins, they'd rarely traveled. Female gargoyles were a rarity. Most of them died giving birth, like Zayne's mother had. And the demons loved to pick them off. Because of that, the females were heavily guarded and well cared for.

Kind of like living in a bejeweled prison, even if they didn't see it that way.

On the flip side, I did understand the males' perspective. Without the females, our race couldn't survive. And without the gargoyles acting as Wardens and keeping the demons in check, what would happen? Demons would take over, plain and simple. Or the Alphas would destroy everything. Happy times.

Thankfully I wasn't under any kind of protection order. That was why I was able to attend public school when none of the other gargoyles could. Being only half-Warden meant I wasn't mating material. My purpose in life wasn't to continue the race. And even if I could mate with a Warden—without taking their soul accidentally—the demonic blood I carried would be passed down, just like the Warden DNA.

And no one wanted that hot mess in their bloodline.

I was more than happy to be able to come and go as I pleased and to help the cause in any way I could, but it was...well, it was hard. I would never truly be a part of the Wardens. And no matter how badly I wanted it, I'd never really be their family.

Something else Roth had been spot-on about.

My chest squeezed as I set my bag on the kitchen table and followed the sound of laughter to the living room. I stepped into the room just as a pint-sized blur of white and gray zoomed past my face. Jumping back, I felt my mouth drop open as a young, dark-haired woman rushed past me, her luminescent spirit trailing behind her.

"Isabelle!" Jasmine yelled. "Get down from there right now!"

The little thing's soul faded enough for me to see her actual body. Isabelle had ahold of the ceiling fan. One wing flapped while the other drooped to the side as the fan spun her around.

Her curly red hair seemed out of place on her chubby gray face. So did the fangs and horns.

"Uh…"

Jasmine stopped and faced me, out of breath. "Oh, Layla. How are you doing?"

I flipped off the switch to the ceiling fan. "Good. You?"

Isabelle giggled as the fan slowed, still flapping that one wing. Jasmine stepped beneath her. "Oh, you know. The twins are two and just learning how to shift. It's been a real joy." She grabbed one of Isabelle's stumpy legs. "Let go—Izzy, let go this instant!"

Yeah, two-year-olds could shift and I couldn't. Embarrassing. "Did you guys get in yesterday?" I asked, thinking of the gargoyles on the roof.

She wrangled in Isabelle, sitting her down on the floor. "No. We just got here. Dez had to go out of town, so he asked Abbot if we could stay here until the clan returns to New York."

"Oh." I peeked behind the couch, spotting the other twin. At first, he was just a little blob of pearly-colored goodness. Then I saw past his soul. He slept in his human form, curled atop a thick blanket. He had his thumb in his mouth. "At least this one is sleeping."

Jasmine laughed softly. "Drake sleeps through anything. This one—" she picked up Isabelle and sat her on the couch "—doesn't like to sleep. Isn't that right, Izzy?"

Isabelle half jumped, half fell off the couch and rushed me. Before I could move, she went down on all fours and sank those sharp little teeth through my flats, biting my toe.

I shrieked, fighting the urge to punt the little freak across the room.

"Izzy!" cried Jasmine, rushing over to us. She grabbed her, but the damn thing had a firm hold on my toe. "Izzy! Do not bite! What have I told you?"

I winced as Jasmine manually removed her daughter's fangs

from my foot. The moment Jasmine put the giggling child down, Isabelle launched herself into the air, straight at me.

"Izzy! Don't!" her mother yelled.

I caught her, taking a wing in the face. She was surprisingly heavy for a two-year-old. I held her at arm's length. "It's okay. She's not bothering me." Now.

"I know." Jasmine floated to my side, wringing her slender hands. "It's just that…"

As realization sank in, I wanted to crawl into a hole. Jasmine was worried that I'd suck her baby's soul out. I'd thought Jasmine had grown to trust me after we first met, but when it came to her babies, that trust had jumped out the window. Part of me couldn't blame her, but…

Sighing, I handed Isabelle over to Jasmine and took a step back. Feeling all kinds of wrong, I forced a smile. "So how long will you be staying here?"

Jasmine cradled the wriggling kid to her chest. Isabelle kept reaching out toward me. "A couple of weeks—a month, tops— and then we'll head back home."

Then it struck me. If Jasmine was here, then that meant her younger and totally available sister was here. And she'd be here for *weeks*. My stomach dropped.

Without saying another word, I wheeled from the room to go on a manhunt—or a female-gargoyle hunt. Whatever. Danika was different from any human girl Zayne might occasionally "date." Way different.

The soft sound of husky laughter floated out of the library I usually occupied during all my copious spare time. An irrational territorial urge surfaced. As I crossed the sparsely decorated sitting room that no one ever used, my hands balled into fists. Jealousy was a bitter acid sweeping through my veins as I stopped before the closed doors. I had no right to barge in on them, but I was no longer in control of myself.

Danika's throaty laugh came again, followed by a deeper

chuckle. I could picture her tossing her long black hair over her shoulder, smiling the way all girls smiled at Zayne, and I pushed open the door.

They stood so close their souls touched.

ZAYNE LEANED AGAINST THE DESK, dusty from disuse, his muscled arms folded across his chest. He had a slight smile on his
face—a fond one. And Danika had one hand on his shoulder,
her face so bright and happy I wanted to throw up on the both
of them. They were the same height, both around the same age.
Admittedly, they'd make a beautiful couple and have tons of
beautiful babies that would shift and wouldn't have any tainted
blood in them.

I hated her.

Zayne looked up, stiffening as his eyes locked with mine.

"Layla? Is that you?" Danika pulled away from Zayne, smiling as her hand trailed down his chest. A soft, rosy flush covered
her high cheekbones. "Your hair has gotten so long."

My hair hadn't grown that much since the last time I'd seen
her, which was three months ago. "Hey." I sounded like I'd
swallowed a bed of nails.

She came across the library, stopping short of embracing
me because we *so* weren't on hugging terms. "How have you
been? How's school?"

The fact that Danika actually liked me made it all the more intolerable. "It's great."

Zayne pushed off the desk. "Did you need something, Layla-bug?"

I felt like the biggest kind of idiot. "I...just wanted to say hi." I turned to Danika, my face burning. "Hi."

Her smile faltered a bit as she glanced at Zayne. "We were just talking about you, actually. Zayne was telling me you were thinking of applying to Columbia?"

I thought about the half-completed college application. "It was a stupid idea."

Zayne frowned. "I thought you said you were going to do it."

I shrugged. "What's the point? I already have a job."

"Layla, there's still a point. You don't have—"

"It's nothing we need to talk about. Sorry for interrupting." I cut Zayne off. "I'll see you guys later."

I hurried away before I made an even bigger fool out of myself, blinking back hot, humiliating tears. My skin was starting to crawl by the time I made it to the fridge. I shouldn't have gone looking for them, because I'd known what I'd find. But apparently I was into torturing myself.

Pulling out the carton of OJ, I also grabbed the roll of sugar-cookie dough. The first gulp of juice was the best. I loved the acidic burn. Sugar helped when the cravings to take a soul hit hard. It was a mortifying need, reminding me of drug addicts.

"Layla."

Closing my eyes, I set the carton on the counter. "Zayne?"

"She's only going to be here a couple of weeks. You could at least try to be nice to her."

I twisted around, focusing on his shoulder. "I *was* being nice to her."

He laughed. "You sounded like you wanted to bite her head off."

Or take her soul. "Whatever." I grabbed a chunk of dough and popped it in my mouth. "You shouldn't keep her waiting."

Zayne reached over, taking the dough from my hands. "She went to help Jasmine with the twins."

"Oh." I turned away, grabbing a glass out of the cupboard, filling it to the top.

"Layla-bug." His breath stirred my hair. "Please don't act like this."

I sucked in air, wanting to lean back into him, but knowing I never could. "I'm not acting like anything. You should go hang out with Danika."

Sighing, he placed a hand on my shoulder, turning me back around. His eyes dropped to the glass I held. "Rough day at school, huh?"

I backed up, hitting the counter. The image of Roth cornering me in the bathroom immediately came to mind. "N-no different than any other day."

Zayne stepped forward, dropping the roll of dough on the counter. "Anything interesting happen?"

Did he know? No, there was no way. He always asked about school. "Um…some girl called me a gargoyle whore."

"What?"

I shrugged. "It happens. Not a big deal."

His gaze sharpened. "Who said that to you?"

"It doesn't matter…." I stopped as he took my glass and watched the muscles of his throat work. He drained half the glass before he handed it back to me. "It's just something stupid they say."

"You're right. It doesn't matter as long as you don't let it bother you."

I shivered, hopelessly drawn into his pale eyes. "I know."

"Cold?" he murmured. "Somebody turned the air on while we slept."

"It's September. It's not hot enough to run the air."

Zayne chuckled as he brushed my hair back over my shoulder. "Layla, our body temperatures run differently than yours. Seventy degrees is steamy to us."

"Mmm. That's why I like you. You're warm."

He took my glass again, but this time he placed it on the counter. Then he grabbed my hand, pulling me toward him. "That's why you like me? Because I'm warm?"

"I guess so."

"I thought for sure there were other reasons," he teased.

My earlier irritation faded. I found myself smiling at him. Zayne always had that effect on me. "Well, you do help me with my homework."

His brows shot up. "Is that all?"

"Hmm." I pretended to think about it. "You're pretty to look at. Does that make you feel better?"

Zayne gaped. "I'm *pretty* to look at?"

I giggled. "Yeah. Stacey also said you're the awesome sauce with an extra side of sauce."

"Really?" He pulled me into his side and draped his arm over my shoulder. It was like being in a headlock, except my body tingled all over. "Do *you* think I'm the awesome sauce?"

"Sure," I gasped.

"How about with extra sauce?"

My cheeks flushed. So did other parts of my body. "I... guess so."

"You guess so?" He leaned back, putting maybe two inches between us. "I think you do."

To my relief, my face didn't feel like it was on fire.

He laughed softly, pulling my hand off my face. "You're done tagging already?"

I blinked slowly. What was he talking about?

The door to the kitchen opened behind us. Zayne dropped my hand as he looked over his shoulder, but his arm remained. He grinned. "Hey, old man."

I twisted around. Abbot stood in the doorway, eyeing his son blandly. He always reminded me of a lion. His hair was lighter than Zayne's, but just as long. I imagined he shared a lot of the same features as his son, but half his face was always covered by a thick beard.

If I looked up the definition of *intimidating,* it would show a picture of Abbot. As the clan leader, he had to be fierce, stern and, at times, deadly. He represented the clan, was the one who met with human officials, and if any of the Wardens messed up, it was Abbot who took the fall. A lot of weight rested on his shoulders, but his back never bowed under the pressure.

Abbot's gaze slid to me. His normally warm eyes were like chips of pale blue ice. "Layla, the school called here this afternoon."

I pursed my lips. "Uh…"

"I was able to get in touch with a Mrs. Cleo before she left for the evening." He folded thick arms across his chest. "She claimed that you ran out of class during an exam. Care to explain why?"

My brain emptied.

Zayne's head jerked up, and without looking, I knew he was frowning. "Why did you run out of class?" he asked.

"I…wasn't feeling well." I gripped the edge of the island. "I didn't eat this morning and I got sick."

"Are you feeling okay now?" he pressed.

I glanced at him. Concern touched his expression. "Yeah, I'm all better."

He glanced over at my forgotten glass of orange juice. A strange look flickered over his face. Without saying a word, he dropped his arm and headed around the island.

"I told this Mrs. Cleo that I was sure you had a good reason for leaving class," Abbot continued. "She agreed such behavior was out of character and has decided to let you make up your exam after school on Friday."

Typically I would have whined about having to spend extra time in school, but I wisely kept my mouth shut. "I'm really sorry."

Abbot's eyes softened. "Next time make sure you let the teacher know you're sick. And call Morris so that you can come home and rest."

Now I really felt bad. I shifted my weight back and forth. "Okay."

Zayne returned to my side, OJ in hand. There was a drawn, brooding pull to his features. He handed me the glass, watching until I finished it off. I felt even worse.

Abbot rested his arms against the counter. "Have you been spending time with Danika, Zayne?"

"Hmm?" Zayne's eyes were still on me.

"You know," I said, setting the glass down, "the girl who was almost standing on top of you in the library."

Zayne's full lips thinned.

Abbot chuckled. "Good to see you two getting along. You know she's of mating age, Zayne, and it's time you think about settling down."

I tried to keep my expression blank as I stared at the empty glass. Zayne settling down? I wanted to hurl.

Zayne groaned. "Father, I just turned twenty-one. Give it a rest."

Abbot arched a brow. "I mated with your mother when I was your age. It's hardly out of the question."

I made a face. "Can't we say 'marry'? Saying 'mate' out loud just sounds gross."

"This isn't your world, Layla. I wouldn't expect you to understand."

Ouch. I flinched back.

Zayne exhaled roughly. "Father, this *is* her world. She's a Warden, too."

Abbot moved from the counter, brushing his hair back. "If

she did understand, the use of the word *mating* would not disturb her. The bonds of marriage are breakable. Mating is for life. Something you—" he looked at Zayne pointedly "—need to start taking seriously. Our clan is dwindling."

Zayne tipped his head back and sighed. "What are you suggesting? That I should go out there right now and devote my life to Danika? Does she have a say in this?"

"I doubt Danika would be displeased." Abbot smiled knowingly. "And yes, I'm suggesting you mate very soon. You aren't getting any younger, and neither am I. You may not love her now, but you'll grow to."

"What?" Zayne laughed.

"I felt...a fondness for your mother when I first mated with her." He rubbed his beard-covered chin thoughtfully. "I did grow to love her. If only we'd had more time together..."

Zayne seemed unaffected by the whole exchange, but I felt close to tears. I murmured something about homework before leaving the kitchen. I didn't need to wait around to see how the conversation wrapped up. Whatever Zayne thought or wanted didn't matter. It hadn't mattered for Abbot or Zayne's mother.

And it sure as Hell didn't matter what I wanted.

The application to Columbia University stared at me from the floor. Scattered beside it were more college applications. Money wasn't an issue. Neither were my grades. Since I couldn't serve the clan by producing more Wardens, my future was my own. Those applications should've filled me with excitement and joy. But the idea of moving away, of becoming someone new and different, was as frightening as it was enthralling.

And now, when I finally had the chance to leave, I didn't want to.

It didn't make any sense. I tucked my hair back and stood. My schoolwork lay on the bed forgotten. If I was honest with myself for two seconds, I'd admit I knew why I didn't want to leave. It was Zayne, and that was stupid. Abbot had been right earlier. It didn't matter how much Warden blood I shared, this wasn't my world. I was kind of like a guest who never left.

I looked around my room. It had everything a girl could want. My own desktop computer and laptop, TV and stereo system, more clothes than I'd ever wear and enough books to lose myself in.

But it was all just stuff…empty.

Unable to stay in my bedroom, I left with no real plan in mind. I just needed to get out of the room—out of the house. Downstairs, I could hear Jasmine and Danika in the kitchen making dinner. The scent of roasted potatoes and the sound of laughter filled the air. Was Zayne with them, cooking alongside Danika?

How sweet.

I passed Morris on the front porch. He glanced up from his newspaper with a questioning look, but that was all. I shoved my hands into the pockets of my jeans and inhaled the scent of decayed leaves and the faint trace of the city's smog.

I cut across the manicured yard, past the stone wall that separated Abbot's property from the woods surrounding the compound. Zayne and I had made this trip so many times as kids that a path had been carved through the grass and rocky soil. We'd escaped here together—me running from the loneliness and Zayne avoiding the rigorous trainings and all the expectations.

When we were younger, the fifteen-minute hike felt like we'd managed to disappear into a different world full of thick cherry trees and maples. It had been our place. Back then, I couldn't imagine a life that didn't include him.

I stopped under the tree house Abbot had built for Zayne long before I came along. There wasn't anything special about it. Kind of like a hut in the trees, but it had this cool eight-by-eight observation deck. Climbing a tree was a Hell of a lot easier when I was a little kid. It took several tries to get into the main part. From there, I crawled through a door roughed into the treated wood. I inched across the platform gingerly, hoping it didn't cave in.

Death by tree house didn't sound like an exciting way to go.

Lying down, I wondered why I'd come here. Was it some twisted way of wanting to be close to Zayne, or did I just want to be a kid again? To go back to a time when I didn't know that seeing colors shimmering around people meant that I wasn't like other Wardens…before I learned that I had tainted blood. Things were easier then. I didn't think about Zayne the way I did now or spend my evenings touching random strangers. I also didn't have an Upper Level demon in my bio class.

A cool breeze picked up a few strands of my hair, tossing them across my face. I shivered and hunkered down in my sweater. For some reason, I remembered what Roth had said about Abbot using me for my ability.

It's not true.

I pulled the necklace out from underneath my sweater. The chain was old and thick. It had a series of ropy loops I knew by heart. In the waning light, I couldn't make out the etchings on the silver ring. Endless knots had been carved into the metal band by someone who obviously had too much time on their hands. I turned the ring over. I'd never seen anything like the gemstone set in the center. It was deep red, almost like a ruby, but the color was off in some areas, darker in others. Sometimes, depending on how I held the ring, it looked as if there was liquid inside the oval stone.

Supposedly the ring had belonged to my mother.

My memories prior to the night Abbot found me were nothing but a blank void. This ring was the only thing that tied me to my real family.

Family was such a strange word. I wasn't even sure I'd had a family to start off with. Had I been with my father at some point, before the foster home? Who knew? And if Abbot did, he wasn't telling. My life started when Abbot found me.

I closed my eyes, inhaling slowly and deeply. Now wasn't the time for self-reflection or a pity party. I tucked the ring back under my sweater, figuring I needed to focus on what I was going to do about Roth.

I was on my own with this one. Ignore him? Sounded like a good idea, but I doubted it would work. Part of me hoped he'd just disappear after warning me not to tag.

I must've dozed off at some point during my plotting, because when I opened my eyes, the sky was dark, my nose was cold and someone was lying beside me.

My heart jumped into my throat, then skipped a beat when I turned my head and soft hair tickled my cheek. "Zayne?"

One eye opened. "What a strange place to nap when you have this great thing called a bed."

"What are you doing here?" I asked.

"You didn't come down for dinner." He lifted his hand and removed a strand of my hair that had drifted across his face. "After a while, I decided to check on you. You weren't in your room, and when I asked Morris if he'd seen you, he pointed toward the woods."

I scrubbed my eyes, clearing away the remnants of my impromptu nap. "What time is it?"

"Almost nine-thirty." He paused. "I was worried about you."

My brows furrowed. "Why?"

Zayne tilted his head toward mine. "Why did you leave class today?"

I stared at him a moment, then I remembered the strange look on his face when he'd seen the glass of OJ. "I wasn't about to suck out a soul, if that's what you're thinking."

He frowned. "Whenever you're craving something sweet—"

"I know." I turned my gaze to the sky. The stars peeked out

from behind the thick branches. "Nothing happened at school today, I swear."

He was quiet for a moment. "Okay. That wasn't the only reason I was worried."

I sighed. "I'm not going to murder Danika in her sleep."

Zayne let out a deep laugh. "I'd hope not. Dad would be pissed if you killed my mate."

Hearing that, I decided there may be a good chance I *would* kill her. "So now you're down with the whole *mating* thing? Going to start making little gargoyle babies soon? That should be fun."

He laughed again, which pissed me off. "Layla-bug, what do you know about making babies?"

I punched him in the stomach as I sat up. His low chuckle turned into a grunt. "I'm not a freaking kid, you ass. I know what sex is."

Zayne reached up and pinched my cheek. "You're like this little—"

I slammed him in the stomach again.

He caught my arm, hauling me to his chest. "Stop being so violent," he murmured lazily.

"Then stop being such an ass." I bit my lower lip.

"I know you're not a kid anymore."

An incredible heat swept through me, odd for such a chilly night. "Whatever. You treat me like I'm ten."

A moment passed and his hand tightened around my arm. "How am I supposed to treat you?"

I wished I had something sexy and flirty to say. Instead I mumbled, "I don't know."

A corner of his mouth turned up. "Danika's not my mate, by the way. I was also joking about that."

I tried to look totally unaffected. "It's what your father wants."

He looked away, sighing. "Anyway, what were we talking about? Oh, yeah. I was worried about where you were because Elijah's here."

I stiffened, forgetting about Danika. "What?"

He closed his eyes. "Yeah, he was one of the group that came in last night. I thought they'd be leaving today, but they're hanging around awhile."

Elijah Faustin belonged to the clan that monitored demon activity along most of the southern coast. He and his son acted like I was the antichrist. "Is Petr with him?"

"Yeah."

My head drooped. Petr was the worst kind of boy. "Why are they here?"

"He's being relocated to the Northeast along with his son and four others."

"So he's going to stay here until Dez gets back?"

Zayne met my stare, his expression suddenly hard. "Petr will not go anywhere near you. I promise you that."

My stomach knotted up. Pulling free, I rolled onto my back. I drew in a shallow breath. "I thought Abbot told them they weren't welcome back here."

"He did, Layla. Father isn't happy about them being here, but he can't turn them away." Zayne moved onto his side, facing me. "Do you remember when we used to pretend this was an observation deck for NASA?"

"I remember you dangling me off the edge a couple of times."

Zayne nudged me. "You loved it. You were always jealous that I could fly and you couldn't."

I cracked a smile. "Who wouldn't be jealous of that?"

He grinned as he looked over his shoulder. "God, it's been years since we've been up here."

"I know." I stretched out my legs, wriggling my toes inside the sneakers. "I kind of miss it."

"Same here." Zayne tugged on the sleeve of my sweater. "We still on for Saturday?"

For years, we'd been visiting a different coffee shop every Saturday morning. He'd keep himself awake to do so, prolonging the moment when he'd return to his room and assume his real form, the one that allowed him to sleep. The only true rest a gargoyle gained was when they turned to stone. "Of course."

"Oh. I almost forgot." He sat up, reaching into the pocket of his jeans. He held a slender rectangular object in his hand. "I did pick this up for you today."

I grabbed the cell out of his hands, squealing. "It's a touch screen! Oh, my God, I promise I won't break it or lose it. Thank you!"

Zayne rolled to his feet. "I went ahead and charged it. All you have to do is program your numbers in there." He grinned down at me. "I took the liberty of programming my number as your first contact."

I stood and hugged him. "Thank you. You *are* the awesome sauce."

He laughed, easing his arms around me. "Ah, I have to buy your love. I see."

"No! Not at all. I'd—" I stopped myself before I said something I couldn't take back, and lifted my gaze. Half of his face was shadowed, but there was a strange look in his eyes. "I mean, you'd still be cool even if you hadn't bought me the phone."

Zayne tucked my hair back behind my ear, his hand lingering on my cheek. Bending at the waist, he pressed his forehead against mine. I felt him take a deep breath, and his hand flattened against the small of my back.

"Make sure you keep the balcony doors in your bedroom locked," he said finally, his voice deeper than normal. "And try not to roam around the house in the middle of the night. Okay?"

"Okay."

He didn't move. A slow burn started to slither under my skin, different than my body reacting to his. I forced myself to take a shallow breath, to focus on Zayne, but my eyes drifted shut. I tried to stop it from happening, but my imagination took hold and ran wild. I pictured his soul—his very spirit—warming the cold, empty places inside me. It would feel better than a kiss, better than anything. I swayed, my body leaning toward his, drawn in by two very different wants.

Zayne dropped his hands, backing off. "Are you okay?"

A tide of hot mortification burned through me. Stepping back, I held the phone between us. "Yeah, I'm fine. We—we should head back."

He studied me a moment, then nodded. I watched him turn and duck back into the tree house. I held my breath, waiting until I heard him drop to the ground below.

I couldn't continue living like this.

But what choice did I have? Go full-throttle demon? That would never be an option.

"Layla?" he called out.

"I'm coming." I lifted my head, and as I started forward, something caught my attention. Frowning, I squinted at the tree branch directly above the observation deck. Something wasn't right about it. The branch seemed thicker, shinier.

Then I saw it.

Curled around the branch was an abnormally long and thick snake. Its diamond-shaped head turned down, and from where I stood, I could see the unmistakable red gleam of the snake's eyes.

I jumped back, gasping.

"What's going on up there?" Zayne asked.

I glanced down for maybe two seconds—that was all—but when I looked up, the snake was gone.

5

BY THE TIME I FOLLOWED Stacey into bio, I wanted to smack her. She wouldn't stop talking about Roth. Like I needed any help wondering if he'd actually show up today. I'd stayed up all night thinking about that damn snake in the tree. Had it been there the whole time, watching me as I slept and listening to my conversation with Zayne?

Creepy.

All of it was made worse by the reminder of how Roth had pressed against me in the bathroom. Because when I thought of him, I thought of how that had felt. No one really got that close to me. Not even Zayne. I wanted to crawl inside my own head, surgically remove the memory and then douse my brain with Clorox.

"He better be," Stacey was saying as she threw herself into her seat. "I didn't sneak out of the house dressed like this for no good reason."

"No doubt." I eyed her short skirt and then her cleavage. "We wouldn't want your boobs to go to waste."

She gave me a sly smile. "I want him to think about me all night."

I pulled out my textbook, dropping it on the desk. "No, you don't."

"I'll decide that for myself." She shifted, tugging her skirt down. "Anyway, I can't believe you don't find him hot. There's something wrong with you."

"There's nothing wrong with me." I looked at her, but her eyes were glued to the door. I sighed. "Stacey, he's really not a good guy."

"Mmm. Even better."

"I'm being serious. He's...he's dangerous. So don't get any perverted ideas in your head."

"Too late." She paused, frowning. "Did he do something to you?"

"It's just a feeling I have."

"I have a lot of feelings when I think about him." She leaned forward, planting her elbows on the table and cupping her chin in her hands. "*Lots* of feelings."

I rolled my eyes. "What about Sam? He's totally in love with you. He'd be a better choice."

"What?" She scrunched her nose. "He is not."

"Seriously, he is." I started doodling on the book, keeping my attention off the door. "He's always staring at you."

Stacey laughed. "He didn't even bat an eye when he saw my skirt—"

"Or lack thereof."

"Exactly. Now, if I wore a binary code on my legs, then he'd notice me."

Mrs. Cleo shuffled in, ending our conversation. I almost keeled over, the relief was that powerful. I didn't even care when Mrs. Cleo eyed me strangely. Roth was gone, I thought, drawing giant smiley faces all over a diagram. Maybe his stupid snake ate him.

Stacey's arm thudded off the desk. "I guess today is just going to suck."

"Sorry," I chirped, twirling my pen between my fingers. "Wanna grab—"

The door swung open just as Mrs. Cleo wheeled out the overhead projector. Roth strolled into class, bio book in hand and a cocky smile plastered across his face. The pen slipped out of my grip, flinging forward and smacking the head of a girl sitting two seats in front of me. She whirled around, throwing up her hands as she shot me a dirty look.

Stacey popped up in her seat, emitting a low squeal.

Winking at Mrs. Cleo, he edged past her. She just shook her head and fiddled with her notes. All eyes were on Roth as he sauntered down the center aisle. Jaws dropped and girls turned in their seats. Some of the guys did, too.

"Hey there," he murmured to Stacey.

"Hi." Her elbows slid across the desk.

Then he turned those golden eyes on me. "Good morning."

"My day is made," Stacey whispered, grinning at Roth as he dropped his book and sat.

"Good for you," I snapped, digging another pen out of my bag.

Mrs. Cleo flipped off the lights. "I haven't graded the tests yet, since some of you will be making up those tests on Friday. Expect your grades and any extra-credit assignments to be handed out on Monday."

Several students groaned while I pictured stabbing my pen into the back of Roth's head.

What had I planned last night? Not a damn thing, because I fell asleep while plotting on the observation deck.

About ten minutes into Mrs. Cleo's dry lecture about cell respiration, Stacey stopped bouncing in her seat. I still hadn't taken my eyes off Roth. He didn't even bother pretending to take notes. At least I held a pen in my hand.

He tipped his chair back until it rested against our table, planting his elbows on my textbook to support his precarious position. Once again, I smelled something sweet, like sugary wine or dark chocolate.

I considered moving his arms, but that would require me to touch him. I could poke him in the arm with my pen—hard. His sleeves were rolled up, revealing really nice arms. Smooth skin stretched over well-defined biceps. And there was Bambi, curling around his arm. I leaned forward, somewhat fascinated by the detail. Each ripple in the snake's skin had been shaded so that it actually looked three dimensional. The underbelly was gray and soft-looking, but I doubted Roth's skin would be very soft. It looked as hard as Warden skin.

The tattoo looked so real.

Because it is real, you idiot.

Just then, the tail twitched and slid over his elbow.

Gasping, I jerked back in my seat. Stacey shot me a weird look.

Roth turned his head. "What are you doing back there?"

My eyes narrowed on him.

"Are you staring at me?"

"No!" I whispered, lying through my teeth.

He eased the chair down, sparing Mrs. Cleo a brief glance before turning sideways in his seat. "I think you are."

Stacey leaned over, grinning. "She was."

I shot her a hateful look. "I was not."

Roth eyed Stacey with renewed interest. "She was? And what was she staring at?"

"I really don't know," Stacey whispered back. "I was too busy staring at your face to notice."

A pleased grin appeared. "Stacey, right?"

She leaned into me. "That's me."

I pushed her back to her side, rolling my eyes. "Turn around," I ordered.

His eyes met mine. "I will when you tell me what you were staring at."

"Not at you." I glanced at the front of the room. Mrs. Cleo flipped over her notes. "Turn around before you get us in trouble."

Roth dipped his head. "Oh, you'd love the kind of trouble I'd get you in."

Stacey sighed—or moaned. "I bet we would."

I clenched the pen. "No. We. Would. Not."

"Speak for yourself, sister." Stacey popped the edge of her pen in her mouth.

He smirked at Stacey. "I like your friend."

The pen cracked in my hand. "Well, I don't like you."

Roth chuckled as he finally turned back around. The rest of the class went like that. Every so often he'd look back at us and grin or whisper something entirely infuriating. When Mrs. Cleo finally turned the overhead lights on, I was ready to scream.

Stacey only blinked, looking like she was coming out of some kind of bizarre trance. I scribbled *hobag* across her notes. She laughed and wrote *virgin ice princess* across mine.

When the bell rang, I already had my stuff packed, ready to make a clean exit. I needed air—preferably air that Roth wasn't sharing. Surprisingly enough, he was already out the door by the time I stood, walking so fast he appeared to be on some sort of mission. Maybe Hell had called him back home? I could only hope.

"What is your problem?" asked Stacey.

I brushed past her, scooping long strands of hair out from underneath my bag's strap. "What? I have a problem because I'm not in heat?"

She made a face. "Well, that just sounds gross."

"You're gross," I threw over my shoulder.

Stacey caught up with me. "Honestly, you have to explain

to me what your problem is with him. I don't get it. Did he ask you to be his baby mama?"

"What?" I made a face. "I already told you. He's just bad news."

"My favorite kind of news," she said as we filed out of the door, "is bad-news boys."

I gripped my bag tighter as a sea of pink and blue souls filled the hallway. A banner hung down, interrupting the flow of the pastel rainbow. "Since when did you start liking bad boys? All your past boyfriends qualified for sainthood."

"Since yesterday," she quipped.

"Well, that's really…" I stopped by the row of lockers, wrinkling my nose. "Do you smell that?"

Stacey sniffed the air, then immediately groaned. "God, it smells like raw sewage. Probably the damn bathroom's backed up."

Other students were starting to pick up on the scent of rotten eggs and soured meat. There were giggles, a few gags. Apprehension stirred in my chest. The smell was foul—too foul—and I couldn't believe it was only now that I was smelling it.

I was going to blame Roth for that, too.

"You'd think they'd cancel classes with a smell like that." Stacey started to tug her shirt up as a shield, but must've realized there wasn't enough material there. She clamped her hand over her mouth, muffling her voice. "This cannot be safe."

A teacher stood outside his class, waving his hand in front of his face. My eyes burned as I turned away from him, trailing behind Stacey. In the stairwell, the smell was stronger.

Stacey glanced at me on the landing. "See you at lunch?"

"Yeah," I replied, stepping out of the way of several taller and bigger seniors. I looked like a freshman standing in their way.

She tugged on the hem of her skirt again with her free hand. "Hopefully the smell is gone by then. If not, I'm starting a protest."

Before I could respond, she was bounding up the stairs. I headed down the steps to the first floor, trying not to gag.

"What the Hell is that smell?" asked a petite girl with a lilac-colored soul. Her hair was blond and pixie short.

"I don't know," I murmured absently. "Our lunch?"

The girl laughed. "Wouldn't surprise me." Then she frowned, squinting at me. "Hey. Aren't you the girl who lives with the Wardens?"

I sighed, wishing the mass of bodies on the steps in front of me would move faster. "Yes."

Her brown eyes widened. "Eva Hasher said you and the old black dude who's always picking you up from school are their human servants."

My mouth dropped open. "What?"

She nodded vigorously. "That's what Eva told me in history class."

"I'm not a servant and neither is Morris," I exclaimed. "I'm adopted. And Morris is part of the family. Big difference."

"Whatever," she said, pushing around me.

A servant? As if. A darker pink soul with stripes of red crept into my vision—Gareth Richmond. The boy who *maybe* stared at my butt.

"This place reeks." He held his notebook over his mouth. "You know the gym is going to smell even worse. Think they'll cancel class, Layla?"

Huh, he *did* know my name.

He lowered his notebook, revealing a megawatt smile. The kind I imagined he used on many girls. "They can't expect us to run laps breathing this crap. You're a pretty good runner, by the way. Why didn't you ever go out for track or something?"

"You…watch me run in class?" I wanted to smack myself after saying that. It sounded like I'd accused him of being a creeper. "I mean, I didn't know you paid attention. Not that you'd pay attention. I just didn't know you knew I could run."

He glanced down the stairs, laughing.

I needed to shut up.

"Yeah, I've seen you run." Gareth caught the door before it smacked into us, holding it open. "I've seen you walk, too."

I couldn't tell if he was teasing or flirting. Or if he just thought I was an idiot. Honestly, I didn't care because all I could think of was Stacey suggesting I hook up with Gareth to start a war with Eva. Talk about awkward thoughts.

"So what are you doing after school?" he asked, falling into step beside me.

Tagging demons. "Um…I've got some errands I have to take care of."

"Oh." He tapped his notebook off his thigh. "I've got football practice after class. I've never seen you at any of the games."

I looked at the empty trophy case by the double doors leading to the gym. "Football isn't really my thing."

"That's a bust. I always throw a party at my parents' house after the games. You'd know that if—"

Someone tall, wearing all black, materialized between us. "She'd know that if she cared, but I doubt she does."

I stepped back quickly, startled by Roth's sudden reappearance.

Gareth had the same response. He was a tall boy, big and brawny, but Roth exuded a kick-ass air. The human boy clamped his mouth shut. Without another word, he inched around us and hurried into the gym, the doors swinging shut behind him. I stood there, dumbfounded as the first warning bell rang. It sounded far away.

"Was it something I said?" Roth mused. "I was just pointing out the obvious."

Slowly, I lifted my head and looked at him.

"What?" He grinned impishly. "Come on. You don't look like the type of girl who watches football, hangs out with the cool crowd and ends up deflowered by the senior jock in the back of his daddy's Beamer."

"Deflowered?"

"Yeah, you know. Losing that pesky thing called virginity."

Fire swept over my skin. I pivoted around, heading toward the gym doors. Wasn't like I didn't know what *deflowered* meant. I just couldn't believe he'd actually used that word in the twenty-first century.

Or that I was even having a conversation about virginity with him.

Roth caught my arm. "Hey. That's a compliment. Trust me. He's on the fast track to Hell anyway. Just like his daddy."

"Good to know," I managed to respond coolly, "but would you please let go of my arm? I have to get to class."

"I've got a better idea." Roth leaned in. Dark locks of hair fell into those golden eyes. "You and I are going to have some fun."

My teeth hurt from how hard I was grinding them. "Not in this lifetime, buddy."

He looked offended. "What do you think I'm suggesting? I wasn't planning on getting you drunk and having my way with you in the back of a Beamer like Gareth is. Then again, I guess it could be worse. He could be planning it in the back of a Kia."

I blinked. "What?"

Roth shrugged, dropping my arm. "Some girl named Eva has him convinced that you put out after one beer."

"What?" My voice was as shrill as the ringing tardy bell.

"I personally don't believe it," he went on blithely, "and I have a Porsche. Not as much leg room as a Beamer, but so much hotter, I'm told."

Porsches were hot, but that wasn't the point. "That bitch told him I put out after one beer?"

"Meow." Roth clawed the air, which looked as ridiculous as it sounded. "Anyway, this is not the fun I had in mind."

I was still stuck on the whole "putting out" thing. "She told another girl I was a freaking servant. I guess I'm a servant who puts out. Oh! And I guess I'm a lightweight, too. I'm gonna kill—"

Roth snapped his fingers in my face. "Focus. Forget about Eva and one-minute boy. We have something we need to do."

"Don't snap your fingers at me," I snarled. "I'm not a dog."

"No." He smiled a little. "You're a half demon who lives with a bunch of stone freaks that kill demons."

"You're the freak, and I'm late for class." I started to turn from him, but remembered last night. "Oh. And keep your stupid snake on a leash."

"Bambi comes and goes as she pleases. I can't help it if she likes hanging out in your tree house."

My hands curled into fists. "Don't come near my house again. The Wardens will kill you."

Roth tipped his head back, laughing deeply. It was a nice laugh, dark and throaty—which made it all the more infuriating. "Oh, there'd be killing, but I wouldn't be the one doing the dying."

I swallowed. "Are you threatening my family?"

"No." He caught my hand this time, easing my fingers out of their fist and then twining them through his own. "Anyway, you can't tell me you haven't smelled the funk that is this high school right now."

Clamping my mouth shut, I glared at him. "What? It's just the sewer or..."

He looked at me like I was about three different kinds of stupid, and my initial suspicions concerning the smell resurfaced. "It can't be..."

"Oh, it is. There's a zombie in the school." A brow arched. "Sounds like the start of a really bad horror movie."

I ignored the last statement. "That can't be it. How would one get in here without being seen?"

Roth shrugged. "Who knows? Anything is possible these

days. My demon spidey senses are telling me it's in one of the boiler rooms downstairs. And since your Warden friends are probably sleeping, I figured we'd check it out before it makes its way upstairs and starts eating students."

I dug in my heels as he started forward. "I'm not checking anything out with you."

"But there's a zombie in the school," he said slowly, "and it's probably hungry."

"And yeah, I know this, but you and I aren't doing anything."

His smile faded. "Aren't you at all curious why a zombie would be in *your* school and what people are going to think when they see something straight from *Night of the Living Dead?*"

I met his stare. "It's not my problem."

"It's not." Roth tipped his head to the side, eyes narrowed. "But it will be the Warden leader's problem when it stumbles upstairs and starts oozing bodily fluids all over everyone while it chomps on body parts. You know how those Alphas expect the Wardens to keep the whole demon thing out of the public eye."

I opened my mouth to protest, but stopped. Dammit. He was right. If that thing made its way upstairs, Abbot would be in a world of trouble. Yet still I stalled. "How do I know you aren't going to throw me at it?"

Roth arched a brow. "Hey, I didn't abandon you to the Seeker, now did I?"

"That doesn't reassure me."

He rolled his eyes, sighing. "You're just going to have to trust me."

I laughed. His head snapped in my direction, eyes slightly wide. "Trust you? A demon? Are you on crack or something?"

His eyes glimmered with…what? Annoyance or amusement? "Crack is whack."

I pressed my lips together tightly, stopping the smile before it could spread across my face and give him the wrong idea. "I can't believe you just said that."

He tipped his chin up. "It's true. No drugs while on the job. Even Hell has its guidelines."

"What is your job exactly?" I asked.

"To deflower you in the back of the most expensive car ever made."

I tried to jerk my hand back, but he held on. "Let go."

"Christ on a crutch." He chuckled deeply. "I was just joking, you prude."

Now I flushed again, because I did feel like a prude. A natural feeling when I'd never kissed a guy before. "Let go of my hand."

Roth heaved a long sigh. "Look. I'm so—I'm sor..." He took a deep breath, trying again. "I'm sorr..."

I turned my head toward him, waiting. "You're what? Sorry?"

He looked chagrined, lips pursed. "I'm...sorr-ree."

"Oh, give me a break. You can't say I'm sorry?"

"No." He looked me straight on, serious. "It's not in a demon's vocab."

"That's rich." I rolled my eyes. "Don't even bother *trying* to say it if you don't mean it."

Roth appeared to consider that. "Deal."

A door across from the gym opened. Assistant Principal McKenzie stepped into the hallway, his drab brown suit at least two sizes too small for his potbelly. He immediately frowned and gained two chins when he spotted us.

"Aren't you supposed to be in gym, Ms. Shaw, and not in the hallway?" he said, loosening the stretched-out belt around his pants. "You may be mixed up with those *things,* but that doesn't give you extra privileges."

Mixed up with those things? They weren't *things.* They were Wardens, and they kept ungrateful asses like McKenzie safe. My fingers reflexively squeezed Roth's as anger and a little sadness flooded me.

These people had no clue.

Roth glanced at me, then at the assistant principal. He ducked his head, smiling demurely. Right then and there, I knew he was about to do something really bad.

Like demon-level bad.

And all I could do was brace for it.

"AND YOU?" Assistant Principal McKenzie continued as he wad-
dled toward us, looking Roth up and down with a distasteful
eye. "Whatever class you're supposed to be in, you need to get
to. Now."

Roth dropped my hand and folded his arms across his chest.
He returned the look, but an odd light radiated from his pupils.
"Assistant Principal McKenzie? As in Willy McKenzie, born
and raised in Winchester, Virginia? Graduated from the Com-
monwealth and married the sweetest little gal from the South."

The man was obviously caught off guard. "I don't know—"

"The same Willy McKenzie who hasn't slept with that sweet
gal since the creation of the DVD, and who has a stash of porn
in his closet at home? And not just any porn." Roth stepped
forward, lowering his voice until it was nothing more than a
whisper. "You know what I'm talking about."

My stomach turned sour. Assistant Principal McKenzie had
questionable soul status—not as obvious as the man on the street
the night I met Roth, but there'd always been something about
him that made me wary.

McKenzie had a totally different reaction. His face turned a mottled shade of red as his jowls flapped. "H-how dare you. Who are you? You—"

Roth raised a finger—his middle finger—silencing him. "You know, I could make you go home and end your miserable life. Or better yet, walk right outside and throw yourself in front of the truck that collects garbage like you. After all, Hell has had its eyes on you for quite some time."

I experienced a moral conflict at that moment. Either I let Roth manipulate the pedophile into offing himself or I stopped him—because, pervert or not, Roth would be stripping the man of his free will.

Crap. This was a tough decision.

"I'm not going to do either of those things," Roth said, surprising me. "But I am going to mess you up. Royally."

My relief was short-lived.

"I'm going to take away the thing you love most in this world—food." Roth smiled beatifically. At the moment, he looked more like an angel than a demon—a mind-numbing beauty that couldn't be trusted. "Every doughnut you see will look like it's sprinkled with a heavenly dose of maggots. Every pizza will remind you of your dead father's face. Hamburgers? Forget 'em. They'll taste like rotten meat. And milk shakes? Soured. Oh. And those jars of chocolate cake icing you hide from your wife? Filled with roaches."

A thin line of drool escaped McKenzie's gaping mouth, dropping down his chin.

"Now go away before I change my mind." Roth waved his hand, dismissing the man.

Stiffly, McKenzie turned around and went back into his office, a strange wet spot spreading down his leg.

"Uh…is he going to remember any of that?" I stepped away from Roth, clutching my bag close to my body. God, this demon's abilities were astronomical. I didn't know whether I was more frightened or impressed.

"Only that food is his worst nightmare now. Seemed kind of fitting, don't you think?"

I raised a brow. "How did you know all of that?"

Roth shrugged, the light fading from his eyes. "We're attuned to all things evil."

"That's not much of an explanation."

"Didn't intend for it to be." He took my hand again. "Now let's get back to business. We've got a zombie to check out."

I bit my lip, weighing my options. I was already way too late to join class and there was a zombie in my school, which I should check out for Abbot's sake. But Roth was a demon—a demon who followed me to school.

Roth sighed beside me. "Look. You do realize I can't really make you do anything you don't want to do, right?"

I peeked up at him. "What do you mean?"

His stare turned incredulous. "Do you know anything about what you are?" He searched my face, gaining the answer to his question. "You aren't susceptible to demon persuasion. Just like I can't sway a demon or a Warden to do something they don't want."

"Oh." How I was supposed to know that was beyond me. It wasn't as if there was a demon operation manual or something. "So why do you want me to check out the zombie thing? Shouldn't the idea of a zombie running amok in a high school be a good thing for you?"

Roth shrugged. "I'm bored."

Irritated, I tried to pull my hand free. "Can you ever give a straight answer?"

Something flashed in his eyes. "Okay. You want the truth? I'm here because of you. Yes, you heard that right. And don't ask me why, because we don't have time right now and you wouldn't believe me anyway. You're *part* Warden and if you get bitten by the zombie, then you will get infected. Maybe not completely batshit crazy like humans, but crazy enough to make my job harder."

My heart rate quadrupled. "Why—why are you here because of me?"

"For the love of all unholy things, why must you be so difficult? I apologized for calling you a prude. I'll even apologize for yesterday. I scared you. I threw your cell in a toilet. See, I was raised in Hell. You could say I'm socially awkward."

Awkward was not one of the descriptions that came to mind for him. He had a sort of fluid grace that was otherworldly and predatory. "This is weird, even for me," I admitted.

"But better than gym class, right?"

Most things were better than gym class. "I want to know why your being here has anything to do with me."

"Like I said, you wouldn't believe me." When I held my ground, he said something too low and quick for me to understand. I wasn't even sure it was English, but it sounded like a curse. "I'm not here to hurt you, okay? I'm the very last thing you should be worried about."

Taken aback by that, I could only stare as realization smacked me upside the head. For some reason—I didn't know why—I... I believed him. Maybe it had to do with the fact that if Roth wanted to harm me, he could've done so by now. Or maybe I was just incredibly stupid and had a death wish. And the idea of going to gym class did suck.

I sighed. "Okay, but you have to tell me why you're here when we're done."

Roth nodded.

My gaze dropped to our clasped hands. Warmth had traveled up my arm, and I really didn't trust that feeling. "And you don't need to hold my hand."

"But what if I get scared?"

"Seriously?"

Several seconds passed and then he released my hand. Scratching his chin, he shrugged. "Okay. It's a deal, but if you want to hold my hand later, you're out of luck."

"I don't think that's going to be a problem."

Roth slipped his hands into the pockets of his black jeans as he rocked back on his heels. "Are you happy now? Can we go?"

"All right," I said. "Fine."

He shot me a wide smile, flashing two perfectly placed dimples I hadn't seen before. He looked almost normal when he smiled like that, but the perfection of his face still seemed unreal.

I tore my gaze from him, walking forward. "Where is it again?"

"The boiler room in the basement. And it's probably going to smell worse down there."

I'd forgotten about the smell somehow. "So you guys keep track of other demons and stuff?"

Roth nodded as he shouldered the double doors open. "Yes."

I caught the door before it slammed shut, easing it closed. "And you let them infect humans even though it's against the rules?"

Heading down the steps, he glanced back. He was humming under his breath, a song that was faintly familiar. "Yes."

I followed him, gripping the rail with damp fingers. Something felt as if it was nesting in my stomach. "The Alphas forbid that kind of stuff. You're only allowed—"

"I know. We're only allowed to nudge humans, but never outright manipulate, infect and/or kill, and blah, blah. Free will is bullshit." He laughed and jumped off the step, landing nimbly on the cement. "We're demons. Rules kind of only apply to us when we want them to."

"Free will isn't bullshit, Roth."

He stopped suddenly in front of me and our eyes locked. "Say it again."

I frowned. "Say what?"

"My name."

"Roth...?"

The dimples appeared again. "Did you know that was the first time you've used my name? I've decided I quite like hearing you say it. But back to my point—free will *is* bullshit. No one really has free will."

I couldn't look away. "That's not true. We all have it."

Roth came up a step, towering over me. I wanted to back down, but I forced myself to stand still. "You have no idea," he said, eyes glinting like chips of tawny jewels. "None of us do. Especially not the Wardens or the demons. We all have orders, ones that we must obey. In the end, we always do what we're told. The idea of free will is a joke."

I felt sorry for him if he truly believed that. "I make choices every day—*my* choices. If you have no free will, then what kind of purpose would you even have in life?"

"What kind of purpose does a demon have? Hmm?" He tapped his chin with the tip of his finger. "Should I coerce a politician to turn dirty or should I save a kitten from a tree today? Wait. I'm a demon. I'm going to—"

"You don't have to be sarcastic."

"I'm not. I'm just giving you an example of how we are who we are—what we're born to be. Our paths are clearly laid out in front of us. There is no changing that. No free will."

"That's your opinion."

He held my gaze for a few more seconds and then smiled. "Come on." He spun around, hurrying down another flight of stairs.

It took me a few seconds to make my legs move. "I'm not anything like you."

Roth laughed in that rough, deep way again.

A brief, satisfying image of me kicking him down the stairs

flashed before me. He was humming again, and I was too annoyed with him to ask what the song was.

The school was old and several stories tall, but it had been remodeled a few years ago. The stairwells were a sign of its true age. Old brick walls crumbled into a red-and-white dust that covered the steps.

We stopped in front of a rusted gray door that said Employees Only. The smell was enough to kill my appetite for the rest of the day. Roth glanced at me, seeming unaffected by the rankness.

"So…can you really tell if someone is going to Hell?" I asked, stalling. I might hurl if he opened the door.

"Pretty much," he responded. "Usually it runs in the family. The apple doesn't fall far from the tree."

"Kind of cliché." I wrinkled my nose as the stink increased the closer we got.

"Most clichés are true." He jiggled the doorknob. "Locked."

"Oh. Darn." I tugged on the chain and fiddled with the ring. "I guess we—" I heard gears grinding and metal give way. I glanced down at Roth's hand as he pulled open the door. "Wow."

"Told you I have many talents," he said, glancing down at the ring. "Interesting piece of jewelry you have there."

I dropped it back under my cardigan, smoothing my hands over my jeans. "Yeah, I guess so."

He turned back to the door, slowly pushing it open. "Oh. Wow. He's definitely down here."

Flickering lights and the worst smell north of Hell greeted us. I clapped a hand over my nose and mouth, the mixture of decomposition and sulfur triggering my gag reflex. I'd rather take a shower in the moldy school stalls than go into this place.

Roth entered first, holding the door open with his booted foot. "Don't wimp out on me."

I let the door slam this time, because the idea of touching

anything down here grossed me out. "How do you think he got in?"

"Don't know."

"Why do you think he's here?"

"Don't know."

"Real helpful," I muttered.

Large metal cabinets full of God knows what cramped the corridor we traveled and the heat dampened my brow with a fine sheet of sweat. The overhead light swayed in the breeze-less room, casting shadows across vacant workbenches and tools scattered across the floor. We squeezed past a stack of old chalk-boards, more white than green.

"I think this is a bad idea," I whispered, fighting the urge to latch on to the back of Roth's shirt.

"And your point is?" Roth pushed open another door lead-ing to a dark room where heavy machinery droned. The door banged into a stack of cardboard boxes.

Out of the darkness, a skeleton fell across the doorway, arms and legs flailing in the damp, musty air. The eye sockets were empty and sightless, jaw hanging open in a silent scream. I let out a hoarse shriek, jumping back.

"It's not real." Roth picked up the skeleton and examined it. "It's what they use in your biology classes. See." He wiggled an off-white bony arm at me. "Totally fake."

My heart didn't agree, but I could see the metal bolts hold-ing the arm bones together. "Oh, sweet baby Jesus…"

Grinning, Roth tossed the skeleton aside. I winced as it bounced, bones clattering when it hit whatever Roth had thrown it at.

And then something growled.

I froze.

Roth flipped on the overhead light. "Whoops," he mur-mured.

It stood in front of the boiler, a fake arm bone in its blackened hand and the rest of the skeleton lying at its feet. Thin wisps of air wriggled out of the patchy skin like brown worms. Areas of its face were missing flesh. A strip on the cheek flapped against the purplish lips, and what skin remained hung from the bones, heavily creased and resembling dried-out beef jerky. It also wore a suit that had most definitely seen better days— days that didn't involve seeping bodily fluids.

Behind the boiler, the only window in the room was broken. That explained how it had gotten into school, but gave us no clue about why it was here.

Roth let out a low whistle.

The zombie's eyes moved to Roth and kept on moving. At least one did. It went right out the eye socket, flying through the air, splattering across the muck-covered floor.

"Oh! Oh, no. No. I didn't sign up for this!" I clamped my hand over my mouth, gagging. "I'm not going near that thing."

Roth stepped forward, eyeing the mess on the floor as if fascinated. "That was pretty gross."

I felt exposed standing in the doorway by myself. Inching closer to Roth, I kept my gaze on the zombie. I'd never seen one in such bad condition. God knows it had to have chomped on people by now, but the Wardens should've been notified through their contacts.

My movement drew the zombie's one good eye. "You," it gurgled.

I stopped. They could talk? Guess George Romero missed out on that. "Me?"

"Hey. Don't look at her. Look at me," ordered Roth, his voice heavy with authority.

It struggled to get its mouth to work right. "You…needs…"

"Um…why is it staring at me?" I gripped the strap on my back until my knuckles hurt.

"Maybe it thinks you're pretty," Roth quipped, stepping back as a rat ran in front of him.

I shot him a hateful look.

The zombie lurched, its left foot sliding forward. I stepped back, bumping into more boxes. "Roth…?"

With slow, purposeful movements, the zombie winged the skeleton arm at Roth's head. Bones in the zombie's body cracked and splintered. Pus leaked out the tear in its jacket.

Roth snatched the arm out of the air, face incredulous. "Did you just throw this at my head? *My head?* Are you insane?"

It lumbered at me, groaning incoherent words.

"Roth!" I screeched, dodging the stinky arm. "This was a terrible idea!"

"You have to rub it in?"

I reached behind me, grabbing a box. I threw it at the zombie, hitting it on the side of the face. An ear fell off, landing on its shoulder. "Yes! Do something!"

Roth crept up behind it, wielding the skeletal limb like a baseball bat. "I'm trying to."

"What are you doing?" I darted to the side as it reached for me. "Don't you have any evil powers of darkness or something?"

"Evil powers of darkness? None I can use here without bringing the whole school down on us."

This seemed ridiculous. "Can't you come up with a better plan?"

Roth scoffed. "Like what?"

"I don't know. Feed it to Bambi or something!"

"What?" Roth lowered the arm, his expression dumbfounded. "Bambi would get indigestion eating something that rotten."

"Roth! I swear to God, I'm—" My sneaker slipped on the gunk and my leg went right out from underneath me. I hit the dirty, wet cement with a loud *oof.* Sprawled out on the floor, I held up my slimy hands. "I'm going to barf. Seriously."

"Move out of the way!" yelled Roth.

My head jerked up as he swung the makeshift weapon. I scrambled back, getting hung up on my book bag. The skeleton arm hit the zombie's head and then went through it. Mottled blood and flesh flew through the air, plopping off the floor... and onto my jeans.

Skin, muscle and bone sank in on itself. The thing sort of imploded, collapsing until nothing was left but a puddle of muck on the floor and the filthy clothing it had worn.

Roth threw the arm down, anger tightening his expression. "That was slightly irritating." He turned around, looking at me. His amber eyes took on a sheen of amusement. "Oh, you've made a mess of yourself."

I stared at my goo-covered pants and hands before fixing Roth with a glare. "I hate you."

"*Hate* is such a strong word." He swaggered to my side, bending down. "Let me help you."

I kicked out, catching him in the shin. "Don't touch me."

He hobbled back, cursing and shaking out his pants leg. "You got brains on my new jeans. Thanks."

Muttering under my breath, I pushed to my feet and grabbed my bag. Luckily, there wasn't any yuck on that, but me? I didn't even want to look at myself, I was that gross. "Well, this was really fun."

"Hey! Don't be upset. The zombie problem has been taken care of."

I pointed at myself with both hands. At the moment, I didn't give a crap about why he was following me. "Look at me. I have zombie spew all over me, thanks to you. And I have classes the rest of the day."

A slow smile spread across his face. "I can take you back to my place. I have a shower you can use. Then maybe we can get a drink and check out my Porsche."

My palms itched to make friends with the sides of his face. "You're disgusting."

He chuckled, turning back to the corpse. "What in the Hell were you doing here?" he said, mostly to himself. "And what did...?" He looked over his shoulder, gaze falling to my chest. His eyes narrowed. "Oh, great."

"Hey! God, you are such a dog!"

Roth arched a brow. "I've been called worse. Go get cleaned up. I'll take care of this."

Drawing in a deep breath, I spun around. I made it to the door before he stopped me. He said something like "lamb" under his breath. Shaking my head, I left him in the boiler room, smelling of rotten zombie.

I spent the rest of the day in my gym clothes with soaking wet hair.

I hated Roth.

Morris looked surprised when I slid into the passenger seat. Typically I tagged every day after school, but today I wasn't feeling it. Unlike yesterday, silence greeted me as I walked into the house and dropped my bag inside the door.

I headed through the foyer, pulling my damp hair into a messy bun. I needed to tell Abbot about the zombie at school. Roth issue aside, the zombie was something serious. There was a good chance that Abbot was still asleep, though.

The last time I'd woken him up, I'd been eight and had only Mr. Snotty for company. I wanted someone to play with me, so I knocked on Abbot's stone shell while he slept.

That hadn't gone over well.

This time was different. He'd have to understand, but I could at least ease his temper with a cup of coffee. It took me a couple of minutes to find the damn coffee grounds and filter, then another five minutes of trying to figure out if I should use the coffee or the cappuccino setting. The thing required a degree in engineering to figure out. I tugged on the stainless-steel lever, frowning. What the Hell did this do?

"It's really not that complicated."

Every muscle in my body locked and yet I managed to drop the little metal measuring spoon. It clattered on the tile floor. I bent down and grabbed the spoon, trying to calm the sudden bundle of nerves in my stomach. My legs felt weak as I straightened.

Petr stood in the doorway. His thick arms crossed a barrel-sized chest. "I see you haven't gained any grace since the last time I saw you."

Coming from anyone else, that dig might have stung. I put the spoon on the counter. Coffee be damned. I stopped a few feet in front of him. "Excuse me."

He didn't move. "And you're just as rude and bitchy."

My chin shot up. Petr was only a year or two older than me, but the dark stubble across his chin and jaw made him look older. "Can you *please* move out of the way?"

Petr stepped aside, leaving about a foot to go through. "Happy?"

I was anything but happy with the idea of my body being in the same zip code as his. I squeezed past him, wincing as my hip rubbed against his leg.

"Thought you were making coffee?" He fell in step behind me. "I could help you."

Ignoring him, I picked up my pace. I wouldn't fall for his cajoling tone again. Not in this lifetime or the next.

Petr stepped around me, blocking my way upstairs—to safety. He sighed. "So who were you making coffee for?"

A flicker of fear curled around my heart. "Can you move? I need to go upstairs."

"You can't talk to me for five minutes?"

Out of habit, I felt for the circular object under my shirt, clasping my hand over it. I tried to move past him. He shadowed my movements. "Petr, please let me by."

Faint sunlight from the nearby window reflected off the

small stud pierced into his hawkish nose. "I can remember a time when you liked talking to me. When you looked forward to when my clan would visit."

A faint flush crept over my face as my grip tightened on my shirt. The ring bit through the clothing, pressing against my palm. I used to have a crush on the jerkwad. "That was before I realized what a creep you are."

The line of his jaw hardened. "I didn't do anything wrong."

"You didn't do anything wrong? I told you to stop and you wouldn't—"

"You were being a tease." His voice dropped low. "And since when do demons really get a say in anything?"

I sucked in air. "I'm a Warden."

He rolled his eyes, laughing. "Oh, I'm sorry. You're only half-demon. Like that makes a difference. Do you know what we usually do to the spawn of demons and humans?"

"Love them and hug them?" I tried to slide past, but he slapped his palm against the wall in front of me.

"We kill them, Layla. Like Abbot was supposed to do with you, but you're just so damn *special*."

I bit down on my lip. He was too close. If I breathed too deeply, I could taste his soul. "I need to go see Zayne."

"Zayne is still resting." He paused. "He stayed up pretty late this morning talking to Danika."

Irrational jealousy flooded my system, which was so stupid considering the current situation. "Then I'm going to see—"

"Jasmine and the twins?" he asked. "Yeah, they're taking a nap. No one is up, Layla. It's just you and me."

I swallowed. "Morris is here. Geoff is up, too."

Petr laughed. "You're so clueless."

A slow burn began under my skin. I held my breath. If there was anyone in this world I wanted to suck a soul out of, it was Petr. Out of everyone, he'd deserve it the most.

His heavy hand landed on my shoulder, forcing me around.

Petr smiled. "You're in so much trouble, you little half-demon bitch."

Anger flooded me and I tried to shake off his hand. Dropping the ring, I prepared to break the no-fighting-a-Warden rule. "Are you threatening me?"

"No. Not at all." He moved his hand to my throat, circling his fingers much tighter than Roth had. Ironic that a demon seemed to have gentler hands than a Warden. "You want to fight me, don't you? Do it. It'll make everything easier for us."

My stomach tumbled over itself. Petr knew I'd get in trouble, and there was more than a hint of cruelty in his pale eyes. Worse yet, I knew that he saw nothing wrong with what he was doing. His actions would never taint his soul, because it was pure, no matter what he did. It was like a free pass to him. Petr pressed forward, his breath too warm against my cheek. "You're going to wish Abbot had snuffed out your miserable little life when you were a baby."

Screw the rules.

I brought my knee up, hitting him where it hurt. Petr let out a low growl and let go, cupping himself. Spinning around, I flew up the stairs without looking back. In the hallway, I came face-to-face with Petr's father. I tried not to react, but the jagged scar that tore through his upper and lower lips was hard not to notice. Abbot had once told me a King demon had given Elijah that scar.

Elijah eyed me with a look of revulsion, but said nothing as I raced around him and into my bedroom, locking the door behind me. Not that it would stop any of them if they decided to come through that door.

ABBOT SAT BEHIND THE DESK, his leg propped over his knee. "You didn't eat very much at dinner. Are you still feeling unwell?"

I threw myself in the chair. I'd managed only a bite or two during the tense dinner. Petr eyeballed me the entire time. "I don't want them here."

Abbot rubbed his fingers across his bearded chin. His sandy hair was pulled back as usual. "Layla, I understand that you're uncomfortable. Elijah has assured me that you will have no problems with Petr."

"Really? That's funny, because Petr cornered me earlier."

His fingers stilled, the pale eyes sharpening. "Did he do anything?"

"It wasn't like...the last time." I shifted uncomfortably, feeling my face burn.

He let out a long, low breath. "Can you just stay away from him for the next week or so?"

I was floored. "I *am* staying away from him. *He* won't stay away from *me!* If he comes near me again, I swear to God I'll take his—"

Abbot slammed his hand down on the desk, causing me to jump in the chair. "You will do no such thing, Layla!"

My heart lurched. "I wasn't being serious. I'm...I'm sorry."

"That is nothing to joke about." He shook his head, speaking as if I was an ill-behaved child. "I'm very disappointed that you'd even consider saying something like that. If any of our visitors overheard you—including Petr's father—the damage would be irreversible."

A messy, icky lump formed in my chest. I hated disappointing Abbot. I owed him so much—a home, safety, a life. I cast my eyes down, twisting the ring between my fingers. "I'm sorry—really I am."

Abbot sighed, and I heard him lean back in his seat. I peeked up, not wanting to add to his long list of worries. He ran his fingers over his brow, eyes closed. "What did you want to talk to me about, Layla?"

Suddenly the whole thing with the zombie didn't seem very important. Neither did Roth's presence. I just wanted to go hide in my bedroom.

"Layla?" he questioned, pulling a fat cigar out of a wooden box on his desk. He never smoked them, but liked to fiddle with them anyway.

"It's nothing," I said finally. "Just something that happened today at school."

His pale brows rose an inch. "You wanted to talk to me about school? I know Zayne has been occupied with Danika's arrival and training, but I have a lot going on right now. Perhaps Jasmine would be interested in chatting with you?"

My face felt like I could fry eggs on it. "I don't want to talk about boys or my grades."

He rolled the cigar between his fingers. "How are your

grades? I assume your teacher is allowing you to make up your test tomorrow?"

I dropped the ring, clutching the arms of my chair in frustration. "My grades are fine. And I have the make—"

"What are you two doing in here?"

I twisted around. Zayne stood in the doorway, his hair falling around his face like sheets of sand. "I'm trying to tell Abbot what happened today at school."

His lazy look turned to surprise. He glanced at his father as a slow grin twisted his lips. "How's that going?"

Abbot sighed heavily, placing the cigar back in the box. "Layla, I have to leave shortly to meet with the police commissioner and the mayor."

"There was a zombie at my school today," I blurted out.

"Huh?" Zayne stopped behind my chair, flicking the back of my ear. I swatted his hand away. "What are you talking about?" he asked.

I met Abbot's suddenly alert gaze. "He was in the boiler room and—"

"How did you know he was there?" Abbot demanded, uncrossing his legs as he leaned forward.

I couldn't tell them about Roth. No way was I opening that door. "I…I smelled him."

Zayne dropped in the seat beside me. "Did anyone see him?"

I cringed. "Trust me, if they did, it would have been on the evening news. He was that bad off."

"Is he still there?" Abbot stood, rolling down the sleeves of his shirt.

"Uh…yes, but I don't think he's going to be a problem. He's nothing but a pile of clothes and goo."

"Wait a minute," Zayne said, frowning as he watched me. "You smelled a zombie, and knowing how dangerous they can be, you decided to go down to a boiler room and check it out?"

I looked at him. Where was he going with this? "Well, yeah, I did."

"And you engaged the zombie? Killing it?"

Well... "Yes."

He shot his father a meaningful look. "Father."

"What?" My eyes bounced between the two.

Abbot walked around the desk, letting out another long sigh. "What are the rules, Layla?"

Unease cramped my stomach muscles. "I don't mess with the dangerous stuff, but—"

"Zayne told me you followed a Poser into the alley the other night," Abbot interrupted, in total father mode. Disappointed-father mode. "And it turned out to be a Seeker."

"I..." I closed my mouth, glancing at Zayne. He avoided my eyes, watching his father. "It's not a big deal."

"Following a Poser or any demon into an alley is a big deal, Layla." Abbot folded his arms, pinning me with a displeased stare. "You know better. No one can see your tags besides us. There is no reason you should be following one into an isolated area. And instead of seeking out the zombie today, you should have called Morris and he would have woken us up."

Jeez. I sank down in my seat. "But—"

"There are no buts, Layla. What would have happened if the zombie was seen by anyone? We are charged with keeping the truth secret. Mankind must have faith that Heaven and Hell exist without proof."

"Maybe we should cut back on her time tagging," Zayne suggested. "We don't need her doing it. Honestly, it's all very lazy of us to rely on her tagging instead of actively searching them out."

I stared at him, seeing my freedom shrivel up in front of me instead of his godly looks. "No one found out about the zombie today!"

"That's not the point," snapped Abbot. "You know better,

Layla. You risked serious consequences by not telling us, not to mention risking your own safety."

His disappointment rang through loud and clear. I shifted uneasily in my seat, feeling about a foot tall.

"We should check out the school tonight," said Zayne. "Have the commissioner contact the superintendent—say it's something routine so there's no suspicion."

"Good call." He gave his son a proud smile.

I bristled. "So I'm not allowed to tag anymore?"

"That's something I need to think about," replied Abbot.

That didn't sound good to me. I hated the idea of not being able to tag. It was the one thing that redeemed the demonic blood in me, or at least made me feel better. Taking that away was like a smack in the face. It also got me out of the house, and with Petr here that was even more important. I apologized once again and left the study. I felt as if I was on the verge of crying and screaming—or punching someone.

Zayne followed me into the hallway. "Hey."

I stopped near the stairs, a rush of anger hitting me hard in the gut. I waited until he stood beside me. "You just had to tell him about the Seeker in the alley. Thanks."

He frowned. "He needed to know, Layla. You weren't being safe and you could've been hurt."

"Then why didn't you say something to me instead of running to your daddy?"

His jaw immediately clenched. "I didn't run to my daddy."

I folded my arms. "That's not how it looks."

Zayne gave me a sigh I was familiar with. It said *you're being childish and getting on my last nerve.*

I ignored it. "Why would you even suggest that I stop tagging? You know how important it is to me."

"Your safety is more important. You know I've never really agreed with them allowing you to run around D.C. by yourself, pursuing demons. It's dangerous."

"I've been tagging since I was thirteen, Zayne. I've never had any problem—"

"Until a few nights ago," he interrupted, cheeks flushing with anger. It was so rare that Zayne ever lost his cool with me, but when he did, it was epic. "And it's more than that. You're young and pretty. Who knows what kind of attention you're attracting out there."

Any other time I would have been thrilled to hear him say I was pretty, but right now, I wanted to take that word and shove it in his face. "I can take care of myself."

He looked at me dead-on. "What I've shown you will only get you so far."

Irritation and the need to prove I wasn't some helpless dweeb provoked what I said next. "And I know how to finish someone off."

Zayne got what I was saying. A look of utter disbelief flickered across his face. "That's the way you'd protect yourself? By taking someone's soul? Nice."

Immediately, I realized my mistake. I came down a step. "I didn't really mean it, Zayne. You know that."

He didn't look too sure. "Whatever. I have things I need to do."

"Like Danika?" I said before I could stop myself.

His eyes fell shut, and when they reopened, they were a sheltered, icy blue. "Real mature. Good night, Layla."

The hot rush of tears clouded my vision as I watched him leave. I was making a mess of everything without even trying. That took talent. I turned around and saw Petr standing just inside the sitting room. The smirk on his face told me that he'd heard our whole exchange—and enjoyed it.

I woke up, heart pounding and throat burning. The sheets twisted around my legs, chafing my skin. Rolling over, I stared at the neon-green light of the alarm clock.

2:52 a.m.

I needed something sweet.

Throwing off the sheets, I stood. My nightgown clung to my damp skin. There wasn't a single light on in the hallway outside my bedroom, but I knew the way by heart. There'd been so many nights when the craving unexpectedly hit hard, leading to dark and silent trips to the kitchen.

I padded down the steps and through the shadowy rooms in a hurry. My legs were starting to feel wobbly, my heart rate spiking. *I can't live like this.*

My arm trembled as I pulled open the door to the fridge. Yellow light washed over my bare legs and the floor. I bent down, impatiently searching for the carton of orange juice among the bottles of water and milk. Annoyed and ready to kick something, I found the OJ behind the eggs.

The carton slipped from my shaking fingers, crashing to the floor and spilling sticky juice all over my toes. Tears welled up and spilled down my cheeks. I was crying over spilled orange juice, for chrissake. It had to be one of my lamest moments of all time.

Sitting next to the sticky puddle, I ignored the cold air from the fridge. God knows how long I sat there before I smacked the door shut. At once, the kitchen was pitched into darkness. I kind of liked it like that. It was just me being ridiculously stupid, and the darkness. No one could witness my hysterics.

Then I heard the soft fluttering of wings, growing louder as they moved toward the kitchen. I stiffened, my very breath halting in my throat. The air stirred around me. I looked up, seeing yellow eyes and fangs surrounded by skin the color and texture of polished granite. The nose was flat, nostrils thin slits. Parting the cascade of dark hair were two horns that curved inward.

Danika was just as striking in her true form as she was in her human.

She dropped beside me, claws tapping on the tile floor as she walked over to the kitchen island and grabbed a roll of paper towels. "Need help?"

It was strange seeing a six-foot gargoyle offer you paper towels.

Danika stared down at me, her dark gray lips curving into a tentative smile.

I hastily wiped my palms under my eyes and then took the wad of towels. "Thanks."

Danika tucked her wings in as she crouched, cleaning up most of the mess with one swipe. "Are you feeling unwell?"

"I'm fine." I picked up the carton. It was empty. Great.

She balled the paper towels, her fingers long and elegant, but those claws could rip through skin, muscle, even metal. "It doesn't seem like you're fine," she said carefully. "Zayne told me that sometimes you...get sick."

My head jerked up. A rush of hot betrayal swept through me. I couldn't even form words.

Danika's face grew pinched. "He's just concerned about you, Layla. He cares about you deeply."

I grabbed the soaked towels and empty carton, standing on shaky legs. "Oh." I laughed harshly. "He does? That's why he told you about my *sickness?*"

She slowly straightened. "He only said something so that I could help in case you needed anything." She backed up, seeing the look on my face. "Layla, I don't judge you. In fact, I think you're incredibly strong."

More tears, hotter than those that had already fallen, burned at the back of my throat. Why I was always eating something sweet was no secret, but only Zayne knew how badly I struggled—up until now. I couldn't believe he'd told Danika. And asked her to keep an eye on me? *Mortifying* seemed like a weak word to describe how I felt.

"Layla, do you need something else? I can go to the store and get some more juice."

I dumped the stuff in the garbage can, shoulders stiff. "I'm not going to jump on you and suck out your soul, if that's what you're worried about."

Danika gasped. "That's not what I meant—not at all. It's just that you look like you need something and I want to help."

I whirled around. She still stood by the fridge, her wings unfurled, reaching at least four feet on either side of her. "I'm fine. You don't have to keep an eye on me." I turned away, but stopped at the door, drawing in a shallow breath. "Tell Zayne I said thanks."

Before Danika could respond, I left the kitchen and went back to my room. I crawled into bed, throwing the covers over my head. Every so often, a spasm ran through my muscles and my leg would jerk. Over and over again, the words ran through my head.

I can't live like this.

8

"ARE YOU FEELING OKAY TODAY?" Stacey asked the moment she sat beside me in bio. "You look like warmed-over crap."

I didn't even bother looking up. "Thanks, buddy."

"Well, I'm sorry, but it's true. You look like you've been up all night crying."

"It's allergies." I shifted forward so my hair blocked most of my face. "You, on the other hand, sound awfully chipper this morning."

"I do, don't I?" Stacey sighed dreamily. "Mom didn't screw up my coffee like she always does. You know how I get when she does, which is almost every freaking morning, but today. No. Today was hazelnut day and my world is bright and shiny. Anyway, what did Zayne do?"

"What?" I lifted my head, frowning.

Her stare was sympathetic. "Zayne is the only person who makes you cry."

"I wasn't crying."

She brushed her bangs back. "Whatever. You need to get over him and get with a hottie." She paused, nodding at the door. "Like him, for example. He'd leave you crying for a whole different reason."

"I wasn't crying over—" I cut myself off when I realized she was gesturing at Roth. "Wait, how would he make me cry?"

Stacey's eyes widened. "Are you for real? Do I need to spell it out for you?"

I glanced back at Roth. Like Stacey, my classmates had stopped what they were doing to just watch him. There was a natural swagger to the way he walked. Suddenly I got what Stacey meant. Turning beet-red, I turned back to my book.

She giggled.

It was a lab day. We were partnered with Roth, much to Stacey's delight. Surprisingly, he ignored me for most of the class and chatted with Stacey. She told him everything except her bra size, and I sincerely believed that if the bell hadn't rung, she would have told him that, too.

My craptastic mood followed me through the rest of the day. At lunch, I pushed my food around my plate while Stacey engaged Eva in an epic stare down.

Sam poked me with his plastic fork. "Hey."

"Hmm?"

"Did you know every northern state has a Springfield as a city?"

I felt a grin tug at my lips. "No, I didn't. Sometimes I wish I had half the memory you do."

His eyes twinkled behind his glasses. "How long do you think Stacey is going to give Eva the stink eye?"

"I can hear you," Stacey responded. "She's been spreading some nasty rumors. I think I'm going to break into her house later and cut her hair off. Then maybe glue it to her face."

Sam grinned. "That's kind of an odd form of retaliation."

"Yeah, that is weird." I took a sip of my water.

Stacey rolled her eyes. "If you heard the shit she's been saying, you'd sign up for the face-gluing."

"Oh, is this about me putting out after one beer or being a servant in my own house?" I twisted the cap back on the water bottle, briefly considering chucking it at Eva's face.

Sam took his glasses off. "I hadn't heard this."

"That's because you don't hear anything, Sam. Eva's been saying some vicious stuff about Layla. I'm not down with that."

A fine shiver ran down my spine, cutting off my response. I looked to my left, shocked to find Roth standing there. This was the first time I'd seen him in the cafeteria. For some reason, I didn't think he ate.

Stacey didn't even try to hide her surprise. "Roth! You came!"

"What?" I felt as confused as Sam looked.

Roth dropped down in the empty seat beside me, a smug grin on his face. "Stacey invited me to lunch during bio. Weren't you paying attention?"

I shot Stacey a disbelieving look. She just smiled. "How nice of you," I said slowly.

Sam's gaze bounced between Stacey and me before settling on Roth. He stuck his hand out awkwardly. I wanted to knock it back. "I'm Sam. Nice to meet you."

Roth shook his hand. "You can call me Roth."

"Roth as in the retirement account?" asked Sam. "Is that what you're named after?"

Dark brows inched up Roth's forehead as he stared at Sam.

"Sorry." Stacey sighed. "Sam has absolutely no social skills. I should've warned you."

Sam's eyes narrowed on Stacey. "What? That's what retirement accounts are called—Roth IRAs. How can you not know that?"

"I'm in high school. Why would I care about retirement? Besides, who would know that but you?" Stacey shot back as she picked up a plastic fork, waving it in his face. "Next you're going to wow us with your knowledge of plastic utensils and how they were created."

"I'm sorry if your lack of knowledge makes you uncomfortable." Sam knocked the fork away, grinning. "It must be hard living with that tiny brain of yours."

Roth nudged me with his elbow. I nearly jumped out of my seat. "Are they always like this?"

I considered ignoring him, but when I glanced at his face, I found I couldn't look away. Seeing him in the school cafeteria was beyond unnerving. I figured he just came to bio and then disappeared. Was he actually attending all day?

"Always," I murmured.

He smiled as his gaze dropped to the table. "So what were you guys talking about before retirement accounts and the creation of utensils?"

"Nothing," I said quickly.

"Eva Hasher—the bitch over there." Stacey gestured with her hand. "She's been talking smack about Layla."

"Thanks." I eyed the doors leading out of the cafeteria desperately.

"I've heard," Roth responded. "So you were planning some sort of revenge?"

"Most definitely," she answered.

"Well, you could always—"

"No." I stopped him. "No revenge necessary, Roth." I was pretty sure his ideas would buy me a one-way ticket to Hell.

He flipped a lock of hair out of his face. It wasn't spiked today, and I kind of liked it like that. It made his face softer. Not that I liked his hair or his face or anything about him. "That's no fun."

Sam glanced at Roth, slipping his glasses back on. "You don't know Stacey. The last time she plotted revenge, it included stealing a can of mace and a car."

Roth's eyes widened. "Wow. Hard-core."

Stacey stretched in the chair, grinning from ear to ear. "What can I say? If I'm going to do bad, I'm going all out."

This seemed to excite the demon, which was hardly surprising. I jumped in before he could say anything. "So...what's everyone doing this weekend?"

Sam shrugged. "I was thinking about going to see a play at the old opera house. Since someone hasn't scored me the interview of the century, I'm doing a piece on folk art instead. God help me."

I rubbed my forehead wearily. "Sorry. I told you not to hold your breath. The Wardens are pretty camera shy, as you might recall."

"Roth, did you know Layla was adopted by Wardens?" Stacey nudged me under the table. "Does that freak you out?"

I wanted to smack her.

"Freak me out?" Roth grinned. "No. I think it's...epic."

Slowly, I looked at him. "Do you?"

His grin turned into a damn near angelic smile. "Oh, yes. I admire the Wardens. Where would any of us be without them?"

I almost laughed. It sounded so ridiculous coming from a demon. But even though I managed to choke back the laughter, my smile appeared before I could do anything about it. His eyes met mine again, but this time the cafeteria faded away. I knew the world continued on around us, and I could hear Stacey and Sam bickering again, but it felt like it was just the two of us. A strange fluttering started in my chest, spreading through my body.

He moved without me realizing, his warm breath dancing over my cheeks, my lips. The air hitched in my lungs. His lips parted, and I wondered what it would be like to run my fingers across them, to feel them.

"What are you thinking?" he murmured, his eyes fluttering down.

I snapped out of my haze, remembering who and *what* I was staring at. Thinking about him in a way I should never be considering. I was supposed to be angry with him about yesterday and the countless other things he'd done in the short time I'd known him.

Feeling dizzy, I bit my lip and focused on what my friends were arguing over. Something to do with pineapples and cherries, but a few seconds later, I sneaked another glance at Roth. His smile was smug, even a bit daring.

And I had a feeling I was in trouble.

After finishing my makeup bio exam, I dumped my books in my locker. Abbot probably didn't want me tagging tonight, but that was what I had planned. Risking his wrath was far better than locking myself in my bedroom or being forced to be around Petr. As I shut the door, I felt an unnatural stirring of air around me. Glancing up, my heart stuttered to a halt.

Roth slouched against the locker beside mine, hands shoved into the pockets of his jeans. "What are you doing?"

"Jeez." I stumbled backward. "You almost gave me a stroke."

One side of his lips curved up. "Whoops."

I shouldered my bag and edged past him, but he easily caught up with me. I pushed open the heavy metal doors, welcoming the cool evening air. "What do you want?"

"I thought you'd like to know that I cleaned up the mess yesterday."

I figured as much, since Abbot and Zayne were supposed to check it out last night and hadn't yanked me out of bed to yell at me about the corpse. "Good for you."

"And you're tagging, right? Even though I asked you nicely not to. I can't let you do that alone."

"Why not?"

"I've already told you why. It's not safe for you."

I bit back the urge to scream. "And why is it not safe for me?"

He said nothing.

Beyond annoyed, I started forward. The streets were thick with commuters hurrying to the metro hubs. Maybe I could lose him in the crowd. A block later, Roth was still at my side. "You're angry with me," he said casually.

"I guess you can say that. I don't really like you."

He chuckled. "I like that you try to be honest."

I glanced at him warily. "I'm not trying. I *am* being honest."

Roth smiled broadly, flashing surprisingly sharp-looking teeth. "That's a lie. A part of you likes me."

I stepped off the curb, irritated. "I'm not the one lying right now."

Unfazed, he reached out and caught my arm, pulling me back just as a taxi zoomed by so fast it whipped at my hair. The cabbie honked his horn, yelling something obscene at me. "Careful," Roth murmured. "I doubt your insides are as pretty as the outside."

I was instantly aware of how my chest felt pressed against him. Warmth inexplicably flooded me, like I was basking in the summer sun. Our eyes locked. As close as we were, I could see that his eyes weren't pure gold, but there were flecks of deep amber in them. They churned crazily, drawing me in. That wild scent of his cloaked us.

My hand curled against his chest. When had my hand landed on his chest? I didn't know, but my gaze had dropped to his mouth. Those lips…so close.

Roth's one-sided smile tipped up higher.

Snapping out of it, I wiggled free. Roth's chuckle raised my hackles. I managed to cross the street without getting hit. My body still tingled from the brief contact.

And that was wrong.

Luckily, I found something to distract me. Standing on the opposite corner was a Fiend.

He was loitering outside a hotel that was under construction, standing next to the red scaffolding that climbed the front of the building. The Fiend looked like any of the number of punk-rock kids that could be found on the streets of D.C.

"You know, you could have said thank-you for saving your life." Roth was suddenly beside me.

I groaned, keeping an eye on the Fiend. "You didn't save my life."

"You almost got plowed by a cab. And if you want to get plowed, I will gladly volunteer my services. I promise you I'll be a lot—"

"Don't even finish that sentence."

"It was just an offer."

"Whatever." I watched the Fiend eyeing a construction worker who was starting to climb down the scaffolding. "If I say thank-you, will you go away?"

"Yes."

"Thank you," I said eagerly.

"I lied."

"What?" I looked up at him, frowning. "That's messed up."

Roth leaned down so that our faces were inches apart. God, he smelled wonderful. I closed my eyes briefly and I swore I could *feel* him smile.

"I'm a demon. I tend to lie from time to time."

I felt my lips twitch into a smile. I quickly turned away to hide it. "I've got things to do, Roth. Go bother someone else."

"You going to tag that Fiend over there?" he asked. We'd stopped outside a game shop a few stores down from the construction site.

I said nothing.

Roth leaned against the redbrick building. "Before you tag the kid and sentence it to death, why don't you see what he's actually going to do."

My eyes narrowed. "Why would I let him do something that I know is going to get someone hurt?"

"How do you know someone is going to get hurt?" Roth cocked his head to the side, sending waves of raven-black hair across his smooth forehead. "You've never actually waited to see what one is going to do, have you?"

I started to lie, but I turned away, focusing on the Fiend. The demon with spiky green hair scrubbed a hand along his jaw as he watched a construction worker hop down and head over to another section blocked off by orange mesh rope. The man picked up some sort of saw, waving it around as he laughed at something his buddy said.

"Just wait and see what happens before you judge him." Roth shrugged. "It won't hurt."

I sent him a sidelong glare. "I'm not judging him."

Roth tipped his head to the side. "Do you want me to pretend I have no idea what dastardly things you do after school?"

"Dastardly?" I rolled my eyes. "I'm just tagging—"

"Which lights them up for the Wardens to take out later," he finished. "So I have no idea how you can think that's not playing judge and jury."

"This is stupid. You want me to let him do something evil? I don't think so."

He seemed to consider that. "You know what I think your problem is?"

"No, but I bet you're going to enlighten me."

"Why, yes, I am. You don't want to see what the Fiend does because you're afraid that it isn't going to be something nefarious, and then you'll have to deal with the fact that your Wardens are murderers and not saviors."

My mouth dropped open, but my stomach also lurched at his words. If what he said was true, it would turn my world upside down. But it couldn't be true. Demons were evil.

"Fine," I snapped. "I'll wait."

Roth flashed a cheeky grin. "Good."

Muttering under my breath, I focused on the Fiend again. I was going to have some 'splainin' to do when it took out an entire sidewalk of commuters. Considering any other option was impossible. My whole life was built around one simple belief: demons deserved to be punished without question.

The Fiend pushed off the marbleized stone and reached out, casually brushing his fingers along the bottom part of the scaffolding, then kept on walking. A second later, a loud groan pierced the noise from the traffic and the scaffolding began to shudder. The workers' heads whipped around. The man dropped his saw and yelled out. Several other workers rushed out from the side of the building, gripping their yellow helmets as the whole scaffolding came down, collapsing like an accordion behind the orange rope.

As the plume of dust settled and curses exploded like gunshots, pedestrians stopped on the sidewalks, some taking pictures with their phones of the mess. And, God, it was a mess. Who knew how long it took to put the scaffolding up, and tools had been attached to it, but they were most likely destroyed when the scaffolding collapsed.

I just stared.

"Hmm," Roth drawled slowly. "That was definitely a setback in the project and some wasted money, but pure, scary-bad evil? Nah, I don't think so."

"It… He probably meant for it to fall onto the sidewalk."

"Keep telling yourself that."

No one had been hurt. Almost like the Fiend had waited for the last man to come down from the scaffolding before he'd touched it. I couldn't process what I'd seen.

Roth draped his arm over my shoulders. "Come on. Let's find another."

I shrugged his arm off as we started down the sidewalk. Roth was humming that damn song again.

"What is that?"

He stopped. "What is what?"

"The song you keep humming."

"Oh." He grinned. "'Paradise City.'"

It took me a few seconds to put it together. "Guns N' Roses?"

"Good stuff," he replied.

We found another Fiend messing with the poles connected to the streetlights. All four sides of the intersection went green at once. Epic fender benders ensued, but again, no one was hurt. The Fiend could've messed with the pedestrian signal, which would have been really bad, but she hadn't.

The whole thing was more mischievous than sinister.

"Want to go for third time's the charm?"

"No," I whispered, unnerved and confused. It was just two demons. It couldn't mean anything.

Roth arched a dark brow. "You want to tag? No? I didn't think so. How about we do something else?"

Stopping at a crosswalk, I shot him a look. "Is that why you ordered me to stop tagging? Because you think the Fiends are harmless?"

"I *know* the Fiends are harmless. Not all demons are. Some of us are really bad, but the ones you're sentencing to death? Nope." He paused as my stomach sank. "But no. My request really doesn't have anything to do with that."

"Then what?"

He didn't answer until we crossed the street, stepping up on the curb. "Are you hungry?"

My stomach grumbled in response. I was always hungry. "Roth…"

"I'll sweeten the deal for you. You eat with me and I'll tell you about the other one who was like you. You'd love to know, wouldn't you?" He flashed a winning smile. "Hang out with me and I'll tell you what I know—at the end of our little adventure. Not before."

I stepped around a cluster of tourists. My curiosity was burning a hole through me, and it was easier to focus on that instead of the possibility of damning relatively harmless Fiends to death. But a deal with a demon was literally making a deal with the devil. "What's the catch?"

Roth looked terribly innocent. "You let me hang out with you. I promise. That's all."

"You've already lied to me." I folded my arms. "How do I know you aren't lying now?"

"I guess that's a risk you have to take."

An elderly couple passed by, smiling at us. Roth gave them one of his most charming smiles while I debated what to do. I doubted Abbot expected any tags tonight since I wasn't even sure I was still allowed to be doing it. Drawing in a shallow breath, I nodded stiffly. "Okay."

His smile slipped into a grin. "Great. I know just the place."

"That worries me," I replied blandly.

"You excite me."

I flushed, busying myself with adjusting the strap on my book bag. Then he reached down, prying my fingers off the strap. I felt my heart skip a beat and my face blaze hotter.

"Are you always like this?" Roth asked, turning my hand over in his.

"Like what?"

"Easily flustered, forever blushing and looking away." He ran the tips of his fingers over my palm. The caress sent a jolt through me, following the pathway of nerves all the way to the tips of my toes. "Like now. You're blushing again."

I slipped my hand free of his. "And you're always annoying and creepy."

He chuckled. Not a fake laugh. Roth was genuinely amused by my insults. Twisted. "There's this little diner by the Verizon Center that has the best muffins in the world."

"You eat muffins?" It struck me as odd. "I figured you drank virgin blood and ate cow hearts."

"What?" Roth laughed again, and the deep sound was pleasant. "What have the Wardens taught you? I love muffins. Want to take the metro or walk it?"

"Walk," I said. "I don't like the subways."

We started off toward F Street, which would take us some time on foot. I kept my gaze trained on the glimmering souls in front of me, aware of Roth on every level. The weirdest thing was, when I looked at him and didn't see a soul, I felt relief instead of horror. Being around souls all day gnawed at me. The emptiness was a reprieve.

But it was something more than that.

Being around Roth was sort of *freeing*. Besides Zayne and the Wardens, he was the only one who knew what I was. Even my best friends had no idea about me. Roth knew, and he didn't care. Zayne and the Wardens cared. Granted, Roth was a full-blooded demon of God knows what, but I didn't have to pretend with him.

"I don't like going underground, either," Roth said after a few moments.

"Why? It should be like going home to you."

"Exactly."

I looked up at him. With his hands shoved into his pockets and the earnest expression on his face, he looked strangely vulnerable. But when he glanced down at me, his eyes bespoke a predator's stare. Shivering, I squinted at the bright sun. "What's it like down there?"

"Hot."

I rolled my eyes. "I figured that much."

Roth pulled an anti-Warden flyer off the back of a bench we passed and handed it to me. "It's kind of like here, but darker. I think it tries to mirror everything topside, but it gets twisted. Not a very scenic place. Lots of cliffs, rivers that have no end and wastelands where cities have crumbled. I don't think you'd like it."

The flyer had the same crudely drawn picture that most did. I tossed it into a nearby trash can. "Do you like it?"

"Do I have a choice?" he asked stonily. I could feel his eyes on me, studying my reaction.

"I'd say so. Either you like it or you don't."

His lips thinned. "I like it here better."

I tried to keep my expression blank as we stopped at another busy intersection. "Do you come here often?"

"More than I should."

"What does that mean?" I tilted my head back, meeting his intense stare.

"It's...real up here." He placed his hand on the small of my back, and the weight burned through my thin sweater in the most...unusually delicious way as he guided me across the street. "So, when did you start tagging?"

I chewed on my lip, unsure of how much I should tell him. "I was thirteen when I started."

His brows furrowed. "It took them that long to realize you could do it?"

"No. After they...found me, they knew I could see souls. I guess I'd babbled about seeing their souls or something. It was an accident that anyone even knew I could tag demons."

"What happened?" he asked, dropping his hand.

"I think I was ten or something, and I was with one of the Wardens," I said. "We were getting something to eat. I saw a person who didn't have an aura and I brushed against her in line. It was like flipping a switch. No one else seemed to notice but the Warden."

"And the rest is history?" Roth sounded smug. "The Wardens find a half demon who can see souls and tag demons. Sounds kind of convenient to me."

"I don't know what you mean by it being convenient. I *am* a Warden, too, you know."

He looked at me. "You can't tell me you never seriously

considered that the reason they keep you around is because of what you can do."

"And the reason you're interested in me has nothing to do with what I can do?" I quipped, feeling rather bold and proud.

"Of course I'm interested in you because of what you do," he replied casually. "I've never pretended otherwise."

I sidestepped a group of kids my age. The girls dressed in short skirts and lacy kneesocks rubbernecked Roth. "They didn't know what I could do when they found me, Roth. So stop trying to make them sound like they're the bad guys."

"I like when people try to classify things into good and bad, as if everything is that clear-cut."

"It is that clear-cut. Your kind is bad. The Wardens are good." My response sounded flat. "They *are* good."

He ran a hand through his hair, causing it to fall haphazardly across his forehead. "And why do you think the Wardens are so good?"

"Their souls are pure, Roth. And they protect people from things like you."

"People with the purest souls are capable of the greatest evils. No one is perfect, no matter what they are or what side they fight for." Roth caught my hand, pulling me around a cluster of tourists with fanny packs. "One of these days I'm going to buy me one of those."

The laugh came out before I could squelch it. "You'd look real sexy in a fanny pack."

His smile warmed his face—warmed *me*. "I'd look sexy in just about anything."

I laughed again, shaking my head. "You're so modest."

Roth winked. "Modesty belongs to losers. Something I am not."

I shook my head, grinning. "I'd tell you that probably earned you a ticket to Hell, but you know…"

Roth tipped his head to the side, chuckling. "Yeah. Yeah. Do you know how many times people have told me to go to Hell?"

"I can only imagine." I caught sight of the top of the Verizon Center.

"It never gets old," Roth mused, smiling softly.

WE TURNED ONTO F STREET and I stepped closer to him, pointing across the road. "When I was little, I used to sit across from the performing-arts center and watch them through the windows. I wish I had a smidgen of their grace and talent. You should see me dance."

"Hmm," Roth murmured, golden eyes twinkling. "I would like to see you dance."

Was it commonplace for a demon to twist every comment into something laced with sexual innuendo? The crowd grew thicker near the arts center, a sure sign there was a concert later. My gaze landed on a couple leaning against the corner of the building. They were locked together, oblivious to the world around them. I could barely tell where one ended and the other began. Envy reared its head, forcing me to look away.

Roth was watching me observe the boy and girl. He smiled wolfishly. "So what does a tag look like?"

"You can't see it?" I smiled. "Well, I'm not telling you."

Roth laughed. "Fair. Can I ask you something else?"

I peeked at him. He was staring straight ahead now, lips pursed. "Sure."

"Do you like doing this? Tagging demons?"

"Yes. I'm doing something good. How many people can say that?" I quickly added, "I like it."

"Doesn't it bother you that your *family* willingly puts you in danger to serve their own purpose?"

Irritation flashed like a glare from the winter sun. "They don't really want me tagging anymore, so they don't willingly put me in danger. I'm glad I can help. Can you say the same about whatever you do? You're evil. You ruin people's lives."

"We aren't talking about me," he countered smoothly. "And what do you mean they don't want you tagging anymore? I think these Wardens and I have something in common."

I clutched the strap around my shoulder, mentally spin-kicking myself in the face. "It's nothing. I'm tired of talking about me."

We stopped in front of the café Roth had spoken of earlier. The fresh cookies and muffins in the window sang to me.

"Hungry?" Roth whispered in my ear.

His closeness was making it difficult to breathe. I could see the edge of the snake's tail poking out of his collar. I lifted my head, swallowing. "Your tattoo moves."

"Bambi gets bored." His breath stirred the hair around my ear.

"Oh," I whispered. "So…does she live on you or some-thing?"

"Or something. Hungry or not?"

That was when I noticed the We Don't Serve Wardens Here sign. Disgust filled me. "I guess I know why you like this place."

His laugh confirmed my suspicions.

"This is just rich." I faced him. "They won't serve Wardens, but they'll serve your kind."

"I know. It's called irony. I love it."

Shaking my head, I headed into the café. Those cookies looked too good to pass up. It was slightly warmer inside the busy eatery. The smell of freshly baked bread filled the air as did the soft chatter of people sitting at bistro-style tables. I ordered a cold-cut sub and two sugar cookies. Roth got a coffee and a blueberry muffin—the muffin still surprised me. We found a table near the back, and I tried not to be weirded out by the fact that I was eating dinner with a demon.

I searched for a normal question to ask as I munched on my sandwich. "How old are you?"

Roth's gaze flicked up from where he was strategically breaking his muffin into several bite-sized pieces. "You wouldn't believe me if I told you."

"Probably not." I grinned. "But try me."

He popped a chunk of muffin in his mouth, chewing slowly. "Eighteen."

"Eighteen…what?" I finished off my sandwich while he stared back, brows raised. "Wait. Are you trying to tell me you're only eighteen years old?"

"Yes."

My mouth gaped. "You mean eighteen in dog years, right?"

Roth laughed. "No. I mean eighteen as in I was born eighteen years ago. I'm a baby demon, basically."

"A baby demon," I repeated slowly. When I thought about babies, the image of something soft and cuddly came to mind. Nothing about Roth was babyish. "You're being serious."

He nodded, brushing the crumbs off his hands. "You look so shocked."

"I don't understand." I picked up one of the cookies.

"Well, technically, we're not really alive. I don't have a soul."

I frowned. "Were you hatched from brimstone or something?"

Roth threw his head back, laughing. "No. I was conceived just like you, but our growth is vastly different."

I shouldn't be curious, but I couldn't help it. "How is it different?"

He leaned forward, grinning as his eyes glimmered. "Well, we are born as babies but within a couple of hours we mature. This—" he gestured at himself "—is just a human form I chose to wear. We all pretty much look alike, to be honest."

"Just like the Wardens, then. You're wearing a human skin. So what do you really look like?"

"As gorgeous as I do now, but a very different shade of skin."

I sighed. "What color?"

Roth picked up his cup as he dipped his chin. He stared at me through thick lashes. "A boy must have some secrets. It keeps the mystery alive."

I rolled my eyes. "Whatever."

"Maybe one day I'll show you."

"I won't be interested then. Sorry." I moved on to my second cookie. "So back to the eighteen thing again. You seem a lot more mature than normal guys. Is that a demon thing?"

"We're omniscient."

I laughed. "Such crap. You're saying you're born all-knowing?"

Roth grinned impishly. "Pretty much. I went from this big—" he held his hands about three feet apart "—to what I am now in about twenty-four hours. Brain grew right along with it."

"That's just weird."

He picked up his coffee, taking a sip. "So what do you know about your other half?"

And he was back to me again. I sighed. "Not that much. They told me my mom was a demon, and that's pretty much it."

"What?" Roth sat back. "You really are that innocent of your heritage. It's cute, but oddly infuriating."

I nibbled on my cookie. "They think it's better that way."

"And you think it's okay for them to keep you completely in the dark when it comes to the other part of you?"

I took another bite, shrugging. "It's not like I claim the other half."

He rolled his eyes. "You know, it kind of reminds me of a dictatorship. The way the Wardens treat you, that is."

"How so?"

"Keep the people in the darkness, away from the truth. Makes them easier to control." He sipped his coffee, watching me over the lid. "It's the same with you." He shrugged. "Not that you seem to care."

"They don't control me." I broke off the cookie roughly, briefly considered throwing it in his face. But that would be a waste of a perfectly good cookie. "And I guess you're on speaking terms with some of the world's most infamous dictators."

"I wouldn't say I talk to them." His lips pursed thoughtfully. "More like shove hot pokers through them when I get bored."

I cringed. "For real?"

"Hell ain't pretty for those who've earned their way."

I thought about that for a moment. "Well, they kind of deserve an eternity of torture." I glanced around the café, over the shimmering souls and framed portraits on the walls. They were pictures of former owners, each old and silver-haired. And then I saw her.

Or I saw her soul first.

Sinner alert. The essence around her was tainted, a kaleidoscope of dark shades. I wondered what she had done. Once her soul faded, I saw that she looked like a normal thirtysomething woman. She was dressed nicely, wore really cute heels and carried a to-die-for purse. Her blond hair was a bit brassy, but cut in a trendy bob. She looked normal. Nothing to be afraid of or to run from, but I knew differently. Evil simmered under the normal facade.

"What is it?" Roth sounded far away.

I swallowed. "Her soul—it's bad."

He seemed to understand. I wondered what he saw: a woman

in nice clothes, or the woman that had sinned so badly her soul was now tainted?

"What do you see?" he asked, as if he was sharing the same thought.

"It's dark. Brown. Like someone took a brush, dipped it in red paint and flicked it around her." I leaned forward, breathless with want. "It's beautiful. Wrong, but beautiful."

"Layla?"

My nails dug into the tabletop. "Yeah?"

"Why don't you tell me about the necklace?"

Roth's voice tugged me back to reality. Tearing my gaze away from the woman, I sucked in a deep breath. I looked down at my cookie, my stomach filling with lava. "What...what do you want to know?"

He smiled. "You wear it all the time, don't you?"

I felt around until my fingers touched the smooth metal of the band. "Yeah, I'm not big on jewelry." As if compelled, I turned back to the woman. She was at the counter, ordering food. "But I wear this all the time."

"Layla, look at me. You don't want to go down that road."

With effort, I focused on him. "I'm sorry. It's just so hard."

His brows furrowed. "You don't need to apologize for something that is natural to you, but taking a human's soul... You can't go back from that."

So many emotions shot through me. First was surprise. Why wouldn't Roth, being what he was, want me to jump out of this chair and suck some soul? But then the bitter lash of sadness followed. "Why do you care?"

Roth said nothing.

I sighed. "It's not natural—what I want from her, or from anybody, for that matter. I can't even get close to a boy, Roth. This is my life." I picked up a cookie, waving it in front of my face. "This is all I have. Sugar. I'm a walking ad for diabetes in the making."

A deep frown pierced his striking face. "Your life is so much more than what you can't do. What about all that you *can* do?"

I laughed, shaking my head. "You don't even know me."

"I know more than you realize."

"Well, that's creepy and you're a demon preaching to me about life. There is something inherently wrong with that."

"I wasn't preaching."

I glanced at the counter. She was gone. I sank down in my chair, the relief as sweet as the cookies. "Anyway, the necklace belonged to my mother. I've always had it. I don't even know why. I mean, it's stupid since she was a demon and didn't even want me. And here I am, running around wearing her ring. Pathetic."

"You're not pathetic."

I cracked a smile, not sure why I'd admitted that. It wasn't even something I'd ever said to Zayne. I took another bite of the cookie and dropped it on the napkin.

Moving as fast as Bambi, Roth reached over the bistro table, caught my hand and brought my fingers to his mouth. Before I could even react, he licked off the tiny specks of sugar the cookie had left behind.

I gasped, but the air got stuck in my throat. Sharp tingles spread down my arm and across my chest, then lower, much lower. A heaviness settled just below my breasts, different and intense, but not unpleasant. "That...that makes me uncomfortable."

Roth peered up at me through thick lashes. "That's because you like it."

A huge part of me did, but I slipped my hand free, glancing around the small bakery. I felt unnaturally hot. "Don't do that again."

He grinned. "But you're so tasty."

I wiped my fingers clean on the napkin. "I think we're done."

He caught my hand again. "No. Don't run off yet. We were just getting started."

My eyes locked with his and I felt...I felt like I was falling. "Getting started with what?"

His fingers slid between mine. "Becoming friends."

I blinked tightly. "We can't be friends."

"Why not?" Roth threaded his fingers through mine. "Is there a rule I'm unaware of?"

Suddenly, I wasn't really sure anymore. He got up to take care of our tab while I tried to figure out what was going on between us. Could I be his friend? Did I even want to try? I probably should've made a run for it while he waited in line, but I didn't.

A middle-aged waitress approached our table. Her soul was a faint pink—a complete contrast to the haggard look on her face and world-weary gleam in her eyes.

She picked up the napkins and empty plates as she glanced over her shoulder to where Roth stood. "That boy looks like he must be a handful."

I flushed, at once very interested in the hem of my shirt. "You could say that."

The waitress snorted and moved on to another table.

"Why are you so red in the face?"

"No reason." I grabbed my bag, standing. "You promised to tell me about the one who could do what I can. I think now is the time."

"It is, isn't it?" He held the door open for me.

In the waning sunlight, all the buildings in the district looked old and unfriendly. We stopped near a small, neatly kept city park. I stared up at him, waiting.

"I know what you want to know, but I have a question to ask first."

Fighting my impatience, I gave him a curt nod of assent.

He dipped his chin again, looking terribly innocent. "You've never been kissed before, have you?"

"That's *so* not your business." I folded my arms as Roth waited for an answer. "I think it's obvious. I can't kiss anyone. You know, the whole soul-sucking thing makes it difficult."

"Not if you're kissing someone who doesn't have a soul."

I made a face. "And why would I kiss someone who doesn't—"

He moved unbelievably fast. I didn't even have a chance to react. One second he was standing a good three feet away from me and the next his hands were gently clasping my cheeks. There was an instant when I wondered how something so strong and deadly could hold anything so carefully, but then he tilted .my head back and lowered his own. My heart rate kicked into hyperdrive. He wasn't going to kiss me. No way—

Roth kissed me.

The brush of his lips was tentative at first, an unhurried sweep of his mouth against mine. Every muscle in my body locked up, but I didn't pull away like I should've, and Roth made a low sound deep in his throat that sent shivers down my spine. His lips caressed mine again, nibbling and clinging to them until they parted on a gasp. He deepened the kiss with a thrust of his tongue. My senses went into overload, firing in every direction. The kiss—it was everything I could've imagined a kiss to be and then some. Sublime. Explosive. My heart fluttered wildly, from a yearning so deep, darts of fear shot through my veins.

"See," he murmured in a thick voice, and he let go, his fingers trailing over my cheeks. "Your life isn't about all you can't do. It's about what you *can* do."

"Your tongue is pierced," I said dumbly.

A wicked gleam filled his gaze. "That's not the only thing pierced."

His words really didn't sink in. Suddenly, I was so angry I thought my head was going to pull an *Exorcist*. He *dared* to kiss me. And I actually liked it? I didn't know who to be more ticked off at—him, or my traitorous body, but wait—where else was he pierced? The last thought caused my brain to play happily in the gutter, and that ticked me off even more.

Roth cocked his head to the side. "Now you've been kissed. One thing off the bucket list."

I hit him.

Cocked back my arm and punched him in the stomach like I was a heavyweight boxer.

He grunted out a choked laugh. "Ouch. That kind of hurt."

"Don't ever do that again!"

Even after I hit him, he still looked pleased with himself. "You know what they say about first kisses."

"You regret them?"

His smile faded. "No. I was going to go with 'you never forget them.'"

Struggling not to hit him again—or laugh—I took a deep breath. "Tell me about the one who was like me, or I am walking away from here."

"You're so dramatic." He shoved his hands into his pockets. "Are you sure you want to know about her?"

I was sure of three things: I was never going to forget that kiss, I needed to know about this demon and I was really getting sick of his know-it-all attitude. "Yes. I'm sure."

"The one who could do what you could was a bit more… invested in her ability," he said, leaning against the back of a bench.

I pursed my lips. No further explanation needed. The one like me enjoyed taking souls.

"She was also very good at what she did, so good that she was one of the most powerful demons to ever walk topside. There were other things she could do besides taking souls."

A bundle of nerves formed in my stomach. "What else could she do?"

Roth shrugged, his gaze fixed over my head. "Things you probably don't want to know about."

My breath caught as unease spread through me like a choking weed. "Who was she, Roth?"

His eyes met mine, and part of me already suspected what the answer was going to be.

"The demon was your mother," he said, his gaze never leaving mine.

"Okay." I swallowed. *Hard*. And I took a step back. "So that explains what I can do. Makes sense, right? Most people get their mom's eyes. I just got her demonic soul-sucking ability. And her ring. What was her name, anyway?"

I wasn't sure I even needed to know her name, because it would make her all the more *real* to me, but I couldn't take back the question.

Roth let out a low breath. "Your mother was known by many names, but most knew her as Lilith. And because of that, you're on Hell's Most Wanted List."

Sitting on the bench, waiting for Morris, I stared straight ahead, not really seeing or hearing anything. Okay, so my mother was a demon who sucked souls. That didn't take a huge leap of intelligence to figure out, but I hadn't expected who she was. Lilith? Like *the* freaking Lilith? The mommy of all things that go bump in the night? There was no way. There had to be another Lilith because that demon hadn't walked topside for a millennium.

Folklore claimed that Lilith was Adam's first wife and had been created like him, but she refused to become subservient to Adam. This caused many epic battles between them, eventually leading to God banishing her from Eden and then creating Eve. Needless to say, Lilith wasn't a happy camper. To get back at Adam and God, she ran off and seduced the archangel Samael. Things went downhill after that.

That much was true, but the rest was mostly bunk from what I'd picked up in the old, crusty religious texts Abbot had in his office. The whole eating-babies myth was utter bull. Lilith never slept with Satan. She never slept with *any* demons. She slept only with one angel, and the rest were all human consorts. But the Alphas weren't too pleased with her in the first place, and after she hooked up with Samael, they punished her.

Every child Lilith spawned from that point on was a monster—succubi, incubi and just about every other demonic creature you could think of. Worst of all, she'd birthed the Lilin, a race of demons who could steal souls with a single touch. They were her first and most powerful children. Around that time was when the first generation of Wardens appeared, created by the Alphas to battle the Lilin. They managed to wipe out the Lilin and capture Lilith. Texts claimed that Lilith had been bound to Hell by one of the Wardens, chained down there together with him for all eternity.

Like most things that Alphas did, that just didn't make sense to me. Through the birthing of so many demons, Lilith turned into one herself—and because the Alphas had punished her, they accidentally created the Lilin, a legion of demons so feared and powerful that they could ensure no human ever made it past the pearly gates.

Humans who died without souls, no matter how good they were in life, existed between Heaven and Hell, stuck in the in-between for all eternity. Plagued with endless thirst and hunger, they turned into violent, vengeful wraiths that even demons were wary of. Wraiths could interact with the living world, and when they did, it usually ended in a gory mess.

Tucking my hair back, I watched a shimmery blue soul trail behind a man in ragged jeans. My mother couldn't be *that* Lilith. Because if she was, what did that really say about me? How could I ever overcome a bloodline like that? And if Lilith was really my mother then Abbot would have to know and there was no way that anyone would let a child of Lilith walk around. Besides, there was the whole problem of her being chained to

Hell. It wasn't like someone let her out to get knocked up and birth a kid.

Hell's Most Wanted List? I shuddered. Was that why the Seeker and a zombie—I cut that thought off. Nothing Roth had told me could be true. What was I even doing considering any of it? Trusting him would be like smacking the Wardens in the face. Demons lied. Even I lied. Well, my lying really didn't have much to do with being a demon, but still.

Roth was just messing with me, trying to get me to stop tagging. And if Hell was after me, then that could be the only true reason.

Squeezing my fingers around the ring, I stopped a groan from escaping. I'd kissed a demon. Or he'd kissed me. The semantics probably didn't matter. Either way, my lips had been all up in a demon's. My first kiss. Dear Lord...

I almost squealed when I spotted the black Yukon, seriously needing a distraction from my troublesome thoughts. I stood and shouldered my bag. A strange shiver wiggled its way down my neck, raising the tiny hairs on my body. It wasn't like the time before while I waited for Morris. This was different.

I turned, scanning the pedestrians on the sidewalk. Blurs of faint pink and blue and a few darker auras, but no one was missing a soul. Craning my neck, I stretched onto the tips of my toes and tried to see around the corner, past the fleet of cabs lining up. There didn't seem to be anything demonic, but still, the feeling was familiar.

Morris honked the horn, drawing my attention. Shaking my head, I darted between two cabs and yanked the passenger door open. The feeling hit me again, like a cold hand traveling around my neck.

Shivering, I climbed into the front seat and pulled the door shut, my eyes on the line of taxis. Something...something wasn't right.

"Do you feel that?" I asked, twisting toward Morris.

He raised his brows and, as usual, said nothing. Sometimes I pretended we had a conversation. I'd even acted it out once or twice for Morris. I liked to think it amused him.

"Well, I feel something weird." I leaned forward as he eased the SUV out into the congested streets. Three cabs pulled out, too, blocking most of the storefronts and sidewalk. "It's like there's a demon nearby, but I don't see any."

Three blocks later and the feeling not only lingered, but grew like an ominous cloud. Malice and evil filled the streets, seeping into the Yukon, its presence choking. Beads of sweat appeared on Morris's creased forehead.

"You feel it now, don't you?" I gripped the edges of my seat. "Morris?"

He nodded, gaze sharp as he veered around a slow-moving truck and then cut in front of it, hitting the exit ramp. Two cabs were right behind us, plus a whole slew of cars were also entering the beltway.

The malicious feeling hung thick and murky. So potent that it felt as if whatever was causing the suffocating feeling was in the backseat, breathing down our necks. *That* was a feeling of raw evil, something I'd never picked up on around a Fiend.

"Morris. I think we need to hurry up and get home."

He was already on it, foot slamming down on the gas as he weaved in and out of the congested traffic. Twisting around in my seat, I peered out the back window—and my heart tripped.

Behind us, a cab was so close I could see its silver cross dangling from the rearview mirror. The fact that the cabbie was inches away from kissing our rear end wasn't a big deal; cabbies were insane when it came to city driving. No, it was the *driver* behind the wheel that sent a shot of fear straight through me.

Now I knew where the bad feeling was coming from.

The space around the hunched driver was blacker than any shadow, thick like oil. Thin slivers of silver, tiny specks of humanity, peeked through the darkness of his soul, barely there.

His soul spread out from him, seeping through the front of the taxi, slipping over the dashboard and crawling over the window.

"Oh, my God," I whispered, feeling the blood drain from my face. "The driver's possessed!"

As soon as the words left my mouth, Morris wrenched the steering wheel to the right. A horn blared. Tires squealed. He slammed down on the brakes, whipping me around as he narrowly avoided clipping the back end of a delivery truck. A series of quick maneuvers later, and several cars were between us and the possessed cabdriver.

I stared at Morris. "Damn. For an old man, you sure know how to drive."

Morris kept a tight grip on the steering wheel, but he smiled in acknowledgment.

A second later, we were on our exit ramp, flying down the road. The Yukon fishtailed as he hung a quick right, and I shrieked, grabbing the "oh, shit" handle. Then the heavy vehicle lurched forward as he put the gas pedal all the way to the floor. We hit the narrow two-lane stretch of private road at breakneck speeds.

And we weren't alone.

The taxi was gaining on us, and then it was in the other lane, going in the wrong direction, inching up on us. My heart jumped in my throat as I stared into the taxi.

The blackness of the man's soul faded, revealing a pale, empty face. The human was on autopilot, completely under the thumb of the demon that had possessed him. Possession, next to murder, was one of the worst crimes, and it was forbidden according to the Law of Balance. Humans lost all free will once a demon breathed its essence into them, possessing them. Only Upper Level demons could possess humans.

Roth? Seemed likely, since he was the only Upper Level demon I'd seen, with the exception of the one that had moved too fast for me to be sure. Dread filled my stomach like lead.

Had Roth possessed this man because I'd refused to stop tagging? If so, I'd just put Morris's life in danger. Anger and guilt swirled inside me, causing my hands to clench until my nails bit into my palms.

Suddenly the taxi was speeding alongside us. Like a pro, Morris kept his gaze trained forward, but a scream built in my throat. My muscles tensed, as if my body already knew what to expect.

Morris swerved. Two wheels went off the road, crunching over dirt. But—oh, God—he was too late. I squeezed my eyes shut, terror seizing me in its tight grip.

The taxi slammed into us.

10

THE IMPACT WAS DEAFENING.

Metal crunched and gave way in an explosion of white that
sent me sideways and then snapped me back. A second before
the airbag smacked into my face, I saw a blur of trees rushing
toward the front of the car.

God bless Morris, because somehow, even with an airbag
in his face, he turned that steering wheel, spinning the vehicle
around so the back end instead of the front slammed into the
thick trunk of an ancient tree. But the impact was no less brutal, throwing us backward.

When we finally stopped moving, I was sure I was going
into cardiac arrest.

"Morris. Morris!" I pushed at the deflating airbag, coughing as white dust plumed. "Are you okay?"

He leaned back, blinking several times as he nodded. White
powder caked his cheeks, but other than a trickle of blood under
his nose, he looked fine.

Turning my attention to the other car, I unhooked my seat
belt with shaky fingers. The entire front of the cab was a mass

of twisted, crunched metal. A body-sized hole was in the windshield. Splotches of a dark red substance coated the edges of the broken glass and splattered the hood.

"Oh, God," I said, letting the seat belt smack back. "I think the other driver was ejected."

Scrambling for my bag to get my cell, I smacked at the damn airbag. I needed to call for help—something. Even though the cabbie had hit us, he was possessed and totally not responsible for his actions. He was an innocent human being, and I had to do something. Traffic didn't come down this road often—

A bloodied, mangled face appeared outside the passenger window. I jerked back, swallowing a scream. Nausea rose swiftly. The face—oh, God—the face was a wreck. Pieces of glass were embedded in his cheeks. The flesh was torn. Rivulets of blood coursed down his face like rain. One eye appeared almost gouged out. His lower lip...it was barely hanging on and his head was bent at an unnatural angle. Dude should be dead, or at least in a coma.

But he was still up and walking.

Not good.

He grabbed the handle and pulled, tearing the Yukon door right off its hinges. He flung it aside and then reached in, bloodied hands shooting straight for me.

One of Morris's arms came around my shoulders as I scrambled out of the seat, but the damn possessed kept coming. Leaning back against Morris, I brought my knees back and slammed both my feet into his ragged shirt, knocking the man back.

The possessed popped back up, determined and single-minded. His hand wrapped around my ankle as I kicked out again, and he yanked, pulling me out of the car. Blood bubbled out of his mouth—out of the freaking *hole* in his throat.

I screamed and slapped my hands down wildly, wrapping them around the gear shift. For a second, my body went up in the air, half out of the Yukon as the possessed pulled like he was willing to rip me clear in two.

Morris shot forward, yanking the glove box open. There was a flash of shiny, black metal and then an explosion rang through the interior of the car. The possessed jerked and let go. I hit the seat and center console on my side. Dull pain shot through my body. Acrid smoke burned my eyes.

The possessed stood still, eyes glazed over, with a bullet hole dead center in his forehead. Then his head fell back and his mouth opened. An inhuman cry escaped him—a cross between a screaming baby and a dog's whine.

Red smoke poured out of the gaping mouth, filling the air with its filth and stench. It kept coming until the last tendril snaked out and a cloud of rolling smoke formed. The possessed toppled over, but the cloud continued to expand. Shapes formed inside it. Fingers and hands pressed out, as if something was seeking a way to escape.

The mass suddenly reared back, and a long oval shape formed, almost like a head. It swung toward us, and panic punched a hole through my chest.

This thing just wouldn't die.

Beyond the mass, the tops of the trees began to shake like Godzilla was about to make an appearance. At this point, anything was possible. Branches waved back and forth, shaking loose the last of the leaves that had been clinging on. They fell like rain, clouding the sky in muted browns and greens.

Something big was coming.

Then, along the edge of the trembling woods crowding the roadway, the fading sun caught and reflected over a thick, shiny onyx tail slithering along the leaf-strewn ground.

My breath caught. Bambi.

The mass pulsated and twisted, but that damn snake was *fast*. Shooting across the ground, it arced into the air, swallowing the evil essence within a second.

And then there was nothing—no essence or giant snake. The horrible scent of sulfur lingered, but it was no longer potent, and the malicious feeling had vanished. There was just the sound of Morris's heavy breathing and my pounding heart.

"Did you see that?" I looked up into Morris's face.

His expression said "see what?" And I wasn't sure if he had seen Bambi, she'd moved so fast.

"Jesus," I murmured.

Morris smiled.

It was chaos in the mansion.

From the moment Morris and I explained what had happened, anger and tension seeped into every room in the sprawling house. A possessed human coming after anyone wasn't good. And the idea of one coming so close to the house had all the Wardens in a tizzy. All except Zayne, because I had no idea where he was.

Even with all the security and the charms blanketing the acres of land the house rested upon, only so much could be done. Because of…well, because of me.

My presence threw off the protective charms. Probably not as much as a full-blooded demon or a possessed would, but the Wardens had to be careful they didn't accidentally take me out.

I had no idea how my day started off somewhat normal— at least normal for me—and ended with my whole belief system being questioned, sharing my very first kiss with a demon, finding out my mother could possibly be *the* Lilith and being chased by a possessed human.

How in the world had things gone so wrong?

Nicolai, a Warden in his mid-twenties who had lost his mate and his child last year during childbirth—like so many of them did—stopped by where I stood on his way to dispose of the body and the wreckage of the two cars.

"Are you okay, Layla?" he asked, placing a hand on my shoulder.

Though Nicolai rarely smiled anymore and was more re-served than the others, he'd always been kind to me when some of the Wardens, even some in the clan, treated me like I wasn't worth the dirt on their boots because of my blood.

I was bruised and shaken, and more than a little freaked out, but I nodded. "I'm fine."

He squeezed my shoulder and headed out, leaving me in a room full of ticked-off Wardens. Tired, I sat down on the couch.

In the center of the six Wardens, Abbot stood in a pure warrior's stance. Legs spread wide, back rod straight and arms folded. Needless to say, he wasn't happy. They were speaking in low voices, and Elijah and his son were there, exchanging dark looks that made their way to me every so often. No doubt Elijah and Petr blamed me.

I'd already been debriefed. Not talked to or comforted, but interrogated about the events. It wasn't a big deal. A possessed human was a crisis. My coping skills weren't a priority.

After telling Abbot and the clan everything I could remember, from the first inkling of something being off to when I realized the poor driver had been possessed, he turned his attention to the men.

"Canvass the city for Upper Level demon activity," he ordered, and several heads nodded in agreement. "Detain *any* demon for questioning. If a demon is possessing humans, then something's brewing. Even a Fiend might know what's going down. Make them talk."

One of the Wardens smirked. Several glances were exchanged, all saying they were looking forward to their night's work.

An uncomfortable twisty feeling unfurled in the pit of my stomach. Dying would be a more pleasant outcome for a demon. If they were captured for questioning... My insides twisted. There was a warehouse in the city where the Wardens detained demons. I'd never been there, but I'd heard the Wardens talking about what went on there and how they made the demons talk.

I hadn't told the clan about Bambi, since Morris hadn't seemed to see her. Guilt chewed my skin raw, but Bambi had come to our aid. There was no telling what that evil essence would've done if the snake hadn't swallowed it.

Tapping my foot, I wrapped my arms around myself and bit down on my lip. Not telling Abbot was wrong. Warden lives could be in danger. *Humans* could be in danger. But I'd been keeping the whole Roth situation to myself so much that I wasn't sure even how to begin. And if Abbot knew about him, he'd pull me out of school. And I hated the part of me that was demon, because it was more concerned with what *I* got and what *I* would lose than how things affected other people.

But that was the catch. Sometimes the demonic blood won out. I knew it was wrong. Totally understood that, but it meant nothing in the end.

"We knew this would happen eventually," growled Elijah. "That this day was—"

Abbot shot him a look that said "shut up," and I wondered what in the Hell the other Warden was talking about. No doubt he was about to blame all of this on my demonic blood.

Closing my eyes, I sucked in a long breath. Immediately, I saw the mangled face of the poor man who had been possessed. As long as I lived, I would never forget what the man looked like. Shuddering, I forced my eyes open, and my gaze searched for one face in particular.

I cleared my throat. "Where's Zayne?"

Geoff, whom I never really saw moving around the house since he seemed to live in the control room, turned to me. His shoulder-length brown hair was pulled back, revealing broad features. When he smiled, there was a dimple in his chin. But he wasn't smiling now. "He's out with Danika and Jasmine. They took the twins to the park with another male."

The bitter burn of jealousy was quick to rise, and so wrong, but it crept over my skin anyway.

Geoff's acute eyes missed nothing. "We've called them, and they are returning immediately."

Casting my gaze to the carpet, I could only wonder and cringe at what Geoff caught on his cameras. If anyone knew everything, it was him.

"Layla?" Abbot's voice drew my attention, and I glanced up to find him standing before me. "You're positive the possessed said nothing to you?"

I shook my head as I watched the clan leave to find and *question* demons. Petr stopped briefly, his eyes narrowing on me, and then he was out the door, following his father. Only Geoff remained. He stood by the door, arms crossed. "No. I don't think it was capable of talking. It had a…" I trailed off, shuddering as I remembered the jagged hole in its throat. "It couldn't talk."

He knelt down, his gaze exceptionally sharp. "And this Seeker who pretended to be a Poser, it didn't say anything?"

My head jerked up. "No. I mean, I think it said 'gotcha' but I can't be sure. Why?"

Abbot looked over at Geoff, who muttered something under his breath.

"What?" I said, clamping my hands together between my knees. "What's going on?"

He pinched the bridge of his nose and stood. "I think it's time that you stop tagging."

I started to protest, but Geoff tipped his chin up and spoke over me. "It's obviously no longer safe for you or the clan, Layla."

Déjà vu smacked into me, and my heart stuttered. "I didn't get hurt—neither did Morris, not really. He doesn't have to pick me up anymore. I can—"

"Within a handful of days, you've had a Seeker, a zombie and a possessed come near you. There is no such thing as a coincidence when dealing with demons. One of them almost made it to our compound, Layla."

An image of Roth popped into my head. "Why…why do you think the demons are coming around me?"

There was a stretch of silence and Abbot said, "It appears they may have discovered your ability." He paused, looking away. A muscle popped in his jaw. "There can't be any other reason."

I couldn't really place it, and maybe it was just a bad case of paranoia, but I had a hard time believing that was all Abbot knew. There was surely more he wasn't willing to say.

"It isn't safe for you right now." Geoff came closer, stopping beside Abbot. "If the demons have caught on to what you can do, you can't tag. It's too dangerous."

"I know how to defend myself. Zayne taught me."

Abbot scoffed. "Whatever my son has taught you isn't enough to face a demon Hell-bent on taking you out, child. You no longer have the element of surprise, which is *all* you had. And you know that."

I wanted to argue, but dammit, he had a point. I knew my limits, but it didn't make any of this suck less. I slumped back against the supple leather of the couch.

"We're going to find out what's going on, Layla." Abbot's voice softened by a degree. "I know how important it is to you that you help in this war, but right now, I can't afford to be worried about your safety. Honestly, I should pull you out of school."

Fear seized me, and I shot to my feet, ready to beg and plead. "Please, Abbot, don't do that. Everything is okay at school. I'm safe there and—"

"I didn't say I was going to do it. At least not right now, but I don't want Morris driving you anymore. One of the clansmen will."

And that was that. I was deemed pretty much on lockdown unless I was at school or one of the Wardens was with me. Which was sort of ironic considering there was an Upper Level demon in my bio class, but now I knew beyond a doubt that if I shared that little ditty, I would end up homeschooled. Part of me understood the precaution.

I went upstairs, leaving Geoff and Abbot to do more of the hushed-conversation thing. Just as I kicked open my bedroom door, I heard the twins' excitable squawking coming from the foyer. Turning around, I prepared myself for the sound of bounding footsteps, for Zayne to rush me and check me over for injuries I didn't have. For him to pull me into one of those mammoth hugs that made everything feel better.

Male voices boomed from downstairs, one of them Zayne's. Anger deepened his voice, and his father's matched his. They weren't arguing, but I heard Danika's soft tone intruding, and then their voices lowered.

I waited.

There were no footsteps coming up the stairs, and the voices trailed off as they moved farther into the house, most likely underground.

A sigh escaped my lips as I stood there, still waiting for Zayne, but he never came up the stairs. He never came.

The next morning, I got up early like I did every Saturday. Sure, I was still upset over everything with Zayne, but it was Saturday morning. There had to be a reason why he never checked on me last night. Most likely Abbot had him leave the mansion immediately to help the rest of the Wardens.

We had plans—we always had plans on Saturday morning. Even with the possibility that demons were looking for me, I'd be okay because I'd be with Zayne. He was the kind of babysitter I could get behind.

And I wanted to ask Zayne about my mother. I figured I could do so without raising any suspicion and I knew he'd tell me the truth. All my life, Zayne had never lied to me. I trusted him and I knew he'd tell me I had nothing to worry about—that my mother was not *the* Lilith.

I waited until eight and went to his bedroom door like I always did. By then he'd already be shifting back into his human skin, opening the door any minute. But the door didn't open at eight. Ten minutes went by. After thirty minutes, I sat down. When the clock chimed nine, I started to feel sick. What if something had happened to him? What if he was hurt or worse?

Unable to wait any longer, I pushed to my feet and raced to the first floor. Abbot wasn't at rest yet. He was with Elijah and a few other men from the clan. I skidded to a stop in front of his study, out of breath.

Abbot lifted his head, a faint look of amusement crossing his face when he spotted me by the door. "Layla?"

Each of the men turned to look at me. Heat suffused my cheeks as I folded my arms across my chest. "Has Zayne returned?" I couldn't ask if he'd been hurt. The words wouldn't form on my lips.

Abbot looked puzzled for only a moment as he stroked his beard. "Oh, today is Saturday, isn't it?"

I nodded.

"I do believe Zayne may have forgotten," Nicolai said in his quiet way.

Elijah leaned against the door, yawning loudly. "Zayne is with Danika. She met up with us just before dawn. I heard them mention something about breakfast."

My gaze darted to Abbot. He looked pleased by the development. Of course, he wanted Zayne to mate with the girl, so he was probably mentally cheering and already picturing bouncing babies, but I couldn't breathe.

Stepping around the chair, Nicolai's eyes landed on me. Sympathy shone on his face, and my heart lurched in the worst way. "Do you want to get breakfast? Or coffee?"

Elijah and his men snickered, which Nicolai ignored.

"That won't be necessary," Abbot said. "You need your rest, Nicolai, and Layla really shouldn't be out after what happened last night."

"I can spare an hour or two for the girl." Nicolai's expression sharpened. "It will bring no harm to anyone, and we'll be fine."

"How charitable," Elijah murmured.

Humiliation brought stinging tears to my eyes. Backing away from the study's entrance, I shook my head. "No. That's… that's okay."

"But—"

I spun around, hurrying away before Nicolai could finish. Zayne had forgotten me. I couldn't believe it. He *never* forgot our Saturdays. Maybe he hadn't. Maybe he'd just replaced me with Danika, a much more suitable companion. I didn't understand, though. He had never paid this much attention to her before.

But he was now.

I started to head toward the front door, but stopped in the foyer. Sunlight streamed in through the windows. Where could I go? Hang out in the tree house again, like a dweeb? I was stuck in this house.

Back in my bedroom, I changed back into my pajamas and crawled into bed. I didn't want to cry. It was weak and stupid to shed tears over something like this, but my cheeks ended up feeling damp anyway and my chest ached. I curled onto my side, fisting the ring in my hand until I drifted back to sleep.

A knock on my bedroom door roused me out of sleep hours later. I pried my eyes open to see that the sun was setting outside my bedroom window. I had slept the day away. The knock came again. I pulled the thick down comforter over my head.

The door cracked open. "Layla-bug?"

I hunkered down, hoping he'd just go away.

A few moments later, the bed shifted under Zayne's weight. He felt around until his hand landed on my head. "Where are you at under these blankets?" He patted the bed a couple of times. "I can't find you."

I hated him for joking.

There was a moment of silence. "You're mad at me."

I squeezed my eyes shut until I saw white light. "You *forgot* me."

Another stretch of silence followed. "I didn't mean to forget you, Layla. After everything that happened last night with the possessed human, all of us were out late. It just…happened."

A weird empty feeling opened up in my chest. "In all the years we've known each other, you've never forgotten me." A dry lump formed in my throat. "I waited for you, you know? Then, like an idiot, I thought something had happened to you. So I embarrassed myself in front of the whole clan."

"I heard that Nicolai offered to take you."

Rehashing that made me feel so much better. "Just go away."

Zayne seized the edge of the blanket, pulling it from my grasp. I desperately clamored for control of the blanket, but Zayne held it away from me. I gave up, falling onto my back. "You suck."

"I'm sorry." He looked exhausted. Faint shadows blossomed under his eyes, his hair was a mess, wavier than normal, and his shirt was rumpled. "Layla, I'm really sorry. I had every intention of coming back here on time. And I wanted to see you—I was worried about you. I just lost track of things."

"You look terrible," I said. "I guessed you stayed up longer than normal, huh?"

Zayne's eyes narrowed. "No longer than I normally would if I'd been with you."

But he hadn't been with me. "Why did you tell Danika to keep an eye on me?"

He blinked. "So that's what this—" he gestured at me "—is all about? You're mad because I asked her to help you if you needed anything?"

"I'm mad because you left me hanging this morning, and yeah, I'm mad because you told her about my problem."

"Layla, everyone here knows what you can do. It's not a secret."

I sat up, pushing the tangled mess of hair out of my face. "Not everyone knows how much I struggle with it! And you know that. But you told Danika."

Confusion rippled across Zayne's features. "I don't get what the big deal is. It's not like we were talking bad about you."

"You don't know what the big deal is?" I climbed out of the bed, ignoring the covers that spilled to the floor. Everything poured out of me. All the anger, frustration and confusion rushed to the surface. And there was biting grief making its way out, too, because it felt like I was *losing* him. "Do you know how embarrassing—how *humiliating* it is for people to think I'm that screwed up? Jesus. Jasmine already thinks I'm going to suck the souls out of her babies and now Danika follows me around in the middle of the night. That is, when she's not following *you* around."

"Jasmine doesn't think that, Layla." He twisted at the waist, thrusting his hand through his hair. "You've just been so wired lately. I thought it would be a good idea in case..."

I flinched. "In case of what, Zayne?"

"Layla, I didn't mean anything by that." He stood, raising his hands helplessly.

For some reason, my gaze fell on an old dollhouse in the corner of my bedroom. After all these years, I'd never had the heart to store it in the attic. Memories of forcing Zayne to play dolls with me seemed so long ago. Why was I holding on to them—on to him—when it was all so very pointless?

"You know, I don't even think this morning or my asking

Danika to help you have anything to do with why you're acting this way," Zayne said, his voice laced with frustration.

I frowned, turning back to him. "And why else would I be mad?"

"You're pissed because Danika is here. You get like this every time she comes to visit, but it's beyond obvious this time around."

My mouth dropped open, and the weird icky, empty feeling spread. "You really think that's it? That's ridiculous. You made me feel like crap four times, Zayne."

"Four? What in the Hell are you talking about?"

I raised my hand, ticking them off my fingers. "You threw me under the bus with the whole tagging thing, which you should be happy over, because after last night, I'm not tagging anymore. You told Danika to look after me *just in case* I go demon on everyone's ass." I knew how crazy this all sounded, but I couldn't stop myself. "You didn't even check on me last night. And you forgot me this morning to spend time with someone else!"

He crossed the room, stopping in front of me. "I suggested that you stop tagging because it's dangerous for you, which turned out to be true, now didn't it? I told Danika to keep an eye on you because I *care* about you. Strange concept, huh?" His pale eyes snapped fire, latching on to mine and holding them. "I didn't come see you last night because I figured you were resting and I left immediately to hunt. And I'm sorry about this morning. I'm not replacing you, Layla. It was an honest mistake."

"But you *are* replacing me!" Realizing what I had said, I clasped my hands over my mouth and backed off. Even worse were the tears building in my eyes.

His expression softened instantly. He reached for me, but I stepped back. Something akin to pain flickered over his face. "That is not the case."

I lowered my hands to my sides. "But you're spending so much time with her. I've barely seen you since she's been here. She's doing everything I…" I stopped, biting the inside of my cheek until I tasted blood. *Stupid, stupid girl.*

"It's only been a few days. She'll be leaving in a couple of weeks." Zayne dragged his fingers through his hair again. "Please don't be like this, Layla."

Our eyes met, and I knew he was waiting for me to tell him it was okay. That I was cool with things now, and I wouldn't be upset over Danika. I didn't say anything, though, because I wasn't okay with it and jealousy and bitterness were like bitter pills exploding in my stomach. This was more than a crush unreturned. He was my friend—the only friend who *really* knew me—and I was *losing* him.

Shaking his head, Zayne shrugged. Then he went to my bedroom door, stopping to look at me over his shoulder. "I am sorry."

"Sorry doesn't make me feel any better," I said just because I wanted to be a bitch.

A muscle ticked along his jaw. Several seconds passed before he spoke. "You know, you're constantly griping about everyone treating you like a kid. It's kind of hard to treat you as a grown woman when you act like this."

Ouch. He could've hit me and it would have hurt less.

For a moment he looked like he regretted saying it, but the expression was lost as he rubbed his hand over his face. He opened the door. "By the way, Father spoke to the Alphas last night."

My heart faltered in my chest. "The Alphas?"

He gave me a curt nod. "They're coming here tomorrow."

Everything else was forgotten in an instant—the whole thing with Lilith, even the sharp ache his words left behind. "Are you meeting with them?"

"No. They only want to speak with Father."

I nodded slowly. "So I shouldn't be here?"

"No. You shouldn't be here."

11

THE ALPHAS REALLY WERE LIKE the boogeyman to anything with a trace of demonic blood in its body. Even the Wardens weren't entirely comfortable around them. I kept an eye on the clock, knowing they'd come before nightfall. I should've already left the house, but I really had no place to go and…and I wanted to see them again.

I puttered around the kitchen while Jasmine tried to get a snack in the twins before she settled them down for the night. Izzy and Drake were at the table, in full gargoyle mode. Their little black horns bobbed up and down as they giggled.

Jasmine stood between them, suddenly stiffening.

Her reaction caused a nervous flutter in my chest. I set my glass of juice down. "Are they here?"

"Not yet." She smoothed her hands over the front of her cap-sleeved blouse. "But the men are preparing for their arrival."

It was weird how they all were connected. Seconds later, I heard them moving around upstairs. I hadn't seen Zayne all day. It was official. He was avoiding me. I needed to see him, because after staring at the ceiling all night, I knew I should apologize. I was putting too much on him, expecting things I shouldn't be. He did care, but the warping was on my side, because what I felt for him was more than I should.

"Where are you going to go?" Jasmine asked, quickly cleaning away the boxes of apple juice and animal crackers.

I tucked my hair back. "I don't know. I'm hoping I can find Zayne before they get here. If not, I guess I'll hang out in the tree house." *Like a loser...*

A tight look pinched her features. "How will you know when they're gone?"

"I don't know. If I can't get ahold of Zayne, I guess someone will call me." At least that was what I hoped. "How long do you—"

A loud rumble cut off my words. Glasses shook in the cabinet. Stainless-steel pots clanged off one another. I backed away from the counter, clasping my hands together. In an instant, all the air sucked straight out of the house. Static permeated the room. I didn't dare move. Even the twins seemed to sense their arrival, staring wide-eyed at their mother.

Alphas sure loved their fancy entrances.

A burst of energy raised the tiny hairs on my body. The rumbling stopped and the air smelled of something musky and sweet. It wouldn't smell like that to everyone. Heaven smelled however you wanted—like what you desired. Roses? Pancakes with maple syrup? Burnt rubber. Whatever. The last time they'd been here, it had smelled like winter mint to me.

Jasmine glanced at me, but I was already moving around the counter. Instinct told me they were in the library. I crept down the hall, stopping several feet away. Soft, luminous light seeped underneath the door, slipping across the maple floors, climbing the buttercream walls. The light pulsated, becoming more of a living entity as tendrils crossed the ceiling, dripping bits of bright light into shiny puddles on the throw rug.

It was the light people saw moments before they died. And

it was beautiful. Heavenly. For some, there was nothing to fear in death. Not when *this* waited for them.

This was as far as I could go. They already knew I was here, somewhere in the house, but I couldn't pull myself away. My throat started to burn, and my skin tingled. It was sheer torture to be near something so pure and not want to…well, devour its essence.

I knew I needed to leave, but I reached out, running the tips of my fingers through the light. Gasping, I jerked my hand back. It was hot—burning. My fingertips were pink and they throbbed. Thin wisps of smoke drifted from my hand.

Stepping back, I held my injured hand to my chest and, well, my chest ached for a whole different reason. I stared at the light as it continued to spread throughout the house, basking everything in its warmth.

I couldn't go into the light. Not now and probably, not ever.

Harsh tears stung my eyes. I turned away then, grabbing my book bag from the now-empty kitchen, and left the house before the Alphas grew tired of my presence and took the choice of leaving from me.

Sitting on the stupid observation deck, I stared down at the screen on my cell phone and let out a juicy curse that would've burned the ears right off the Alphas. Dusk had fallen and tiny stars were starting to peek through.

Zayne hadn't answered the first two times I'd called a half an hour ago.

Glancing down at my hand, I frowned at the bright pink skin on my fingers. Only I'd be dumb enough to try to touch heavenly light.

I reached around my neck and tugged on the chain so that the odd stone dangled just below my fingers. Smoothing my thumb over the jewel, I wasn't able to stop the shudder of repulsion. I wanted to rip the ring off the chain and toss it into the bushes. I almost did, but when my fingers curled around it, I...I just couldn't do it. Even if my mother was *the* Lilith, even if she hadn't wanted me, I couldn't throw the only thing I had of hers away.

Pushing my backpack aside, I wiggled through the opening and climbed down the boards nailed into the trunk of the tree.

After calling Stacey and getting no answer, I got a quick text back from her saying she was at the movies. Envious, I kicked a thick root breaking through the ground and I did it again—called Zayne.

The phone continued to ring several times and Zayne still didn't answer. I cut the call off when his voice mail picked up. My heart rate kicked up, like it did every time he didn't answer. Maybe it was a bit psycho stalker-ish, but even as mad as he was at me, he had to know that I was basically camped out in the damn tree house until someone remembered to call me.

Five minutes went by and I tried him again, hating myself for it. Because seriously, I was slipping into that desperate land again, the one inhabited by girls who made fools out of themselves over boys—boys who didn't want them or couldn't have them. My stomach was flopping all over the place, like it had last night, right before I said all those stupid, stupid things.

After the second ring, the call went straight to his voice mail. What the...?

My stomach stilled—I stilled.

Everything around me seemed to go quiet as I listened to the automatic voice mail picking up. Numb, I pressed the end-call button and slowly lowered my hand. He'd sent me to voice mail. He'd actually sent my call to voice mail.

Who knows how long I stood there. It probably would've been much longer if I hadn't heard the twig snap behind me.

Whipping around, I felt my heart drop to my sneakers. Petr stood in front of me, his hands shoved into the pockets of his jeans. The air had turned chilly, but he wore only a thin shirt. I couldn't make out the design in the encroaching darkness.

Petr laughed—snickered really. "This is really too easy."

"What is?" I took a step back, but kept my eyes trained on his.

A razor-sharp smile cut into his lips. "You're out here? Hanging out in a tree house? How incredibly lame is that?"

Unease quickly flipped to annoyance. "What are you doing here?"

Petr looked around pointedly. "What does it look like? Bearing witness to your pathetic existence one last time."

A ball of ice formed in my chest. "You were told to leave me alone."

"Yeah, see, that's the funny thing. I was told a lot of things." He walked around me slowly, head down, much like the predator a Warden was. "How does it feel to be left outside like a mangy dog? Unwanted? Even Zayne seems to have grown tired of you."

His words cut deep, because in a way, they were kind of true, except I was more like an unwanted mule than a mangy dog. But I refused to show any hurt. "How does it feel to be a perverted excuse for a male?"

Petr's eyes narrowed into thin slits as he made another wide circle. "You know what's so funny about all of this?"

"No. But I guess you're going to tell me?"

He smirked. "You don't even know why the Alphas are here. You don't even know the real reason why the demons are sniffing after you."

I curled my hand around the cell, feeling my pulse spike. "And you're going to tell me?"

He shot forward so fast, I didn't even see him move. Wrapping a long finger around the chain of my necklace, he tugged on it hard enough for it to bite into my skin. His gaze dropped to where the ring dangled. "You don't even know what this is."

Pulling the necklace out of his grip, I stepped back. Something in his words struck a deep nerve. Did he know about Lilith? It really didn't matter. Alphas in the house be damned, I started around him.

He grabbed my arm. "Where do you think you're going?"

I looked down at his hand, stomping down the sudden rush of dread. Showing fear was never a good idea. "Let go of me."

Petr sneered, and warnings fired off left and right. Too far away from the mansion to be heard if I screamed, I also knew that anyone who'd come to my aid was otherwise occupied.

I squared my shoulders. "Do you remember what happened last time?"

Unconsciously, his hand went to the faint scar along his jaw. Zayne had given him that.

"I'm going to do worse to you than break your jaw if you don't let go of me."

Petr's cold laugh came like a punch in the stomach, and a sinking, drowning feeling threatened to swallow me. "This should've been done a long time ago, but I'm glad it wasn't. I'm going to have fun fixing it."

In a cold moment of striking clarity, I realized that Petr wasn't here to just talk crap to me. He was here to *kill* me. With that knowledge, I inhaled sharply, but panic punched the air out of my lungs. "You won't get away with this."

"Ah, I think I'll be fine."

Instinct kicked in. Lurching to the side, I surprised him and his grip loosened. Somehow I remembered that I held my phone in my hand. I tapped on the screen blindly, praying that it dialed someone—anyone. Before he could recover, I brought my knee up and slammed it into his stomach.

Breaking loose, I whirled around, but he got a handful of my hair, yanking my head back. Petr went for the phone, twisting my wrist until I lost my grip on it. He threw it into the nearby bushes.

Terror rushed through me, as did pure rage. I swung at him,

digging my nails into his cheek. Petr yelped and let go. I kicked out, clipping his leg.

Petr shot around me, slamming his fist into me and knocking me to the ground. The fresh burst of pain stunned me, but I crawled forward. He caught my shoulder, flipping me onto my back.

To the left of us, the bushes suddenly rattled wildly, drawing Petr's attention. He reared up, just as I twisted and something—something shiny-black with big fangs—shot from the foliage. *Bambi?* I didn't even question why the snake was here, but I prayed she ate Petr.

Bambi darted across the clearing, mouth open and fangs gleaming. Growling deep in his throat, Petr whipped around, catching the snake just below its head. She hissed and snapped out, but with a ripe curse, he threw the snake against a nearby tree. Bambi hit the trunk with a nasty, sickening thud and fell to the ground in a messy, unmoving lump.

Real terror spread its way through me like a virus. I swung, aiming for any part of him I could make contact with.

"You stupid little demon bitch," Petr spat, catching my arm. "A familiar—you have a *familiar* hanging around you? Even Abbot will thank me for this."

A scream caught in my throat as I kneed him in the stomach. Petr grunted and then his fist snaked out, crashing into my face. The ringing in my ears blocked out all sound. I sucked in air and blood, thrashing under his weight. I was reduced to struggling like a wild animal.

"Stop. Just stop," Petr said, pushing my head back. "This will go so much easier if you just don't fight."

A different kind of instinct struggled to rise inside me—not Warden, but a part of me that was more powerful than the will to survive. Petr thought he had me defenseless under him? Let him believe that. All I needed was for him to lower his head just another inch or two. The demon inside me roared its approval.

"That's it." The scratches on his cheek stretched, seeping blood. "This has to be done. The entire world will be better off if you're dead."

Confusion and the spicy cologne he wore suffocated me. My skin felt like it was stretched to the limit. The demon inside me clawed to get out.

"You're going to beg." His gaze flicked up, pale eyes heated. "They all do. Beg right before we send them back to Hell." His hand moved lower, bruising. "No pride. And that's the way it should be. Look at you now."

Tears of frustration and fear ran down my cheeks, mixing with dirt and blood, but they had no effect on Petr. I couldn't do this—couldn't just lie here and wait. I reared up, clutching the short hairs on the back of his head and forcing his mouth toward mine.

Petr crammed his hand over my mouth, forcing my head back down. "Oh, no, you aren't going to do that."

Full-blown panic set it. His hand crushed my split lip, and I couldn't breathe. I beat my fists against his arms, his chest. The thin material of my camisole ripped, and then his fingers were wrapping around my throat. I felt every pebble digging into my back, and out of the mass of jumbled thoughts, I remembered what Roth had said. *People with the purest souls are capable of the greatest evils. No one is perfect, no matter what they are or what side they fight for.*

Truer words had never been spoken.

Desperation clouded my senses. I dug my nails into his hand, but no matter how I tried, I couldn't breathe. My limbs felt heavy as I choked on my own tears. His fingers bruised as he tried to pry my legs apart, but I squeezed them tighter and tighter. I stared up at the darkening sky, the moon a pale, distant shadow.

Defiance burst through me. I craned my neck, his hands slipped and I bit down as hard as I could. His skin popped between my teeth and warm blood gushed. Petr jerked back, howling. The blow he landed cracked my head on the hard ground. Starbursts clouded my vision.

Don't pass out. Don't pass out.

I pried my eyes open and they stung unnaturally. Something inside of me snapped. Maybe it was the demon finally. It didn't matter what it was. I reared off the ground, clenching the sides of his face. My movement stunned him, giving me enough time to latch my mouth on to his. I inhaled deeply, feeling the first wisp of his soul.

I breathed in again, and he went wild, beating my arms, my chest. I held on, dragging his soul bit by bit inside me as he moaned. He didn't taste like I thought a pure soul would. It felt thick, heavy with blood and hatred.

Petr was shifting, his fingers clawing at my neck, wrapping around the silver chain. The last of his soul struggled against me, but I coaxed it out and into me. Petr jerked away, and the moment his mouth left mine, a ragged sob escaped me.

Back bowed and arms thrown out to the side, Petr's skin turned sallow. Veins bulged along his throat and then darkened, like ink had been injected into his blood. Darkened vessels traveled up his cheeks and down the bare skin of his arm. He shuddered once, and then he rose onto the tips of his toes as if he was nothing more than a puppet.

Feeling too warm and more than a little off balance, I tried to stand, but my legs wouldn't cooperate even though dull instincts were flaring to life. *Get away. Get away.* Whatever was happening with Petr wasn't normal, but the soul—ah—tasting a soul was like taking a hit of the purest drug out there. Warmth buzzed through my veins, dulling the numerous aches and erasing the fear. I'd tasted a soul before, but never taken one completely.

Humans would waste away within minutes of losing their souls, turning into wraiths. Apparently Wardens did something completely different.

I willed my muscles to work, managing to sit up. Light-headed, I struggled to focus through the rushing tide of heat. Muscles relaxed and loosened. The world above spun, but Petr...

His body contorted and he threw his head back, mouth gaping open in a silent howl. Fangs punched out between his pale gray lips. Clothing stretched and tore. Petr was shifting. Maybe I hadn't taken his soul. Maybe I was hallucinating.

Bones popped and skin ripped. Petr's wings unfurled from his back, spanning six feet on either side of him. His body jerked into the final stages of transformation. He stilled for a moment and then his chin snapped down.

Petr's eyes were bloodred.

And that...well, that wasn't right.

My palms slid across the soil and I ended up flat on my back. A tiny giggle escaped my slack lips. Blood pounding, I tried to sit up again. Deep down I knew I should've been afraid, but nothing could hurt me now. I could kiss the sky if I wanted to.

The ground trembled as Petr stepped forward, a low growl rumbling up through him. He extended a heavily muscled arm, and his hands formed deadly claws. Lips pulled back in a snarl, he dropped into a crouch.

Something bigger and faster pulled away from the shadows, heading straight for us. In my mixed-up head, I wondered if it was another Warden coming to help Petr finish what he'd started.

Petr straightened, whipping toward the fast-approaching shadow, but he was too late.

The blur solidified in an instant. The facial features were familiar but sharper, as if the skin had thinned over bone. Pupils stretched vertically and irises glowed yellow.

Petr's body spasmed and he let out a hoarse cry. Hot, wet warmth sprayed into the air, dotting my jeans and my stomach. A metallic scent flooded the air.

"That's for being a bastard," Roth said, and then he yanked his arm back. A long spiny structure dangled from his hand—a spine. "And that is for throwing Bambi."

12

TOO STUNNED AND OUT OF it to say much of anything, I watched Roth drop the spine on the ground. His lip was curled in disgust as he stepped over Petr's body and knelt before me.

"Are you okay?" he asked, and when I didn't answer, he reached forward with a bloodied hand. His gaze dropped to it and he muttered something under his breath. Pulling his hand back, he wiped it on his jeans. "Layla?"

His face didn't seem so sharp now, but those eyes still glowed yellow. The high had peaked and was starting to drift away like an idle breeze. Sharp bursts of pain were popping up all over my body. I opened my mouth, but only air came out.

My gaze drifted toward the body.

"Don't look," he said, placing a hand on my leg.

I jerked away, my breathing starting to pick up again.

"Okay," Roth said, glancing over to where Bambi was stirring to life. He turned his gaze back to me, whistling low, and the snake rose up and traveled halfway to Roth before turning into a dark cloud. The smoke traveled up his arm and settled against his skin, the tail of the tattoo wrapping around his elbow. Roth kept his eyes fixed on me. "Layla, say something."

I blinked slowly. "Thank...you."

A muscle popped in his jaw as his gaze held mine a moment longer, and then he turned back to the body. "I need to take care of this and then I'll...I'll take care of you."

Roth picked up the body and the other parts, quickly disappearing into the thick brush of the woods. Rolling onto my side, I managed to pull myself up so I leaned against the base of a tree. Disjointed thoughts trailed endlessly through my head.

I'd taken a soul—a pure soul.

My stomach cramped. The soft glow that had surrounded me disappeared and I shivered uncontrollably.

I'd taken a soul.

Roth materialized out of nowhere, the front of his jeans damp and his hands clear of blood. He must've washed them in the nearby stream. Without saying a word, he approached me slowly, as if worried about frightening me. He slipped an arm under my knees and lifted me, and it occurred to me that I should probably ask where he was taking me. But I just wanted to be away from here, as far away as possible.

His body changed against mine, hardened much like a Warden's would. Heat radiated from his skin and there was the familiar sound of skin separating. Wings so dark they almost blended into the night spread out from his body, arcing gracefully. At the tips were horns, curved and sharpened into fine points. The wings had to be at least ten feet wide. The biggest I'd ever seen.

I pulled back a little and sucked in a sharp breath. His skin was the color of polished onyx, more skeletal than skin. Unlike the Wardens, there were no cranial horns. Just smooth black skin. A cold stab of fear pierced my heart. Seeing Roth in his true form was a sharp reminder of what he really was—a demon.

But I was part demon and Petr...Petr had been a Warden, and

he'd wanted to kill me. Things were no longer so black-and-white to me.

I lifted my gaze to Roth's face.

Golden eyes met mine, and it was as if he knew what I was thinking. "Funny how much demons and Wardens look alike, huh?"

I didn't respond, but one side of his lips tipped up in total Roth fashion. "Close your eyes, Layla. This is going to be fast."

He didn't give me much of a chance to protest. With his free hand, he tucked my head into the space between his throat and shoulder. He dropped into a crouch and a powerful tremble rocked his body a moment before he launched into the sky.

Pulse pounding, I squeezed my eyes shut and burrowed in. Only Zayne had ever done this—taken me into the sky. It required a lot of trust on my end. If Roth decided to drop me, it wasn't like I was going to sprout wings and save myself from going splat. And even though I doubted that was part of his master plan, my anxiety level skyrocketed and pushed my already-thumping heart into overdrive.

Roth tightened his hold and he murmured something that was lost in the wind. The flight to wherever Roth was taking me was a blur, but it did kill the remaining buzz. When he finally landed, my entire body thrummed with pain. I was shaking so badly I didn't even realize that he'd shifted back into human form until he leaned back and I could see his face.

"You hanging in there?" he asked. The pupils of his honey-colored eyes were still stretched vertically.

I nodded or at least I think I did. Over his shoulder, I could see nothing but apartment buildings, lit up like a chessboard. "Where are...we?" I winced as pain shot through my jaw.

"My place."

His place? Roth didn't elaborate as he started forward. It took me a few seconds to realize that we were in a narrow alley behind a rather large building. The door before us swung open, and a man appeared in the darkness.

He looked like he was in his mid-twenties. Icy blond hair was pulled back in a low ponytail, but the finely arched brows were dark. His eyes were like Roth's, the color of rich honey. He was most definitely a demon, but he held the door open. "This is a surprise," he said.

"Shut up, Cayman."

Cayman's steps matched Roth's. We were in a stairwell, heading up. "Should I be concerned? Because if that's who I think it is and she looks like that because of something you did, I really need to know before I have a fleet of Wardens tearing up my building."

I wondered how bad I looked and how this guy knew who I was. "He didn't do this."

"That's somewhat of a relief, but…"

Roth rounded a level. "The Wardens are of no concern at this moment."

The other demon arched a brow. "That would be your opinion—and an invalid one. The Wardens—"

"Didn't I already tell you to shut up?"

Cayman grinned as he slid around us, opening the door to the fifteenth floor. "And since when do I ever listen to you?"

Roth grunted. "Good point."

He stepped aside, hand on the door. "Can I get you guys anything?"

"Not at the moment." But Roth stopped and faced the other demon. "I'll be down to see you later. Don't worry. I'll fill you in."

Humor glimmered in the demon's eyes. "Great. I'm in need of some good gossip."

And then he was gone, like he'd poofed out of the hallway. Roth started down the hallway. "I…I can…walk."

"I'd prefer that you didn't right now, and besides, we're here."

Here was a door painted black. It opened on its own, and as soon as we stepped through, an overhead light flicked on and bright light spilled across the room. I blinked until my eyes adjusted.

His home away from Hell was pretty nice. A large loft fit for a king, to be exact. The walls were painted white, and they were bare with the exception of a few macabre, abstract paintings. There was a bed in the middle, covered with black and red sheets. A TV was mounted on the wall, and below it were several stacks of DVDs and books. There was a piano in the corner beside a closed door.

Any other time I would've made a beeline for the books and DVDs, but when he gently sat me down on the bed, I stayed there, feeling numb and empty.

"Why did he do this?" Roth's voice was eerily calm.

"Is…is Bambi okay?" I asked instead.

Roth frowned. "Bambi is fine."

It was strange to feel relief over a demon snake. "She helped me twice." I lifted my gaze. "You helped me twice."

"Like I said, Bambi seems to like you. She keeps an eye on you…"

When I can't seemed like the unspoken part of the sentence. I lowered my gaze, so very confused about freaking everything. Were all demons really evil? How could they be when one rescued me from the one thing meant to protect everyone?

"Answer my question, Layla."

I hesitated. Because…because I wasn't sure I could say why Petr did what he did. I wasn't ready to speak those words, because it made everything painfully real. And at that moment, I didn't think I could handle them.

He stared at me a moment and then stalked over to a low sitting chair. He pulled a thick blanket off the back. "Here." He carefully dropped it over my shoulders. "You look cold."

I slowly let go of my torn clothes, sinking my fingers into

the rich softness, pulling it around me. I didn't know what kind of material it was. Maybe cashmere? It was black, though, which fit him.

Roth lingered again, not saying anything, and then he spun around. I watched the intricate play of his muscles as he reached down and tugged his dirty shirt up over his head. Muscles in his arms flexed as he tossed it to the floor. There was a large tattoo along the side of his body: four lines of eloquently written scripture in a language I'd never seen before.

Even in the state of mind I was in, I couldn't help but appreciate all that Roth had going on. When he turned to grab a shirt out of a pile of neatly stacked clothes, I got an eyeful of his front. He was all muscle, chiseled and lean. Graceful. His pants hung low, and it looked as if someone had pressed their fingers into the skin next to his hips, leaving behind indentations. The dips and planes of his stomach looked unreal.

Bambi was wrapped around his biceps, and there was an odd, circular tat over his right pec. Yet another tattoo was carved over his stomach. It appeared to be a dragon, with its head reared back and jaws open. Wings were tucked against its scaly back and the tail disappeared below the waistband of his pants.

I needed to look away, but my eyes were glued to where that tail must've been.

Roth pulled a clean shirt on, and I let out a breath. He moved to a small kitchen area and opened up a cabinet. He returned to my side, unscrewing a bottle. "You should drink some of this. It will help."

I accepted it, taking a long swallow. The liquor burned my lips and the inside of my mouth as he disappeared into what I assumed was a bathroom, but it warmed my insides wonderfully. I heard the water turn on a few moments later. When he reappeared, I stared at the towel in his hand. "What are you doing?"

"Cleaning up your face." Roth crouched, his eyes roaming over me. "Does it hurt to talk?"

It hurt not to talk. "A little." I took another drink, gasping as the liquid dribbled over my torn skin. Roth took the bottle from me, setting it out of my reach. I sighed.

"How do you normally heal?" he asked.

"Faster than a human, but not like the Wardens or...like you," I answered. Hopefully most of the bruises would be gone by midweek. Not that my injuries were even a problem. I had bigger things to worry about.

He dabbed the towel under my lip with surprising gentleness. "I want to know why he did this, Layla. I need to know."

Looking away, I squeezed my eyes shut. Raw pain tore through my chest like a real wound. I knew—God, I knew—that it wasn't just Petr who wanted me dead. The whole thing seemed like a big setup—the Alphas, the clansmen being nowhere nearby, and even Zayne not answering his phone. Betrayal cut so deep, it splintered my very core.

Gentle fingers pressed under my chin, turning my head to the side. "Talk to me, Layla."

I opened my eyes and blinked back tears. "He wanted... he wanted to kill me. He said the world would be better off without me."

A muscle spasmed along Roth's jaw and his eyes flared a tawny color, but his touch remained so soft that it didn't seem like it was him holding my chin. "Did he say why?"

"He said I should've been killed when the Wardens first found me. Petr's always hated me, but this...this was more." I told Roth everything that had happened, stopping every few moments to rest my aching jaw. "I didn't have a choice."

"A choice about what?" he asked. "You didn't kill him. I did. And I'd like to do it again."

I shook my head and it hurt. "I took his soul, Roth. I don't understand what happened. He didn't waste away like a human would. He turned and his eyes were red."

He stilled, looking me straight in the eye. "You took his soul?"

Tears pricked my eyes.

"Layla," he said gently. "Did you take his soul completely?"

"I think so." My voice cracked. "Yes. Yes, I did."

The hue of his eyes darkened. "You did what you had to do. There is no guilt in what happened. Do you understand me? He was…hurting you. The bastard deserved to die."

I said nothing to that, and Roth smoothed the cloth over my brow. He was quiet and meticulous as he worked. I watched the muscle in his jaw tick away, his pupils slowly but surely going back to normal by the time he left and returned with a fresh towel.

"How bad is it?" I asked when I couldn't take the silence any longer.

Roth smiled for the first time since he'd found me. "It's not as bad as it could be. Your lip is split, and there's going to be one Hell of a bruise on your jaw—" he skimmed his fingers over my brow "—and here. You're more durable than you look."

I should've felt relief, but I couldn't. All I could feel were Petr's hands on me and the way he'd looked after I took his soul. Roth gently started to part the edge of the blanket and my grip tightened. "What are you doing?"

"I'm making sure you're okay."

"No." I leaned away from him, feeling the walls start to close in around me. "I'm fine."

"I'm not going to hurt you." Roth placed his hand on my shoulder carefully, but I still winced at the ache traveling down my arm. His eyes hardened. "You're letting me check you over. I'm not going to hurt you, okay? I promise."

I stared at him for what seemed like eternity, then I nodded and let go of the blanket. Roth didn't wait for me to change my mind. He slipped the blanket off my shoulders and when I heard his sharp inhalation, I wanted to grab it again. I felt him move the cloth under my neck, dip between the shredded halves of my camisole.

"He scratched you," Roth explained after a few moments. "Was he in his true form when he did this?"

"No." I opened my eyes. "He started to shift when I got ahold of his soul and then he turned completely afterward."

Before Roth could respond, I felt something soft and warm brush against my ankle. I looked down in surprise. A tiny white kitten stared up at me, eyes as blue as the sky. "Kitten?"

"Yes. It's a kitten."

Stunned that Roth would have something so cute, I ignored the wave of dizziness and bent around him, reaching for the tiny ball of fur. Its soft purr was like a miniature engine. Another one popped out from underneath the bed. Black, fluffy and the same size as the other kitten, it shimmied out and pounced on the back of the white one. They rolled, hissing and swatting at one another. I glanced at Roth. "Two?"

He shook his head, pointing back to the head of the bed. "Three."

A third peeked around the corner of a pillow, a mixture of black and white. It trotted up to me, sweeping at my fingers with surprisingly sharp claws. "I…can't believe you have kittens." I wiggled my fingers and the little guy strained to reach them. "What're their names?"

Roth snorted. "That one is Fury. The white one is Nitro and the black one is named Thor."

"What? You called these cuties something like that, but named a giant snake Bambi?"

He bent forward, placing a kiss on my shoulder. It was so fast I wasn't sure he'd actually done it. "There's sweetness in evil," he said. "And remember, looks can be deceiving."

I lowered my fingers, running them over the kitten's little head.

"I wouldn't do that if I—"

Fury sank its claws and teeth into my hand. I yelped, jerking my hand back. It remained latched on, a squirming ball of vamp kitty.

Roth grabbed the fluff of fur, gently removing it from my hand. "Bad kitty," he said, dropping it next to its siblings.

I stared at the demonic furball as it licked its bloody claws, and then shifted my gaze to Roth. "I don't understand."

"Let's just say that they weren't always this cute and cuddly-looking. They can get pretty big when provoked, but even in this form, Hellhounds are afraid of them," Roth said.

The white one jumped on the bed, stretched out little legs and yawned. It eyed me as if it wasn't sure what I was doing there.

Roth caught my hand, bringing the finger the kitten had injured to his lips. He pressed a kiss to the blemished skin, surprising me once more. "You're going to be fine."

I could feel the tears welling up in my eyes again. "What... what am I going to do? I took a soul—*a pure soul.*"

Roth sat beside me. "It will be okay."

A strangled laugh escaped me. "You don't understand. I'm not allowed...to take souls. Not in any situation."

"It's not something to worry about right now," he said firmly. "I'll take care of it."

I wanted to believe him so badly, but I couldn't see how he could take care of anything. What had been done couldn't be reversed.

Roth reached out, cupping the side of my jaw that didn't feel like it was on fire. "This will all work out. It will." There was a pause. "Look. You have a little visitor."

I glanced down. The white kitten rubbed against my side, staring up at me with slanted blue eyes. I itched to pick it up and hold it close, but I valued my fingers. It went back to rubbing my hip, as if it dared me to pet it.

Emotion clogged my throat as I realized I hadn't thanked him properly. "Why are you helping me? I mean, thank you—I can never thank you enough for coming when you did. I just…" I just didn't understand how a demon could be the one to save me from a Warden.

He shrugged, dropping his hand. "I'm a lot of things, Layla. But even I have my limits."

Silence fell between us, and Roth went back to cleaning up the rest of my wounds. He was good at this—taking care of someone. I doubted it was something he learned in Hell.

When he finished, he gave me a pair of his sweats and a shirt to wear. On the walk to his bathroom, I ached and felt awkward. In his bright bathroom, I stared at my reflection. My eyes seemed larger than normal, a brighter gray that bordered on looking wild. The right side of my jaw was already turning a deep purple. It matched the bruise forming just below my hairline. The skin had split there, but it didn't look like I needed stitches. My lip looked like a Botox injection gone horribly wrong.

I shook off my clothes, wincing not just from the pain but from the sight of the blue and light violet splotches covering my shoulders and chest. Petr's claw marks started under my throat, three deep slashes about four inches long. I quickly changed, unable to look at myself any longer.

Roth was at the window when I returned. He turned around and tried for a wolfish grin. "I always knew you'd look great in my pants."

I hadn't thought I'd laugh again, but I did then. It sounded weak. "That's real original."

He pushed off the wall and gestured at the closed door I'd noticed before. "I want to show you something. You think you're up for it?"

Intrigued despite myself, I nodded. He opened the door and motioned me forward. I followed him up the narrow staircase.

He stopped at a door and glanced over his shoulder. "Promise me you won't walk off the ledge."

I would've rolled my eyes if it wouldn't have hurt. "I promise."

He didn't quite look like he believed me, but he opened the door. Cool air pulled me forward. I limped past him.

"Don't walk off the rooftop. Please." He followed behind me. "I wouldn't want to scrape your remains off the pavement below."

Soft, billowy white tents rolled in the perfumed breeze. Under them were several lounge chairs and small tables, but it was the neatly manicured flower garden that caught and held my attention. Vases of every size and shape lined the rooftop. I didn't know most of the flowers, but I did see roses and lilies everywhere.

"Is this yours?" I asked.

"All of this is mine."

I stopped by a large pot, running my fingers over the heavy petals. In the dark, I couldn't tell if the flower was purple or red. But it smelled sweet and tangy. "You garden?"

"I get bored." His breath danced off my cheek. "I find that it's a viable way of passing time."

I hadn't heard him come up directly behind me. I turned around halfway, inclining my head. "A demon who gardens?"

One corner of his lips quirked. "I've seen crazier things."

"Is that so?"

Roth tilted his head to the side. "You'd be surprised. I know a few of my kind who do taxes whenever they're topside, some who teach gym. We demons do love a good game of dodgeball."

I made a feeble attempt at a laugh. "I knew…there was something up with my gym teacher."

"If I didn't know better, I'd think Mrs. Cleo was a Hellhound in disguise."

I drifted away from him, focusing on the dazzling display of lights from the hundreds of buildings surrounding us. Off in the distance, I could see the tower of the Nancy Hanks Center. I shivered as I turned back to Roth.

He was so close, but I hadn't heard him move. "You should sit."

He didn't give me much of an option, guiding me over to one of the lounges. I ended up on my back within seconds, embraced by the thick pillows. The high was gone. The adrenaline had seeped away, and all that was left behind were bone-deep aches and too many questions.

Roth sat beside me, his hip pressing against my leg. "How are you feeling?"

What a broad question. "Everything is…so screwed up."

"It is."

Shifting my gaze to him, I almost laughed again. His brutal honesty was something else. Under the white canopy, the moonlight reflected off his striking face. Our gazes locked. "I don't know what I'm supposed to do from here."

His stare was unwavering. "Have you ever known what you're supposed to do?"

Good question. I broke eye contact. "You're a strange demon."

"I'll take that as a compliment."

I smiled a little. "You're actually nothing like any demon I know."

"Is that so?" He ran the tips of his fingers up my arm, over the slant of my collarbone, stopping short of where the skin was torn. "I find that hard to image. We demons are all alike. We covet pretty things, corrupt what is pure and whole, take what we can never have. You should have a whole fan club made up of demons."

His touch was lulling, comforting. I yawned. "You'd be a member of my demon-horde fan club?"

Roth laughed softly. "Oh, I think I'd be the president." He eased down beside me, onto his side. "Would you like that?"

I knew what he was doing. Distracting me. It was working. "Can I be serious for a moment?"

His hand skipped to my other shoulder. "You can be whatever you like."

"You really aren't all that bad…for a demon, you know."

"I wouldn't go that far." He stretched out beside me, propping himself up on his elbow. "They don't come any badder than me."

"Whatever," I murmured. Several moments passed. "I—"

"I know. I do. There probably isn't a question I don't have an answer for. And we do need to talk. What you know now is nothing but a drop in the messed-up bucket. And what you're going to learn is going to turn your world upside down." He paused, and my heart skipped a beat. "But we don't need to do this right now. You need to sleep. I'll be here when you wake up."

As I watched him through thinly slitted eyes, I realized I didn't know jack. I had no idea if I was ever going to be able to go home. If I'd ever really had a home. I didn't know how far the betrayal ran, if it included others who'd watched me grow up. I didn't even know what tomorrow was going to bring. But I did know that as unlikely as it was, I was safe right now, and I trusted Roth—a demon.

So I nodded and closed my eyes. Roth started humming "Paradise City" again, and I found it oddly comforting. In the moments before I drifted off to sleep, I swore I felt his hand brush my cheek.

13

WHEN I AWOKE, it was near dawn and the sky beyond the softly rolling canopies still clung to night. The events of the previous day rolled through my mind with startling clarity. My heart rate picked up, but I didn't move. My body wasn't the problem—the aches had dulled, and even the throbbing in my face was nothing compared to a few hours ago. It was just that I knew the Wardens would've realized I was missing by now. They would've started looking for me and for Petr. Zayne...I couldn't even think of him right now.

Nothing would ever be the same.

The heat of the lean, hard body pressed against mine was a stark reminder of that fact. Roth's chest rose and fell steadily against my side. Our legs were tangled together. His arm was thrown over my waist. The closeness, as crazy as it was, pushed away everything else that was important. I'd never woken up in the arms of a boy before. When Zayne and I were kids, we'd bunk together, but this...this was *so* different. Languid warmth started in my toes and traveled up my body at an alarming speed, flaring tightly at each point our bodies met.

I thought of the kiss we'd shared—my first kiss. I was as breathless as I'd be practicing evasive techniques. Considering everything that was happening and had happened already, it seemed like the last thing I should be thinking about.

But it was as automatic as breathing. My lips tingled from the memory. I doubted Roth even thought twice about it, but I had quite a few times since Friday.

I turned my head ever so slightly and sucked in a soft breath.

Roth was on his side, like he'd been before I'd fallen asleep. His face was relaxed, lips parted. I wanted to touch the line of his jaw, the curve of his brow, and I had no idea why. But my fingers tingled with the desire to do so. At rest like this, the harsh edge to his beauty was absent. In that moment, he was what I believed angels might look like.

Then he opened his mouth.

"You shouldn't look at me that way," he murmured.

A different kind of heat swamped my cheeks and I cleared my throat. "I'm not looking at you in any way."

He gave his customary lopsided smile. "I know what you're thinking."

"You do?"

An eye opened. The pupils were stretched vertically, and I shivered—not out of fear, but from something else entirely. He reached out, brushing a few strands of hair back from my face. His hand lingered on my cheek, surprisingly gentle compared to what came out of his mouth next. "Just so you know, your virtue isn't safe with me. So when you look like you want me to devour every inch of your mouth, I will without an ounce of regret. However, I doubt you'll feel the same afterward."

"How do you know what I'll regret?"

The moment those words left my mouth, I knew I probably should've kept that comment to myself. Both of Roth's eyes opened and fixed on me. Then he moved incredibly fast.

Hovering above me, he stared down at me with eyes that were a mosaic of every shade of gold imaginable. "I know a lot."

"You barely know me."

"I've watched you for a long time, always a few steps behind you. I wasn't trying to be creepy when I told you that before." He ran his finger along the hem of the borrowed shirt, his knuckles brushing the swell of my chest. "You know what I saw?"

I blinked slowly. "What?"

He stopped messing with the hem and slid his hand along the curve of my ribs as he bent his head down. His lips moved against my ear. "I saw something in you that you desperately try to hide from everyone. Something that reminded me of myself."

I drew in a shallow breath, mouth dry.

Roth pressed his lips against my temple, sliding his hand under the edge of the shirt. I jumped when his fingers touched my belly. "You always seemed lonely. Even when you were with your friends, you were lonely."

My chest spasmed. "And you…you're lonely?"

"What do you think?" He shifted so that one leg was between mine. "But it doesn't really matter. I'm not lonely right now. Neither are you."

I wanted to pursue the conversation, but his hand traveled up my stomach, stopping at the edge of my bra. My body had a mind of its own and it arched against his hand, willing him further without really knowing why. His eyes met mine. There was something hot and calculating about his gaze—feral and predatory.

Roth's gaze landed on my mouth, and I felt his chest rise sharply against mine. A soft breeze kicked up, stirring the canopies. They rolled noiselessly, revealing the sky. I knew he was going to kiss me then. The intent was in his stare, in the way he lowered his head to mine and parted his lips. I reached up, placing my hand on his cheek. His skin was warm, hotter than mine.

Roth pressed against me and my heart beat crazy fast. Our bodies were nearly flush, pieced together, and his musky, wild scent enveloped me. There was a brief moment when his lower body rocked against mine, and every nerve I had came alive, but then he sighed a sound full of regret and rolled off me.

Rolled right on off me.

Standing beside the lounge, he stretched his arms up over his head, flashing a tantalizing glimpse of his abs and the dragon tattoo. "I'll get us some coffee. We need to talk."

There was no chance to respond. He was just gone. Poofed like Cayman had in the hall the night before. What the Hell?

Sitting up, I pressed my palm against my forehead and groaned. I used his absence to gather my wits and calm my chaotic pulse. Five minutes later he returned with two cups of steaming coffee.

I blinked. "That was fast."

"Being a demon has its benefits. Never have to worry about traffic jams." He popped open the tab and handed it over. "Be careful. It's hot."

I murmured my thanks. "What time is it?"

"A little after five in the morning," he said. "I'm thinking about skipping school today. You should."

I smiled wearily. "Yeah. I don't think school is going to happen."

"Rebel."

Saying nothing to that, I took a sip of the coffee. French vanilla? My favorite. Just how closely had Roth been watching?

He sat beside me, stretching out long legs. "Seriously, though, how are you feeling?"

"Better. My face doesn't hurt as much." I peeked up, wondering if he'd felt anything before he rolled off me and disappeared into thin air or if he'd just been messing with me. "How does it look?"

Roth's gaze drifted over me, and I had a feeling he wasn't really paying attention to the bruises. "It looks better."

There was another stretch of silence, and I reached for my necklace out of habit.

It wasn't there.

"My necklace?" Dismay hit me. "Petr ripped it off. I have to—"

"I forgot." Roth leaned back and reached into his pocket. "I saw it on the ground and grabbed it. The chain is broken."

I took it from his palm. Squeezing my hand around the ring, I wanted to cry like a fat, angry baby. "Thank you," I whispered. "This ring..."

"It means a lot."

I looked up. "It does."

Roth shook his head. "You don't know how important it really is."

The ring seemed to burn against my palm and I looked down, slowly opening my hand. In the blossoming sunlight, the stone looked like it was full of black liquid. I thought back to what Roth had told me about my ring and then I thought about what Petr had said.

I looked up and found Roth watching me. A full minute passed before he spoke. "You must be so lonely."

"We're back to that again?"

He frowned. "You live with the very creatures obligated to kill you on sight. One of them tried, and who knows how many more want that same fate for you? You've probably spent your entire life wanting to be like them, knowing that you can never be. And the only thing you have to remind you of your real family is a ring that belongs to the only part of you that you refuse to claim. Nothing else, right? No memories. Not even what it felt like for your father to hold you, or a memory of what his voice sounded like."

I sat back, a dry lump in my throat. The low hum of traffic

on the street below muffled the gasp that escaped my tightly pressed lips.

Roth nodded without looking at me. "I've tried to imagine what it's like for you, wanting to belong so desperately and yet knowing you never can."

"Wow," I whispered, looking away. "Thanks for the reality check. Are you the demon of downers?"

He looked at me then. "Why were you out in the woods last night?"

The change in subject caught me off guard. "The Alphas were at the house. It's not good for me to be around when they visit."

"Ah, the Seraphim—warriors of justice and blah, blah, bullshit." Roth shook his head, smiling ruefully. "What a nasty lot of bastards, if you ask me."

"I'm sure they'd say the same thing about you."

"Of course they would." He dropped my hand and took a sip of his coffee. A moment passed as he watched a leafy plant sway in the breeze. It looked like a Venus flytrap. "The Seeker, the zombie and the possessed…that sounds like the start of a really bad joke, doesn't it?"

It did.

"But they all had something in common. You."

"I figured as much, but I don't understand why. What does it have to do with the ring or my mother?"

"Hell is looking for you," he said, rather casually.

"You said that before and I…"

"Didn't believe me?" When I nodded, he closed his eyes. "I wasn't lying. Hell only looks for someone when that person has something that interests them. We do like to covet things. I've told you that."

"But I don't have anything they could want."

"You do."

I shifted on the lounge, pushing down the sudden urge to

get up and run. "And you? It's the same reason why you started looking for me?"

"Yes."

"Why?" I placed the half-drunk cup of coffee on the roof and held the ring close to my chest.

He gave me another quick grin. "I've told you. I've been watching you for months, years really."

Years? My brain couldn't wrap itself around that idea.

He returned to staring at the plant. "I found you long ago, way before your most recent birthday, before any of the demons became aware of you. I guess the real question is, what makes you so special that Hell is looking for you? You're half-demon. So what?"

For some reason, I started to feel lamer than I normally did. "Okay."

"But—" he held up his hand "—half demons don't really have any demonic power. They're just bat-shit crazy. You know, the kids that pull wings off of butterflies and burn down their houses for fun? Usually while they're still inside the burning house. Not the smartest bunch, but hey, it happens. Not everyone is created equal."

I pursed my lips. "I don't think I'm special."

Roth looked at me again. "But you are. You're a half demon that is also half *Warden*. Do you even know what they really are?"

"Well, people call them gargoyles, but—"

"Not what they're labeled, but how they were created?"

I ran my fingers over the curve of the band. "They were created to fight the Lilin."

He busted into laughter—deep, amused chuckles.

Embarrassment flooded me. "Then why were they created, smart-ass?"

"Don't ever let them make you feel like they're better than you." Roth shook his head, still smiling. "They aren't. They aren't better than any of us." He laughed again, sounding less amused. "They're His big-ass mistake, and He gave them a pure soul to make up for it."

"None of that makes any sense."

"And it's not my place to explain it to you. There are so many rules. You know that. Ask your dear adopted dickhead of a father. I doubt he'd tell you the truth, or has ever told you the truth, for that matter."

"Not like you're doing a good job of telling me the truth, either."

"It's not in my nature to do so." Setting his cup down, he leaned back on his elbows and peered up at me through dark lashes. "Believe it or not, there are rules that even the Boss follows. Not all of Hell's children follow them, but there are things I cannot and will not do."

"Wait. The Boss—do you mean…?"

"The Boss?" he repeated. "Yes. The big one downstairs."

"Do…do you work for him?"

He flashed another demure smile. "Why, yes, I do."

Good God, what was I doing wanting him to kiss me earlier?

Roth sighed as if he knew exactly what I was thinking. "Say you had something I wanted? I can't just take it from you."

I shook my head, confused. "Why not? A succubus takes energy without the person knowing."

"That's different. The succubus isn't killing the human. Just tasting their essence, and for the most part, the human doesn't mind." He winked. "But I'm old-school. Just like the Boss. Humans have to have their free will and all that nonsense."

"I thought you didn't believe in free will?"

"I don't, but that doesn't mean the Boss doesn't." He shook his head. "Look, we've gotten way off topic here. You know that I work for the Boss and that I'm here on a job, so to speak."

Even though I knew there had to be a reason why Roth popped out of nowhere and started following me, sour disappointment still curdled in my stomach. What was I thinking?

That he saw me chowing down on a Big Mac and just had to know me? "I'm your job?"

His dark gaze flickered to mine and held. "Yes."

Slowly nodding, I let out a low breath. "Why?"

"I'm here to keep you safe from those who are looking for you. And by those, I mean demons a lot bigger and badder than what you normally deal with."

I stared at him so long that I think my eyes crossed, and then I burst into laughter. So hard, tears tracked down my face, blurring his scowl.

"Why are you laughing?" he demanded. "It better not be because you doubt my ability to keep your ass—a very lovely ass, by the way—safe. Because I think I've proved that I can."

"It's not that. It's just that you're a demon."

His expression turned bland. "Yes. I know I'm a demon. Thanks for the clarification."

"Demons don't protect anyone or anything." I waved my hand dismissively, still chuckling.

"Well, obviously they do, because I've saved you multiple times."

Wiping a few tears off my face, I quieted down. "I know. And I appreciate it. Thank you. But it's just so...so ass-backward."

Impatience flashed in his eyes, darkening them until the brown flecks almost disappeared. "Demons will protect just about anything *if* it's in their best interest. Or namely, Hell's best interest."

"And why would protecting me be in Hell's best interest?"

Roth's eyes narrowed. "I was going to try to break this to you gently, but screw it. I told you what your mother could do. I even told you her name."

My humor dried up right then and there as I stared at him.

A bit of smugness seeped into his face. "And I bet you went through every stage of denial and then some, but Lilith is your mother."

"You mean a demon named Lilith." I still refused to believe anything else. It was just some random demon with an unfortunate name.

"No. I mean *the* demon named Lilith," he corrected. "She's your mommy."

"That's not possible." I shook my head. "She's chained in Hell!"

Now it was Roth's turn to laugh like a demented seal. "And who started those rumors? The Wardens? Lilith was in Hell, but she broke loose seventeen years and nine months ago, give or take a week or two, which by the way, corresponds directly with what?"

I did the quick math, which put that date right around my birthday. My stomach roiled.

"She went topside, engaged in a little naughty action, got pregnant and popped out a pretty little baby that looked just like her."

"I look like her?" My head got stuck on the wrong thing.

Roth reached over, picking up a strand of my hair, twisting the pale locks around his long fingers. "She had your coloring from what I remember. I only saw her once before she was taken care of."

"Taken care of?" I whispered, already knowing the answer.

"When she escaped, the Boss had a pretty good idea of what she was up to. Where he has her now, she's not getting out of."

A dull ache pierced my temples. I rubbed at them, never more confused in my life. Should I feel better that Lilith wasn't dead, being that she was my mother? But being trapped in Hell by Satan himself had to suck and my mom...she was Lilith. I wasn't sure how to feel, and I knew it was about to get a whole lot worse.

"Have you ever heard of *The Lesser Key of Solomon*?" he asked.

Lifting my gaze, I shook my head. "No."

"It's the real deal—a book cataloging all the demons. It has their incantations, how to summon them, how to tell them apart, ways to trap a demon and all kinds of fun stuff. Lilith can't be summoned." He paused, watching me closely. "Neither can her original children."

My head felt like it was about to explode. "The Lilin?"

When he nodded, my stomach plummeted like my popularity status. "But everything has a loophole, and there's a really big one concerning the Lilin," he continued. "In the original *Lesser Key,* it describes how one can create the Lilin. It's like a seal that needs to be broken—an incantation."

"Oh, my God…"

Roth was all serious at this point. "The incantation has these stages, like most spells do. We know they involve spilling the blood of a child of Lilith's, and the—well, the dead blood of Lilith herself. There's more—a third or fourth thing, but we don't know for sure. Whatever those things are, if they're all completed, then the Lilin will be born again upon Earth."

My hands fell to my lap. Several moments passed. "And the child. That's me? There's no one else?"

He nodded again. "And the whole spilling-of-the-blood thing—well, not to be a downer, but since the Boss doesn't know if it means a pinprick of your blood or your death, he's not willing to risk it."

"Gee. Tell him thanks."

A smirk graced his lips. "The dead blood…" Leaning over, his agile fingers skipped along my wrist, eliciting a shiver in its wake. He worked my hand open, and the odd ruby-colored ring was exposed. "This stone isn't a gemstone. It contains the dead blood of Lilith."

"What? Ew! How do you know?"

"Because Lilith used to wear this ring, and only the child of Lilith can carry her blood without experiencing some seriously ill effects,'" he said, gently closing my fingers around the ring. "So we know where two of the things are, but the rest…it's in the Key."

"And where is the Key?"

"Good question." Roth leaned back, closing his eyes. "Don't know. And the Boss doesn't know what the third and fourth things are, but he's concerned that other demons—Dukes and Princes—may since Lilith was chummy with several of them. Getting out of Hell and having you was on purpose, her last big 'eff you' to the Heavens and Hell."

Wow. That did wonders for a girl's self-esteem.

"I don't get it," I said, curling my hands inward until my nails pressed into the flesh of my palm. "The Lilin are…they are insane and crazy scary, but wouldn't your Boss want that? It would be Hell on Earth basically."

Roth choked out a laugh. "No one wins in this case. When humans are stripped of their souls, they waste away and turn into wraiths. They don't go to Heaven or Hell. And the Boss knows he can't control the Lilin. He could barely control Lilith." Roth's beautiful lips twisted in a wry grin. "And trust me, you haven't witnessed a pissing contest yet if you haven't seen Lilith and the Boss go toe-to-toe."

I tried to wrap my head around this. "So…?"

"The last thing that Hell wants is for the Lilin to be running amok on Earth." He tapped his fingers on his knee, brows knitted. "And so here I am, making sure your blood doesn't spill and neither does the blood in the ring while trying to figure out what the other stuff is before *that* happens. Oh, and there's the whole issue of trying to discover exactly who wants the Lilin to be reborn. I'm a busy demon."

My mouth worked, but no words came out. We sat there for several minutes, the only noise the soft tapping of his fingers and the cars below. Mind. Blown. My mother was *the* Lilith. I was too tired to deny the truth to that. Mommy dearest apparently conceived me as a way to give everyone the middle finger. Blood spilling didn't sound fun, no matter which way you looked at it.

"Why now?" I asked.

"It's the timing of your birth. Supposedly the incantation can only work after you turn seventeen." He paused. "The Boss wasn't sure if Lilith had been successful in the sense that you..."

I stared at him, horrified when I realized what he was getting at. "That I wasn't killed once..." I swallowed, thinking of what Petr had said. "Once the Wardens found me?"

Roth nodded. "No one knew where Lilith had gone or where you'd been born. The world's a pretty big place. I'd found you before, but your birthday was still far off. When the Boss knew we were months away from your birthday, he sent me up again to see if you were still...uh, well, yeah."

"Alive," I whispered.

He plowed on. "When I reported back, the Boss ordered me to keep an eye on you. See, the Boss and the demons that Lilith hung with aren't the only ones who've heard of the incantation. Others have, as well, and they see you as a risk. They know the Alphas will obliterate every demon topside if the Lilin are reborn. They want to take you out—the Seeker, the zombie and the possessed human."

"So some demons may want me to raise the Lilin and others want to kill me because—" And it struck me then, with the force of a cement brick. Ice froze my veins just as a hot rush of betrayal swept through me like a rising tide. "Abbot has to know this."

Roth said nothing.

I swallowed, but the lump in my throat refused to budge. "He must have known this whole entire time. I mean, there's no way. The Alphas...and that's why Petr tried to kill me. It's probably why he and his father have always hated me, because of what I'm linked to."

In the looming silence, tears burned my eyes. I clenched my fists until my knuckles ached, refusing to let them fall. At no point had Abbot believed that I deserved to know the truth about what I was, what I could become a part of. And if Zayne knew, I didn't think I could ever get over that.

"Layla…"

Roth said my name so softly that I had to look at him, and when I did, our gazes locked. Part of me wondered at that very moment what he saw when he looked at me like that—like he wasn't exactly sure what I was or what he was really even doing here. And this had to be confusing for him. He was a demon, after all. I also wondered why I even cared, but the last thing I wanted to be seen as was a girl on the verge of tears. Which I was.

Sucking in a shrill breath, I eased my fingers open, and the ring bounced around my loose fist. Because I had no other place to put it, I slipped it onto my right ring finger. Part of me expected the action to spark Armageddon, but nothing happened. Not even a weird sensation or a shiver.

How anticlimactic.

Slowly but surely, my brain started to turn everything over. It probably took longer than necessary, but I was proud to know that my eyes were dry even though my throat felt raw. "We need to find that Key."

"We do. Knowing what's needed in the incantation gives us a fighting chance. I have some leads." He paused, and I could feel his stare on me again. "You can't tell the Wardens about any of this."

I barked out a short laugh. "I don't even know how I'm supposed to go home. Once they find out what I did to Petr—"

"They will never know." Roth caught the edge of my chin, forcing me to look at him. His eyes were a furious shade of amber. "Because you will not tell them what really happened."

"But—"

"You will tell them part of the truth," he said. "Petr attacked you. You defended yourself, but it was me who killed him. You will not mention taking his soul."

Stunned, I stared at him. "But they'll come after you."

Roth chuckled deeply. "Let them try."

I pulled away and stood, unable to sit any longer. Smoothing my hands over what I was sure was a tangled mess of hair, I started to pace between a potted apple tree and something that resembled a lilac bush that hadn't bloomed. "I'm not telling the Wardens that you killed Petr."

His lips slipped into a scowl. "I can take care of myself. I'm rather hard to find when I don't want to be and even harder to kill."

"I get that, but no. I'll tell them it was a demon, but not you. I'm not giving them your name." Once those words left my tongue, my conviction was cemented.

Roth stared at me, obviously bewildered. "I know I'm telling you to lie about the whole soul thing, but that makes sense. They'd kill you. But you're willing to lie about me? You do realize what that means?"

"Of course," I snapped, tucking my hair back. Not telling them about Roth was a betrayal. It could even be seen as me taking sides, and if the Wardens ever found out that I knew who killed Petr and hid the truth, I was as good as dead.

"I think you like me," Roth said suddenly.

I stopped pacing and my heart did a funny little jump. "What? No."

He tilted his head to the side, his lips spreading into a teasing grin. "The way you lie to yourself is sort of cute."

"I'm not lying."

"Hmm…" He sat up, eyes glimmering with mirth. "You wanted me to kiss you earlier."

Heat flooded my cheeks. "No. I did not."

"You're right. You wanted me to do much, much more."

Now that heat was spreading elsewhere. "You're insane. I don't want that—you." The words sounded lame to my own ears. "You saved my life. Sending the Wardens after you isn't a way to repay that." There. That sounded better.

Roth chuckled. "Okay."

"Don't 'okay' me." I took a deep breath.

"Okay."

I shot him a glare.

"What?" he said innocently. Then he got all serious-faced again. "What are you going to do?"

Glancing up at the overcast sky, I shook my head. Besides the obvious, which was finding out where the Key was and staying away from the demon who wanted to use me as part of a bizarre incantation, I assumed he meant with the home situation.

"I don't know what to do," I admitted, my voice a tiny whisper. "I can't hide from them forever. And as long as they don't know about the soul thing, I should be okay. Zayne—"

"Zayne?" Roth was frowning again. "The big, blond oaf?"

"I don't think he can be categorized as an oaf," I said drily. "How do you—Never mind. Watching me. Got it."

"You can't trust them. You may be close with Stony and crew, but they have to know what you are. You're not safe there." He ran the tips of his fingers along the cushion beside him, drawing my attention. Hadn't he touched me like that last night? I shivered and looked away. "If you go home, Layla, you're going to have to pretend you don't know any different."

"I can't believe it," I said, and when he sent me a look, I shook my head. "Zayne—he couldn't have known. He…"

"He's a Warden, Layla. His loyalty—"

"No. You don't understand. I'm not naive or stupid, but I know Zayne wouldn't have kept something like this from me."

"Why? Because you care for him?"

I was about to ask how he knew that, but then I remembered Bambi had been chilling about the tree house. "Of course I care about Zayne. He's the only one who's ever really known me. I can be myself around him and…" I trailed off, because the falsity of what I was saying sank in. I really couldn't be what I truly was with Zayne, either. "Anyway, he would've told me the truth."

He cocked his head to the side. "Because he cares about you, too?"

"He does, but not in the way I'm sure you're insinuating."

"Actually, he does *like* you." When I frowned, he laughed. "And I do mean *like you,* like you."

I scoffed. "How would you know? You—"

"Don't know Stony? You're right, but you forget that I did watch you for some time. I've seen you around him, and I've seen the way he looks at you. Sure, a relationship between you two is as hopeless as the debt problem facing—"

"Jeez, okay. I know that." I sighed.

"But it doesn't stop someone from wanting another person they can never have." His gaze turned acute. "Even if Stony doesn't know the truth, and you trust him with your life and blah, blah, you can't tell him anything."

A big, heavy ball of dread settled in my stomach.

"Layla?"

I nodded. "I'm not going to tell them."

"Good," he said, standing. He smiled, but I couldn't bring myself to return the gesture. I couldn't shake the feeling that I'd just sealed my fate.

14

LEAVING ROTH'S LOFT HADN'T BEEN EASY. For a second or two, I didn't think he was going to let me go. He hadn't voiced any direct opposition to me going home, but I could tell he wasn't a big fan of the idea. But if I stayed with him it would only be a matter of time before the Wardens found me.

They'd kill Roth, and even though I had no idea how I felt about him, I didn't want him to die.

Roth wanted to take me as close to home as he could get me, but I wasn't ready to go there. I wasn't sure where I wanted to go, but I needed to be alone. He'd followed me outside his loft and I discovered we were in one of the new skyrises outside the Palisades. Along the Potomac River, it was one of the wealthiest sections in D.C.

I guessed being a demon paid well.

I started walking and I didn't stop or look behind me to see if Roth followed. I knew I wouldn't see him, but I also knew he was there. And as I walked, my brain replayed everything over until my stomach churned relentlessly. Coffee may not have been a great idea.

Two hours later, I sat down on one of the benches outside the Smithsonian Institution. Even in the early-morning hours, the great lawn was full of runners and tourists. The first few people to pass me by cast worried looks in my direction. With my busted face and borrowed clothing, I probably looked like a poster child for what happens when kids run away.

I kept my chin down, letting my hair shield most of my face, and no one approached me. Perfect. It was a cold morning and I hunkered down in Roth's shirt, weary to the soul. In a matter of hours, everything had changed. My thoughts were scattered; my entire world felt broken. Roth had probably been amazed that I hadn't freaked out after he'd told me everything, but now I was knee-deep in freak-out mode.

How were we supposed to find an ancient book when no one knew where it was? How could I stay safe from a demon when no one knew who that demon was? And better yet, how could I ever go home?

Going home was the plan. That was why I'd left Roth's loft. Well, it wasn't the only reason. I needed space from him, too, because things were different between us. Like a bargain had been struck—a deal. But it was more than that. Whatever had sprung up between us this morning still made me feel like I was coming out of my skin, and Roth had been right. I *had* wanted him to kiss me.

God, I couldn't think about that right now.

What I wanted to do was rage. I wanted to throw something—kick someone, namely Abbot—and break something valuable. Lots of valuable things. I wanted to stand on the bench and scream until my voice gave out. Anger roared through me like a rabid dog and I wanted to unleash it, but under that fury, something bitter and dank stirred. There was more to the twisting in my stomach than just the bundle of nerves. I knew what would be coming in a matter of hours. I needed something sweet, like juice, but that would require money.

Within a couple of hours, a deep ache would settle in my bones. My skin would feel icy, but my insides would catch fire. As twisted as it sounded, I welcomed the sickness that came after tasting a soul. It was a rough form of punishment, but one I deserved.

I inhaled the brisk morning air and closed my eyes. I couldn't afford to break down. What could happen was bigger than my feelings of betrayal or anger. If this demon succeeded, the apocalypse would seem like a sweet-sixteen party in comparison. I needed to be strong—stronger than what could be gained from rigorous workouts.

The low rumble of a finely tuned engine forced my eyes open. Strange that in a bustling city with the low hum of chatter, drone of passing cars and blaring horns, I'd recognize the sound of Zayne's 1969 Chevy Impala anywhere.

I peeked through a sheet of whitish-blond hair just as Zayne climbed out of the driver's seat. The aura around him was so pure it looked like a halo. He slammed the door shut and turned, his gaze immediately finding the bench I sat on.

My breath whooshed out like I'd been sucker punched. A thousand thoughts ran through my mind as Zayne rounded the Impala. He came to a complete stop when he saw me, his body going rigid, and then he started forward again, his pace picking up until he broke out in a dead run.

Zayne was beside the bench in an instant, uncaring of all the eyes on us, and then his arms were around me, squeezing so tight that I bit down on my lip to keep the squeak of pain from coming out.

"Oh, my God," he said, his voice hoarse in my ear. "I can't..." A fine tremor coursed through his large body, and his hand pressed against my back, then slid up, burying deep in my hair.

Over Zayne's shoulder, I finally saw Roth. He was near one of the bare cherry-blossom trees, just standing there. Our eyes met for a brief moment, and then he turned around, crossing the lawn and heading east on the sidewalk, hands shoved into the pockets of his jeans. For Zayne not to have sensed the demon's presence was a testament to his state, and I hated that he'd been that worried.

A strange urge hit me then. I wanted to go after Roth, but that didn't make any sense. I knew he'd been watching me and that was all he was doing, but...

Zayne tugged me closer, tucking me into the crook of his neck, and he held on. Slowly, I lifted my arms, placed my hands on his back and fisted his shirt. Another shudder rocked his body. I don't know how long we stayed like that. It could've been seconds or minutes, but his warmth eased some of the chill, and for a moment, I could pretend that this was a week ago and this was Zayne—*my Zayne*—and everything was going to be okay.

But then he pulled back, his hands trailing to my shoulders. "Where have you been? What happened?"

Having no idea where to start, I kept my chin down.

"Layla," he said, placing his hands on either side of my face. I winced when his fingers pressed against my temple, but I didn't pull away. Zayne lifted my head and his eyes widened in shock. A rush of wild emotion cut across his face. Anger was the most apparent, turning his eyes an electric blue. Tension formed around his mouth. A muscle popped as his jaw worked. He slid his hands off my face, keeping my hair back. "Petr did this?"

My chest tightened with fear and dismay. "How...how did you know?"

His chest rose harshly. "He hasn't been seen since last night. Not since Morris said he saw him heading into the woods. I found your bag in the tree house and your phone was lying on the ground. There was...there was blood on it—your blood. We've been tearing this city apart looking for you. God, I thought the worst. I thought..." He swallowed thickly. "Jesus Christ, Layla..."

I opened my mouth, but nothing came out. The look in Zayne's eyes was frightening. "Are you okay?" he asked, and then he cursed. "That's a stupid question. Obviously, you're not okay. How badly are you hurt? Do you need to go to the hospital? Have you been out all night? Should I—"

"I'm okay." My voice cracked as I wrapped my fingers around his wrists. I'd never seen him like this before. "I'm okay."

He stared at me, and I suddenly recognized the emotion churning in his eyes. Horror. "God, Layla, he…he *hurt* you."

There was no denying that when my face still looked like I'd run into a wall. "I'm all right."

"It's not all right. He *hit* you." And then his gaze dropped, and I knew he saw the tips of the three angry slashes. He sucked in a ragged breath and a violent spasm shot through him. A low growl rumbled from his chest. "What form was he in?"

"Zayne." I put my hand on his trembling arm. "You're starting to phase."

"Answer me!'" he shouted, making me jump. A few people cast glances our way. He swore and lowered his voice. "I'm sorry. Did he—"

"No." I was quick to answer. "He tried to kill me, but he— Zayne, you're shifting."

Zayne was on the verge of losing complete control and going into full gargoyle mode. His skin had taken on a gray tint. While humans were accustomed to seeing them around at night, I doubted they'd expect one in front of the Smithsonian on a Monday morning.

"How did you find me?" I asked, hoping to distract him.

His wild gaze landed on me. "What?"

I squeezed his arm with as much force as I could. His skin was already hardening. "How did you know I was here?"

A few seconds passed. "It was a last-ditch effort. I checked everywhere and then I remembered how much you liked it here." He blinked and his eyes returned to normal, skin becoming more golden by the second. "Hell, Layla-bug, I've been out of my mind."

"I'm sorry." I threaded my fingers through his. "I couldn't go home and I didn't have a phone. I just…"

"Don't apologize." He reached out, trailing his fingers around the corner of my lip and then feathering across the bruise on my jaw. "I'm going to kill that son of a bitch."

I dropped my hands into my lap. "That won't be necessary."

"The Hell it won't be!" Fury sharpened his voice. "This isn't okay. Breaking his jaw won't make it better. His father—"

"He's dead, Zayne." I twisted my fingers together. "Petr's dead."

Silence. So much silence that I had to look at him and my stomach dropped. He had that wild look in his eyes again. "I didn't kill him," I said in a rush. "He came after me while the Alphas were here. It was like he was *sent* to kill me, Zayne. It wasn't just him messing with me and it getting out of hand." I told him everything Petr had said, barely taking a breath. "And I would've died, but—"

Zayne took my hand—the one with the ring—and I flinched. "But what, Layla?"

"I didn't kill him." That much was true. "A demon showed up. He came out of nowhere and he killed Petr."

He grew very still.

Lying to Zayne sucked. It made my chest feel raw and achy. "I don't know why. I don't know who it was. I don't even know what he did with Petr's body." Fear rose on a breath of cold air. Very real considering what the Wardens would do if they learned I'd taken Petr's soul and what they'd do to Roth. "And afterward, I was so confused and I knew what the Wardens would think—what Abbot would think. I'd be blamed, because Petr is a Warden. So I just—"

"Stop," Zayne said, squeezing my hand gently. "You're not going to be blamed for what Petr brought on himself. I'm not going to let anything happen to you. You should've come to me. You didn't have to be out here, dealing with this by yourself. I would've—" He cut himself off with a low moan.

"I'm sorry," I said, because I didn't know what else to say.

"God, Layla, don't apologize." A haunted look crept into his eyes right before he averted his gaze. He leaned back, thrusting fingers through his hair. It looked like he'd done that many times already. "Did you try to call me afterward?"

I knew immediately what he was getting at and my heart ached. "No. I was calling you before...before it happened."

Zayne swore swiftly. "If I had answered—"

"Don't," I pleaded.

He shook his head, brows furrowed as if he was in some kind of pain. "If I had answered the phone, this wouldn't have happened. I *knew* you had no place to go, but I was still so angry with you. *Shit!* No wonder you didn't come home. You must've been so scared. Layla, I'm—"

"You couldn't have done anything." I wiggled closer. Who knew what would've happened if Zayne had answered his phone. Petr may not have gotten me alone, but there would be other chances. "It would have happened no matter what. He wanted to kill me. He needed to kill me. That isn't your fault."

Zayne didn't respond immediately, and when he did speak, his voice was gruff. "I'll tell my father what you've told me so you don't have to go through this again, but he's going to want to talk to you. He's going to want to know exactly what Petr said to you and what the demon looked like."

Unease blossomed into thick apprehension. "I know."

He sighed and looked at me. Dark shadows spread under his eyes. "Everyone has been so worried. Father's been beside himself—the whole clan. Let me take you home." He held out his arm as he stood. "Layla?"

I rose on shaky legs and went into the shelter of his body. Zayne held me close as we walked back to his car. When I looked up, he smiled, but the haunted look was still there and I knew that no matter how many times I reassured him that he couldn't have prevented this, it wouldn't make a difference. Just like Zayne could call the house I'd spent the past ten years living in "home," but it would never mean that to me again.

Most of the clan was moving about the house when Zayne brought me home, and it was hard looking at them and wondering if some of them were disappointed that I was still standing.

Goes without saying that Elijah and the members of his clan had vacated the compound the moment Zayne had called his father and told him that he'd found me and what had happened. Two of the clansmen were currently looking for them, but I doubted Elijah would be found, or that anything would happen to him.

Trying to kill a half demon, even unsanctioned, probably only earned a Warden a smack on the hand.

Besides Morris, who'd squeezed me to death when I got out of Zayne's car, Nicolai was the first to break ranks. With a genuine smile of relief, he hugged me. "I'm glad you made it back to us."

I believed him. Even Geoff looked relieved, along with Abbot. The rest...eh, not so much. Then again, I wasn't really close to the others. We were like ships passing in the night.

Zayne had been right about his father wanting to question me. Most of what happened came from Zayne, but Abbot wanted to hear the details of the demon intervention from me. Lying to Zayne made my skin feel itchy and wrong, but with Abbot, it made my paranoia hit an all-new high. Luckily, it was just the three of us, so it didn't completely feel like an inquisition.

"And you've never seen this demon before?" Abbot asked. Sitting next to me on the couch, he didn't look convinced as he stroked his beard.

I decided to throw a little more of the truth out there. Parts that couldn't hurt. "The demon didn't look normal."

Zayne's brows furrowed. "What do you mean?"

"He sort of looked like the Wardens." I really hoped there was some OJ in the fridge.

"An Upper Level demon," Zayne said, looking at his father.

"So maybe I have seen him before, but not in that form."

Abbot stared at me for several long moments. "Why don't you head upstairs. I'll send Jasmine up to take a look at you, make sure everything is okay."

Sweet relief shot through me even though I knew this wasn't the end of the conversation. I was free for the time being. "I'm sorry for any trouble this—"

"Stop apologizing," Zayne said, eyes flaring that deep teal blue again. "None of this is your fault."

Abbot placed his hand on my shoulder and squeezed gently. He wasn't a hugging type of guy, so it was the closest thing to an embrace I'd ever get. Emotion clogged my throat, a vile mixture of guilt, anger and betrayal. I was lying, but so was Abbot. Looking at him now, my gaze crawling over his weathered-but-handsome face, I had to wonder if he'd ever been honest with me.

And what he had to gain by keeping the child of Lilith alive.

"I'm sorry that we allowed Petr into this house," Abbot said as I stood, his pale eyes sharp. "This home is a safe haven, and he breached that."

"And his clan," Zayne added, voice rough with anger. "It's awfully convenient that they bolted the moment they realized Layla was alive."

"It is." Abbot stood, too. "We'll get to the bottom of this."

I nodded and turned to leave, doubting that Elijah would suffer any extreme consequences if he or any of his clan were in on the plan to snuff me out. I knew they had to be, because while Petr loathed my very existence, he wouldn't have gone after me without his father's support.

"Layla," Abbot called out, and I stopped at the door. "Just one last thing."

My stomach tumbled. "Okay."

Abbot smiled tightly. "Where did you get the clothes you're wearing?"

Hours later, my stomach still churned. Between the sickness that brewed after tasting a soul and the fact that I *knew* I was so busted, I didn't venture far from the bathroom.

The clothing—holy crap—how could I have forgotten that? How could Roth not have caught that? The too-big sweatpants and the shirt with some '80s hair band emblazed across the front were so obviously not mine.

And what had I told Abbot? That they were old gym clothes I had in my backpack? What kind of lame-o lie was that? Why would I have men's clothing in my book bag, and why would I've changed into the clothes, but left my bag in the tree house?

I wanted to smack myself.

Hopefully, Abbot chalked it up to me being traumatized, but I doubted it. He wasn't stupid. The way he'd smiled and the knowing gleam in his eyes told me he knew better. So why didn't he call me out? Waiting for him to do so was worse.

Ten minutes later, I was gripping the sides of the toilet and emptying out what Jasmine had managed to get me to eat after checking me over. "Jesus," I gasped as another cramp rolled through me. Dry heaves racked my body until my eyes watered.

Then the soul came up.

Slicing its way up my throat, it dug in with tiny hooks, refusing to let go. My stomach clenched, doubling me over. Finally, white smoke expelled from my mouth. As the last of Petr's soul left my body, I shuddered, collapsing against the bathroom wall.

Petr's soul floated in the air above me, a sad and twisted

thing. Like a dark cloud before a violent storm, it swirled and churned. I could see neatly stacked yellow towels behind it, the little baskets I kept my makeup in. The soul's mere presence tainted the walls.

"I'm sorry," I whispered hoarsely, pulling my knees to my chest. As much as I hated Petr, I didn't want this for him. What he had turned into after I'd taken his soul was something straight out of nightmares, and without his soul there was no chance for him to ever find peace in Heaven. Humans turned into wraiths. I had no idea what happened to Wardens who died without their souls.

Soaked with sweat, I flushed the toilet and stood on weak legs. Leaning over, I turned on the shower. Steam filled the bathroom, breaking the black mass up. It evaporated in the hot mist, like it had never been there. I stripped off my clothes and took my second shower of the day. Glancing down, I stared at the ring on my finger. Part of me still wanted to get rid of the thing—throw it away or hide it.

With wet fingers, I tried to slide the ring off. It wouldn't budge. Wiggling it didn't work, either. Holding it in the steady stream did nothing. Nothing I did would get the ring off my finger. It was strange, because it wasn't like it was too tight. I could move it around, but just couldn't get it off.

Great. I'd probably somehow set the incantation into motion by putting the damn ring on, and now my finger would have to be chopped off.

I stayed in the shower until my skin wrinkled, but the taint still lingered.

The chills would be next.

I'd just finished pulling on my pajamas when there was a knock on my bedroom door. Tugging my wet hair out from underneath my shirt, I sat on my bed. "Come in."

Zayne stepped in, a blur of white at first. When his essence faded, I saw the strands of blond hair shielding his face as he shut the door behind him. A light blue sweater stretched over his chest, nearly matching the color of his eyes.

When he looked up and saw me, he stilled. "You look like crap."

I laughed, the sound of it raspy. "Thanks."

"Here's your phone. It works fine and I...I cleaned it up," he said, placing it on the nightstand. He sat beside me on the bed. I shied away, putting some distance between us. He caught my movement, his shoulders stiffening.

"Layla," he pleaded.

"I'm just tired after everything." I busied myself with getting my legs under the blanket. "Maybe I'm getting the flu or—"

Zayne grabbed my hand. "Layla, you didn't. Please tell me you didn't."

I pulled my hand free. "No! No. I'm just coming down with something and I'm tired. It's been a long night and day."

He pressed forward, trapping me between his body and the headboard. "You need to tell me if you did, Layla. If you took someone's soul last night, even Petr's, I need to know."

"No," I whispered, curling my fingers into the blanket.

His eyes searched mine intently and then he lowered his head. A soft sigh escaped his tightly pressed lips. "You'd tell me the truth, wouldn't you?"

I shivered. "Yes."

Zayne lifted his head, his steady gaze meeting mine once more. "And you trust me? You know I'd never turn you over to the Alphas, that I'd never do that to you. So please don't lie to me now. Please promise me you're not lying to me."

"I promise." The lie felt sour in my mouth. I looked away, unable to hold his gaze. I recognized that there was a good chance that Zayne knew, just like he knew when I'd done it before.

He let out a breath as he stared at his hand, fisted around the comforter. "Do you need anything?"

Shaking my head, I shifted down on my back and shivered. "I'll be okay."

Zayne fell silent for several minutes. When he spoke I could feel his eyes on me. "I talked to Jasmine."

I cringed.

He swallowed. "She said you were pretty bruised up."

Jasmine had gasped and murmured something unintelligible after she'd helped me strip out of my clothes and seen the smorgasbord of bruises.

"She told me the claw marks shouldn't scar, though." His voice carried a tide of anger. "I'm glad Petr is dead. I just wish I had been the one to kill him."

I looked at him sharply. "You don't really mean that."

"Yes. I do." His eyes flared a startling teal color. "The only thing I wish more is that you never had to experience what you did."

Having no idea what the appropriate response to that was, I sat back and said nothing while wanting to say *everything*.

Silence stretched out and then he said, "I'm sorry about Saturday morning."

"Zayne, you don't—"

"No, let me finish. It was a terrible move on my part. I could've called you—I should've answered the phone when you called yesterday—and it wasn't my place to suggest you stop tagging."

"I'm not tagging anymore." The possessed human pretty much sealed that deal.

"That doesn't matter. I know how much tagging meant to you."

I rolled onto my side, nudging him with my covered elbow. "Yeah, but I was being a total bitch. You were just worried I'd get myself killed or something."

Zayne ran a hand through his hair, clasping the back of his neck. Muscles flexed and rolled under his shirt. Then he reached down, brushing strands of damp hair off my cheek. "You sure you don't need anything? Juice or some fruit?"

"No." It was too late for that. I snuggled down, chilled to my very bones. I couldn't remember how long it had lasted the time before. Two days? More? I squeezed my eyes shut, praying it would only be a day or so. I wanted to talk to him about Hell and Lilith, but I couldn't figure out a way to do so that wouldn't be tantamount to throwing myself in front of a loaded bus.

"Do...do you have to leave?" I asked, even though I couldn't tell him a thing.

He smiled for the first time since he'd walked into the room. "Scoot over."

I wiggled around, giving him room. Zayne kept enough space between us, but I pulled the edge of the covers up, hiding my mouth. He gave me his lopsided grin and I recalled what Roth had said. That Zayne *liked* me. For a second, I didn't feel like I was burning and freezing all at once. "So what did the Alphas want?"

Zayne stretched on his side, propping his head up with his arm. "Apparently there's been an increase in Upper Level demon movement in D.C. and the surrounding cities." He rubbed the bridge of his nose, scrunching up his face. "More than the Alphas have seen in centuries."

I stopped fidgeting with the blankets. I may have stopped breathing for a few seconds.

"It's nothing for you to really worry about," he reassured me quickly, misjudging my reaction. "They're our problem, one we will take care of."

"But...why would they be coming topside? Why so many?" A different kind of coldness seeped through my veins.

Zayne rolled onto his side, facing me. "The Alphas think they're planning something. Possibly another rebellion, but no one is sure. All of us are to be on the lookout for them. Like my father had ordered after the possessed human attacked you and Morris, we've been ordered to question them first before we send them back to Hell."

My throat dried. What if they caught Roth? I pulled my hand out from under the blanket, running it over my forehead. Dampness clung to my skin. Abbot had told me about the last rebellion when I was a little kid. It occurred during the Spanish Influenza. No one really knew how many people had died from the flu or from demonic possession. Was this what some of the demons wanted? For the Lilin to be reborn and another rebellion to occur?

"Hey," Zayne said, inching closer. "It's okay. You don't have anything to worry about."

"Huh?"

"You're so pale, Layla." He reached over, pulling the blankets around my shoulders.

"Oh. I told you I'm tired." I rolled onto my back, stretching out the sudden cramping in my legs.

"Maybe you should stay home from school tomorrow," he suggested.

Sounded like a plan. "Maybe."

He didn't respond for a while. "Layla?"

I turned my head, meeting his steady gaze. I tried to smile, but it came off more like a grimace. "Yeppers?"

"I know this is more than you being tired or what Petr did."

The air fled my lungs.

Leaning on his elbow, he placed his hand on my cheek. "I know that what you probably did was done because you were defending yourself. Or maybe it was afterward because of what Petr did. And I can't even begin to imagine how hard it is for you, but I know you're stronger than this. And I know you don't want to live like this. You're not a demon, Layla. You're a Warden. You're better than this."

I felt my lower lip begin to tremble. *Don't cry. Don't cry.* My voice came out broken and small. "I'm so sorry. I didn't mean to. I just wanted him to *stop* and—"

"Shh…" Zayne closed his eyes and a muscle popped in his jaw. "I know. It's okay."

Tears burned my eyes. "I won't do it again. I promise. I'm just so sorry."

Zayne pressed his lips against my forehead. "I know." He pulled away, turning off the bedside lamp and settling back now. "Get some rest. I'll stay here until I have to leave."

I curled onto my side again, reaching for his hand blindly. He took it, threading his fingers through mine. "I'm sorry," I whispered again. Sorry for yelling at him, sorry for taking Petr's soul and, most of all, sorry for all the lies.

15

I STAYED HOME TUESDAY, spending most of the day in bed. By the time school started on Wednesday, the worst of the bruises on my face had faded and the hardest part of the sickness had passed.

Stacey was waiting for me at my locker. Her mouth dropped open when she saw me. "Okay. I know you said you were in a car accident on Friday, but you look like you need to see a doctor."

Apparently I still looked like crap.

I kicked my locker door shut and followed her into bio. Roth was a no-show, and by the time lunch rolled around, he was still MIA. Between feeling like I was crawling out of my skin and wondering where Roth was, all I wanted to do was go back to hiding in my bed. The Wardens had been given orders to hunt down the Upper Level demons invading the city. Had they caught Roth? My breath stalled out every time I considered that.

I reasoned that my concern was only rooted in the fact that he was the only one who knew that Hell was after me and why. I needed Roth alive and whole. That was the only reason why I was concerned. *Yeah. Right.*

At lunch, Stacey's thoughts mirrored my own. "I wonder where Roth has been. He hasn't been to school since Friday, either."

I said nothing.

"At first, I thought that maybe you caved to the wild lust between you two and ran off with him and eloped."

I almost choked on my half-frozen pizza. "You are insane."

Stacey shrugged. "What? You can't tell me that if you were alone with him you wouldn't jump his bones."

"I was alone with him, and I didn't." My eyes popped wide a second after those words left my mouth. "Crap," I muttered.

She clutched my arm. "Oh, my God, details—I need details right now."

Nothing short of a zombie chewing on her head would distract Stacey now, and even then I wasn't sure if she'd let it go. Coming up with a quick excuse, I played it off. "I ran into him over the weekend and we hung out."

"In public or at his place?"

"At his place, but it wasn't a big deal." I squirmed. No way in Hell was I telling her that he'd kissed me. I'd never hear the end of it. "Aren't you going to Wick It tonight?" I asked, hoping to change the subject.

Sitting down, Sam rolled his eyes. "Who would want to? It's poetry-slam night, which means everyone who thinks they can form a couplet will be there."

"Don't be jealous," Stacey said, "because I didn't invite you. And back to Layla."

"What about Layla?" Sam eyeballed the rest of my pizza.

I slid my plate toward him. "Nothing."

"Nothing," gasped Stacey. "She spent time alone with Roth— time at *his* place. Was it in his bedroom? Did you see his bed? Wait. Let me start with the most pressing question—did you lose your virginity finally?"

"Jesus, Stacey, why are you so interested in her virginity status?" asked Sam.

"Yeah, I'm wondering the same thing." I tucked my hair back. "But to answer your question, no, I didn't put out. It wasn't anything like that."

"Look, you're my best friend. I'm obligated to take an interest in your sexual activity." She paused, grinning. "Or lack thereof."

I rolled my eyes.

"That's kind of disturbing." Sam elbowed Stacey as he grabbed a handful of her Tater Tots.

"Wait. It's not 'like that' when we're referring to the hottest guy to walk these halls?" Stacey sat back, throwing her hands up. "You're unreal." Another startled look crossed her face before I could respond. "Did you see his bed? Holy Mary, mother of baby Jesus, were you actually *on* his bed?"

I turned a thousand shades of red. "Stacey..."

"Your face tells me you did see his bed, probably even sat on it. What was it like?" She leaned forward, eyes eager. "Did it smell like him? Like sex? Did he have silk sheets? Come on, he had to have satin or silk."

"Really?" Sam put his drink down, scowling at her. "Did you just ask her if his bed smelled like sex? Who cares what his bed smells like?"

"I do," Stacey exclaimed, eyes wide.

"It didn't smell like sex," I mumbled, scratching the side of my face.

Stacey scoffed. "You don't even know what sex smells like."

I kind of wanted to strangle her. "Can we just—"

"You know what? You're acting just like the rest of the stupid girls here." Sam grabbed his bag, stood and slung it over his shoulder. "He's good-looking. Awesome. You don't have to go all stalker on him."

Stacey's mouth dropped open.

I stared up at Sam, suddenly feeling very sorry for him. I started to stand. "Sam—"

Cheeks flushed, he shook his head. "I'll see you guys in English. Peace."

We watched him dump his lunch, then head out the double doors. I turned to Stacey, biting my lip. She watched the doors like she expected him to walk back through and yell "I'm just joking!" and laugh.

When he didn't, she fell back in her seat, dragging her fingers through her hair. "What the Hell was that?"

"Stacey, Sam has liked you since we were freshmen. It's obvious."

She snorted. "How can something like that be obvious to you and not me? Up until Roth, you didn't think boys had a pulse."

"This isn't about me, you jerk."

"You have to be wrong." She shook her head as she tossed a Tater Tot on her tray. "Sam doesn't think about me that way. He can't. We've been friends for years."

I thought about Zayne. "Just because you've been friends with someone doesn't mean they don't think of you as something more. Sam's cute, Stacey. And he's smart."

"Yeah," she said slowly. "But it's *Sam*."

"Whatever."

She arched a brow. "Forget the Sam thing for the time being. Do you like Roth? I mean, you don't hang out with any guys besides Sam or Zayne. This is kind of epic."

"It's not epic." I downed the rest of my drink, still thirsty.

"So you do like him?"

I eyed her drink. "No—I don't know. You gonna drink that?"

Stacey handed me her bottle of water. "What do you mean you don't know?"

"It's hard to explain." I wiped the back of my hand over my mouth. "Roth isn't like other guys."

"You're telling me," she said drily.

I laughed, but it quickly faded. I wanted to tell Stacey about Roth—about everything. What he was. What I was. It wouldn't be a stretch for her to believe it, not after the Wardens went public. People probably already expected the truth. The need to just talk, to be honest for once, hit me hard.

"Layla? Are you feeling okay?" Concern pinched her brow. "I know it was just a car accident, but you look sick."

"Yeah, I think I'm just coming down with something." I forced a smile. "No big deal."

The bell rang, forcing our conversation and my need to tell her the truth to end. We gathered up our trash, and as we headed out, Stacey stopped me outside the cafeteria. I swallowed thickly. Souls—souls were everywhere.

Then I noticed the blush crawling across Stacey's face. She never blushed. Never. "What's up?" I asked.

She fiddled with the strap on her bag, exhaling. The puff of air lifted her bangs for a moment. "You really think Sam likes me?"

In spite of everything, I smiled. "Yeah, I do."

Stacey nodded, focusing on the stream of students. "He's not bad-looking."

"No."

"And he's not a jackass," she continued. "He's not like Gareth or any other guy who just wants to get in a girl's pants."

"He's so much better than Gareth," I agreed.

"He is," she said, pausing. A troubled look pulled at her features. "Layla, do you think I hurt his feelings? I didn't mean to."

I grabbed her hand, squeezing. "I know. And I think Sam knows that, too."

She squeezed my hand back and then slipped free. Turning around, she grinned as she headed down the hallway backward. "Well. This is an interesting development."

I grinned. "It is. What are you going to do about it?"

Stacey shrugged, but her eyes were shining. "Who knows? I'll call you later, okay?"

We broke apart after that, heading in different directions. I spent the rest of the day looking over my shoulder, expecting Roth to pop up. He never did, and the gnawing in my stomach expanded until I could barely concentrate in class, or later that day on the conversation at the dinner table. None of the Wardens spoke of catching any Upper Level demons, but they didn't typically let me in on that kind of stuff.

Abbot didn't address the clothing issue either or even broach the topic of Petr's attack and the subsequent demonic involvement. Waiting for him to say something, to confront my lies, was driving me insane. In my own home, with all these secrets building between everyone, I felt like an outsider and uneasy in my own skin.

Not to mention I was trying to keep myself from freaking out. Knowing there were demons out to either use me in some kind of bizarre incantation or kill me made me jumpy. What also didn't help was the fact that Elijah was still out there. When it was quiet, my imagination got the best of me.

Thursday morning, I'd officially decided that the craziest thing to happen over the past couple of weeks had nothing to do with learning I was the child of the Lilith or that I could somehow raise a horde of soul-eating demons. Or that there was more than a crap ton of demons who wanted me dead. Nope. The craziest thing was Stacey.

She was acting weird and surprisingly subdued. She didn't talk about sex or boys within the first five seconds of a conversation. In English on Wednesday, after the lunch fallout with Sam, she'd laughed at everything he said, which was awkward to watch. Sam kept sending me looks, and I tried to ignore them. I had a feeling it had to do with her newfound knowledge of his crush on her.

Not that she'd admit to it.

Grabbing her bio text, she kicked her locker door shut. "You still look sick. You should go see a doctor, Layla."

I rolled my eyes. "Don't change the subject. You've been acting like a weirdo since lunch yesterday."

Stacey turned around, leaning against the locker as she looked at me with raised brows. "You're weird every day. You disappear when you're supposed to meet up with us. You hang out with the hottest guy on the planet and say 'it's not like that.' Hello. You're the weird friend here."

I winced. All of that was true. "Whatever."

She pushed off the locker, linking her arm through mine. "I just don't want Sam to think I'm...one of those girls anymore."

"But you *are* one of those girls," I said slowly. The steady stream of shimmery souls demanded my attention, but I focused. "And Sam likes you for who you are."

"Obviously he doesn't."

I hip-bumped her. "You're being silly."

She opened her mouth, but stopped as a tall body crossed our path. I knew before looking up that it was Roth. That sweet, musky scent could belong to no one else.

"Hey there," Stacey said, recovering. "We thought you'd died or something."

I lifted my head, feeling off-kilter when our eyes met. His gaze traveled over me. I looked pretty frumpy today, wearing loose jeans and a hoodie that had seen better days. A slight frown appeared on his full lips.

"You two missed my face that much?" Roth teased, his eyes fixed on me.

"Where have you been?" The words came out before I could stop them and, God, did I feel like a tool.

Roth shrugged. "I had some things to take care of. Speaking of which—" he turned to Stacey "—I'd like to steal her away from you if you don't mind."

"I try to tell my mom all the time I have stuff to do, but I still have to go to school." Stacey slid her arm from mine, pursing her lips. "I wish I had your parents. Just let me come to school when I feel like it. But anyway, you're not planning on showing for bio?"

"No." He winked as he lowered his voice. "I'm going to be a rebel and skip class *again*."

"Ooh," Stacey cooed. "And you want to corrupt my wholesome, pure friend?"

Arms dangling at my sides, I sighed.

His golden gaze heated. "Corruption *is* my middle name."

"Well, you can only steal and corrupt my friend *if* she wants to be stolen and corrupted."

Enough was enough. "Hey, guys, I'm right here, remember? Shouldn't I get a say in this decision?"

He arched a brow at me. "Do you want to be stolen and corrupted?"

I had a feeling I was already corrupted just by his mere presence. "Why not."

"Great!" Stacey chirped, backing off and gesturing wildly behind Roth. She was doing something with her hand and mouth that I knew Roth would be oh so down for. I tried to ignore her. "But promise to return her, okay?"

"I don't know." Roth stepped around, dropping his arm over my shoulders. "I may steal her away from you permanently."

I couldn't stop the shiver that went through me. The way Roth's hand tightened on my shoulders told me he hadn't missed it, either.

"Whatever." Stacey gave us a short wave and flounced off toward bio.

Roth's hand slid off my shoulder, grasping my hand. "You look terrible."

I couldn't tell if my cheeks were burning. I already felt unnaturally hot for a whole slew of wrong reasons. "Thanks. Everyone keeps telling me that."

He tugged on my messy ponytail with his free hand. "Did you even shower this morning?"

"Yes. Jeez. Where have you been, Roth?"

"Why are you sick?" he asked instead. "You look like you haven't slept since I last saw you. You couldn't have missed me that much."

"Man, you're self-centered. It has nothing to do with you. I get like this after..."

"After what?" He leaned in, waiting.

I looked away, lowering my voice. "If I taste a soul, it makes me sick afterward. Only for like a day or so, but taking a soul seems to last longer."

Roth let go of my hand. "Why?"

"It's like withdrawal or something," I said. Roth was unnaturally quiet as he watched me, expression pensive. "What?"

He blinked. "Nothing. I'm really not planning on going to bio."

"I figured as much." Taking a breath, I decided to corrupt myself. "Where are you planning on going?"

He flashed a quick grin, which made me think he was about to say something perverted, but he surprised me. "Come find out. What I've been doing the last couple of days has to do with you."

"Lovely."

Roth took my hand, his skin pleasantly warm against mine, and I didn't pitch a fit about the hand-holding thing. He led me into a nearby stairwell and then down a flight of steps, into the old part of the school where there were a couple of empty offices and a decrepit gymnasium that smelled like mold. Thankfully the boiler rooms were on the other side of the school. With all the cubbyholes in the bottom part of the school, it was a notorious hangout spot for the stoners.

It didn't surprise me that Roth knew where to go in the school if you didn't want to be found.

He stopped in the bottom stairwell. Torn orange safety tape hung from the gym's double doors, hanging against the dull gray metal. One of the windows was covered with so much muck it looked tinted. The walls of the stairwell hadn't fared much better. Entire sections were missing paint, exposing the cement walls.

Roth stopped and took both of my hands in his. "I've missed you."

My heart did a weird little jump. Stupid heart. I needed to focus. With all the lying in bed I'd done the past three days, it gave me time to think about what he'd revealed. "Roth, we need to talk about what you told me."

"We're talking." He dipped his head, brushing his cheek against mine.

"This is not talking." Not that I didn't enjoy it. "And I really do have questions."

"So ask away. I can multitask." He tugged me forward, circling an arm around my waist. Dipping his head to where my neck sloped, he inhaled deeply. "Can't you?"

I shivered against him, my fingers curling into the front of his shirt. I didn't think so, but I was willing to try. "Where have you been?"

"Where have *you* been?" His hands dropped to my hips, grip tightening deliciously. "You weren't at school on Tuesday."

"How do you know?"

"I know a lot of things."

I sighed. "I stayed home. I figured with being sick and with the…bruises, it was best to take another day off."

"Good idea." A slight frown appeared on his lips as he lifted one hand, trailing a finger along my temple. "It's barely noticeable." His gaze dropped to my mouth, and I felt my lips part. "And your lip looks…"

"What?"

The frown turned into a slow, seductive grin. "Well, it looks good enough to nibble."

I sucked in an unsteady breath, trying to calm the wild beating in my chest. "Roth, come on."

"What?" He gave me an innocent look. "I'm just saying I could do all kinds—"

"Got it. Anyway, back to my question."

"Hmm…" Roth moved his hands to my waist. Warmth flared from where his fingers pressed in through the hoodie. "How was everything when you returned?"

Distracted once more, I answered his question. "It was… okay, but I forgot to change back into my clothes before I left your place." At his raised brows, I reminded him of the borrowed clothes and how Abbot had asked about them. "I don't think he believed what I'd told him, but he hasn't pushed it."

Roth didn't appear too concerned. "I am sure he knows the truth—about everything. But what can he say without exposing all the lies he's fed you?" His hands slid up an inch, resting just under my rib cage. "And besides, he's not going to kill you or anything."

I scrunched up my nose. "I sure hope not."

He chuckled softly. "I don't think your fearless leader will do anything to upset Stony. Speaking of which, Stony seemed relieved to see you on Monday."

"He was…" I shook my head. "I told you. I've known Zayne for most of my life. We're close."

"He seemed *really* relieved to see you on Monday." His thumbs moved in slow, idle circles that made it difficult to concentrate. "I think I've only seen a Warden run that fast if it was actually chasing after a demon."

I felt heat creep back into my face as I gripped his wrists. "Roth, I don't want to talk about Zayne."

"Why don't you want to talk about Stony?"

Irritation flared hotly. "I don't know, because there are more important things to talk about?"

Roth dipped his head again, and when he spoke, his breath

was warm against my ear. "But I want to talk about Stony. Remember when I said he cared for you, Layla?"

My grip on his wrists tightened. "Yes. Like I said—"

"You've known him all your life. I get that." His lips brushed the space below my ear, and I gasped. "But has it ever been… like this?"

Before I could even ask "like what," Roth's lips traveled across my cheekbone. Tiny, fiery shivers darted along my nerves. His lips brushed the corner of mine, and my pulse fluttered wildly. I was so far out of my league with him it wasn't funny. "Is it like *this,* Layla?"

Like this? Ah, the touching…the almost kissing. "No." I barely recognized my own voice. "I can't…"

"Can't what?" The very edges of his teeth came down on my lower lip. A little nip, like he'd mentioned before, and my entire body arched against his. "Can't what, Layla?"

"I can't be this close to him," I admitted in a breathy voice.

Roth's lips curved into a smile against mine. "What a shame."

The lack of sincerity was epic. "I'm sure you really feel that way."

He laughed, and this time, when he pulled back and bent his head again, his lips were against my pulse. This was ridiculous. We needed to talk about stuff. Important stuff. I wasn't skipping class to do…well, whatever this was with Roth. But damn, what he was doing was all fresh and new to me.

And it felt so unbelievably good—this wild anticipation he was building, a promise that could actually go somewhere. The fierce yearning was like a tempest inside me, swirling and spinning me up so high that I knew the fall would break something valuable. Because this was different—this wasn't built on hopeless fantasies. Realizing that was as thrilling as it was terrifying.

With effort I didn't realize I had, I broke away. Roth quirked an eyebrow as he dropped his hands to his sides. His eyes were a heated tawny, consuming in their intensity and frightening in their ability to draw me in, make me forget all that really freaking important stuff.

Clearing my throat, I looked away. "Okay. Back to my question."

"What did you want to know?" Amusement clung to his words. "I forgot."

"I'm sure you did." I sighed, wondering if I was ever going to get Roth to stay on target. "Where have you been?"

He leaned against the wall, crossing his arms. "I had to go home."

"Home as in...?" I lowered my voice even though there was no one else around. "Hell?"

Roth nodded. "I needed to check in and I thought it would be a good chance to ask around, see if anyone knows which demon is pulling the strings."

I switched my bag to my other arm. "Did you find out anything?"

"Everyone is pretty tight-lipped about it. No one is willing to say who it is, which tells me it's someone with a lot of reach."

"Obviously an Upper Level demon like you?"

"But definitely not as awesome as me." He winked, and, God help me, he actually looked good doing it. "But I didn't come back empty-handed. I was right about the whole *Lesser Key* thing. The exact incantation to raise the Lilin is in that Key, and a lot of demons are looking for it, on both sides."

It clicked together. "That's why there are so many Upper Level demons around here."

"Do tell?"

I nodded. "That's what I hear."

"And where did you hear that?" When I didn't say anything, Roth pushed off the wall. His slow, precise steps forced me backward, until I was flush with the wall. Tiny flecks of paint floated into the air. "Sharing is caring, Layla."

Telling Roth what the Wardens knew wasn't easy. Guilt

settled in my stomach like cement blocks, but I trusted him. Besides saving me from Petr and Lord only knows how many other times, he'd never asked me to trust him. Not once. Maybe for that reason alone, I trusted him.

"We're in this together, right?" I said, glancing up at him. "I mean, we're going to figure out the demon behind this and stop it?"

Roth's eyes met mine. "You and me are like peanut butter and jelly when it comes to this."

My lips twitched. "Okay, because I don't feel right telling you this, but I…I trust you." Pausing, I took a big gulp of air. "The Alphas have said there's been a lot of Upper Level demon movement in the city. The Wardens are trying to capture and detain. I thought…well, anyway, what's going on is on the Alphas' radar."

He turned his head, a lopsided smile playing across his lips. "You thought they caught me? Me?" He let out a loud laugh. "I'm flattered by your concern, but that's nothing you'd ever have to worry about."

I was pretty sure my face was burning, so I focused on the pot leaf someone had carved into the wall behind him. "I wasn't worried about you, you douchebag."

"Uh-huh. Keep telling yourself that."

My patience started to fade. "So it's obvious that the demons are looking for the Key, right?"

Roth got all up in my personal space once more. Why did he always have to get so damn close? And should I be complaining? "Right," he murmured. His hand curved around my shoulder, and I inhaled deeply. A heartbeat passed between us, and my body tensed. "That's not the only thing I've learned."

"Really?"

He nodded. "We need to find the Key before anyone else does. And finding an ancient book that's probably well protected isn't going to be easy. But I do have a lead."

"Okay? What's the lead?"

Reaching out, he caught an escaped strand of hair and twisted it around his finger. The paleness stood out in stark contrast to the darker tone of his skin. "There is a seer nearby."

I snatched my hair back. "A psychic?"

Roth snorted. "Not a psychic–hotline kind of psychic. A seer who has a one-way connection upstairs and downstairs. If anyone knows who the demon is or where the Key is located, the seer will."

I was still doubtful. "Seers are protected by the Alphas. How would a demon know where one is located?"

"I said I got a lead. I didn't say it was easy." Roth stepped back, shoving his hands into his pockets. I opened my mouth, but he cut me off. "And before you ask, you *don't* want to know what I had to go through to get this lead."

Dammit. I did want to ask. "So where is the seer?"

"Just outside of Manassas," he answered.

"So not very far at all." A bubble of nervous excitement rose. "We can go now."

"Whoa." Roth held up his hands. "I'm all about you skipping school and committing acts of general mayhem. I am a demon, after all, but 'we' are not doing anything."

"We aren't?" I couldn't believe it. "Why?"

The look on his face said he wanted to pat me atop the head. "Because I'm probably not the only demon who has done unspeakable things to gain the location of the seer. It could be dangerous."

I folded my arms, digging in. "Everything could be potentially dangerous right now. Going to school? A zombie could show up again and try to take me back to its evil leader. A demon could possess a teacher. I could get demon-napped on the way home from school today."

A frown appeared. "Well, that brings on the warm fuzzies."

I rolled my eyes. "Look, I'm not going to stand on the sidelines and let everyone else risk their lives for me and do all the hard work while I sit in history class."

"Well, if you're against sitting in school, you could always go to my apartment and keep my bed company until I get back."

There was a good chance I was going to hit him. "This has to do with me—my life. We're in this together. That means we're going to the seer together."

"Layla—"

"I'm sorry, but I'm not taking no for an answer. I'm going with you. So deal with it."

Roth stared at me, looking sort of stunned. "I didn't know you had it in you."

"What?"

He tapped the tip of my nose. "You're feisty underneath all that fluff."

"I'm not sure if I should be offended or not," I grumbled.

"Not." He said something under his breath in a different language and then extended his hand. "Then come on. Let's do this. Together."

16

SKIPPING SCHOOL FOR, WELL, for the very first time to see a seer had trouble written all over it. So did the way Roth drove his Porsche, like he was the only person who had the right to be on the road. Naturally, "Paradise City" was blaring from the speakers.

"You may be an immortal demon," I said, holding on to the seat belt's chest strap, "but I'm not."

He flashed a wild sort of grin that made me think really stupid things. "You'll be fine."

The possibility of dying in a massive car accident aside, this was far better than sitting around pretending that nothing was going on. I was being active. In a way, I was taking care of this myself with Roth's help and that eased the panicky restlessness that had been building inside me.

As we entered Manassas, Roth did the unexpected and pulled into the lot of the first grocery store we came upon. I stared at him as he cut the engine. "You need to get groceries, like right now?"

Roth sent me a look but didn't answer. Sighing, I got out of the car and followed him into the market. I half expected someone to jump out at us and demand why we weren't in school, but once inside the store, I saw about six other teenagers and figured we'd blend right in.

He stopped in the poultry section, frowning.

"What are you looking for?" I asked, curious.

"A chicken," he said, poking around the shelves. "Preferably a live chicken, but doesn't look like that's going to happen."

I leaned closer to him. "Do I want to know why you want a live chicken right now?"

"I thought it would make a good traveling companion." He smirked when my eyes narrowed. "You should always bring a token of thanks when you visit a seer. I've heard that chickens make a good gift." He picked up a wrapped whole chicken that claimed it was raised on a farm. "Everyone loves Perdue, right?"

"This is so weird."

A lopsided grin appeared. "You haven't seen anything yet."

Ten minutes later, we were back on the road, heading toward the Manassas Battlefield with our Perdue chicken. I wasn't sure what to expect, but when we passed the old wooden fences and stone walls and pulled into the driveway of a house that looked like it probably had bullet holes in it *from* the Civil War battle, I tried to prepare myself for the bizarreness that was about to go down.

Roth strode ahead of me, his eyes scanning the neatly trimmed bushes lining the walkway like he expected a garden gnome to attack us. We stepped up on the porch. A swing to the far left moved in the slight breeze. There was a wooden scarecrow sitting on a pumpkin hanging from the door.

The door opened before Roth could even raise his hand to knock.

A woman appeared. Once the faint blue hue of her soul faded, I got a good look at her. Her blond hair was pulled up in an elegant twist. Fine lines surrounded razor-sharp gray eyes. Her makeup was immaculate. Her light pink cardigan and linen trousers were free from wrinkles. She was even rocking a pearl necklace.

Totally not what I expected.

She swept a cool gaze over us and then settled on Roth. Her lips thinned. "I am not happy about this."

He arched a dark brow. "I'd say I'm sorry, but I wouldn't mean it."

I opened my mouth to apologize, because that kind of attitude wasn't going to get us anywhere, but the woman stepped aside nonetheless. "In the den," she said, gesturing to her right.

Carrying the chicken in a plastic bag, Roth went down a narrow hall first. The house smelled nice, like roasted apple. Sounds of a video game radiated from the den, and as we stepped inside the large room, my gaze went straight to the TV.

Assassin's Creed. Sam would dig this place.

"I appreciate the chicken, but it's not quite what you'd bring a seer."

My jaw hit the floor.

At first it was just a blur of pearly white goodness—a pure soul. Seeing a human with a pure soul was like winning the lottery; that was how rarely they were sighted outside the Warden race. My mouth dried and my throat constricted. A bone-deep yearning kicked me right in the stomach, one that didn't go away when the soul faded, revealing the seer. Roth put his hand on the small of my back, and I hadn't realized I'd stepped forward until then. The look on his face said, "don't eat the soul of the seer," but honestly, the only thing that eased the craving was the shock that rippled through me when I turned back to the seer.

Sitting cross-legged in front of the TV was a boy about nine or ten years old, game controller in hand. It couldn't be...

Roth shifted his weight. "Sorry, but you'd be surprised how hard it is to get a live chicken on such short notice."

The game on the TV paused, and the little boy turned toward us. Several golden curls tumbled onto his forehead. He had a cherub's face. Dimple in the chin and all. "It's a good thing I'm craving roast chicken anyway."

"*You're* the seer?" I asked, dumbfounded. "Why aren't you in school?"

"I'm a seer. Do you think I actually need to go to school?"

"No," I mumbled. "Guess not."

"You seem shocked." Bright blue eyes landed on me, and I took a step back, hitting the arm of the boxy, plaid couch. The center of his pupils were white. "You shouldn't be, child of Lilith. If anything is truly shocking in this room, it's the fact that you are here. With a demon."

My mouth was gaping like a fish out of water. I had no idea what to say. The seer was a kid.

His mother cleared her throat as she stepped up behind us and took the chicken from Roth. "I'd offer drinks, but I don't expect the two of you to be here long." She paused. "Tony, what did I tell you about sitting so close to the screen? You're going to ruin your eyes."

I turned to Roth slowly, and his lips twitched.

Tony's little face scrunched up. "My eyes will be fine. I've *seen* it."

Well, that ended that part of the conversation. His mom left us alone with the seer, and when he stood, he only came up to Roth's hip. This was beyond weird.

"I know why you're here," he said, crossing chubby arms. "You want to know who wants to raise the Lilin. That I don't know. And if I did, I wouldn't tell you. I'd like to make it to an age when I can grow facial hair."

Roth's eyes narrowed. "How is it that a seer doesn't know who wants to raise the Lilin?"

"How is it that a demon of your stature doesn't know? If you don't know, why would you expect that I would? I look into things I *want* to look into and things that affect me. Like I knew you were coming here today with a Perdue chicken, so I told Mom not to bother laying anything out. I also know that if I took a peek at the demon behind this, my eyes would be sitting in a jar on someone's mantel like a trophy. And I prefer to keep them intact."

It was sort of disturbing to hear a child talk like that.

Tony cocked his head to the side as he eyed me. "And you should be really careful."

Hair all over my body stood. "Why?"

"Besides the obvious?" he asked. "All the time you fight what you truly are. It must be exhausting. So much so that when it comes time to truly fight, you'll be too worn down for much of anything."

I sucked in a soft breath. "I—"

"Didn't come here for my advice? I know. You want to know where *The Lesser Key of Solomon* is." Tony gave a world-weary sigh that sounded way too strange coming from a kid. "Did you know that a Warden and a demon hid the Key? It's the only time the two have ever worked together. The two races will be working together in the future again."

Impatience radiated from Roth and it gave his voice a steel edge. "Do you know where the Key is, seer?"

Tony's pupils flared. "Let me ask you a question. Who do you think stands to gain from raising the Lilin?"

I glanced at Roth and said, "I don't see how anyone has anything to gain. The Lilin can't be controlled."

"Not exactly true," the seer responded. "The Lilin can be controlled by Lilith, but that's neither here nor there. If the Lilin are set loose, no one will stop them. And you're right. No one will be able to stop them once unleashed."

"So?" Roth folded his arms. "You already know the answer to that question. Why ask?"

The boy smiled, flashing small, straight teeth. "Because I

posed the question to get you to think, but apparently trying to get a demon to think is asking too much."

Roth's eyes narrowed and he took a step forward. I knew he wasn't above picking up a pint-sized seer and throwing him across the room. I jumped in. "Why do you think a demon is trying to do this?"

The seer didn't take his eyes off Roth. "Only one thing can result from this, and that's the start of the apocalypse." He sounded as if he was discussing a cartoon. No big deal. "If the Lilin walk the Earth again, the Alphas will step in. They will try to take out every demon topside, which will start a war. And a war between the Alphas and demons sounds familiar, doesn't it? Armageddon ain't scheduled to kick off for another couple hundred years, but the Lilin will fast-track that little party with the Four Horsemen."

My stomach dropped. "The demon wants to start the apocalypse?"

"That *is* what I just said." The kid turned his back and picked up the game controller. "Sorry, buds, but demons don't run things topside, and the only way they can is by kicking off the apocalypse and hoping to win. It's a risky gamble to take, but..." He looked over his shoulder at Roth. "You know how bad Hell sucks. Demons want out. And some are willing to destroy the whole world to get out. You can't tell me you haven't thought about what it would be like to be able to come topside whenever you want and not have to worry about the Wardens hunting you down. Freedom—that's all any living creature wants."

The knots in my stomach tripled, magnified by the fact that Roth didn't deny what the seer said. Would he really risk the world? Who was I kidding? Roth would, because he was a demon and demons operated on a self-serving sort of basis. But Hell did have to suck on a massive level, so who was I to judge?

"All I have to say is, if this demon succeeds, mankind better hope that God's more New Testament than Old Testament, because shit's about to get real."

"Tony!" His mother's voice rang out from somewhere in the house. "Watch your language!"

Roth smirked. "Yeah, watch your mouth, kid."

His cheeks flushed, and I had the feeling that he was about to kick us out before we got any information. "Can you tell us where the *Lesser Key* is?"

Tony took a deep breath and exhaled loudly through his nose. "Why should I tell you anything? *He* hasn't been very nice."

"I'm not nice to anyone," Roth replied casually.

"You're nice to her," the boy pointed out.

Roth lowered his voice. "That's because she's pretty. One day, when you grow up, you'll understand why."

"One day, you're going to find yourself chained in the fiery pits of Hell, and I'm going to be laughing," Tony shot back.

Instead of laughing it off or trying to outsnark the ten-year-old, Roth paled and straightened as if someone had put steel in his spine. An emotion flickered across his face, something like terror, and my unease multiplied. It was brief, gone before I could really say he had that moment of vulnerability.

A tight smile appeared on Tony's face. "Find where the monolith is cast back during the full moon and you'll find the entrance to where the true *Lesser Key* is seated. Now, as you can see, I have some butt to kick—"

"Wait. That made no sense whatsoever," I interrupted. I had no idea what a monolith was. So much for all the time I spent in the library.

"It makes perfect sense." He waved the game controller. "And I'm busy."

On what planet did that cloak-and-dagger sentence have any meaning? "Can't you just tell us where it's located?"

"And draw you a map, too?"

"That would be great," I replied drily.

Tony made an exasperated sound and clenched the game controller. "I can't tell you exactly where the Key is located."

"Because that would be too easy," Roth muttered under his breath.

"No. Because those are the rules," the seer said. "If I tell you guys exactly where the Key is located, then I have to give the same information to the next demon that strolls through the doors. I can't pick sides or even come across like I have. I've told you enough for you to figure it out." He plopped down in front of the door. "So go figure it out. Like now."

"But there's a good chance the other demon knows what it takes to raise the Lilin," I protested.

"Then you better get crack-a-lackin'." Tony restarted the game. An arrow zoomed across the widescreen, smacking into the gap between a knight's armor. "Don't let the door hit you where the good Lord split ya."

"Well, that was about seven different kinds of weird," I said, staring out the window. Gray walls separating the beltway from the neighboring subdivisions blurred. "Do you have any idea what he was talking about? The monolith?" I glanced back at my phone, at the results of my Web search for *monolith*. "A monolith is a massive rock. Any idea where a handy massive rock would be?"

"No."

I looked at him. Since we'd left the seer's house, he hadn't said much of anything. "Are you okay?"

His gaze flicked up to the rearview mirror. "As okay as I can be."

Biting down on my lip, I sat back. "Do you believe him?"

"What part?"

"The part where he said you'd be chained in the fiery pits of Hell?" I felt cold saying those words.

"No." Roth laughed, but something about the sound made

me even colder. "Anyway, we need to figure out what he meant about the monolith and casting back. We need the Key."

I nodded, turning my attention back to the road as Roth cut in front of a taxi. A quick glance at the clock in the dashboard told me that if we headed back to school now, we'd get there just before lunch. Going back to class like I hadn't just met a ten-year-old seer and been given a riddle I had no hopes of figuring out. And we'd made no headway on discovering the demon behind any of this.

"Do you want to go back to class?" Roth asked.

"You sure you can't read minds?" He angled the Porsche around a car in front of us, and my eyes popped wide as we narrowly avoided clipping the front end. "Or drive," I added under my breath.

Roth grinned. "I'm sure. Though I'd be curious to know what goes on in your head."

Right now I was wondering if we'd make it back to the city alive. "No. I don't want to go back to school," I admitted.

"Look how the mighty have fallen." His voice dropped, teasing in nature. "I was totally planning on showing up in time for math."

"Sure you were."

Hitting the exit at breakneck speeds, he laughed softly. "We can go back to my place."

My stomach tumbled, and not because he'd slammed on the brakes. "I don't know about that."

Roth cast me a sidelong look. "What? Are you worried that I'm taking you back to my lair to have my way with you?"

Heat blossomed across my cheeks. "No."

"Damn. That was my master plan." He hung a right. "Roaming around town isn't really smart considering there's a demon after you. So it's either school or my place."

Feeling like an inept preteen, I shrugged stiffly. "Your place is fine."

"I thought we could use the time to figure out what the seer said about where the Key was kept."

Sounded like a good plan, but nervous excitement buzzed through me like a hummingbird for all the wrong reasons.

Roth coasted the Porsche into a dark parking garage. Curious, I looked at him. "This isn't your place."

"I know, but it's only a few blocks away." He turned off the engine. "This baby isn't getting parked along the street. Someone might touch it."

His love for his car made him so human in that moment, it was hard not to smile. He got out of the car and had opened my door before I could even blink.

Bowing at the waist, he extended his arm. "May I escort you?"

I couldn't hide my smile then. Placing my hand in his, I let him pull me out of the car. He threaded his fingers through mine, and I felt like I was on a roller coaster. "So what do you do with your car when you're…uh, downstairs?"

"Remember Cayman? He's a good friend. Keeps an eye on it."

Glancing down at our joined hands, I almost tripped over a crack in the pavement. "You have friends?"

"Ow."

I cracked a grin. "What? It's an honest question."

"There's some like me who live in my apartment building. I trust them."

"Really?"

He nodded, tugging me down the incline leading to the lower levels of the parking garage. Overhead lights spaced every few feet cast patches of light along the aisles, reflecting off the hoods of cars. "So, yeah, Cayman takes care of my baby while I'm downtown."

"Cayman seems an odd name for a demon."

He laughed deeply. "Cayman is an infernal ruler who remains topside. He, like most infernal rulers, is a demon manager. He keeps them in check and reports back with weekly and monthly updates. He's also like an assistant to me."

So middle management existed even in Hell.

I shook my head as we rounded the second level and, as if by unspoken agreement, both of us came to a complete stop. A bone-deep dread settled in my stomach like stones. My feet felt rooted to the cement. Roth dropped my hand and stepped forward, his eyes narrowed.

Before I could ask what was happening, the overhead lights began to flicker. Then, in rapid succession, they blew out one after another, showering sparks like raindrops. Each explosion was like a gunshot. Only one light remained, wavering rapidly.

Thick shadows seeped from between the cars, shooting up the walls. A clicking noise filled the air as the shadows crawled up, swallowing the red EXIT sign and covering half the ceiling. The shadows rippled and pulsed, and for a stuttered heartbeat, they swelled like an overripe berry and then stilled.

Roth cursed.

As though a string had been cut, the shadows dropped, blanketing the floor before us in a thick, boiling oil slick. Out of the mess, columns shot into the air, over a dozen of them taking form in a nanosecond. Their bodies hunched over, lumps protruding from their skin and bony backs. Fingers bent and sharpened into claws. Pointy ears flattened and horns broke through hairless scalps. Their skin was a pasty gray and wrinkled in heavy layers, nearly overcoming the red, beady eyes. Thick, ratlike tails slapped off the ground.

Rack demons were from the inner bowels of Hell—the kind that spent an eternity torturing souls. And we were completely surrounded.

17

THERE WAS A REASON WHY these kinds of demons were never topside, and it wasn't their good looks. Racks fed off the pain of others, and if they didn't have souls to torture, they didn't sit around and wait.

Roth groaned. "Okay. Which one of you was fed after midnight? Because you're worse than a mogwai."

"Mogwais are cute," I couldn't help but protest. "These things are not."

"But mogwais turn into mohawked gremlins, so…"

I shot him a look as I took a step back, nearly gagging on the rank smell of sulfur. "Uh, do you think they want to capture me or kill me?"

"You know, at this point, I'm not sure it matters." Roth's voice was grim.

One of the Racks opened its mouth, revealing a mouthful of serrated, sharklike teeth. It made a series of cringing clicks, and whatever language it spoke was completely lost on me, but Roth's brows shot up.

"I think they want to take you somewhere. Perhaps on a

honeymoon retreat?" He shook out his hands. "Yeah, I don't think so. Let's do this."

And that was like ringing the dinner bell for some really hungry salvage-yard dogs. As one, the demons launched themselves at Roth.

I started forward, but Roth's harsh voice rang out. "Stay out of this, Layla!"

Then he dropped low and kicked out, catching the first demon and knocking its bent legs right out from underneath it. Moving lightning quick, he sprung up as the demon staggered to its feet. Roth reached out, avoiding the thing's snapping jaws, and placed his hand on its forehead.

A flash of red light came from Roth's palm, dousing the Rack's head. Whatever was in Roth's touch or the light, it was like gasoline. Fire lit up the demon, glowing from its eye sockets and open mouth. Half a second later, the Rack was a pile of ash.

"Jeez," I whispered.

Throwing a wink over his shoulder at me, Roth shot forward, taking out three Rack demons with a swipe of his arm. Fire swarmed them, incinerating their bodies. Three more came forward, dropping low and hissing.

They advanced on Roth. He stood there, head cocked to the side, and then he lifted his right arm. From the sleeve of his sweater, a twisty, dark entity spilled into the space before him.

The shadow broke into a thousand marble-sized dots and then they hit the floor, shooting together faster than the eye could track.

"Bambi," I whispered.

In a heartbeat, the huge snake was coiled between the Rack demons and Roth, raising its diamond-shaped head high, until it was poised directly above the Rack demons.

The approaching Racks fell back a step.

"It's dinnertime, baby," Roth said. "And Papa brought you to an all-you-can-eat buffet."

Bambi shot forward, striking the closest Rack demon. The thing screamed as Bambi's fangs tore through skin and meat. I swallowed hard, wanting to look away from the disturbing sight, but unable to. My stomach roiled as an inky-black substance flew through the air, splattering off the pavement.

Stalking the remaining demons, Roth let out a low laugh that brought chills to my skin. He toyed with them, drawing two of the Racks out and then striking, clearly enjoying himself.

Bambi's huge body was slithering across the scuffed pavement as she tracked another Rack that dared to advance. But Roth—oh, God—he was surrounded now. There was no way he could take out six Racks on his own, no matter how awesome his fiery touch of death was.

Sucking in a breath, I ignored Roth's order and pushed down the fear. There was no way I could stand here and do nothing.

"Hey," I called out. "What about me?"

Three of the Racks swung toward me, their mouths dropping open in a silent scream.

"No!" Roth yelled out.

They rushed me.

"Crap," I muttered, heart tumbling over itself.

Muscles tightened in my stomach and legs as I tried to remember all of Zayne's boring self-defense lessons. He used to preach about getting in the zone or something lame like that, anticipating the enemy's next move. Which I was pretty sure involved one or more Rack demons eating my leg.

The first one reached me and instinct finally took over. I jumped back, twisting halfway as I kicked out, catching the Rack in the stomach. It went down on one knee. No time to celebrate that small victory.

Spinning around, I threw out my arm in a clean sweep, catching the next Rack demon in the throat. The frail bone crunched as it staggered back a step and then shot toward me.

Throwing back my arm, I closed my hand and coldcocked the ugly bastard in its jaw.

The Rack demon went down, out cold like a mofo.

I looked up, meeting Roth's stunned gaze. "What? I can throw a punch."

Pride and something else filled his eyes—something like attraction churned in the tawny depths. As if seeing me punch a demon was tantamount to seeing me in a string bikini, and that was kind of weird. But then that look vanished and fear seeped in, expanding his pupils.

"Layla!"

Hot, wretched breath hissed along the side of my cheek.

Jerking around, I came face-to-face with a Rack demon. Making the ear-bleeding clicking noise, it shot toward me, reaching out with one clawed hand.

Oh, Hell to the no.

Spinning around, I started to dip like Zayne had taught me. I felt the Rack grab the open air above me. Darting under its arm, I started to bring my knee up, but the demon changed sides. Before the words "oh, crap" could form, pins and needles of pain exploded along my spine.

Fire sliced through my palms and my jeans tore along my knees as I hit the cold cement. A cry punched out a second before weight hit me once more. Throwing my head back, I ended up a second away from eating pavement.

Raw, unbridled panic clawed up my throat as the Rack got a handful of my hair and then grabbed the hand that bore Lilith's ring.

And then it let go so fast that my head snapped forward. It flew through the air and hit something behind me—maybe a car? Flipping over, I saw Bambi streak across the pavement, hitting the Rack before it could regain its footing. I scanned the parking garage, seeing some piles of ash and some gross-looking gunk, but no more demons.

Roth knelt in front of me, grabbing my wrists. "What the Hell were you thinking, Layla?"

"What?" I tried to pull free, but he flipped my hands over, inspecting my scuffed palms. "I wasn't just going to stand there. I know how to fight."

His eyes narrowed on the pink skin and then flipped up to mine. "Who taught you all that? Stony the gargoyle?"

I made a face. "His name is Zayne, and yes."

Roth shook his head as his thumb smoothed around my palms. "Watching you kick ass was incredibly hot—like really, *really* hot. But if you ever do anything like that again, I will throw you over my shoulders and spank your—"

"You finish that sentence and I'm going to introduce my knee to a certain part of your anatomy."

His gaze dropped and he winced. "Okay. You win. I've seen your kicks."

I started to respond, but Bambi slithered up and placed its horse-sized head on my shoulder. Every muscle in my body locked up and I squeezed my eyes shut. There was a puff of air, stirring the hair along my temple. Bambi's forked tongue shot out, tickling the side of my neck.

"Hey, look, Bambi likes you."

I pried one eye open. "And if she didn't?"

"Oh, you'd know, 'cause she would've eaten you by now."

My palms stung a little, but all in all, it could have been worse. Both of us were alive and Bambi was back where she belonged, on Roth's skin. Someone was increasing their efforts, and by bringing Rack demons into the mix, things would only get worse from here.

"Do you think your place is safe?"

"No demon would dare to come any closer to my place. And before you accuse me of having an unnecessary ego, there are too many demons here that would get all angry-faced if their turf was invaded."

I sure hoped that was the case. I really didn't want a round two with Racks. Adrenaline still coursed through my veins, kicking my heart against my ribs. If I had been alone tagging demons and run into them... I didn't even want to think about that. Usually demons were nocturnal because it was easier for them to blend in among humans when the sun started to set. For the Racks to be out like that? So not good.

My eyes were peeled wide as we headed through the front door of the apartment building into a brightly lit lobby. The last time I'd been here, I'd gone out the side entrance, so all of this was new to me.

A huge golden chandelier hung from the center of the mural-covered ceiling. The painting was...uh, interesting? Angels covered the vast ceiling, depicted in hard-core battle scenes. They were fighting one another with fiery swords. Some were falling through frothy white clouds. Time had been spent on their expressions. The grimaces of pain and the righteous gleam in their eyes looked far too real.

Yikes.

Old-school leather couches and chairs were spaced under the lighting fixture. The air carried a faint and not unpleasant smell of coffee and tobacco, and it looked like there was a coffee shop or something behind the darkened doors straight across the lobby.

It all had a very old-Hollywood hotel feel to it. I almost expected the ghost of Marilyn Monroe to appear out of thin air. The lobby wasn't empty, but I was sure nobody here was rocking any human DNA.

Demons were everywhere, sprawled along the couches, talking on cell phones, curled up in chairs, reading books, and some were clustered in small groups.

Roth placed a hand on my back, steering me toward the stairs. "No elevator?" I asked.

"None that you'd want to get on." At the look on my face, he smiled. "The elevators here only go down."

Whoa. I'd known there were...*doorways* all around the city and the world. Common sense said there had to be, because how else would demons go back and forth? But no one, and especially not the Wardens, knew where they were, and I'd definitely never seen one. The fact that Roth would bring me here and tell me there was a portal was astronomically stupid.

In the stairwell, he slid me a knowing look. "I trust that you will not tell Stony about our elevator system."

The thing was, I wasn't planning to. I kept thinking of the Fiends and those in the lobby. They all looked so...so normal.

"Layla?" he questioned.

"I won't." And I meant that. "Besides, I've kept my mouth shut about everything else and I'm supposed to be at school right now."

He nodded and we headed upstairs. Seeing his loft again—his bed—left me feeling out of sorts. While Roth went over to his piano, I mumbled something about going to the bath-room and ducked inside it. My face felt ungodly hot, my pulse out of control.

His bathroom was nice, surprisingly tidy and spacious. I hadn't noticed that last time. Matching black towels hung be-side the clawed tub and shower stall. The faucets were gilded in gold. I had a feeling it was real gold, too. I took my time, trying to calm the pounding in my chest.

I'm here to talk about where the Lesser Key *could be. That's all. The fact that I want him to kiss me has absolutely nothing to do with this visit. At all—and I don't really want him to kiss me.*

God, my inner monologue sounded nuts.

When I opened the door, he was sitting by the piano, idly teasing the black kitten with one hand and a glass of—*was that wine?*—in the other. Late-morning sunlight from the nearby windows cast a halo around him. No boy should look as good as he did, and especially no demon. I busied myself looking around his room, suddenly shy. There was something intimate about being in his loft again.

Roth looked up, eyeing me over the rim of his glass. "There's a glass here for you if you wish."

I inched closer to him. "No, thank you. Your…place is nice. I'm not sure if I told you that last time."

He chuckled and stood. "Figured you wouldn't." He stopped in front of me, pulling my hand away from my hair. "Stop fidgeting. I'm not going to ravish you."

Feeling myself turn three shades of red, I sidled over to the rows of books stacked on shelves. A second later, he was beside me. This time I only jumped a little. Roth's half grin was both smug and mischievous. Humming under his breath, he ran a finger over the spines of the various books in a languid manner that made me think of him touching me that way. I let out a quiet breath, grateful he wasn't looking at me. When Roth stopped on one, he pulled a thin volume out. As he strolled past me, he winked.

"What do you have?" I asked, sitting in his desk chair.

Without looking at me, Roth brought the book to the bed, where he flopped down on his side. The thin novel dangled from two fingers. "This is a commercial copy of *The Lesser Key of Solomon*. Want to take a look-see?"

I rolled closer to the bed. "A commercial copy?"

He nodded. "Yep, for all the little Satanist wannabes out there. It's incomplete, obviously. But it goes over the list of all the major players. I've looked over it a dozen times. Maybe I'm missing something."

Reaching the foot of the bed, I held out my hand. "Let me see."

"Join me."

I stared at him a moment, then rolled my eyes. Standing, I cautiously approached where he lay. "Okay?"

"Uh-uh." He pulled the book back. "Sit with me."

I scowled at him. "Why?"

"Because I'm lonely."

"That's ridiculous. I'm *right* here."

His lashes lowered. "But that's too far away, Layla."

My hands curled into fists as a teasing grin appeared on his lips. He wasn't going to budge. Muttering under my breath, I sat beside him.

"Thank you."

"Whatever. Can I see the book now?"

Roth handed it over. The book was narrow and couldn't be more than a hundred pages. A circle and star were drawn onto the front cover.

"The real deal has the symbol engraved and the cover looks like aged beef jerky," he explained. "Bound in human skin."

It was all I could do not to drop the replica in my hand. "Ew."

"Yep. That's how they rolled back in the day."

I flipped open the book and let out a low whistle. "Nice."

I was studying a hand-drawn picture of a half human, half blackbird. The caption beneath proclaimed its name to be Caym, the grand President of Hell, ruler of thirty legions. "'Master of logic and pun,'" I read. "He looks like a freak."

"You should see him in person."

On the opposite page was a half-complete incantation to summon and banish the demon back to Hell. I fell quiet as Roth reached over and flipped through the pages, listening as he made a comment here and there.

I stopped on a demon called Paimon.

"'Ranked first and principal King of Hell, he rules over the West. He commands two hundred legions.' Wow," I said.

"That he does, but he is—or was—high-ranking. Basically the Boss's assistant. He was the most loyal to the Boss."

"'Was'?" I couldn't stop staring at the drawing. It was a man with some kind of dark headdress, riding upon a camel. Or a horse with back problems. One or the other.

"He and the Boss had a falling-out centuries ago."

My little old ears perked right up. "A big enough falling-out that he could be behind this?"

"Half of the demons have been on the outs with the Boss a time or two." Roth sat up fluidly, his shoulder against mine. "See the wonky-doodle banishing spell on the opposite page that was no doubt stolen from an episode of *Supernatural?*"

I grinned.

"The real book has a real spell, which includes—can you guess?—a real demon trap. That's why this book is so powerful. If the stone-cold crew—your Wardens—got ahold of this, they could really get rid of demons."

The gasp came out of me before I could stop it. "What about—"

"Me?" Roth gave a lopsided shrug. "They could try."

I tucked my hair back. "And you're okay with that?"

He barked out a laugh. "I'm hard to catch."

Watching him for a moment, I turned back to the book and changed the subject. Thinking about Roth being banished wigged me out more than it should. "It still surprises me that Hell even follows the rules, you know? It just seems counter-intuitive."

"Whatever agreement the Boss has with Him has stood for over two thousand years. We try to play by the rules, and the Alphas don't wipe us off the planet." He turned the page, settling on a list of lower demons that could be summoned for favors. "There has to be good and bad in the world. There has to be a choice. And you're also half-demon. Believe it or not, the Boss doesn't like us fighting among ourselves. Believes it's a waste of time and purpose. But when one of his kind starts breaking the rules, he's not a happy camper."

I snickered. "Yeah, because you should be spending time corrupting human souls instead."

"You're right," Roth answered, continuously flipping through the pages. "How are you feeling? Are you hurting from going kung-fu master on the demons?"

I shook my head. "No. Everything is healed up from…well, you know what from. And my hands feel okay."

Roth nodded as he flipped to the next page, but I was no longer looking at the book. I was watching him, studying him really. "I owe you an apology."

He glanced up, hand hovering over the book. "I'm in no real need of apologies. I find they're given out far too often to mean anything."

"I'm sorry," I said anyway. "I shouldn't have given you so much crap in the beginning."

Roth fell quiet and I took over flipping through the pages. Demons and more demons, and then one caught my eye. "Hey!" I cried out as Roth made a grab for the thin book. "No! Don't!" I planted my hands on the book.

Roth pulled on the edge. "Layla."

"If you keep pulling it, you're going to rip it apart." I pressed down harder. "Let me see it."

He stared at me for what seemed like an eternity, his eyes flaring. "Fine." He let go of the book, sitting back on his haunches.

I made a face, flipping the book back around. The drawing was that of a young man wearing an unremarkable silver crown. He had wings that were nearly as long as his body. Wings just as dramatic as the ones I saw on Roth. On one arm, a black snake curled, and there was a Hellhound stationed by his feet.

He was also nude and anatomically drawn.

My cheeks flushed. "Astaroth, the Crown…Prince of Hell?"

Roth said nothing.

"'Astaroth is a very powerful demon of the First Hierarchy, who seduces by means of laziness, vanity and rationalized philosophies.'" I snorted. "Sounds like you. 'He also has the power to make mortals invisible and can give power over serpents to mortals.'"

Roth sighed. "Are you done?"

"No." I laughed, reading over the partial incantation to summon. It involved getting naked and the blood of a virgin. No surprise there. There was no banishment spell. Though there was a seal that sort of looked like a messed-up compass. "How do I get rid of you?"

"All demons of the First Hierarchy have no known spells of banishment. You'd have to use a devil's trap on a full moon, which is explained in the *Lesser Key*. But a devil's trap doesn't just banish a demon. It sends them to the fiery pits. That is like death to us."

I looked at him, my amusement slowly fading. A muscle ticked along his jaw as he stared across the room, out the windows. "What?" I gave a short laugh. "This isn't really you. It can't be."

He turned his head back to me, brows furrowed. "What do you think my full name is?"

"Whatever. You're only eighteen and…" And I trailed off as I glanced back at the picture. The Roth sitting in front of me couldn't be the Crown Prince of Hell. Then it struck me and I wanted to kung fu the book straight into his face. "You've been lying to me."

"No. I was born eighteen years ago." Roth shook his head. "You don't understand."

"You're right. I don't. This might be a fake, but the *Lesser Key* is older than dirt. How could you be in it?"

"I am just one of many," he said, voice flat and cold. "Those who came before me met untimely ends or no longer served their purpose." He smiled, but it lacked everything that made it human. "I am the most *recent* Crown Prince."

I sat back. "So…you're like a replacement?"

"An identical replacement." He laughed humorlessly. "Each

Roth before me looked just like me, talked like me and was probably almost as charming. So yeah, I'm a replacement."

"Is it like that with the other demons?"

Roth dragged his fingers through his hair. "No. Demons can't really die, but the fiery pits are our equivalent of death. All the former Princes are there, suffering in ways you couldn't even imagine. I can hear their screams. Kind of serves as a good reminder to behave." He shrugged casually, but I knew this whole thing bothered him. "So you see, I have lied a bit. I'm practically not even real."

I closed the book, wanting to push it off the bed. Roth still sat beside me, stiff as stone. He was a replacement, created because the one before him had failed at something or had fallen prey to a devil's trap. I couldn't begin to imagine what that must feel like. Was he even his own person or an accumulation of the dozens, if not hundreds, that came before him?

I felt terrible for him. While I had barely scratched the surface of my heritage, Roth knew far too much about his own.

Silence stretched out. I could hear the kittens under the bed, purring like little freight trains. I dared a look at him and found him watching me intently. Our gazes locked.

He took a deep breath. "What?"

"I'm...I'm just sorry."

Roth opened his mouth and then closed it. Several seconds passed before he spoke. "You shouldn't feel sorry for me. I don't."

I didn't believe him. Suddenly so many things made sense. "That's bullshit."

His eyes popped wide.

"It's why you like it up here so much. You don't want to be down there. You want to be up here, where everything is real." I leaned forward, keeping his gaze. "Because you're real and not just another Roth when you're here."

He blinked and then laughed. "Maybe that would be the

case if I actually cared about that kind of stuff. I am what I am. I'm—"

"You're a demon. I know." I climbed onto my knees, facing him. "You always say that. Like you're trying to convince yourself that's the only thing you are, and I know that's not the case. You are more than that, more than just another Roth."

"Oh, here you go." Roth flopped on his back, grinning up at the ceiling. "Next you're going to tell me I have a conscience."

I rolled my eyes. "I wouldn't go that far, but—"

His chuckle cut me off. "You have no clue. Just because I like it topside doesn't mean anything other than that I like places that don't smell like rotten egg and aren't a billion degrees."

"You're such a liar."

He rose onto his elbows, his laughter fading into a smirk. "And you're so incredibly naive. I can't believe you feel sorry for me. I don't even have a heart."

I pushed his shoulders. He fell onto his back not because I'd exerted any real power, but mainly from surprise. It was all over his face. "You're such an asshat. I'm ready to leave."

Roth shot up and caught my arms, pressing me down in half a second. He hovered above me. "Why do you get mad when I tell you the truth?"

"It's not the truth!" I tried to get up again, but he had me pinned. "I don't understand why you have to lie. You're not all bad."

"I have reasons for doing what I do." His gaze drifted off my face, down my body. "None of them are angelic. All of them self-serving."

"No," I whispered. I knew it wasn't true. "You're more than just the next Prince."

He leaned down and we were chest to chest. His face was a mere inch or two from mine. Air hitched in my throat. "I am only the next Crown Prince. That's what I am—all I am."

"It's not."

Roth didn't respond as he softened his grip and trailed his fingers down my arm. His hand skipped to my waist, then to my hip. Heat followed his touch, eliciting a sharp pang of yearning and even fear. He brought his gaze up, and the intensity in his stare had a magnetic pull. That heady tension was here, pulling us together. I was tired of ignoring it, tired of believing it was wrong when it was what I wanted—what I needed.

Because Roth was more than just a demon and I was more than just a girl caught between two races.

Slowly, I lifted my hand and placed it against his cheek. Only his chest moved, rising unsteadily. It was then that I realized he was just as affected as I was by whatever it was between us. It wasn't just a game or a job. It was more than teasing and flirting. "You're more than just another Roth. You're more than that. You're—"

Roth's lips brushed mine. I sucked in a startled breath, freezing underneath him. It wasn't much of a kiss, just a tentative caress, surprisingly soft and gentle. He didn't push it or deepen the contact. He just hovered there, the butterfly kiss doing more to me than anything ever had.

And I wanted more, so much more.

ROTH LIFTED HIS HEAD AND stared down at me. There wasn't so much a question in his stare as a feral promise of things I probably couldn't even begin to comprehend.

I placed my shaking hands on his chest. To push him away or pull him closer, I didn't know. So many thoughts jumbled together. I wanted this, but I didn't know what *this* was. The day by the park with Roth had been my very first kiss, and I wasn't even sure if that counted as a real kiss. Oh, it had been good—really good—but had it been born out of passion? I didn't think so. If anything, he'd kissed me to just prove that he could.

But now he'd really kiss me. I knew it in my bones.

I moved my trembling hands to his shoulders. I didn't push hard, but Roth released me immediately, the muscles in his arms bulging as he breathed raggedly.

"What?" His voice was deep and endless.

Heart pounding, I pulled my hands back, folding them across my chest. My shirt was bunched up, our legs still tangled together. His eyes...they seemed to glow golden. "I think...I don't know about this."

Roth was very still for a moment, and then he nodded. I bit down on my lip as he rolled onto his side. I expected him to get up or be upset that I'd pulled the brakes before *anything* got started. Hell, a huge part of *me* was upset. Why had I stopped him?

"I'm sorry," I whispered as I sat up and tugged down my shirt. "It's just I've never—"

"It's okay." The bed dipped as Roth gathered me in his arms and pulled me back down to the bed. He stretched out, keeping me pressed close to his side. "It's really okay."

The black-and-white kitten jumped on the edge of the bed, rubbing against Roth's foot and then mine, drawing our attention. The distraction was a good thing, because it felt like a swarm of butterflies had erupted in my stomach.

The kitten stilled, staring up at me with bright blue eyes. I waited for it to bite my foot or sink its claw into my skin, but it seemed to grow bored with me. It curled up in a tiny ball at the foot of the bed, quickly joined by the other two kittens.

Several moments passed in silence as I tried to get my heart under control and make sense of the warring degrees of disappointment and relief. Then Roth started to talk about random, mundane things. Like the television shows he missed while down under. "We don't get cable down there," he said. "Only satellite, and as soon as someone sends up a ball of flames, which is *all* the freaking time, it goes out."

He told me how he and Cayman ended up being friends. Cayman apparently oversaw the portal and the apartment building. He'd hit on Roth, and Roth ended up with a loft above the bar after explaining he liked girls. Not sure how that one worked out, but I didn't even question it.

And then he told me about his mom.

"You have a mother?" I asked, laughing, because it struck me as funny. I still pictured him hatching from an egg fully grown.

"Yes, I have a mother and a father. You do know how babies are made?"

I kind of wanted to show him that I knew exactly how babies were made. "What's her name?"

"Oh, she has many names, and she's been around a long, long time."

I frowned. Why did that sound familiar?

"But I call her Lucy," he added.

"Not Mom?"

"Hell to the no. If you ever met that woman—and believe me, you don't ever want to meet her—you'd understand why. She's very...old-school. And controlling."

"Like Abbot?" I was too content to move and knock my hair out of my face. I tried blowing it off, but that didn't work.

"Yeah, like Abbot." He brushed my hair back, his fingers lingering on my cheek. "But I think Abbot actually cares about you."

I frowned against his chest. "If he loved me, he wouldn't have lied to me."

"He lies to protect you." A soft sigh shuddered through him. "That's different."

Part of me wanted to question why all of a sudden he was Team Abbot, but I let it slide. "What is she like?"

Roth tipped my head up, his thumb trailing over my lower lip. "She's...something."

We were quiet for a few minutes. "I have to head back soon."

"Stony picking you up from school?"

"It's not safe for Morris to pick me up anymore." I don't know why, but I felt like I needed to give a reason—a valid reason. "So, yeah, Zayne's picking me up."

His arm tightened around my waist. "Maybe I should introduce myself."

"Yeah, I don't think that's a good idea."

He smirked. "I think it's a brilliant idea."

Disentangling myself, I sat up and straightened my shirt. A split second later, Roth's hand was curved around my cheek. I hadn't even seen him move. "You're beautiful like this—your cheeks flushed and eyes wide."

My heart did a dumb little dance. "Sweet-talking me into a meet and greet with Zayne isn't going to work."

He dropped his hand and pulled back. "Damn. I need a new plan."

I pushed off the bed and backed up. "We really do need to head back."

Roth gave a deep, heaving sigh and then stood, stretching his arms above his head. His pants hung low, revealing more of the dragon's tail and the finger-width indentations beside his hips.

He caught me staring. "See something you like?"

I shot him a bland look, and then we, well, we stared at each other awkwardly. Everything had changed between us, even though I couldn't pinpoint the exact moment when or be sure what it really meant. But later on, when I was pretending to come out of school and was heading toward Zayne's Impala, I realized two things.

The weird spasming in my chest that happened whenever I thought of Roth was probably not going to go away anytime soon. And the whole reason for going to Roth's loft had been lost to me the moment his lips had so carefully touched mine. If we continued this way, we were so screwed.

Things were sort of normal over the next week. If *normal* now meant having a demon in class and spending whatever free time I did have trying to figure out where a demonic book was kept. Both Roth and I were either overlooking the obvious or we weren't the brightest stars in the sky, because we were coming up empty-handed.

Other than the whole demonic problem, it was a good thing

Zayne was chauffeuring me back and forth to school. No one had found or heard from Elijah and his clan members. They hadn't returned to their district, and Zayne believed they were still somewhere near the city. Deep down I knew we hadn't seen the last of Elijah, but he wasn't the biggest problem. With each passing day, I felt like we were running out of time. It wouldn't be long before another demon showed up. I was constantly looking over my shoulder.

At lunch on Thursday, Sam flipped over a newspaper in front of me. The headline read "WARDENS? SHOULD THEY STAY OR SHOULD THEY GO? Church of God's Children weighs in."

I picked up the newspaper with a disgusted sigh and scanned the page. Every so often the Church of God's Children held a rally against the Wardens and then made headlines. They'd been doing it ever since the public had found out about the Wardens' existence.

Roth practically radiated glee as he peered over my shoulder. He'd been eating lunch with us when we didn't skip to do some digging on what the seer had meant or who the demon was.

"They need to start doing interviews," Sam said. "Or idiots like these are going to have them burned on the cross."

"What's wrong with a good bonfire?" Roth asked, nudging me with his knee under the table.

I punched him in the leg.

Reaching across the table, Sam grabbed a handful of my chips. "Did you read this crap?"

"I really didn't pay that close attention." I placed the paper on the table.

Stacey leaned in, glancing down at the paper between us. "What the Hell? It says, and I quote, 'The Wardens resemble the very creatures that have been banished from Heaven and sent into Hell. They are sinners cloaking themselves as saints.' Okay. What drugs are these people on, and where can I get some?"

"Look." Roth pointed at the third paragraph as he slipped an arm around my waist. Because of all the touching, half the school thought Roth and I were together. I wasn't sure *what* we were. No labels had been dealt out. "The Church says the Wardens are a sign of the apocalypse. Neat."

Sam snorted. "I'm going to be pissed if there's an apocalypse and there isn't one single zombie."

Roth opened his mouth as he removed his arm from around my waist, but I cut him off. "Fanatics are insane."

Sam glanced at Stacey. "You going to eat those chips?"

"Since when do you ask before you take?" I grabbed Roth's hand, which was sneaking up my leg. "You just help yourself to my plate."

Pink crept across Sam's cheeks. "Do you know that the average adult burns two hundred calories during thirty minutes of sex?" The pink increased to red as his eyes widened behind his glasses. "I don't know why I just said that."

I tried to smother my giggles with my hand, but failed.

Stacey's jaw hit the floor.

Roth's brows rose. "Sex on the brain, bud?"

Sam mumbled something and cleared his throat. "Anyway, did you know bananas are radioactive?"

"Wow." Stacey shook her head, but she was grinning. "You are just full of random stuff."

"Yeah, the banana thing is really…" I jerked up straight, spine rigid. Roth sent me a weird look, but I ignored it. Sam really was a fountain of random knowledge. How had I not thought of this before? Excitement shot through me like an arrow. "Hey, I heard this riddle on the radio the other morning and it's been bothering me ever since."

Interest gleamed in Sam's eyes. "Hit me."

"Okay. I think it's referencing somewhere in the city, a place where a monolith is cast back." I was practically bouncing in my seat once Roth caught on. "Any idea what it could be?"

Sam stared at me for a moment, and then he laughed, smacking his hands off the white table. "Are you serious?"

I didn't get what was so funny. "Yeah, I'm serious."

Roth picked up a plastic fork. "I'm assuming you know where this place is?"

"Of course! How can you not know? It's so obvious. Only a…" Sam trailed off when it looked like Roth was going to turn the fork into a projectile. "All right, maybe it's not *that* obvious."

"Sam," I said, growing impatient.

He pushed his glasses up his nose. "Look, the riddle is worded obliquely to throw you off track. So clearly the key lies in deciphering more common meanings for some of its clues. For example, what's another word for a monolith? A monument. And a synonym for cast back? Reflected. So what you're really being asked is to find a place where a monument is reflected. And we all know where that is."

"Dude." Stacey eyed him peevishly. "Not all of us."

Sam sighed. "Do I have to spell everything out? It's the Washington Monument. And its reflection is in the…reflecting pool. See? Kind of obvious, right?"

Roth muttered, "Obviously not."

I wanted to hug Sam. "You're awesome! Thank you so much."

"I *am* awesome." Sam grinned. "I know."

Glancing at Roth, I grabbed my tray. "Hey, guys, see you in English?"

"Sure," Stacey murmured, still staring at Sam.

I'd bet twenty dollars she was back to thinking about burning two hundred calories. Roth and I dumped our food and sneaked off to our stairwell by the old gymnasium. Flecks of paint peeled around the rusted handrails.

"I'm so hoping you're wanting to test out that two-hundred-calorie thing."

I shot him a bland look. "No, Roth. Good try."

"Ah, a demon can hope, can't he?"

"We know where the *Lesser Key* is now." I tucked my hair back. "God, I can't believe we didn't figure that out. Hello! This is good news."

"I know." He caught the piece of hair I was messing with and wrapped it around his finger. "But I'm really stuck on the two-hundred-calorie idea."

I slapped his hand away. "Roth!"

"Fine. Fine." Roth caught the wild strand of hair again. "Who knew all that useless information Sam has up in his head would actually be…useful."

"I know." I laughed. "Now we just need a full moon."

"We're in luck. There's one on Saturday night."

My lips turned down. "How in the world do you know that off the top of your head?"

Roth tugged me forward. "Demons and full moons go together like peas and carrots."

I placed my hands on his chest to keep some space between us. "That's the stupidest thing I've ever heard."

He grinned. "Want to hear the best thing?"

God only knows what was going to come out of his mouth. My eyes flicked up, meeting his. "What?"

"Hmm?" He pressed forward and I inched away. "Remember what you were trying to convince me of that day at my place?"

My back hit the old cement wall. "About you not being just another Roth?"

Roth dropped my hair only to place the tips of his fingers on my chin. A spark of electricity made its way down to my toes. Tilting my head back, he stared down at me with a mischievous grin. "When I said I wasn't a real boy?"

"Yes."

He smirked as he leaned forward. I tried to clamp my legs

shut, but his thigh slid between mine. "I think I'm definitely becoming a real boy."

Oh, sweet Jesus...

The bell rang, signaling the end of lunch. It sounded so far away. "Roth..."

"What?" He lowered his head, rubbing his nose against mine. His lips hovered just inches from my mouth. Our bodies were flush, hitting at every point that fried my senses. He lowered his head, brushing his lips across my cheekbone, over my earlobe. He nipped, catching the sensitive skin. I gasped, fingers curling into the front of his shirt.

Roth let go and stepped back. "Stop distracting me."

I gaped. "What? I'm not doing anything. It's you—"

"You're just too irresistible." His grin went up a notch. "But back to the important stuff."

I was so tempted to hit him. I folded my arms. "Yeah, back to the important stuff."

"I can go for the Key on Saturday."

"I'm going with you," I threw in.

Roth sighed. "I knew you were going to say that, but there's a little problem with you wanting to do that. How are you going to get out of a Warden stronghold in the middle of the night to do this?"

"I can sneak out." At his pointed look, I groaned. "Okay. I probably can't sneak out, but I could try to get them to let me spend the night with Stacey."

"And they're really going to allow that?"

"I don't know." I readjusted the strap of my bag. "But I want to at least try."

Roth exhaled loudly. "Okay. Try it. Text me and let me know." He inclined his head, holding the door open. "Think you can walk to class, or are your knees too weak?"

I narrowed my eyes, brushing past him. "My knees aren't weak. And you have a big ego."

"That's not the only thing that's bi—"

"Shut up! TMI, Roth, TMI." I threw up my hand. "I'll let you know."

Roth fell back into the throng of students while I made my way to class. I'd lied. My knees were totally weak.

I MADE MY TENTH PASS in front of Abbot's closed-off study. Getting him to agree to let me stay with Stacey on Saturday would take a small miracle. Even though there hadn't been any demon attacks since the Rack demons, and the Wardens didn't even know about that, I seriously doubted he was going to allow this.

But I had to try.

Zayne rounded a corner and stopped when he saw me. Back from working out, his gray shirt was damp and clung to his tapered waist. He grinned. "What are you doing, Layla-bug?"

"Waiting for Abbot to get done talking with Nicolai and Geoff." I glanced at the oak door, willing it to open. When nothing happened, I plopped down on the bottom step. "It's taking *forever*."

"How long have they been in there?"

"Since dinner ended." I scooted over, making room for his massive body. "Your father has been having a lot of closed-door meetings lately."

Zayne sat down, dropping his elbows on his bent knees. "Yeah."

"You don't know anything about it?" I glanced at him.

"No." He laughed under his breath. "Father's up to something, but I don't know what."

A shiver danced all over me. Hopefully, whatever his father was up to had nothing to do with me.

"You okay?" he asked, nudging my leg with his.

"Peachy." Smiling, I tugged my hair back from my face and twisted it over my shoulder. "You?"

His brows furrowed. "I'm okay."

Meeting his eyes for a moment, I nodded and refocused on his father's door. Ever since Petr's attack, things had been different between Zayne and me. He seemed to always be watching me, waiting for the inevitable hysterical breakdown...or for me to fall off the wagon and start sucking souls by the truckload. Maybe that wasn't fair. Zayne was just worried.

"You're different."

My stomach knotted at the unexpected comment. "Huh?"

Zayne's head tilted to the side. "You just seem different... to me."

The cold knots tightened and it felt like someone had thrown a rope around my chest. "What do you mean?"

"It's hard to explain." He laughed again, the sound unsure. "And I can't put my finger on it." His hand found the bundle of hair resting on my shoulder. He didn't tug or wrap his fingers around the strands like he normally would. He threaded his fingers through the hair, feeling it, and I grew very still. "Maybe it's me."

Suddenly images of Roth flipped through my head—of the kiss in the park and all those almost kisses that came afterward. Because, besides the secrets I'd been keeping, the only thing different about me was the fact that I'd...I'd been kissed. But it couldn't be that. There was no way Zayne would know that. It wasn't like it was written on my forehead.

Oh, dear God, what if he did somehow know? Zayne did seem to know everything.

I shook my head, which caused his hand to drop to my shoulder. "I'm the same lame—"

"You're not lame." His hand curved over my shoulder. "You've never been lame."

I grinned, trying to lighten the mood. "Well, actually I'm sort of lame like a—"

"Don't." Zayne shook his head back and forth. "I hate when you say things like that. And what I hate more is that you actually believe it."

I opened my mouth, but my denials withered up like a dead flower. There were so many things that made Zayne different from me. Sometimes it seemed like we were total opposites. Insecurities resurfaced like old friends you didn't want to see. I wasn't like Zayne. I could never be like him, no matter how hard I tried. Izzy and Drake could phase at two and here I was, seventeen, and couldn't do it. I looked away, compiling a mental list of my faults taller than the Eiffel Tower.

Strange thing was, when I was with Roth I didn't wander down this troubling road.

Zayne muttered something and then his arm slipped around my bent shoulders. Tugging me closer, he tucked me against his side and rested his chin atop my head. I closed my eyes, inhaling the crisp winter-mint scent of him. We stayed like that until I heard heavy steps approaching the closed door.

Pulling away from Zayne, I ignored the sudden draft that crept down my body and stood. Nicolai and Geoff exited first, winking at me as they headed toward the doors under the stairwell that led to the underground levels.

Abbot glanced at his son and me. "I assume one or both of you are waiting for me?"

"Me." I stepped forward, twisting my fingers behind my

back, more nervous than a turkey at Christmas. "I was hoping to ask you for a favor."

He folded his arms.

"Well, it's not really a favor at all. More like a request." Warmth cascaded over my cheeks. There was something about this man that always turned me into a blabbering idiot. Glancing over my shoulder, I saw that Zayne listened with interest from his reclined position on the steps. I sighed. "There's this big exam in bio on Monday." Lie. "And since there haven't been any demon attacks lately…" Lie. "I was hoping I could spend the night at Stacey's house on Saturday to study."

Lie. Lie. Lie.

Before Abbot could even respond, Zayne swooped in. "There haven't been any attacks because you haven't been anywhere for them to get to you."

Well…

I sent Zayne a shut-up-or-die look. "If Zayne takes me over to her house and drops me off, he can totally scout out the neighborhood—"

"Oh, wait a sec." Zayne was on his feet in a nanosecond. "Don't volunteer me in this craziness. There's no way you're staying overnight after everything that's happened."

I scowled. "I didn't realize I was asking you for permission."

His glare matched mine. "You shouldn't even be suggesting something like this right now."

Taking a deep breath, I turned back to Abbot. "Please. I really need to study and—"

"I can help you study," Zayne said, planting his hands on his hips.

"No. You can't. You aren't in my class."

Zayne tilted his head. "But I've taken biology, and it was probably a lot harder than what you're studying in school."

My position mimicked his. "Well, thank you for the update, but I need to study what the poor public school is teaching me with Stacey." Giving my best puppy-dog eyes, I was seconds away from begging. "I promise that the moment anything seems shady or suspicious, I'll call the whole clan. I won't—"

"Aren't you at all worried about putting your friend in danger?" Zayne asked, and damn him, I wanted to jump on his back like a monkey. "Layla, be reasonable."

"How about *you* be reasonable? I can't stay in the house forever and only go to school! Do you want me to fail?" Yeah, that was kind of low but I was desperate. "Because I'm going to fail if I don't study."

"No one wants you to fail," Abbot said with a sigh. He pinched the bridge of his nose, a gesture he did whenever Zayne and I got into petty arguments in front of him, but there was a shrewdness to his gaze. "I don't think going to your friend's house on Saturday is that bad an idea."

"Really?" I squealed at about the same time Zayne shouted, "What?"

Abbot frowned at his son. "Yes. I think it will be okay. You need to be able to study and would probably like some time alone with your friend." His stare turned pointed. "Especially after everything that has happened."

Surprise flitted through me. Abbot had been abducted by aliens. This was way too easy, but I knew better than to look a gift horse in the mouth.

"Thank you," I said quickly, stopping myself from running up and hugging Abbot.

"I don't think this is a good idea." Shock deepened Zayne's voice.

"Well, I think it would be a good idea for you to drive her to Stacey's and pick her up since you're so vigilant when it comes to Layla." Abbot flicked a piece of lint off his trousers. "If anything happens, Layla knows to contact us immediately."

I nodded eagerly, but a huge part of me did feel bad for lying, especially since concern was written all over Zayne's face as he kicked his shoulders back against the buttercream walls. My only comfort was the fact that I was lying for the greater good. That had to make up for it.

Abbot left us in the hallway, and I turned to make a clean getaway. Zayne caught my arm before I could hit the first step. "I still think this is a really bad move," he said.

"It's going to be fine. I promise."

"I don't like this."

"But you're going to drop me off and pick me up." I wiggled free. "And you'll make sure everything is fine."

Zayne's eyes narrowed. "You're up to something."

My stomach plummeted as I moved up a step. "I wish I was up to something. Alas, my life is not that exciting."

"Isn't it?" He took the bottom step and towered over me. "Has Stacey ever really studied for an exam?"

Dammit. All those times I'd told him stories about Stacey and school were coming back to haunt me, but I held my ground. "Well, that's why I'm studying with her. By helping her, I'm helping myself."

Zayne snorted. "You're so full of it."

"Am not!" I poked him in the chest. "What else would I be doing other than studying with Stacey? Not like I'd be invited to a party." Playing on Zayne's sympathy was a really wretched thing to do. "And obviously, I'm not sneaking off to meet a guy."

"Layla—"

"I'm just going to study with Stacey. That's all."

A look of annoyance flashed across his face, like he was already planning on regretting this. "You're a brat."

Shooting him a grin, I ran up the stairs to text Roth and let him know Saturday night was a go.

Stacey was more than okay with me using her to "hang out with Roth," and I kind of felt bad afterward. Not because I was using her as a decoy, but because she was way too excited about the idea of me going on an overnight "date" with Roth. While it wasn't a date and I really didn't plan on it being an overnight thing, the idea of spending the night with Roth made me want to giggle *and* break out in hives. Sometimes I thought Stacey was more excited about the prospect of me having a boyfriend than I was.

When Zayne dropped me off at Stacey's a little before seven on Saturday night, I watched him do a couple more passes from the living-room window in Stacey's brownstone. After the fifth one, I rolled my eyes.

"You sure he doesn't know what you're doing?" Stacey asked, propping her little brother on her hip. Her mom was out with her boyfriend, date night apparently, which worked out perfectly. "Or is he moonlighting as a stalker?"

"He's just being overprotective." And really, really annoying. "But I think he's done now."

Stacey arched a brow as she put her brother on the overstuffed couch. "So...you're wearing that?"

Leaving the window, I turned and glanced down at myself. "What's wrong with jeans and a sweater?"

"Really?" She sighed as she picked up a little elephant. "If I were you, I'd be wearing the least amount of clothing that's legal."

"This is okay." I didn't think wearing a skirt and having my boobs fall out while going to God knows where to retrieve the Key would be a good thing. Then again, Roth probably thought it was a great thing. "It's cute."

"It's boring." She waved the toy in her brother's face, causing him to giggle. "Like really boring."

Was it? I tugged on the hem of my sweater and then rolled my eyes. Boring or not, it didn't matter. Walking over to where I'd left my bag, I dug out my phone. At some point, Roth had gotten hold of my cell and replaced Zayne's name with Stony and listed his own number under Sexy Beast. What a tool.

I grinned.

Sending him a quick text telling him I was ready, I turned back to Stacey. She was holding the toy just out of the baby's reach. She finally handed it over. "I'm actually proud of you. Sneaking out with a boy like a normal teenage girl would."

I made a face. "Only you would be proud of something like that."

Stacey came up to me and smoothed the sides of my hair down. The waves were a disaster today. "It's like a rite of passage. Promise me you'll call me in the morning and tell me everything. All the details, and there better be a ton of sexy details."

"I'm coming back tonight." I knocked her hands away.

"Sure you are," she said. A horn blew outside the brownstone, and her eyes opened wide. She tugged up the hem of my sweater, exposing a thin section of my belly, and then pushed me toward the door. I was leaving my bag here with her. Not like I'd really be doing any studying. "I'm not waiting up."

Tugging my sweater back down, I sent her a look. "You better let me in later tonight."

She winked as she opened the door. Roth's silver Porsche purred along the curb. As the tinted window rolled down and Roth appeared, Stacey gave him a wave. "Now go. Make mama proud."

"Proud how?" I shouldered the bag.

Stacey arched a brow. "Use your imagination. Just remember, you can only be young and dumb once. And that is a fine specimen to be young and dumb with."

"You're such a perv." I gave her a quick hug and left before she started talking to Roth about making her proud, too.

Hurrying down the front steps, I stopped at the curb and made sure I didn't feel the presence of any Wardens. When I didn't, I breathed out a sigh of relief. The last thing we needed was for Zayne to check on me now.

Roth grinned as I slid into the front seat. "Why is your face so red?"

I hated Stacey sometimes. "No reason," I muttered. "Where are we going?"

To make it seem like Roth and I were actually doing the date thing, we had several hours before the moon would be out and it would be late enough to check out the reflecting pool. "I thought we'd head back to my place after grabbing something to eat. That should kill a couple of hours."

Gripping the edges of the leather seat, I nodded as my stomach twisted. We ended up at Chan, a couple of blocks from Roth's apartment. I spotted a few Fiends and even a Poser. It took everything in me not to tag the Poser demon. Doing so would draw attention to me from both the demons and the Wardens.

Once back at Roth's loft, he put the little boxes of leftover rice in his fridge and then kicked off his shoes. Unsure of what to do, I sat on the edge of the bed. The kittens were huddled together in a small ball atop the piano.

Roth leaned against the wall, a small smile on his face. "You're nervous."

"No, I'm not."

He laughed. "I can smell your nervousness, Layla. You can't lie about that."

Well, then. I tugged my knees up to my chest and looped my arms around my legs. "Aren't you at all nervous? What if the Key isn't there? What if it is and it's guarded? I doubt we're just going to be able to walk in and grab it."

"I wasn't talking about that." He pushed off the wall and prowled over to where I sat. Sitting down beside me, he placed his hands on either side of my bare feet. "But to answer your question, no, I'm not nervous. No matter what's thrown at us, I'll be able to handle it."

"Well, aren't you special. Cocky much?"

"I'm all kinds of special, but you know that." Leaning in, he placed his chin on one of my knees. "You're nervous because you're here with me."

With him this close, it was hard to think up a good lie. "You make me nervous."

That slow smile of his spread across his full lips as he rose, leaving little distance between our mouths. "You should be nervous."

"That's reassuring." I wanted to lean back, but I held myself in place.

Roth chuckled under his breath and then stood. Strolling over to the shelves, he pulled out a DVD and then looked over his shoulder. "Movie?"

Flustered, I nodded.

After popping the movie in, he settled down on the bed next to me, stretched out like a lazy cat bathing in the sun. About a minute into the film, I recognized it. *"Devil's Advocate?"*

He smirked.

"Nice choice." I sighed, shaking my head.

"Just watch it and enjoy."

Try as I might, I could barely focus on the movie. Between glancing at the clock beside the bed and attempting to ignore Roth, I was strung high and tight. My brain kept going back to what Stacey had said. Real helpful stuff there, but she kind of had a point. I could only be young and dumb once.

And there was a really limited pool of those I could be young and dumb with.

Sneaking a glance at Roth, my gaze got hung up on those impossibly long lashes. With his eyes open to thin slits, his lashes fanned the skin under his eyes. The broad expanse of his smooth cheeks begged for me to touch them. His lips were slightly parted. Just a tiny gleam on the bolt in his tongue shone. Recalling the slick coolness of the bolt, I squeezed my eyes shut.

He really was a fine specimen, too.

A tight bundle of nerves coiled, and my heart rate kicked up. Having no idea what I was thinking or about to do, I took a deep breath and wiggled down until I was lying on my side next to Roth. There was some space between us, but the whole front of my body tingled as if we were touching.

Opening my eyes, I focused on the TV. Keanu had just bought a new apartment in New York City. Stuff was about to go downhill fast. My ability to pay attention to the movie lasted about a minute, giving way to the sharp yearning building inside me.

I wiggled closer, so that my thigh touched his. Roth had been breathing normally up until that moment, but now he seemed to stop breathing altogether. A single dark eyebrow rose.

I still really didn't know what I was doing or why. Was it because I just wanted to be like a normal teenage girl for once? To be young and dumb? Or was I seeking a way to forget about what we were about to do and the very uncertain future?

Or was it because I simply wanted Roth?

The moment that question formed in my thoughts there was no denying the truth behind it. A chill started in the middle of my back and spread to my legs and arms. It was more than just being able to kiss him. There was something about Roth that spoke to me, all of me. Something I wasn't sure I'd felt before.

My hand was moving before I even knew what I was doing. I placed it on his stomach, just below his chest. I was still. Roth was still. Both of us were staring at the movie, and I knew he was like me in that moment, not really paying attention.

"Layla..."

The low growl in his voice sent shivers through me. I started to pull my hand back, but he caught it in a grip that was firm but gentle.

"What are you doing?" he asked.

Air caught in my throat and I couldn't answer, couldn't put

forth the words explaining what I was doing, what I wanted. Another deep sound came from Roth and then he moved lightning quick. A heartbeat later, I was on my back and he was above me, his muscles flexing under the shirt he wore as he held himself up.

His eyes crashed into mine, and they were like two citrines. He read something in my gaze. He had to, because a shudder rolled through his body. "I'm a demon, Layla. What I see in your eyes and what I sense from your body is something I will take. Make no mistake. I'll give you one chance. Close your eyes, and I'll let this go."

I felt weak under his consuming stare, but I didn't close my eyes.

"Layla." He said my name as if it hurt him.

And then he kissed me. Not like the first time in the park. Not like the other time on this very bed. He captured my lips in a lingering kiss. I moaned at the first taste of him, sweet like chocolate. Little shivers of pleasure and panic shot through me when he deepened the kiss and I felt the coolness of the bolt in his tongue. My body sparked to life; my heart swelled and thundered. The rush of sensations crawling across my body was maddening, beautiful and scary.

I dug my hands into his hair, not at all surprised to find it soft to the touch. Roth pressed down, hooking my leg around his waist. I gasped against his mouth. His hand slipped under my shirt, his fingers skimming over my skin, sending a rush of blood to every part of me.

I wanted to touch him the way he was touching me. Roth moaned when I wiggled, slipping my hands under his shirt. His stomach was hard, dipped and rippled in all the right places. He broke away long enough to tug his shirt over his head. He hovered above me for a moment, powerful and strong. It wasn't the first time I'd seen him shirtless, but I still marveled at his beauty. Even Bambi, who covered his arm, and the dragon rising across his stomach were beautiful to me. I wondered what he thought of me, but we were kissing again as he eased me back down, dropping a kiss against my cheek, then my eyelids while I tried to get control of my pounding heart.

Roth cradled my face then, our lips barely touching again and again. My sweater came off in a heady tug and pull. I ran my fingertips down his chest to the button on his jeans. He had the same thing in mind, because he was between my legs, and I was swimming in raw sensations. Pleasure and uncertainty spiked together. I had no experience in any of this.

For a brief moment, Roth froze above me. His eyes squeezed tight and his head thrust back toward the ceiling. I didn't realize that he was exercising any control until it broke.

His arms tightened around me, crushing me against his chest as his hips rocked against mine. We were skin to skin in some areas, tangled together, and each breath we took, the other seemed to inhale. Our chests rose; our hearts pounded. His skin was hard and smooth under my clenching fingers. He gripped my hips, tilting me up and bringing us closer together. When he kissed me again, it was that deep, scorching kind of kiss that pushed me to the edge of the cliff. I was ready to jump off headfirst, to finally *feel* everything I'd always believed to be denied to me.

My fingers dug into the smooth skin of his biceps as his free hand trailed down my stomach, fingers circling my belly button and then lower, under the band of my jeans. Every muscle in my body locked up in a strange way. Not a bad way, but it was intense, too much and not enough. "Roth, I…I don't know…"

"It's okay," he whispered against the corner of my lip. "This is about you. Yeah, this is totally about you." He sounded surprised by his own words, and when he spoke again, his voice was hoarse as he pressed his forehead against mine. "You undo me. You have no idea how you undo me."

Before I could process what that meant, his hand started

to move and his wrist twisted and the cells in my body tightened to an almost painful point. I couldn't control it. My body moved of its own accord, my back arching. A rush of sensations hit me all at once. That edge I'd been teetering on? I toppled right over as those cells seemed to scrabble out in every direction. Roth knew the moment to kiss me, his lips silencing the sounds I would be embarrassed over later.

He held me through it. Hours passed while I slowly pieced myself back together. Maybe it was only minutes. It didn't matter. My heart thundered. I felt glorious. Alive. Better than after tasting a soul.

Our eyes met, and I smiled a little. Something fractured in his gaze as his fingers trailed over my cheek. "What I would give…"

Roth didn't finish the thought, and my brain was still too fuzzy to figure out his meaning. He pressed his lips to my flushed forehead and slowly rolled over onto his back. I followed him, not as graceful. My leg ended up tangled with his.

Roth held up a hand, his chest rising and falling rapidly. "I need a minute."

I opened my mouth and then clamped it shut. Flushing, I started to pull back, but his arm snaked around my waist, holding me in place.

"Okay. Maybe I need more than a minute." His voice was tight and strained, thick.

I may have be inexperienced, but I wasn't completely naive. "Why…why did you stop?"

"I don't know." He gave a short laugh. "I really don't know, but it's all right. Yeah, it'll be all right."

I squeezed my eyes shut for a moment and then I let myself relax against his side, taking comfort in the steady rise and fall of his chest. I felt his hand smooth over my cheek, tucking my hair back behind my ear. My breath hitched in my throat, and when I opened my eyes, he was staring at me in a way I didn't understand.

Unable to hold his gaze, mine flitted down over his bare chest and stomach. The detail on the dragon was as amazing as Bambi. Iridescent blue and green scales glimmered in the natural light streaming through the window, its body rippling over the dips and hard planes of his stomach. As Roth breathed, it seemed like the dragon took a breath. The dragon's eyes matched Roth's, a beautiful golden hue that glowed within.

"If you keep staring down there like that, it's not going to be all right."

I flushed and hastily averted my gaze, but it didn't stay away long. Rising up on my elbow, it took everything for me not to touch it. "The tattoo—does it come off you like Bambi?"

"Only when I'm very, very angry." Roth lifted his arms above his head and his back bowed, causing the dragon tattoo to stretch along with him. "And even then, I don't let him off unless there's no other option."

"Does he have a name?"

Roth arched a brow. "Thumper."

I laughed out loud. "What is it with you and Disney names?"

"I like the name." He sat up quickly and pressed a kiss to the back of my shoulder, and then he settled back down, curving an arm around my waist. His hand landed on my hip with astonishing ease. "You can touch it if you want."

I did.

Following the outline of the wing, I thought it would be rough or at least raised from the skin, but it was as smooth as the rest of Roth. I skimmed over the belly of the dragon and drifted down to where the tail disappeared under the waist of Roth's jeans.

He sucked in a deep breath. "All right, maybe the touching thing is a bad idea."

I jerked my hand back and peeked at him. He was staring at the ceiling, a muscle feathering along his jaw. "Sorry."

One side of his lips tipped up. "You...you surprised me. I figured you'd be wearing white."

"What?" Then it struck me. My bra was red. I smacked him on the chest. "I'm not a purity princess, for crying out loud."

"No. No, you're definitely not." He rolled onto his side, facing me. A funny smile played on his lips. Roth suddenly looked young and...completely at ease. "You're actually a wild little thing."

I shook my head. "I'm not sure about that."

"You have no idea." His voice was rough and he tugged me down so I was lying half on his chest. He wrapped his fingers around my chin and brought my lips to his. The answer was in a slow-burning deep kiss that tripped up my heart. His hand slid off my chin to the nape of my neck, holding me to him as the kisses left me breathless and dazed.

Then he lifted up and all the sensual laziness was gone from his beautiful face. My pulse jumped and a cold chill snaked its way down my spine.

Roth took a deep breath. "It's time."

20

WE'D LEFT A LITTLE BEFORE MIDNIGHT, parking several blocks away from the monument. A Porsche like Roth's would draw too much attention, and I was already worried that we'd stumble across a Warden. They'd be out hunting demons...demons like Roth.

Starting off on Constitution Avenue, I wasn't surprised by the amount of foot traffic for this time of night. Most were humans barhopping, but mixed in among them were a few with no souls. One Fiend, her wine-colored hair pulled up in a high ponytail, was hailing a cab, which struck me as odd. Beside her was a human male, and I wondered if he knew what he was standing next to.

As we got closer to the National Mall, the full moon was high in the sky, fat and bloated. Roth took my hand in his and I glanced at him. "What? Are you scared again?"

"Ha. Actually, I'm making us invisible."

"What?" I glanced down at myself, expecting to see through my leg. "I don't feel invisible."

"And what does invisible feel like, Layla?" Amusement colored his tone.

I made a face at him.

Roth smirked. "The National Mall closed about half an hour ago. The last thing we need is a park ranger getting all up in our business."

He had a good point. "We're invisible now?"

Sending me a quick grin, he pulled me right in front of two young men who were loitering alongside the street. Under the street lamps, the ends of their cigarettes flared red as they inhaled. We walked right in front of them, so close I could see the tiny stud in the one guy's nose. They didn't even blink when Roth flipped them off. No reaction whatsoever. To them, we weren't there.

Farther down the street, I finally found my voice. "That is so cool."

"It is."

We crossed the wide street and the tops of the sandstone museums peeked through the starry night sky. "Do you do the invisible thing often?"

"Would you if you could do it?" he asked.

"Probably," I admitted, trying to ignore how warm his hand felt in mine.

Tight knots formed in my stomach as the Washington Monument came into view. Having no idea what was going to happen, I was expecting some kind of Indiana Jones booby traps lying in wait.

When we made it to the Lincoln Memorial, the moon was behind a thick cloud and the reflecting pool was vast and dark, still as always. Trees lined the pool, and the wet, musty smell of the Potomac teased my nose.

I waited until a park ranger moved on before I spoke. "What now?"

Roth glanced up. "We wait until the moon comes back out."

A minute and ten thousand years later, the cloud rolled on

and the silvery light of the moon was revealed inch by inch. Swallowing hard, I watched the water, wondering if we really did have the right place.

In the pale light of the full moon, the Washington Monument's reflection started at the center of the pool farthest from where we stood in front of the Lincoln Memorial. The pillar sped across the pool as the reflection grew, until the pointed end reached the edge of where we stood.

I held my breath.

And nothing happened. No doorway suddenly appeared. Horns didn't hail. Indiana Jones didn't appear out of thin air. Nothing.

I looked at Roth. "Okay. This is really anticlimactic."

He frowned as he scanned the area. "We've got to be missing something."

"Maybe Sam was wrong or the seer was just messing with us." The level of disappointment I was feeling sucked. "Because everything looks the same…. Wait." I took a step forward, still holding on to Roth's hand as I knelt at the edge of the pool. "Is it just me or does the water where the monument is reflected look sort of…shimmery?"

"Shimmery?"

"Yeah," I replied. It was faint, but it looked like someone had tossed buckets of glitter on the water. "You don't see it?" I looked up at him.

His eyes were narrowed. "I do, but that could just be the water."

With my free hand, I reached down and dipped my fingers into the water and jerked my hand back. "What the *Hell?*"

"What?" Roth was kneeling in a second, his eyes glowing in the darkness. "What?"

It was way too hard to explain. The water…wasn't water at all. My fingers had gone completely through it and were dry as the desert. "Put your fingers in it."

The look on his face said he had a really disgusting comment to follow that up with, but he wisely kept his mouth shut. Using his other hand, he put his fingers into the pool.

Roth laughed. "Holy crap, the water…"

"Isn't there!" Amazed, I shook my head. "Do you think the whole thing is an optical illusion?"

"Can't be. There are idiots who jump in this thing all the time. It has to be some kind of enchantment that's reacting to us." He moved his hand along the fake water, covering about a six-foot space until he must've hit the real deal, because a small ripple moved across the pool. "It's in this space." His gaze followed the center of the pool and then flicked up. "It's the entire length of the reflection."

I hoped so, because I was pretty sure the pool was at least eighteen feet deep and drowning didn't sound like a lot of fun.

"You ready to do this?"

Not really, but I nodded as I stood. Roth went first, testing the theory of the water not really being water. His boot and then his jean-clad leg disappeared. There was no ripple or movement.

He smiled. "There's a step, and it's not wet." He moved farther down until the darkness swallowed him up to his thigh and our arms were stretched as far as they'd go. "It's okay. Whatever this is, it's not really here."

Taking a deep breath, I took the first step. Water didn't soak through my sneaker or my jeans, and then I took another step and I was inches from Roth. "This is so damn weird."

"I've seen weirder."

Part of me wanted more of an explanation than that, but then I'd just be delaying the inevitable, which was my head going under whatever this stuff was. When the darkness reached my shoulders, I shuddered. It was like stepping through thick fog that had substance you could feel but couldn't grab on to. My gaze flicked up, meeting Roth's, and he smiled reassuringly. Out of habit, I held my breath as I slipped under.

The crashing weight of thousands of gallons of water didn't come down on me. My hair was still a dry, wavy mess falling over my shoulders and down my back. I inhaled through my nose and didn't choke on water. There was a wet, musty smell that tickled the back of my throat.

"Open your eyes, Layla." Roth's voice was close to my ear.

I pried one eye open and my jaw dropped. "Crap on a cracker…"

He chuckled as he let go of my hand. "Elegantly put."

We were inside the reflecting pool, or at least that was what I assumed, but it was like being in a different world.

Lit torches lined the tunnel every few feet on both sides, casting flickering shadows over the damp pathway. The roof above us wasn't really a roof, just the bottom of whatever the substance was that we'd come through.

"I'm going to hazard a guess and say we're on the right track," I said, smoothing my damp palms along my jeans. "Or we drowned and are hallucinating."

Roth's chuckle was as dark as the tunnel. "Come on. Let's get this over with."

We started down the tunnel, our footsteps echoing off the cement walls. Roth was humming what I now thought of as his song. Walking for what felt like forever, we had to be nearing the museums when we came to a spot where the tunnel branched off into two sections.

"Too bad there wasn't a map we could've picked up for this," Roth joked as he started toward the right. About six feet down, he stopped and backtracked. "This door is cemented over. So I'm going to hope that's not where we're heading."

Left with no other option, we chose the tunnel to the right. Wrapping my arms around my chest, I shivered in the cold and damp air. Another block or so down the corridor, it curved to the right. Up ahead was an old wooden door. With its wide wooden planks and steel joints, it looked like something straight out of medieval times.

"Any second, a Knight Templar is going to come barreling out that door," I said.

Roth's lips curved up at the corner. "That would actually be kind of entertaining."

"Wouldn't it be? And then he'll ask us to choose—"

A gust of wind whipped down the tunnel, lifting my hair and causing the torches to flicker in a mad dance. All the fine hairs on my body rose as I twisted around. "Roth..."

The sound of something clicking on cement rose in a crescendo, like a wave of superfast tap dancers. I took a step back, my stomach sinking to my toes. The clicking grew, drowning out the sound of my pounding heart.

"LUDs," Roth said, hands curling into fists.

"What?"

"Little Ugly Demons," he explained. "You've seen *The Princess Bride,* right?"

"Uh, yeah."

Roth grimaced. "Remember those really big rats in the dark woods?"

My eyes popped wide. "Oh, dear."

"Yeah, so try to get that door open. Like real fast."

Spinning around, I darted toward the door and let out a ripe curse. The thing wasn't locked, but it had a steel bar across the front. Wrapping my hands around the bottom, I tried to lift it. Even with the demon and Warden strength in me, the thing didn't budge.

"Uh, Roth, this isn't—" The words faded as the clicking gave way to chattering. I turned, seeing shapes barreling down the tunnel.

A scream got stuck in my throat as Roth cursed.

Rising about three feet in the air, LUDs were like rats that

walked on two legs. Their long snouts gaped wide, revealing mouths full of shark teeth. Beady red eyes gleamed in the
shadows. Clawed hands outstretched as their tails smacked off
the ground.

"Good God," I whispered, backing up.

"This is about to get real ugly," Roth said, all kinds of Cap-
tain Obvious.

A LUD sprang into the air, launching straight at Roth. He
darted to the right and the furry creature smacked into the
wall. It hit the floor, its little legs flopping and arms failing as
it tried to get back on its feet.

Okay. Obviously they weren't the smartest creatures, but
what I didn't understand was why they were attacking us. They
were from Hell, and didn't Hell want us to find the *Lesser Key?*
And even if they were being controlled by the demon responsible, why would he want to stop us at this point? If he didn't
know what the incantation was, the information was in the
Lesser Key. It didn't make sense, but it wasn't like I could press
Pause and ask any questions.

Roth sent a LUD flying into the nearby wall with a sickening crunch. Another landed on his back. He bent over, tossing it back into a cluster of other LUDs. There were dozens of
them, snapping at Roth's legs and arms as he whirled around,
kicking out. One ripped a jagged tear through his jeans.

There was no way we could fend them all off. Not with
our backs to a dead end in the form of the heaviest door in the
world. We were trapped.

My gaze swung to the torches.

Pushing away from the door, I ran over to the wall and
stretched up, grabbing the slimy base of the torch. A smaller
LUD grabbed hold of my leg, climbing up. Letting out a high-
pitched shriek, I shook my leg until the damn thing lost its grip
and fell onto its belly.

It sprung up and spun toward me, hissing like a cobra. I

swung the torch around, wincing as the first of the flames licked the creature's furry body. It was like holding a match to gasoline. Flames covered the LUD. The bitter smell of burnt hair rose swiftly.

The LUD let out a piglike squeal and ran in little circles until it slammed into the wall and fell to the floor, collapsing into reddish-tinted ashes.

Roth grabbed the LUD shooting toward his throat and slammed it into another one jumping into the air. They were swarming him, biting and grabbing ahold of his clothes with their claws. Two were on his back.

Rushing to his side, I held the torch back as I grabbed one of the furry freaks by the scruff of its neck and pulled it off. The thing wriggled and snapped at air. I threw it aside and caught the other one before it made it to his head. Tossing it to the floor, I shuddered and was in desperate need of some antibacterial solution and intense therapy.

Roth sent me a grateful smile as he grabbed the torch from me. "Thanks."

Dipping down, he shoved the torch out. The flames jumped to the nearest LUD. Squealing, the LUD flailed and knocked into another. From there it was a chain reaction. They kept running into each other, spreading the flames like a virus.

He turned back to the door. "Hold this and keep them back while I try to get it open."

"Got it." I followed him to the door, keeping an eye on the squealing mass of furry bodies and ashes. My gaze shot to Roth, quickly checking him over for injuries. Blood dotted his white shirt. My stomach twisted. "You're hurt."

"I'll be fine." He grabbed the steel bar. Muscles in his back bunched as he lifted the bar. "Just keep those little bastards back."

Swinging back, I grimaced. "I don't think they'll be a problem. They're all dead."

"Until more come." He grunted as he got the bar out of the latch. "Jesus. What is this thing made of?"

I stepped back, giving him room as he dropped the bar on the floor. The impact resonated through the tunnel, cracking the floor. A moment later, the clicking sounds began again.

"Ugh," I muttered.

"Come on." Roth grabbed my free hand as he pulled the door open. A wave of frigid air blasted us as we stepped inside. Letting go, he slammed the door shut a second before bodies hit the other side of the door. "God, they just keep coming."

Swallowing hard, I turned to see another freaking tunnel. At the end was another door. We rushed toward it, and I kept looking over my shoulder, expecting the LUDs to take down the door behind us. Roth lifted another massive steel bar and dropped it, causing me to jump when the sound pierced the tunnel. He ripped open the door.

Shadows swarmed out of the door. No—not shadows. Wings beat the air. Roth whirled and grabbed my arm. Startled, I dropped the torch as he pulled me into a small enclave, pressing me back against the wall with his body.

"Bats," I whispered against his chest, gripping his sides.

He nodded. "Lots of bats."

They squeaked and their wings flapped like a disturbing chorus that sent shivers down my spine. The sounds went on for what felt like forever, but eventually I became aware of something else. Roth's body was pressed against mine so tightly I couldn't tell where he ended and I began.

His hands dropped to my hips, fingers sliding up under the hem of my sweater. His thumb traced idle circles against my skin as the fluttering continued in the hall and picked up in my chest.

He made a sound deep in his throat. "Forget the Key. Let's stay right where we are."

"You're so bad," I said.

His deep chuckle rumbled through me. "You haven't seen anything yet."

I tilted my head up and his mouth landed on mine. I wasn't prepared for the intensity in the kiss, but I quickly caught up. My lips parted as the piercing slipped inside, dragging across my lower lip. A strangled, needful sound rose up to break the silence.

That meant...

Roth lifted his head, breathing deeply. The hall had quieted. When he stepped back, I willed my heart to slow and followed him out of the alcove. It took a few seconds to form words. "Where did the bats go?"

Roth lifted his chin. "My guess is they went through the crack in the ceiling." Picking up the forgotten torch, he moved toward the open door.

I followed him through the opening. It was a small, circular chamber dimly lit by torches. Toward the back of the chamber was an archway leading to another tunnel. Roth held his torch close to the wall, casting light on strange carvings etched into the cement.

"What is it?" I asked.

"The old language," he said, moving the torch farther along.

"Latin?" The words covered the entire chamber, from ceiling to the floor.

Roth snorted. "No. This predates Latin. The Key has to be here." He turned to the center of the room and knelt. "What do we have here?"

I peered over his shoulder. A square about three feet wide in diameter was cut into the floor. In the center of the square were two handprints. Both roughly about the same size, and something about the prints reminded me of a Warden's hands. The fingers were long and slender, palms wide.

Just like Roth's hands in his true form.

Roth placed the torch on the floor and glanced up at me. "Put your hand in one of the prints."

I got down on my knees beside him and watched him stretch out and place his hand in the one on the left. I thought about what the seer had said about a Warden and demon working together to hide the Key. I fitted my hand to the print. Mine was much smaller.

A low rumbling started underneath the chamber, and I started to move back but Roth said, "Don't. It's working."

Tiny rocks fell to the chamber floor. A crack broke out across the ceiling. Dust plumed, catching in the flames, turning into tiny sparks that glided through the air. Man, I hoped this chamber didn't cave in on us.

The square trembled and then began to rise. I pulled my hand back then, as did Roth. Standing together, we took a step back as the hunk of cement erupted out the floor in a loud groan of cement grinding.

"Bingo," Roth said.

In the middle of the cement block was a cubby, and in that cubby was what could only be the original *Lesser Key of Solomon*.

Roth swiped up the torch and held it close. The cover was just like he'd said before. It looked like aged beef jerky. Bound in human skin—really old human skin.

I already wanted to hurl.

Carved into the cover was the same symbol that had been on the replica Roth had. A circle with a star in the middle was outlined in gold. The star was slightly crooked to the right, making it off center. Tiny numbers and letters were carved near the four points.

Roth handed me the torch, which I took gladly. No way did I want to touch that thing. I watched him reach inside and gingerly place his hands on either side of the book. It would totally suck if the thing imploded in dust, and I almost laughed at the image, except in reality it wouldn't be so funny.

Roth stepped back with the *Lesser Key* in his hand. The crack in the ceiling suddenly exploded. Chunks of the roof crashed to the floor. Roth jumped forward, grabbing my arm and pulling me out of the way of a large section. It hit where I'd just been standing.

Another piece came down, blocking the way we'd come in. Horror poured in, as thick as the dust filling the cavern. "Roth!"

He grabbed my hand and pulled me around the raised square. We darted under the archway. "Do you know where this goes?" I yelled.

There was a wild sort of laugh. "No. But it has to go somewhere."

Somewhere was better than where we were. We hit the tunnel at a dead run. The entire chamber came down behind us, triggering some sort of faulty seam in the craftsmanship. Or maybe it had been designed this way. That once the *Lesser Key* was moved, the whole thing would collapse, trapping the Key and whoever took it.

Hearts pounding, we raced down the tunnel, hanging a right when we came to an intersection. A plume of dust and rocks chased us through the maze of tunnels, snapping at our heels. I stumbled once, nearly face-planting the floor, but Roth caught me at the last minute, hauling me to my feet.

When we finally passed under a larger archway, there was a drop. We landed roughly, stumbling over tracks. Gaining my balance, I turned just as the very last section of the tunnel came down, sealing it off.

I let out a harsh breath. "Well, we won't be returning the book, will we?"

"No." Roth stepped off the track and placed the book up on a ledge. He grabbed my waist and lifted me up. "There you go."

Scrambling along the ledge, I stood and realized we were in the subway system. In the distance, there was a flashing light. "My God, we have to be miles from the Monument."

Roth was beside me in an indecent amount of time, *Lesser*

Key in hand. I glanced at him. Exhilaration lit his eyes. "That was kind of fun, right?" he said. "It got the heart pumping."

"That wasn't fun! There were rats walking on two legs. Bats! And then the whole thing came—"

He moved so fast there was no chance to prepare myself. One second he was there, and then he was curving a hand around the nape of my neck. "You need something," he said, and when I stared at him, he added, "Your face."

"My face?"

"It's in need of my kisses."

I started to laugh, but his lips found mine as if they were made specifically to do so. My mouth parted on a gasp and the kiss deepened, stealing my breath. His fingers dug into my neck in a firm hold. Time slowed to a crawl and his mouth never left mine, his lips soaking up my responses like he was starved for water. The kiss felt good—really good—and it made me think of what we'd done back in his loft.

But reality got in the way. When he did pull back the slightest bit, he rested his forehead against mine. Those beautiful eyes were closed. "We need to get out of here and take a crack at the book."

"Boo," I murmured, but I disentangled myself and walked ahead, giving my heart time to slow its rhythm, along with my body. There were much more important things we had to focus on. I wasn't surprised when Roth caught up with me easily. "I can't believe we actually got the book, huh?"

"I didn't doubt it for one second." He stepped in front of me as we entered a narrow tunnel that opened up into a metro station stop. "We make a good team."

There was that stupid fluttering in my chest again. A team—like we were together. And, dear Lord, the girlie-girl part of me was doing a very happy dance, which was ridiculous, because a future together was riddled with problems. There was the problem that I was part Warden and the whole "my kind was meant to kill his kind" thing, but it was more than that. Roth couldn't stay up here forever. He was just doing a job.

And we were getting closer to his job being completed.

Once we came out of the metro station, I realized we were a couple of blocks from Union Station. The musky smell of the tunnel lingered on us, and I drew in a deep breath of the somewhat-fresh air as I stared up at the stars peeking out from behind the clouds.

I squinted.

One of the stars was falling.

Dread formed like a cannonball in my stomach and then exploded a second too late. It wasn't a star falling.

It was a Warden.

21

HE DROPPED FROM THE SKY, landing gracefully in front of us.

The impact shook nearby parked cars, added another pothole in the street and sent what few humans were on the street running for cover. His wings were unfurled, spanning eight feet or more. The broad chest, the color of granite, was heavily scarred, but the face was smooth and handsome.

Nicolai.

His yellow eyes, pupils slanted like a cat's, slid toward Roth. He let out a growl that shook inside my chest. "Demon."

"Congrats," Roth said tightly. "You know your species. Want a cookie?"

The Warden's eyes narrowed and a voice I'd never heard from Nicolai came out. "How dare you speak to me, *alandlik* demon?"

The switch to Estonian, Nicolai's native language, caught me off guard. And honestly, out of everything, I had no idea why it did. My brain was slow to process what was happening, and before it could catch up, another shadow dropped.

"Layla," he said, rising off the ground and hovering about like a twisted angel. His wings made no sound as they moved through air. All he said was my name, but there was so much weight behind that one word that he had to know. Everything.

Fear hit me in the gut, but not for me.

Nicolai swung toward Roth, baring fangs. There was a second, a sliver of time, when my eyes locked with Roth's and the air was punched from my lungs. Roth stared at me like he couldn't believe it. Betrayal ran deep in his stare, slicing through me.

"No," I whispered hoarsely.

Roth turned at the last second, deflecting Nicolai's attack with a single swipe of his arm. "You really don't want to do that," he snarled. His pupils dilated as he pushed Nicolai back. "Seriously."

"You have no idea who you're messing with," the Warden growled.

Roth laughed coldly. "Aw, hate to break it to you, but you're not a special snowflake."

Only he could be a smart-ass in such a dire situation.

The two went at it. I had no idea how Roth held on to the *Lesser Key* as he went toe-to-toe with Nicolai. The fight was brutal. Punches flew. Claws tore through clothing and skin. Blood—the same tint and texture—flew from both of them.

I couldn't let this happen.

"Stop! Please!" I shot forward, but out of nowhere, Abbot grabbed me from behind. He must have arrived when I wasn't looking. "You need to stop. He's not—"

"A demon?" Abbot rasped in my ear. "Have you forgotten what blood courses through you?"

I dug my fingers into Abbot's arms, which did nothing. His skin was like stone. I stomped my foot down and he cursed loudly. His grip loosened and I broke free, rushing toward where the demon and Warden battled.

I didn't make it.

Abbot was on me in a second. Catching me by the arm, he

flung me back from the two. Unprepared for the power, I lost my footing and hit the sidewalk with a crack. Pain radiated over my knees and I let out a sharp gasp.

Roth whirled with a roar. His eyes glowed that iridescent yellow. The distraction cost him. Another Warden dropped beside him, wrenching the *Lesser Key* from his hands. Roth didn't seem to care. Charging forward, he slammed into Abbot in his human form, taking the Warden down in a flurry of snapping jaws and wings.

I staggered to my feet, heart sinking. Roth was surrounded. Even as powerful as he was, there was no way he could take all the Wardens on. Not unless he unleashed Bambi or the dragon, but then I couldn't bear to see any of my family hurt, either.

Air stirred around me and heat blew along my back. I knew without looking that Zayne had arrived.

"Get her out of here," Abbot ordered, never taking his eyes off Roth.

Roth popped to his feet and backed off, breathing heavily as three Wardens circled him. Blood ran from his nose and mouth.

Go, I mouthed as Zayne threw an arm around my waist, and I begged silently for him to listen. Behind me, Zayne tensed and then he launched into the air. Right before the night swallowed everything below, I saw Roth flicker out of existence.

Zayne hadn't spoken to me. Not once since we'd landed on the balcony outside my bedroom. Not even as he left me in my room and locked the bedroom door from the outside.

Hands shaking, I shoved them under my arms and paced the length of my bedroom. How had they known where we'd be? It was way too convenient that all of them appeared at once, especially Abbot. We couldn't have been followed. I would've sensed them.

God, I was so screwed. The only relief I felt was that Roth

had gotten away, but I'd seen the look in his eyes. He believed I'd betrayed him. Which wasn't a hard conclusion to jump to.

Squeezing my eyes shut when a door slammed somewhere in the house, I knew he wasn't what I needed to worry about right now. I could tell them how Roth had been there to help me—help us. I could convince them.

But me? Oh, dear, this wasn't going to be good. I'd lied to them. I'd protected a demon. There would be no limits to their anger. And Zayne... My chest spasmed as I thought of him, of the stiff way he'd carried me here and set me down, the un-natural rigidness to his spine as he walked out of the room.

Sitting down on the edge of the bed, I dropped my head into my hands. I never wanted to hurt Zayne or for him to be disappointed in me. Even with the whole story, I knew it wouldn't change much. I'd never kept secrets from him before.

But had *he* been keeping secrets from *me*?

My heart hurt to think that he knew all along who my mother was and what that meant. There were so many lies between all of us that the truth was covered in a web.

When a knock sounded on my door, my heart jumped. I stood on shaky legs and went to it. Nicolai waited on the other side in his human form. A faint red bruise shadowed his jaw. His left eye was swollen and painful-looking.

"Nicolai—"

He held up his hand. "There is nothing you can say right now, little one."

I was struck silent, full of shame in spite of the fact that I hadn't been conspiring against them. That what was going on was nothing like that.

Ushered into Abbot's study in silence, I found that I hated how he watched me, like I was a stranger beside him. Worse yet, an enemy to be wary of. Abbot showed up a few minutes later, and he wasn't alone. Zayne was with him, and by the pale, stricken look on his face, I knew that whatever Abbot suspected, he'd filled him in on it.

Zayne wouldn't even look at me. Not once since Abbot slammed the door shut and crossed the room, stopping in front of me. Zayne didn't even blink when I jumped. All he did was stand behind the desk, his gaze fixed to the wall somewhere behind me.

Out of everything that happened that night, I'm pretty sure that was the worst.

"All I can trust myself to say right now is that you are so very lucky we were able to retrieve *The Lesser Key of Solomon*." Abbot loomed over me, his mere presence suffocating. He was bruised, too. Not as badly as Nicolai, but redness marred his brow. "If we hadn't, there'd be no way of preventing the Alphas from becoming involved."

My fingers still trembled as I tucked my hair back. "You don't understand."

"You're right. I don't. I cannot fathom what you were thinking by aiding a demon in retrieving *The Lesser Key of Solomon*."

"He was helping me. He's not like—"

"Don't even finish that sentence." Rage deepened his voice. "Because if you say he's not like other demons, I may not be able to control myself."

"But he's not. You don't understand. Let me explain—"

Abbot shot forward, grabbing the arms of the chair I sat on. I shrank back from the anger mottling his face. Over his shoulder, I saw both Nicolai and Zayne step forward and I wasn't sure if they were coming to my aid or were about to help Abbot choke me.

"I am so disappointed, I am sickened by it," he seethed. "How could you, Layla? I raised you better than this, as if you were a child of my own blood, and this is how you repay me?"

I flinched. "Please let me explain, Abbot. It's not what you think." My gaze darted to Zayne, but he looked away. "Please."

Abbot stared at me for a moment and then pushed back, folding his arms. I took his silence as a reluctant yes. "I wasn't working with a demon to conspire against you. I'm part demon, right? But I'm not like other demons."

"That's what I had always believed," he replied coldly.

I sucked in a sharp breath. That hurt. "He helped me, saving me from the Seeker that I ran into." Taking a deep breath, I told him almost everything, leaving out the more personal stuff that would surely send the Wardens through the roof. "He was sent from Hell to make sure a demon didn't raise—"

"Raise the Lilin?" he said. "And he told you what you are? How important the incantation in the *Lesser Key* is? Did he tell you that's why the Key was hidden all that time ago? To ensure that no one would ever be able to bring the Lilin back to this Earth?"

"Yes. He told me everything. We needed the Key to see what was in the incantation. He wasn't using it to raise the Lilin."

"And you believed him?" Abbot knelt in front of me, forcing his gaze to mine. "Why would you trust a demon, Layla?"

A knot lodged in my throat. "Because he hasn't lied to me, and he has come to my aid—"

"Was he the demon that killed Petr?"

The room was so silent you could hear a grasshopper sneeze. "Yes."

"Did Petr even attack you or was that a lie?"

I gasped in outrage. "Yes! Petr attacked me. Why would I lie about that?"

Abbot's eyes flared a brilliant azure. "You have been doing nothing but lying since you met this demon! Why would I assume there was one truth mixed in among the lies?"

I don't know what he said that did it, and maybe it was a combination of fear and frustration because I couldn't get a single sentence out, but my control snapped. I shot to my feet so fast that Abbot stood and backed up—he actually backed up from me. Anger rushed over my skin like static. "You jump down my throat when you've been lying to me since the beginning!"

Abbot's nostrils flared.

"What? You don't have anything to say about that?" I took a step forward, empowered by the anger. There was so much fury, it was like a second soul inside of me. "You've known all along who my mother was and what could happen! You've told just as many lies as I have!" I cast a dark glare around the room. The hurt was unbearable when my eyes landed on Zayne. "All of you have been lying to me!"

"We were trying to protect you," Nicolai said.

"How was keeping me in the dark going to protect me? There are demons out there looking for me! And not the one you attacked tonight! If it wasn't for him, we'd probably have Lilin running all over the world right now, or I'd be dead."

"I thought keeping you away from the truth was better than you knowing the stain you carry in your blood," Abbot said.

I flinched. "The stain in my blood?"

"You are Lilith's daughter."

"I'm also a Warden!"

Anger snapped from Abbot's eyes. "A Warden would never have worked with a demon!"

"Father," Zayne growled.

I was too caught up in my anger to recognize that Zayne was now talking. "Obviously a Warden has done more than just worked with a demon before! Hello? How else am I here?"

"Did you sleep with the demon?" Abbot demanded.

I was so caught off guard by *that* question that most of the anger was zapped out of me. "What?"

"Are you still a virgin?"

Whoa. The level of awkwardness in the room mirrored the tension and rage. "What does that have to do with anything?"

"Answer me!" Abbot roared.

I blanched and then flushed. "I didn't sleep with him or anyone. Jesus." Abbot's shoulders slumped with relief, so much so that my suspicion went through the roof. "Why? What's the big deal?"

Zayne's body was taut. "Yeah, I'd like to know what the big deal is myself."

His father scoffed. "Why else would a demon her age be hovering around her? Her innocence or the loss of such is a part of the incantation."

"What?" My voice hit an all-new high. "I have to remain a freaking virgin?" And then the bigger picture formed. "You know what's in the incantation?"

The three males in the room were now definitely not looking at me as Abbot spoke. "Yes. We had to know so that we could prevent it from being carried out."

I wondered how in the world they expected to do that when they never felt the need to tell me anything. "What is it?"

Abbot arched a brow. "Did your demon not tell you?"

Irritation pricked me. *"My demon* didn't know what was in the incantation. That's why we were getting the book, so we'd know how to stop it." And I was pretty sure if Roth had known that part, he so would've said something.

There was a pause. "The incantation requires the blood of Lilith dead, and the loss of your innocence. Not just the status of your…well, we've established that, but your innocence is also tied to your demonic ability. Its loss is total if you've taken a soul."

My mouth dried. "A soul?"

Abbot nodded. "Besides the moral implications of you taking a soul, that's why it is so important that you never debase yourself."

I wasn't sure if he was talking about the sex thing or the taking-a-soul part. I threw myself into the chair, numb. Oh, my God, I had taken a soul, which meant that three of the four things required for the incantation to work were already set in motion.

"I think we need to take a few seconds," Zayne said, focusing on his father. "Layla would never have done any of this if it wasn't for that demon. She's a Warden, but she's young and—"

"Naive?" Abbot shot back, hands curling into fists. "She knows better than to allow a demon to use her. She is not blameless."

"She is not completely at fault, either," Zayne argued, and while I wanted to point out I wasn't naive, I kept my mouth shut. "She has never..." He didn't look at me, but I saw him swallow. "She's never had..."

It struck me then what he was trying to say. "Never had anyone pay attention to me before?"

Zayne didn't respond, but I knew that was what he was trying to say, and my chest squeezed painfully. Damn, that was insulting, and unintentionally hurtful.

"Regardless, she knows better." Abbot let out a disgusted breath. "You should've come to us in the beginning."

I looked up. "You should've told me the truth."

We were at a stalemate. Both of us had lied. Both of us should've come to each other. A whole bunch of shoulda, coulda, woulda. Silence stretched out, and I didn't know what else to say. I'd told Abbot everything—well, almost everything—and he didn't believe me. My earlier conviction that I could convince him was dust in the wind.

"How did you know?" I asked quietly.

He cocked his head to the side. "I knew you were up to something the moment you came home that morning in those clothes. I didn't know what exactly, but I knew it was only a matter of time before *this* happened," he said. "It's why I let you go to Stacey's house tonight."

Dammit. I knew Abbot had caved too easily on that. "If you knew I was planning this, then why did you let it happen?"

"Let it happen?" Abbot's laugh was harsh. "We got the *Lesser*

Key, and it is safe now. We wanted the demon, too, but we will find him."

I glanced at Zayne. Standing stoically in the corner, he might try to defend me but he still would not look at me.

"What is his name, Layla?" Abbot asked.

My gaze darted back to him and I swallowed hard. "Why? You don't believe me. You think he's out to—"

"He's a demon! He used you, Layla, like a demon would. Do you not understand? Only a demon and a Warden working together could retrieve the *Lesser Key.* He needed a Warden and you were all too happy to oblige." Abbot's great body shook with the next breath he took. "There was enough blood in you for it to work."

"I know that," I ground out. "But he's—"

"You cannot be this naive, Layla. How do you know he wasn't working against us? That he wasn't *the* demon trying to retrieve the Key? Maybe he needed to know the incantation and he used you to get it."

I wanted to stop his words, because the moment they hit the air between us, the damage was done. What didn't help was the fact that I'd never seen this other demon. The only time I'd even seen another Upper Level demon had been that brief glimpse as I waited for Morris to pick me up.

"He used you. It was only a matter of time before he manipulated you into taking a soul and losing your innocence."

"You don't know that." I closed my eyes. "He had…" I shook my head. Roth had had plenty of opportunity to press the issue of sex. Hell, look what had happened right before we'd left to get the Key. Considering how beautiful and amazing I'd felt, I probably would've given him the green light to go all the way.

"He had what?" Abbot asked.

"Nothing." I squared my shoulders. There was power in knowing a demon's name. With some black candles and bad intentions, one could summon a demon by their name. There was no way I'd risk that. "I'm not telling you his name."

That went over as expected.

Voices rose. Abbot looked as if he was going to strangle the ever-loving crap out of me. But I held my ground. I would not betray Roth even though it appeared that I was betraying the Wardens.

"It doesn't matter," I said, exhausted. It was nearly 4:00 a.m. and there seemed to be no end in sight to any of this. "What does matter is the demon who wants to raise the Lilin. What are we going to do about him?"

"We?" Abbot scoffed. "There is no 'we' in any of this. And there is no need for concern. We have the *Lesser Key*, and while you're too incredibly naive to believe that you were already with the demon responsible, we know better."

I stared at him, dumbfounded. "It *isn't* him. God! Why won't any of you listen to me? It's not him, and the real culprit could already know what's needed."

Abbot shook his head as his eyes narrowed. "You will tell me his name. Maybe not tonight, but you will." Grabbing my wrists, he hauled me out of the chair.

Zayne shot forward, coming to our side. "Father, you are hurting her."

He was. As his gaze flicked down to his hands, his brows pinched together, and then he released me. He backed away, drawing in a deep breath. "Needless to say, you're grounded."

For some reason, I sort of wanted to laugh at that. Good thing I didn't, because I doubted Abbot would find the humor in the fact that he'd grounded me.

"For life," he added.

Oh.

Zayne wrapped his hand around my upper arm in a much gentler grip. There'd be bruises on my wrists later. "Take her to her room," Abbot said, sending me one last dark look. "And pray I don't change my mind and make use of the cells in the city."

I shuddered. As angry as Abbot was, I hoped that was just an idle threat.

Handed over to Zayne, I let him lead me out of the room. Out in the hall, I dared a peek at him. Things were not looking good. "Would he really put me in one of the cells?"

He didn't answer until we were halfway up the burgundy carpeted stairs. "I don't know."

Not very reassuring. I slowed my steps. I was tired, but I wasn't looking forward to being locked in my room until I was ninety. "Zayne—"

"I know what you're thinking," he said. A muscle popped in his jaw. "That I knew about the damn Lilith thing. I didn't. If I did, I would've told you as soon as you could've comprehended what it meant."

I tripped over my feet, partly out of relief that he hadn't known. And the other part? A surge of guilt slammed into me like a bullet heading straight for the heart. In that moment, I believed that Zayne would've told me if he'd known. He would've trusted me and he would've put me before his father.

I hadn't put him before Roth.

Zayne stopped by my door. He closed his eyes for a moment and then turned to me. "Part of me can understand why you didn't go to my father, but you could've come to me. I would've..."

"You would've what?" I kept my voice low. "Would you have believed me? Or would you have told Abbot?"

His pale gaze met mine. "I don't know. I guess we'll never know."

I pressed my lips together as regret swelled, threatening to suffocate me. Zayne had never really let me down in the past. Yes, he'd stepped in when I didn't want him to at times, and there was the stuff with Danika, but he'd never done anything that made me think I couldn't trust him.

Squeezing my eyes against the burn of tears, I took an unsteady breath. "I screwed up, Zayne. I screwed up so bad with you. I'm sorry."

"Yeah," he said in a low, hoarse voice. "Yeah, you did."

ALL MEALS WERE SERVED IN my room on Sunday. My school-bag was retrieved from Stacey's house by Zayne. My phone was confiscated, but not before I could delete Roth's contact from it. So were my laptop and TV. I expected Nicolai to remove my books, but he must've taken pity on me because he left them behind.

I tried talking to him, but he wasn't having it.

Besides the brief moments he'd been there, the only visitor I had was Danika when she brought my food. She didn't speak to me, and I wondered if she'd been ordered not to. Abbot showed up for another round of "what is his name." When I didn't tell him, he slammed the door so hard the windows in my room rattled.

I didn't see Zayne again until Monday morning. He knocked once before opening the door. That was how I knew it was him. "Get ready for school," he said, staring at the floor.

"Abbot's letting me go to school?" Stunned, I stared at him.

"I do believe he's looking into homeschooling, but for now he figures school is enough of a punishment."

Thank God I hadn't told them about Roth being there.

Scrambling off the bed, I set a record for showering and getting dressed. Hope sparked, and I tried to keep my excitement at a minimum. Zayne didn't speak to me on the way to school, except for one last parting shot.

"Don't even think about sneaking out of school, either. Abbot will be checking in throughout the day."

He peeled away before I could say a word.

Sighing, I turned and hurried into the building.

Stacey was at my locker when I got there. "Okay. You have to tell me everything. Starting with why Zayne showed up to get your bag and why you never called me yesterday."

"I got busted." I dug out my bio book. "And I'm grounded for life."

"How?" she gasped.

"One of the Wardens saw us." I shut my locker, hating that I was telling yet another lie after everything that had gone down this weekend. "The rest is history."

"That's so unfair. You don't even do anything bad and the one time you do, you get caught." She shook her head. "God hates you."

"You're telling me."

Looping her arm through mine, she pouted. "So, move on to the better stuff. Did you at least get to hang out with Roth a little?"

"A little, but nothing…nothing happened. We got caught pretty quickly." I changed the subject quickly, too nervous to talk about Roth when I *should* be seeing him in a minute or so.

Except once I was seated in bio and the final tardy bell rang, Roth was a no-show. Anxiety slipped over me like a second skin, growing worse when lunch came and there still was no sign of Roth.

"I hope Abbot didn't kill him and hide his body," Stacey commented. "Because the Wardens can be a bit scary, you know."

My appetite was officially slaughtered.

"What happened?" Sam asked, straightening his glasses.

As Stacey launched into a rapid recap of how I'd gotten busted over the weekend, I kept glancing at the open double doors at the front of the cafeteria. Palms sweaty and stomach twisted into knots, I waited.

I waited for Roth, but he never showed.

As the days turned into a week and there was still no sign of Roth and no change at home, I wasn't sure what to believe anymore. Roth's own words came back to haunt me over and over again. *I'm a demon. All I do is lie.*

Could he have been lying to me since the beginning, using me to get the Key so that he could raise the Lilin? Was that why I hadn't heard from him or seen him?

No—no way. Roth hadn't manipulated me. There was no way everything had been a ploy. I couldn't believe that. Or maybe I just couldn't let myself believe that. It hurt too much to even consider. But in dark moments, those questions got the best of me.

Some days I thought I caught that unique, wild scent of his. In the hallways between classes, or outside as I headed to where Zayne was parked. I looked everywhere for him, but I never saw him. Never heard him humming "Paradise City."

Things had not warmed up between Zayne and me. Other than when I basically forced a response out of him, he wasn't keen on the whole idea of speaking to me. I was still sequestered in my bedroom, but the few times I was allowed out, he was with Danika or the other Wardens.

The cravings hit hard during the night. Probably had to do with the anxiety and the stress of everything, but my door was always locked. As was the balcony, and the windows had been nailed shut from the outside, like they were afraid I might jump out the window or something. Without access to juice or something sweet, the nights sucked.

Strangely, the need to cave to my demon side had barely been a concern while Roth had been around. The yearning had always been there, but it had been faint and easily manageable. As if his presence had helped control it. Or maybe it was something else. I really didn't know.

After a particularly grueling night when I ended up pacing myself into exhaustion, Zayne breached the silence between us on the morning ride to school. "You look like crap."

I shrugged, picking at a string on my jeans. "Long night."

He didn't say anything immediately, but I could feel his eyes on me when we pulled up in front of the large brick face of the school. "Been having a lot of long nights?" When I didn't answer, he drew in a deep breath. "How bad, Layla?"

"It's nothing." I opened the door and climbed out, squinting in the harsh morning glare of the November sun. "I'll see you later."

Just because my luck was outstanding, the first person I ran into was Eva, with her perfectly coiffed hair. The knowledge that I hadn't even bothered to wash my hair this morning along with the fact that her soul seemed darker, more red streaks than pink, meant she was the last person I needed to be in close proximity to.

"Get out of my way, freak."

My feet were cemented to the floor. All I could see was her soul and the darkness. A burning picked up in my throat and stomach, like acid.

Eva glanced around and then snapped her fingers in my face. "Seriously? Are you standing here for a reason?"

Thick and dangerous, the dark craving swelled from deep within. I turned, counting my breaths until the worst of it faded, and then I put one foot in front of the other. The day dragged—I dragged. Day eight of no Roth.

Later that night, when the need hit me in my sleep and woke me up, I turned onto my side, keeping my eyes closed. *Not again. Please not again.* Insides balled into knots. The fire started on my skin. A chill broke out.

I opened my eyes and blinked back tears. Jumping from the window was starting to sound better by the day.

Sitting up, I looked around the bedroom. My gaze passed over an odd shape on my desk and then swung back. I frowned, not recognizing whatever was there. Throwing the sheet off, I stood and stumbled toward the desk.

As soon as my eyes made out what it was, I clamped my hand over my mouth.

There was a pitcher of OJ sitting next to a glass and a roll of unopened sugar-cookie dough.

Zayne had been here while I slept. It was the only explanation.

There was no stopping the tears. They coursed down my cheeks, soaking the hem of my shirt. I don't know why I was crying so hard, but it was the ugly kind of sobs. Maybe it was because this tiny act of kindness on Zayne's end said that he didn't hate me. Not entirely. And maybe it was more than that. Some of the tears were for Abbot, the only father I'd ever known. Right now, I was sure he regretted bringing me home that day so many years ago. Maybe some of those tears were for Roth, because the longer I went without him, the more weight was added to Abbot's words. If there really was another demon out there wanting to raise the Lilin, wouldn't Roth still be around, making sure I didn't end up hanging from an upside-down cross?

But he wasn't around.

He'd left.

On Tuesday it felt like a cracked-out drummer had taken up residency in my head. My whole face ached from the cry fest. I could barely pay attention to anything Stacey was talking about in bio. By some small miracle, she hadn't asked about Roth yet today.

Stacey may be boy crazy, but she wasn't stupid. She thought it was odd that after being busted with him, he'd disappear. I bet she didn't think her comment about the Wardens killing Roth was so funny now.

I couldn't focus on the notes on the overhead projector. Instead, I drew a bigfoot along the margin in my notebook. Halfway through class, I caught *that* scent again—Roth's scent—the sweet and wild flavor that reminded me of his kisses.

Placing my pencil down, I glanced around the class. There was no Roth, but the scent was still there. Great. On top of everything else, I was officially losing my mind.

Mrs. Cleo flipped another screen on the projector and then ambled back to her stool. I ended up staring aimlessly at the chalkboard until the bell rang.

In between classes, I headed to the bathroom. I don't know why I sat in the stall until everyone left and the tardy bell rang. I just couldn't sit through another class. Once I was sure the bathroom was clear, I kicked open the stall door.

Dropping my schoolbag on the floor, I clutched the rim of the sink and stared at my own wide eyes in the mirror. Strands of icy blond hair curled around my overly pale cheeks, and I thought I looked a bit deranged, standing there like an idiot.

I turned the tap, dipping my hands under the rush of cool water. I washed my face, hoping to cool the fire burning through me. It helped a little.

The door to the bathroom creaked open as I grabbed several rough brown paper towels. I swung around, but no one stood in front of the door that was easing shut. Frowning at the sense of déjà vu, my gaze moved away from the door and over the empty bathroom stalls.

A surprised gasp caught in my throat.

Perched atop the second bathroom door was a crow—a very

large, very black crow. Its yellow beak had to be half the size of my hand.

My school kind of had a sucky security policy since they didn't have many problems, but I couldn't imagine a crow that big getting into the building…or how it had been able to open the bathroom door.

"What the…?" I stepped back, hitting the edge of the sink.

The crow cawed loudly, the sound as disturbing as it was fascinating. Launching itself into the air, its black wings spread out as it glided to the space between me and the stall. My eyes widened as the crow hovered before me for a second and then… expanded.

Really, *really* expanded.

The dark belly elongated and the wings took on armlike shapes. The beak sank in and fingers replaced the sharp-looking talons. *Roth?* Filled with hope, I stepped forward, ready to rush and embrace him.

I drew up short as the man appeared, dressed in leather pants and a loose, flowing white shirt. Mixed among shoulder-length black hair were feathers.

I blinked slowly. So not Roth.

The man smiled. "My name is Caym. I rule thirty demons, loyal to Hell only."

"Oh, crap," I whispered. What in the Hell was up with demons and the girls' bathroom?

Caym's opaque eyes fixed on mine. "Do not be afraid. This will only hurt for a few moments." Then he reached for me.

Reacting on instinct, I threw my arm out, catching him in the throat. The demon made a strangled sound, but I didn't wait to see if I'd done any real damage. For the millionth time in my life, I cursed my inability to phase as I darted toward the door.

He grabbed a handful of my hair, twisting the strands around his thick fist as he yanked. A scream built in my throat, powerful and sure to draw attention. I opened my mouth, preparing to let it loose when Caym's hand clamped around my throat, cutting the scream off.

"Don't fight it," he cajoled, letting go of my hair. "It'll be easier that way."

I clawed at the hand around my throat, sinking my fingernails deep into his skin as Caym lifted me until my feet dangled in the air. I gripped his hands, trying to loosen them as I gagged. *No air!* I couldn't breathe, couldn't get the fingers off my neck.

"Now," he said, moving his free hand to my forehead. Warning bells went off. "Just relax and—"

I kicked out wildly, catching the demon in the stomach hard enough to startle him. He let go and I fell backward. My hip crashed into the rim of the sink and the side of my head smacked off the ceramic. A fresh burst of red-hot pain shot through me, knocking what little precious air I had out of my lungs. I hit the dirty tile of the bathroom floor hard. Gasping for air, I rose to my elbow and reached one hand up to the side of my throbbing head in a daze. My hand came back red.

Red? I pushed through the pain and confusion, scrambling under the sink before Caym could grab me again. Wasn't the best hidey-hole, but it was all I had.

"You shouldn't have done that," he seethed, kneeling down and grabbing my flailing leg. "Now you've pissed me off."

"You weren't pissed when you tried to strangle me?" I grabbed on to the metal under the sink.

The bathroom door swung open before Caym could respond to that, and I immediately caught the scent of a familiar sweet musk. My heart tripped over. Hope, along with something far more powerful, rose like a tide.

Roth stood in the doorway, his golden eyes slowly moving from me to the demon. "Caym, I didn't expect to find you in the girls' bathroom."

23

I ALMOST COULDN'T BELIEVE THAT I was seeing him.

"Extreme times call for extreme measures," Caym replied with an odd smile as he tugged on my leg again and pulled me another inch out from underneath the sink.

I kicked out my free leg, catching him in the knee. Caym let go, stumbled backward and straightened. The anger blew off him in waves of heat.

"That doesn't look like it's working," Roth commented, brows raised.

Caym sighed. "It's been one of those centuries, brother. I can't catch a damn break."

"Roth," I said, his name coming out a croak. He didn't take his eyes off the other demon. He was too busy *chatting* with him. Any hope I had deflated like a balloon.

"I can see that." His stare lowered and thick lashes fanned his cheeks. A small smile pulled at his lips, and when he spoke, his voice was soft, yet deep and powerful. "You know I can't let you take her."

"What?" demanded Caym. "You know what the risk is! She

must be dealt with or all of us will die if the Lilin are raised. You can't stop me."

Roth shrugged. "But I can."

His brows furrowed as he stared at him, and then understanding dawned on his face. The air around him started to shimmer, but it was too late. Roth shot forward, and he was just so damn fast. His hands were around the other demon's neck in a second. He twisted.

The crack was deafening, swallowing Caym's scream.

A thick black mist exploded, stinging my eyes. And it stank—*really* stank. I covered my mouth, gagging as the vapors expelled from the demon—or what was left of the demon—blew the window at the back of the bathroom out. Shards of glass clattered off the floor and then the fire alarms went off, ear-piercingly shrill.

The smoke filled the bathroom, turning everything black. Out of the darkness, I felt warm hands touch my cheeks. I jerked back, unable to see past the fire in his eyes.

"It's all right. It's me," Roth said, sliding his hands to my shoulders. "Are you okay?"

I coughed. "I can't see...anything."

Roth bent, picking something up off the floor, and then he slid an arm around my waist. "You're bleeding."

"I hit my head."

He lifted me to my feet. "On the sink you were hiding under?"

"Yeah, well, things weren't going too well in here." I let him guide me out of the heavy smog and into the hallway. I dragged in a deep breath and soaked up the clean air, but the smoke billowed out into the hall. I was having trouble making sense of the shapes in front of me. "Roth, where have you been? I've been so worried."

"I've been around" was all he said.

Kids were rushing out of the classrooms, half-hysterical.

I thought I heard someone yell "Bomb!" in the barely controlled chaos.

I felt Roth let go and my hands reached out blindly. "Roth...? I can't see."

"I'm here." Roth wrapped an arm around my waist, half carrying me down the hall.

I stumbled alongside him, dumbfounded by his sudden reappearance and still reeling from my encounter with the demon. The pounding in my head was lessening, but the sting in my eyes made it impossible to see.

His grip tightened. "Hold on. We're almost outside."

A burst of bright light caused me to wince as the double doors were opened. Teachers called out, ordering students to cross the street and stay in the park. Chilly air caressed my cheeks and soothed some of the burn.

Roth guided me to the ground. "How are you feeling?"

All around me, I could hear kids coughing, some calling their parents and others crying. I guessed I was faring better than them. "My eyes are burning. How come you can still see?"

"I closed my eyes."

"Gee," I muttered, rubbing the palms of my hands against my eyes. "I guess you're smarter than me."

"Nah. I just expected it to happen. You didn't. Just keep blinking," Roth ordered softly, pulling my hands down and holding my wrists in one hand. "It should clear up in a few minutes if you can keep your fingers out of them for three seconds."

My eyes still watered something fierce. "Roth..."

"I don't want to talk about that stuff right now," he said.

I swallowed hard. "I didn't betray you. I swear. I had no idea they were going to be there."

There was a pause. "You're part Warden. I'd expect no less from you."

Pressure clamped down on my chest. "I'm also part demon."

"What? Is that side of you now as important as the Warden side?"

I didn't answer, because I wasn't sure.

"Did you tell them my name?" he asked, his voice surprisingly gentle. "I'd at least like a heads-up before I get sucked into a summoning spell."

"No, I didn't tell them your name." Keeping my head lowered to avoid the bright glare of the sun, I drew in a deep breath and willed the hurt to go away. "You'd already know if I did."

"True." He shifted so that I could feel him behind me. He still held my wrists, as if he expected that I would immediately start clawing at my eyes. "Too bad you're missing this. Everyone is freaking out. The police and firemen are inside."

I wished I could see something. "Does anyone look hurt? Stacey and Sam were in there."

Roth sighed. "Everyone is fine. I promise you. It was just smoke. It won't kill anyone. And I also grabbed your book bag from the bathroom. It's right beside you."

My vision was starting to clear. Twisting around, I looked at Roth, and instead of seeing a blur, I saw honey-colored eyes and dark lashes. It struck me then. All the times I thought I caught his scent hadn't been my imagination. "You've been here this entire time."

Roth didn't answer.

"You've just been invisible." I kept my voice low. "But you've been *here*."

A funny little smile tipped his lips up, and I started to push the topic, because I wanted him to admit it—I needed him to admit it—but his fingers slid over my cheek. His touch elicited a hundred delicious tingles that started in my belly and spread. Our eyes locked, and I suddenly found it difficult to breathe or even remember what we were talking about.

His gaze flickered away from mine and he sighed. "Here comes the cavalry, a hundred years too late."

Caught up in Roth, I hadn't sensed another Warden's presence until he was right on top of us.

"Let her go," came Zayne's voice.

There wasn't a chance for me to be surprised about Zayne being there, because Roth's grip tightened. "Or what?" he said. "Are you going to go all stony on me and force me to go demon on your ass? Where does that leave us? I'm sure the Alphas won't appreciate a showdown in front of a bunch of impressionable youth."

Zayne growled low in his throat. "I'm willing to risk it."

"I'm sure you are."

But Roth let go of my wrists and strong hands gripped my arms, hauling me to my feet. I yelped in surprise and a bit of pain as the fingers dug deep. I caught the scent of winter mint right before Zayne spun me in his arms.

He looked furious and the emotion went up a notch when he got an eyeful of the egg growing on my head.

Roth eyed us from under the shade of the trees, his lips twisted into a smirk as Zayne smoothed my hair back and checked out the knot beneath it. "Her head will be fine," Roth said. "The arm you nearly twisted off is another story."

Zayne's grip relaxed. "Shut up."

Roth came to his feet fluidly. "I don't think I like your tone."

"And I don't like your face," Zayne returned.

"My head—my arm is fine. I'm fine." I wiggled free, ignoring the wave of dizziness. "My eyes still burn a bit, but now I can see."

Zayne grasped my shoulders. "Why couldn't you see? What happened?"

"The sulfur," answered Roth, stepping closer and speaking low. He had no fear of Zayne. None whatsoever, and I didn't know if I should be proud of him for that or angry. "There was a demon inside the school. And no, not me. He wanted to kill her, so you should be keeping a better eye on her. Then I wouldn't have to step in."

Zayne snarled, taking a step toward him.

The half smile on Roth's face spread as they went toe-to-toe. They were about the same height, but Roth was a few inches taller while Zayne was broader. I glanced around, realizing a few kids were starting to stare.

The amount of testosterone the two were throwing off was ridiculous. I squeezed in between them. "Contrary to popular belief, you two are not the enemies here."

Roth chuckled. "And he obviously can't keep you out of trouble."

There was a good chance Zayne was going to choke slam Roth. "I'm going to enjoy ripping your throat out."

"Yeah, yeah." Roth took a step back, his gaze drifting to me. "You need to protect her or wraiths won't even have a chance to rip your throat out. You get what I'm saying?"

I opened my mouth to tell them both I didn't need them to protect me, but Roth had pivoted around and disappeared into the throng of students. I stared at the spot where he'd stood until Zayne pulled me against him. I let out a muffled squeak.

"Shit. Are you sure you're okay?"

"Yes." I pushed against his chest to get some air, but there was no moving him. Reasoning he could only squish me for so long, I dropped my arms and waited for him to let go.

When he finally did, Zayne grabbed my bag off the ground and took my hand. A muscle ticked along his jaw as he stared straight ahead. "I'm taking you home."

"He didn't hurt me, Zayne. It wasn't him." When there was no response, I squeezed his hand. "Zayne…"

"It doesn't matter right now," he said. "What does is that the bastard was right. We haven't been keeping you safe. And if he's truly the one who has, then there is something messed up about that."

* ★ ★

Jasmine held a cloth that smelled of antiseptic an inch from my face. "This may sting a bit."

I figured it couldn't sting any more than my eyes had. Even now they were still sensitive as I tracked Abbot's clipped movements in the kitchen from where I sat in the sunroom. She placed the cloth against my temple and I winced.

"Sorry," she whispered with a sympathetic smile.

Nodding, I held myself still as she swiped the material over the knot. Things could be worse, considering Caym wanted to kill me.

Zayne stood by, arms crossed. "Father, it goes against everything I know to say this, but we must give consideration to what Layla has been telling us. This demon—"

"I know," Abbot snapped.

I tried to hide my smile and failed. Jasmine's eyes narrowed on me. Any satisfaction was short-lived.

"She cannot go back to that school or go anywhere without a Warden accompanying her until we get to the bottom of this." Abbot faced me, rubbing his beard. "And don't even think to argue with me over this."

I withered under his stare. "But what will you tell the school?"

"That you have mono or some other human disease. Really, it doesn't matter. Your schoolwork will be sent here in the meantime." He turned to where Geoff stood. "Have you heard anything from the police commissioner?"

Geoff nodded. "No one knows what truly happened at the school. They are filing a report that it was a prank gone wrong—a smoke bomb. But this was a close call. If the demon had gotten her out—"

"Or if my friend hadn't shown up," I threw in just for kicks.

Abbot's gaze slammed into me. "Even if by some bizarre chance this demon isn't out to raise the Lilin, he is not and never will be your friend."

"Anyway," Geoff said drily. "The exposure would've been beyond damaging."

Jasmine brushed my hair back and continued to dab at my temple as she glanced at the doorway. Danika came in, carrying Izzy, whose little head was resting on her shoulder.

"Drake?" Jasmine inquired.

"Still asleep." Danika hefted Izzy a little higher. "This one won't sleep unless she's being held, and I don't want to miss this conversation."

It took everything for me not to roll my eyes.

She moved to stand beside Zayne, and I couldn't help but think that they already looked like a family, especially with Izzy in Danika's arms. I kind of wished there was black demon smoke in my eyes again. "What I don't understand is how we've been unable to capture any Upper Level demons," she said, smoothing a hand over the child's curls.

"Demons know when to hide," Abbot grumbled.

"It makes sense." Zayne looked at me and then glanced away quickly. "All the Upper Level movement around the city, I mean. A demon trying to raise the Lilin is bound to bring others by the masses."

"True, but foolish of them. They're safer down below, where Wardens can't get them." Geoff sat down in one of the chairs and stretched out his long legs.

Hearing them discuss this seriously was odd to me, but I jumped in. "They want to start the apocalypse."

Abbot muttered under his breath. "Child, the apocalypse—"

"Isn't supposed to happen now, or only God knows when it will be. Yeah, I know. But here's the deal. No one benefits from the Lilin being reborn, right?" With all the eyes on me now, I felt exposed sitting there having Jasmine fussing over my head like I was an invalid.

Ducking out of her grasp, I stood and moved behind the wicker chair I'd been sitting in. "When a Lilin takes a soul, the human turns into a wraith. Neither Heaven nor Hell gets the human. And that's why even Hell doesn't want the Lilin to be reborn." I'd tried explaining this before, but everyone had been so angry with me I was sure none of them had listened. "But some of the demons want out of Hell. They want to be able to come topside and not have to follow the rules or worry about the Wardens. They know that if the Lilin are reborn, the Alphas will step in and go after every demon. They aren't going to go down without a fight. Mankind is going to find out about demons. There will be a war, which will most likely move the apocalypse ahead of schedule."

No one spoke for a few moments. Then Geoff broke the silence. "It's risky, but demons have never been worried about that gamble before."

Danika handed off the sleeping tot to Jasmine. "Kind of like the crazy boyfriend, right? If I can't have Earth, then no one can."

I almost grinned at that comparison.

"When can the incantation be complete?" Zayne asked.

"There is no set time." Abbot picked at a leafy blossom from one of the nearby plants. "It can only occur after Layla turns seventeen. Or at least that is how the text has been translated."

"I can't stay holed up forever. I'll go crazy."

"You have no other choice," Abbot replied.

Irritation coated my skin and I snapped, "Now you believe me?"

"I'm not sure what to believe at this point." He broke off a dead leaf and closed his fist around it. "All of this is just theories. None of it is backed by evidence or truth."

I threw my hands up. "It is the truth. It's what I've been telling you since the beginning."

"There is another way," Zayne said before his father could unleash what was no doubt a verbal lashing the likes of which

I'd never seen before. "We find the demon responsible and send it back to Hell."

"I like that idea." I folded my arms to keep from hitting something.

"That's a good idea, but the problem is there are hordes of demons out there." Geoff pinched the bridge of his nose. "We could start summoning them from the *Lesser Key,* but that would take us years."

"The demon..." Zayne took a deep breath. "Your friend doesn't know who the demon is?"

I knew how much it must've cost Zayne to call Roth my friend, and I appreciated it. "No. That's something he was trying to find out, but no one is talking. Either there're a lot of demons supporting this, or they're scared of whoever is behind it."

"That's not reassuring," Danika said.

Zayne's brows arched in agreement. "We could see if he's made any progress since—"

"Absolutely not!" his father thundered. "We are not working with a demon."

"Father—"

"No, Zayne." Abbot prowled to the door and stopped. Anger mottled his cheeks. "That is a path I am not willing to go down for any reason. History has proved that doing so ends in treachery."

I knew then that no matter what Roth could do, or any demon, for that matter, Abbot's views would never change. They were too deeply rooted in him, to the point of blind bigotry. Nothing short of a miracle would change his beliefs. Most Wardens were like that, especially the older ones.

My gaze fell to Zayne. He wasn't ready to let it go. "Layla's life is in danger. So are the lives of thousands, if not millions, of humans."

"As if I don't know that?" Abbot crossed the room in a flash, stopping in front of his son. "Is it desperate times call for desperate measures? We've been here before, on the brink of the world falling apart. This is nothing new. And trusting a demon will only aid in that destruction."

"It's not going to happen." Geoff stood, placing his hands on his hips. "We've seen firsthand what trusting a demon will do."

"That we have." Abbot looked at me over his shoulder, his expression unreadable. "After all, Elijah foolishly trusted a demon once before."

"What?" I laughed. "Elijah would kill himself before he trusted a demon."

Abbot faced me fully. "Now he would, and he has good reason for his caution. A little over seventeen years ago he made the mistake of trusting one—a demon who claimed that she would rather be dead than be what she was. No one but Elijah knows the whole story, but one thing is certain. He lay with her, and in the end the demon got what she wanted."

I opened my mouth, then clamped it shut. A cold wind swept down my spine. Denials formed on the tip of my tongue but no words came out.

"The demon he trusted was Lilith," Abbot said. "And because Elijah trusted her, he helped create the one thing that could destroy the world. You."

I'D NEVER BEEN THE PASSING–out kind before, but I almost kissed the floor after that little bomb was dropped. Shaken and a whole lot disturbed, I sat back down.

"Elijah's her father?" Shock colored Zayne's tone. "You have got to be kidding me."

"I am not." Abbot took a weary breath. "He didn't know the demon was Lilith until we found Layla in the foster home years later."

I blinked slowly, but the room wouldn't come into focus. "He knew I was his daughter?"

"He did."

"But he…he *hates* me." I sank back into the floral cushions. "He's always hated me." The moment the words left my mouth, I finally understood why. "God, I must've reminded him…"

"Of his lapse in judgment?" Abbot came to my side, his voice low. "He could never reconcile the part of you that was him."

My head spun. "Didn't he want to kill me when you all found me?"

Abbot looked away.

I sucked in an unsteady breath. "He did. Wow. I don't even…" My eyes searched Abbot's face for an answer. "You stopped him from killing me and you knew he was my father?"

Again, Abbot said nothing. It was Geoff who stepped forward. "The scar Elijah carries is not from a demon. Abbot stopped him that night and took you in. After all, you carry a Warden's blood in you."

"Oh, my God…" I shook my head. "This is…"

Too much.

Everyone's eyes were on me, a mixture of surprise and pity. It was too much, learning all this and not having a moment to really let it sink in without an audience.

I stood and blindly made my way around Abbot. Someone called my name, but I didn't stop until I was in my bedroom.

Sitting down on my bed, I stared at the spot on my wall. Nothing else seemed to matter at that moment. Elijah was my father—the Warden who hated me with the power of a thousand suns; the very same Warden who wanted me dead. He'd probably ordered Petr to kill me.

Oh, my God…

Nausea rose sharply. Petr had been my half brother. That disgusting son of a…

I'd taken my own brother's soul.

Lying on my side, I curled into a ball and squeezed my eyes shut against the burning that had nothing to do with what had happened in school. A tremor started in my leg, working its way up to my fingers. I tucked them against my chest.

How did one deal with something like this? I doubted there were coping skills I just hadn't learned yet. I didn't know what sickened me more. That my own father wanted to kill me or that I'd taken my brother's soul.

Over the next couple of days, I really didn't come to any great understanding of everything that had been revealed to me.

There was no comprehending it. The only thing I could do was not think about it. That didn't work out so easily. It was like trying not to breathe. At the strangest moments, it would pop into my head and I couldn't get it out.

My own father wanted me dead.

The knowledge overshadowed everything, leaving me numb to the core. Part of me could understand Elijah's hatred because of what I reminded him of, but I was still his daughter. All these years I'd built up this fantasy surrounding my father, convincing myself that even though I was part demon, my father still loved me. That something unfortunate had happened to him and I had gotten lost in the tragedy.

Now that dream had been blown to bits.

The whole thing with Petr also weighed on me. The fact that he was my half brother didn't change my opinion of the monster, but I wondered if, had I known who he was to me, I would've done the same thing.

I wasn't sure.

Zayne had sneaked in my laptop the day after everything had gone down in the sunroom. I guessed I was still grounded, but he felt bad for me. After sending a quick email to Stacey letting her know that I was sick and didn't know when I'd be back at school, I lost all interest in the internet.

I wanted to be stronger than all of this, but never in my life had I wished as badly as I did then that I could be something or someone else.

I don't know what got into me Friday evening. I was standing in front of that damn dollhouse and I *hated* it.

Wrapping my fingers along the top floor, I pulled hard enough to tear the story right out of the house. It wasn't enough. The back of my neck tingled as I grabbed the roof and tore it right off the sides. Holding it, I briefly considered swinging the section like a bat, taking out the walls.

"What are you doing?"

I squeaked and spun around. Zayne stood in the doorway, eyebrows raised. His hair was wet from the shower. I flushed. "Um, I'm not doing anything." I glanced down at the toy roof. "Well…"

His gaze moved behind me. "If you didn't want the toy house in your bedroom anymore, I could've removed it for you."

Gently, I set the roof on the floor. "I don't know."

He cocked his head to the side.

I sighed. "I don't know what I'm doing."

Zayne stared at me for what felt like forever. "Good."

"Good?" The fact that he'd walked in on me going cray-cray on my toy house didn't seem like a good thing.

"I have something for you to do. It involves ice cream."

My eyes went wide. "Ice cream?"

A small smile appeared. "Yeah, I thought we could go get some."

Excitement rushed through me like a summer storm. It was like Christmas Day. I could get out of the house and it involved ice cream. But the joy faded quickly. "Abbot will never let me."

"He's all right with it as long as I'm with you."

"Do you think it'll be okay?" I asked, too afraid to get happy again. "What if something happens?"

"A demon isn't going to come after you while I'm with you." The confidence in his voice erased any concerns. Zayne was right. It would be suicidal if one did. "It seems like an ice-cream kind of night. You game?" he asked.

When it came to ice cream, I was always game.

I loved riding in Zayne's vintage Impala. The rumble it made, the looks it got. In a sea of Mercedes and BMWs, nothing stood out more than a 1969 cherry-red Impala. He'd let me drive it once, on my sixteenth birthday. Driving proved to be too much with all the shimmery souls serving as an epic distraction. I'd rear-ended a police cruiser.

I hadn't gotten behind a wheel since.

We stopped at a convenience store to pick up a pack of Twizzlers. I puked a little in my mouth when Zayne brought them into the ice-cream parlor. "That's so gross," I muttered.

He gave me an innocent look. "Don't knock it till you try it."

"I'll never dip Twizzlers into chocolate ice cream."

Zayne shoved me playfully and stole my place in line. I shoved him back, but he didn't move a centimeter. The souls around us were various degrees of pastel colors, soft and, thankfully, uninteresting to me. And no demons were in sight. Score. He ordered a bowl of chocolate ice cream and I got a banana split, the same thing I always ordered.

Pleasant temperatures for November had driven people to the shop in droves. Indian summer or whatever Zayne called it. We were lucky to find a small booth to squeeze into. This shop was one of my favorite places to go in the city, a mom-and-pop business shoved in the middle of a modern downtown, and it felt good being here. The floors were checkered black-and-white, the booths and tables were red and family photos adorned the walls. What was not to love?

It felt like a home.

I watched Zayne gleefully dip the ropy stick in his chocolate. He caught my eye and winked. "Sure you don't want a bite?"

I made a face. "No, thank you."

He offered the candy to me, a thick glob of chocolate syrup dripping off the end. It splattered against the table. "You might just like it."

I took a bite of my banana split instead. Shrugging, Zayne popped it in his mouth and sighed. I studied him. "Do you think I'm pretty much going to be on house arrest until I turn eighteen?"

"Afraid so," he replied. "Father isn't budging on anything."

"That's what I feared."

He poked my hand with a Twizzler he hadn't dipped yet. "I'll break you free as often as I can."

"Thank you." I forced a smile. "So…how are things with you and Danika?"

His brows knitted as he focused on his bowl of ice cream like it held the answers to life. "Good. She's a…great girl."

"She's freaking hot. I'd kill to have her body." I glanced down at my food. "Come to think of it, how many calories are in this thing?"

Zayne's eyes flicked up. They seemed brighter than usual. "You're…perfect just the way you are."

I rolled my eyes. "Have you been watching *Bridget Jones's Diary?*"

He studied me a few more seconds and then went back to his dessert. There was stiffness in his shoulders that hadn't been there before, as if he was suddenly carrying some unseen weight. Like an idiot, I kept talking. "I overheard Jasmine and Danika talking. She said you two hadn't talked about your future… together."

It seemed like his shoulders tensed even more. "No. We haven't."

I poked a cherry around. "So are you still planning to buck the system?"

Zayne ran a hand over his head, squinting. "I don't look at it that way. If I'm going to mat—if I'm going to marry, I want to do it on my own terms."

"And what does Abbot have to say about that?" I offered him the cherry, which he took. "Or have you been stalling?"

He shrugged as he studied the cherry's stem. "I've just been avoiding it."

"But you haven't been avoiding Danika," I pointed out. "You like her. So what's the deal?"

"It's not about me liking her or not." He sat back in the booth, hands bouncing restlessly off the table as he stared at the tubs of ice cream behind the glass. "She's a great girl. I have fun with her, but I really don't want to talk about her right now."

"Oh." Sort of knew where this was heading.

He shot me a knowing look. "I'd ask how you've been holding up, but I think the dollhouse answers that."

I sighed. "I'm trying not to think about it. It's not working. I mean…"

"It's heavy stuff?"

I cracked a smile. "Yeah, it's pretty heavy." Poking a slice of banana around, I shook my head. "Zayne, I…"

"What?" he asked after a few seconds.

Looking up, I met his stare before I lost my nerve. "I haven't been completely honest."

"Really?" he said drily. "Could've fooled me."

I flushed. "I am sorry, Zayne. Not because I got caught, but because I know it hurt you and it was wrong. I should've trusted you."

"I know." His hand landed on mine and squeezed gently. "I was pissed—part of me is still pissed—but it is what it is."

Hoping he still wanted to breathe the same air as I did after he learned what I'd done, I pulled my hand back and cast my eyes to my now-soupy ice cream. I decided to approach it like ripping a Band-Aid off. "I took Petr's soul."

Zayne leaned forward, his brows furrowing as if he didn't quite understand what I'd said, and then he sat back. His hands slid off the table as his throat worked. Silence hit like a bomb.

"I know you sort of guessed it when I came home and I was sick." My fingers twisted around the spoon. "I was defending myself. He was going to kill me. I didn't want to. God, it was the last thing I wanted to do, but he just kept coming after me and I didn't know what else to do. It did something to him, Zayne. He didn't turn into a wraith like a human would. He morphed, but his eyes were red. I'm so sorry. Please don't—"

"Layla," he said quietly. He grabbed the hand clenching the

spoon and gentled unraveled my fingers from around the handle. "I know you did it to defend yourself and it wasn't something you intended to do."

"But the look on your face," I whispered.

He smiled, but it was strained. "I was shocked. Like you said, I suspected something, but I thought you might have tasted the soul. I didn't know it went...all the way."

Shame was a pail of rusted nails I'd swallowed. I couldn't help but feel it, even though I knew that I'd most likely be dead if I hadn't taken his soul, giving me a reprieve until Roth had shown up. "You're disappointed, aren't you?"

"Oh, Layla, it has nothing to do with me being disappointed. You defended yourself, and I wish you hadn't needed to. Not because of what you are." He kept his voice low. "But because I know how sick it makes you. I hate seeing you like that. I *hate* seeing you like this."

Using my free hand, I swiped under my eye. God, I was crying.

"See? You're blaming yourself because of what you did. And I hate that you're doing that to yourself."

"But you said I was better than this."

He flinched. "God, I wish I'd never said that to you. And you know, the way you look at yourself—it's partly our fault."

I frowned. "What do you mean?"

Sitting back, he lifted his hands. "We raised you to hate that part of you. Maybe that wasn't the right thing to do. I'm not sure anymore. I'm not sure of anything." He thrust his fingers through his hair. "I do know that I'm not disappointed in you. I don't hate you. I could never hate you. Even if you don't see the true pleasure of Twizzlers dipped in chocolate."

I choked out a laugh as I blinked back more tears. "Funny."

His smile was a little more real. "You ready to get out of here?"

Sniffling, I nodded. We gathered up our trash, and once

outside, Zayne draped his arm over my shoulders as we walked to where he was parked. It was good to be like this with him, having that connection again. It did wonders, warming that chilled spot in my chest.

Zayne made sure I was tucked safely in the passenger side before he slipped around the front of the car and got in. It made me smile.

Listening to music on the way home, I laughed as Zayne sang along to a pop song on the radio. He was a lot of things, but a singer was not one of them. As we reached the private stretch of road leading to the compound, he glanced over at me. Something foreign was reflected in those eyes—a quality I'd seen before, but I'd never understood what it meant until... until Roth had come along. There was a swelling feeling in my stomach as he turned his gaze back to the road.

"Jesus!" he shouted, slamming on the brakes.

Something landed on the hood of Zayne's Impala, shattering the windshield.

At first I thought an overgrown gorilla had escaped the zoo and dropped out of one of the many nearby trees. Then I saw the serrated teeth and smelled the sulfur. I screamed—really screamed.

It was a Hellion.

A big, hairy, stinky Hellion that had just done some major damage to Zayne's precious Impala. Matted, coarse hair covered its massive body. The enormous ram horns were what had shattered the windshield. But I had to be seeing things. Hellions weren't allowed topside for obvious reasons.

Zayne threw his arm out, pressing me back against the seat as the Hellion tried to reach inside the car. Its horns were getting caught on the metal and it seemed too stupid to figure out that it only needed to lower its head to fit through.

The Hellion roared. It was like having a T. rex scream in your face.

"Zayne!" I screeched as its thick front claws swiped inches from my face. "Zayne!"

"Layla, I need you to listen to me." He unbuckled his seat belt with one hand. "I need you to be calm."

The Hellion's claws shredded Zayne's forearm, drawing blood. Zayne didn't even flinch.

"Oh, my God," I whispered, watching the rivulets of blood drip from his arm onto my lap. "Zayne, your arm."

"Layla, you're going to have to make a run for it when I tell you to. Okay?" he said urgently. He reached for the button on my seat belt, releasing it. "When I tell you to run, you run and you don't look back and you don't try to fight. You cannot fight this thing."

I didn't want to leave him, not with that thing on the attack. Hellions were notorious killers. They could rip Wardens limb from limb using their brute strength. "But I can hel—"

Another wide sweep of clawed fingers almost got me. Zayne pulled me toward him and down, pressing my cheek against his thigh. "Keep down," he ordered. "Just listen for my command. You know these woods. Get home and get my father. Don't stop. That's how you can help me."

My heart pounded in my chest. I nodded as best I could.

Zayne's hand slipped over my cheek and through my hair. I squeezed my eyes shut as the Hellion howled once more. Then Zayne was opening the door and I was falling into his seat. The car shook as the Hellion switched gears, spotting Zayne outside of the car.

It laughed, a guttural sound.

I knew I should have stayed fixed to the seat, but I sat up as the Hellion jumped from the car. I thought Zayne would hesitate, knowing that I was nearby. But he didn't.

Zayne shifted.

The wings were the first to sprout, arcing high in the sky behind him and unfolding around his body. I could only see the side of his face, but that alone was dramatic enough. His skin turned a dark gray and his jaw widened as his nose flattened. Two horns grew, much like the Hellion's horns, but Zayne's were black as night and beautiful in an odd way. They curled back from his head, a fierce sight. As if to remind me that he was still Zayne, a breeze played with his blond hair, blowing it around the horns.

I sucked in air, a gasp that shouldn't have been heard, but Zayne turned a fraction of an inch toward me. Pain streaked across his face as our eyes locked for only a second. Out of the corner of my eyes, I saw the Hellion move.

"Zayne!" I screamed, clutching the dashboard.

He whipped back to the Hellion, catching the beefy hand before it could get a grip on him. Still holding the beast, Zayne leaned back and planted his foot in the Hellion's midsection. The Hellion flew back several feet, grunting. It picked itself back up and rushed Zayne. They collided with enough force to shake ground and car.

Bending at the knees, Zayne pushed himself into the air, bringing the Hellion with him. From the heights of the massive oaks, Zayne arced in the sky and shot back down to the ground. They slammed into the soil, their impact eating away several feet of road. Zayne stood, wrapping a muscled arm around the beast's neck.

"Go," he yelled in a voice that was his, but wasn't. "Run! Go!"

I threw open the door, half falling out of it. Spinning around, I took Zayne in. There was something dark—blood?—leaking from his nose, a patchy area of skin on his cheek that seemed a darker gray. The Hellion struggled against his hold, jaws snapping.

"Go," Zayne ordered. "Please."

The Hellion latched on to Zayne's arm. The last thing I saw was Zayne hurling through the air. With a scream stuck in my throat, I whirled around and ran. I tried to tell myself that I wasn't running away and that I was going to get help, but each step that took me farther from Zayne felt like a punch in the chest. What if he got seriously hurt?

What if he died?

I couldn't let myself think of that. I ran on, knowing the best thing I could do was warn the clan. Branches snapped at my face, pulled at my clothing. Several times I tripped over a rock or an upturned root, catching myself with my hands and then pushing back up. It was like a cheesy horror movie, except what was behind me wasn't some dead dude in a hockey mask. I'd actually prefer that guy over the Hellion, machete, high body count and all.

I kept going, throat seizing and muscles burning. Part of me realized I should have taken Zayne up on his offer to run with him. I was hideously out of shape.

Hot wind kicked up, scattering fallen leaves in the air. They rained down, a chorus of dark reds and browns. A snapping sound cracked through the night, followed by another and another.

I felt something whip through the air a second before it wrapped around my leg, dragging me down. I hit the hard soil elbows first. Wincing, I rolled onto my back. Thick tree roots climbed both my legs, squeezing until I was sure it would snap the bones in half. Frantic, I grabbed the end of a coarse root and started unwinding it with shaking hands. It yanked me forward, knocking me flat. Small rocks dug into my back as I was dragged over the ground. Arms flailing, I tried to grab ahold of the small bushes. When I finally came to a halt, the smell of sulfur was suffocating.

He stood above me a second later, occupying a space that had been empty. There was no soul—nothing around him— and I knew he was an Upper Level demon. His dark hair was buzzed into a Mohawk, the tips colored bloodred. He looked only to be in his mid-twenties and he wore a pin-striped suit, which, besides the fact that it looked ridiculous in the dark woods, was something straight out of old mobster movies. He even had a red satiny tie and matching hankie. A short, hysterical laugh escaped me.

And I realized I'd briefly seen him before. The day I'd waited for Morris to pick me up—he'd been the demon watching me.

"My name is Paimon. I'm the great and powerful King, ruler of two hundred legions," he said in a distinctively Southern accent. I found myself wondering the weirdest things right then. Did Hell have a north and south? Because this dude was *Southern*. He bowed at the waist, a parody of elegance. "And you are Layla, child of the Warden Elijah and the demon Lilith. Finally, after all this time, I'm pleased to make your acquaintance."

Paimon—I recognized him from the *Lesser Key,* the one on the camel/horse. It took no stretch of the imagination to conclude that I was now face-to-face with the demon who sought to raise the Lilin.

"Shit." I jerked up, desperately trying to untangle my legs.

He raised a hand and I was pinned back, staring up at the cloudless night sky. "Let's not make this difficult, darlin'."

I gulped in air, moving my hands over the ground. I grabbed a rock, squeezing until the rough edges bit into my palm.

"I'm feeling a bit gracious, so I'm going to give you an opportunity I've never given anyone. You come along with me without being too much of an inconvenience—" he flashed a perfect set of white teeth "—and I won't make a crown out of the bones of everyone you love. I can promise you riches beyond your imagination, the freedom to be whatever you want to be and a life envied by all."

The rock felt heavy in my hand and I almost laughed again. "You want to raise the Lilin?"

"Ah, I'm glad I don't have to explain my desire. Though I

did have this whole speech planned." He winked one crimson eye. "There's always time later, darlin'."

Fear knotted my stomach, but I forced as much bravado into my voice as possible. "And after you use me to raise the Lilin, you're seriously going to let me live?"

"Maybe," he replied. "Depends on how happy you make me."

"Yeah, you can go to Hell."

Paimon turned his head away and then faced me again. His skin melted away, revealing a red skull and eye sockets full of flames. His mouth gaped open, long and distorted. The howling sound that came from him turned my soul cold. I screamed until my voice left me, unable to move more than an inch backward.

Then he was the handsome man again, smiling. "Darlin', you're a means to an end—an end that works wonderfully in my favor." Paimon crouched beside me, tipping his head to the side. "Now, you can make this easy or very, very hard."

I took a deep breath, but couldn't seem to get enough air in my lungs. I was worried about Zayne and knew that if I let Paimon capture me, I'd never have a chance to get him help. "Okay. Can—can you get these creepy roots off my legs?"

Another brief smile and Paimon waved his hand. The roots trembled, withered up and became nothing more than ashes within seconds. "I'm so glad you're going to ma—"

I swung my arm around with all my strength, slamming the rock into his temple. His head snapped in the other direction, but a second later he was looking at me and laughing. *Laughing.* Flames licked from the wound where blood should have flowed.

Paimon grabbed my arm in a viselike grip. "Now, that wasn't very nice, darlin'."

I stared at his burning head. "Jesus."

"Not quite." He hauled me to my feet. "Say good-night."

I opened my mouth, but before I could make a sound, my world went dark.

25

THINGS PIECED THEMSELVES BACK TOGETHER SLOWLY. Sensation led the way, which was the first indication that something was very wrong. I couldn't move my arms or legs. They were bound to the cold floor, the rope tight and cutting into my wrists as I strained forward.

Oh, crap.

Smell came next. The moldy scent was familiar, poking around in my head, but I couldn't wiggle an exact memory free. When I was able to pry my eyes open, I was staring up at exposed metal rafters.

Candles didn't cast much light, but in the flickering dance of shadows I could make out a basketball hoop without a backboard. My gaze dropped and tracked the visible scuff marks until they disappeared in a white line drawn in chalk—a circle. Straight lines streaked out, meeting the circle. I turned my head, wincing at the dull ache in my temples. More lines on the other side of me.

A pentagram slightly crooked. Oh, this was bad.

I was in the old gymnasium on the lowest level of my school, tied down in the middle of a pentagram and *was that chanting?* God. Craning my neck, I tried to see beyond the hundreds of white candles following the circumference of the circle.

In the shadows, there were *things* moving. Their soft chattering and piglike squeals turned my insides cold. Rack demons.

"You're awake. Good." A deep Southern drawl came out from the shadows. "Let's get this show on the road."

My chin snapped down, to my toes. Paimon had removed the jacket and untucked the red shirt. He came to the edge of the circle, stopped and glanced down. He took a step back, and my suspicion soared. "You're not going to come in here?" I asked.

Paimon tipped his head back and chuckled. "That pretty little lopsided pentagram can easily be converted into a devil's trap, and my Hermès loafers are not going one inch beyond that chalk."

My hands curled into fists and I could feel the ring biting into skin. "That's going to make doing this incantation hard, isn't it?"

"Not at all, darlin'," he said, kneeling down. That Mohawk of his had to be at least two feet high. "That's what lackeys are for. Oh, lackey!"

To my left, another form pulled free from the shadows. I hadn't seen him before, but his smile was beyond creepy. I swallowed as my eyes darted between the two demons. No one was going to show up and save the day. I didn't know if Zayne had survived the Hellion. Roth probably didn't even know I'd been taken. And unless I could Houdini my way out of these ropes, I wasn't going to be able to do much to defend myself. At that moment I knew three things. I was screwed. Mankind was screwed. The entire universe was screwed.

"I confess I've been disappointed with Naberius. He should've been able to retrieve you without me stepping in. Show her how displeased I was."

The lackey waved his left hand. Four of his fingers were

missing. Only the middle one remained. "They'll grow back. Slowly."

"Painfully," Paimon added with a gleeful smile. He rose fluidly. "Anyway, Naberius, spill the blood of Lilith. I don't have all night."

Like a dutiful little tool, Naberius stepped carefully over the circle and knelt. My heart dropped. "Wait." Naberius grabbed my hand with that one finger. Metal glinted in his other hand. "Wait, I said!"

Paimon sighed. "Are you going to beg now? Come over to the dark side? You already had your chance, darlin'. When I get done, I'm going to kill you. Well, I'll probably have a little fun with you first, but I will kill you."

Panic clawed its way up my throat, but I knew if I caved to it, that would be the end. Heart pounding, I tried to tug the arm closest to Naberius, but the rope gave no slack. "Why?"

"Why?" He mimicked my voice.

"Why do you want to do this?" My mouth was dry. "Do you really want to start the apocalypse? Do you really think this is going to work?"

Paimon tipped his head to the side. "The apocalypse?" His laugh was deep and it echoed through the gymnasium. "Oh, darlin', is that what the Wardens think?"

"It's what Hell thinks, too."

"The Boss thinks that? Fabulous. While the apocalypse sounds like a good time, I could give a flying rat's ass about that."

Surprise shot through me. "You...you don't want out of Hell?"

"Oh, what demon doesn't want out of Hell? Take me, for example. I've served the Boss for over two thousand years. I'd like nothing more than to say au revoir to that life, but I'm not here because of what I want. I'm here for what I need. Just like you, another means to an end."

"I—I don't understand." I really didn't.

His lips, wide and expressive, twisted into a smirk. "It's rather ironic that you don't. Kind of sad, too."

"Is it?" Naberius was messing with my hand, trying to turn the ring around. "Then explain it to me? If I'm going to die, I'd like to know the real reason behind it."

Paimon looked over his shoulder and then his gaze slid back to me. "Have you ever been in love?"

"What?" I so wasn't expecting that question.

"I said, have you ever been in love?"

"I…" I didn't know. I loved Zayne, but I didn't know what kind of love that was, and Roth… I thought I could be in love with him, if given time. Or maybe I already was, in a little way. "I don't know."

"Interesting," the demon answered. "When you're in love, you'd risk anything to ensure your loved one's happiness. Even the end of the world." He shrugged. "When you're separated from the one you love, you'd do anything to be reacquainted with that person. Anything. What? You look so shocked. Did you think demons couldn't fall in love? We can. Our love is a little dark and twisted. We love until death. Most wouldn't want to be on the receiving end of our affections, but we feel what we feel all the same."

I had no idea what him being in love had to do with raising the Lilin, unless he thought his lover would be reincarnated into one.

His eyes rolled. "I can tell you still haven't figured it out. It's your mother, darlin'. That's why it's ironic."

"Lilith?" I squeaked.

"You can't call her Mother? I'm sure that would warm her cold heart."

"No. No, I cannot."

He prowled along the chalk circle. "Your mother is being kept in the fiery pits—exactly where a devil's trap will send a demon. With the Boss in Hell, no one goes near the pits or gets out. And the only way I can get her out is to lure the Boss topside. Apocalypse now or later, the Boss will venture topside if the Lilin are there. And a minute with my beloved is worth the risk of an eternity without her."

"Which leaves the pits unguarded," I finished. When Paimon clapped his approval, I was stunned. All of this had been to free Lilith because he *loved* her? That was so twisted and...

"Naberius?"

"Wait!" Terror was starting to overcome the panic, which was way worse. "How do you know the incantation will work? You don't even have the *Lesser Key*."

Paimon frowned. "Like I need the *Lesser Key*. I had Lilith— I helped her get free so she could have you."

"You love her, so you helped her get knocked up by someone else?"

"It's the only way that we can truly be together." He shrugged. "And you're ready. I can see the taint of your soul."

I didn't know what surprised me more: that the demon could see my soul, *that I had a soul* or that he thought it was tainted. I just stared at him as I continued to twist the wrist of my left hand, hoping to slide it free.

"When I learned that the Boss was sending Astaroth topside, I was sure it was my birthday. Obviously the Boss thought I needed the *Lesser Key* and he sent him to help me obtain it." He threw his head back and laughed loudly. "Can it get any easier for me? All I needed was time for Roth to get in your pants. And it really was only a matter of time. He is a demon, after all. I can smell your carnal sin, Layla."

I didn't know what carnal sin he was smelling, but it wasn't that. I started to point that out, because that put a major kink in his plans. My *status* was intact, and if he figured it out, there was no stopping him from remedying the problem himself.

I was screwed, but mankind and Earth weren't if I let him believe this. The incantation wouldn't work. The Lilin wouldn't be reborn and he wouldn't get to free Lilith. Numbness settled into my bones as I stared at the demon. I was most likely going to die, but there was the bigger picture. Maybe it was the Warden blood in me that made my fate easier to accept, because I wasn't ready to die. There was so much of life I hadn't experienced. It wasn't fair.

Or maybe it was the humanity I'd picked up from Stacey and Sam.

Letting my head fall back against the cold floor, I stared up into the dark rafters. Beside me, Naberius finally got the jeweled part of the ring to face the right way. He brought the blunt edge of the knife down, cracking its surface.

I bit down as pain exploded along my hand and then cool, sticky wetness spilled across my fingers. The moment the liquid dripped onto the floor inside the circle, the candles flickered.

The chattering and chanting stopped.

"The dead blood of Lilith," Paimon said. "The live blood of Lilith's child."

A quick flick of Naberius's hand, and a sting sliced over my wrist. The cut wasn't deep at all. Really just a pinprick as tiny beads of blood flowed. A thin stream ran down my arm, pooling in the fleshy part of my elbow.

"Now," Paimon said. "There's just the question of your taking a soul."

He didn't know that had already happened? I opened my eyes as a new anxiety burst through me. Paimon yelled something in a coarse, deep language. Movement followed, and I strained to see behind me.

Shadows broke free, and as they came closer to the candlelight, I cried out. *No. No. No.* This couldn't be happening. I struggled wildly against the ropes.

Four Rack demons approached, two sets each carrying a hunched-over body. One set held Zayne and the other set held Roth. Both guys looked as if they'd played kissy face with a meat grinder. Their clothing was torn. Blood streaked their necks and chests.

Paimon smiled like a pleased parent. "Are you wondering how I got the Rack demons to do my bidding?"

"No," I said hoarsely.

"Think about all the suffering they'll be able to feed on once the Lilin turn Earth into a playground," he said anyway. "Naberius?"

Standing, the demon backed out of the circle, careful not to disturb the chalk or candles. In his hand, that knife…

The candles flickered again, and my gaze darted to my arm. One drop of my blood had hit the floor and burned through it like acid. There was no time to wonder why.

"Let's go back to my question about love," Paimon said, coming to stand behind the Rack demons that held Roth and Zayne. "Do you love them? What if I wanted you to take the Warden's soul?"

A low buzzing picked up in my ears as I met the blatant cruelty in Paimon's eyes. "No."

"I didn't think you would agree so easily." Paimon watched Naberius walk around Roth. His dark head was bowed and his shoulders barely moving. There wasn't even a reaction as Naberius slipped the knife under Roth's still chin. "They caught him coming to the Warden's rescue. How utterly ridiculous is that? A demon helping out a Warden? Then again, he was probably coming to save you."

I pulled on the ropes until my skin and muscles burned. "Let them go."

"Oh, I plan to." Paimon smiled. "If you don't take the Warden's soul, then Naberius here will gladly cut the Crown Prince's head right off."

"And I really, really want to do that," Naberius added.

A pounding heart joined the buzzing in my ears. Horror poured into me. "No. You can't—you can't do this."

Paimon laughed. "I can and I will. Either you take the Warden's soul or I kill Roth. Now, I know how incredibly naive and stupid teenage girls are. But surely you're not going to want to watch your first get beheaded, are you?"

Roth wasn't my first—no one was my first, but that didn't mean I could allow this to happen. Potent, helpless fury rolled through me, stretching my skin tight.

"And he won't just die," Paimon continued. "Oh, he'll feel it." Moving lightning quick, he grabbed a handful of Roth's hair and yanked his head back. "Won't you, Your Highness?"

A shudder rolled through Roth's body and his eyes opened. "Screw you," he spat.

"How terribly boring." Paimon let go of Roth's head, but it didn't fall back. His eyes met mine. They were surprisingly alert for someone who looked like he was in such bad shape. Paimon glanced at Zayne. "Roth will end up in the fiery pits, which is worse than death."

Terror formed painful knots in my stomach. I couldn't take Zayne's soul and watch him turn into the monster that Petr had. And I couldn't let them kill Roth.

"What is your answer, Layla?"

A low, terrible rumble came from Roth's chest. "Layla…"

My gaze swung back to him. His eyes were dilated, glowing. "I can't."

"Don't," he growled. "Don't do—" The knife moved in, pressing against his neck until fresh blood welled up.

"Stop!" I screamed. My hands tried to curl into fists, but I couldn't make them move. "Just stop!"

Paimon raised a hand and Naberius backed up. "Yes?"

"Layla, don't say another word! You—" Naberius's fist silenced Roth.

"I don't need to take his soul," I gasped out. "I've already taken a soul—a pure soul."

Paimon stared at me for a moment and then he barked out a loud laugh. "Well, well. This is an interesting development."

"Yes. Yes! It was a Warden. I took his soul." My breath was coming out too fast and in a strange pattern. One breath in. Two breaths out.

"Huh. I didn't see that one coming." He looked perplexed, and I wondered if that was the taint he'd sensed and mistaken for the whole carnal-activity thing. It didn't matter, though. He snapped his fingers.

The Rack demons dropped Zayne on the floor and he lay there, an unmoving lump of flesh and bone. A second later, Naberius was behind him and had grabbed a handful of blond hair and yanked Zayne's head back, exposing his throat.

"Well, even with all that said and done, you know what they say about Wardens?" Paimon's slow smile stretched across his face. "The only good one..."

Naberius waved the wicked-looking dagger, placing the deadly sharp edge to Zayne's throat. "Is a dead one," the other demon finished.

"No!" I screamed, and my back bowed.

Zayne's bloodshot eyes opened into thin slits.

I threw my head back and my own scream deafened me. So many images flickered through my mind like a photo album, coming together and crashing gloriously in a moment of raw pain greater than any I'd known.

The rage unlocked the demon inside me.

As I wrenched forward, the ropes around my arms stretched. Thread unraveled, splitting at the ends, and then the twine broke. My legs were freed next. Seconds later, I was standing. Air didn't pass through my throat. Fire did, scorching my insides and spilling through my veins. I was burning from the inside out. Muscles tightened. Hands curved into claws. My vision sharpened and tinted the world in red. Bones broke in a burst of pain and then fused back together. Static clung to skin that felt stretched too thin. Pieces of clothing tore as my body shifted, expanded with ropy muscles and grew. My sneakers split wide open and fell to the side.

Tiny strands of hair rose all around my head. Pain exploded along my back, but it was the good kind of pain—the kind that brought sweet relief as my wings unfurled, arcing high in the air above me.

As I lifted my hands, shock fluttered through me. My skin was black and gray, marbleized in a shifting blend of both species. A beautiful mixture of the Warden and the demon long since buried deep inside me.

"Get her!" screamed Paimon.

The Rack demons that had been holding Zayne shot toward me just as Roth reared back, breaking free of the demons holding him.

On autopilot, controlled by something innate and binding, I didn't even think. Raising my head, I bared my teeth and hissed.

I caught the first Rack demon by the throat, digging my claws in. There was a satisfying crack and I dropped it. The second Rack demon I toyed with, catching it by the neck and lifting it into the air. The hoarse, piglike squealing brought a toothy smile to my face. Wheeling around, I tossed it through the wall above the bleachers.

Stepping out over the candles, I stretched out my wings.

Bloodied and beat up like no tomorrow, Roth grinned at me as he dropped one of the Rack demons. "You're still hot as a stone freak." His gaze dropped. "Maybe even hotter. Damn."

"Get them!" Paimon roared. "Kill them! Do something!"

My head swung toward where he stood beside Zayne. Launching off the floor, I landed in front of the demon. Swinging my arm around, I backhanded him, throwing him into the air and spinning him around.

I knelt beside Zayne, gingerly rolling him onto his back. "Zayne?"

His eyes were open, blinking furiously. "I'm okay. The cut's not deep at all." He folded his hand around mine—his human hand over mine. The contrast was all the more startling because of our role reversal. His gaze traveled up my arm, where the sleeves of my sweater had split at the seams. His lips parted as he got a good eyeful. "You're…"

"Layla!" Roth yelled.

Twisting at the waist, I swiped out at the Rack demon gunning for me. The thing went down, but there were dozens, if not hundreds, more. The whole gymnasium was full of them. And behind them, bigger and hairier creatures roared.

Hellions.

"I'm okay." Zayne staggered to his feet. "I can fight."

"I sure hope so." Roth lifted his arm and Bambi came off his skin, coiling on the floor between us. "Because if you're just going to lay there and bleed, you suck."

Then Roth shifted. His skin turned the color of obsidian, sleek and shiny. He was bigger than both Zayne, who was now in full gargoyle mode, and me. The skin tone was different and he wasn't rocking any horns, but the resemblance between us was still uncanny.

The three of us turned as one.

Beyond Paimon and Naberius, a whole horde of demons waited.

They charged forward. A chaotic mess of bodies, and there was no time to think as bodies crashed into one another. Taking down a Rack demon, I ducked out of the way of a Hellion, clearing a path for Bambi, who shot through the air and sank its fangs into the beast's neck. The snake coiled itself around the Hellion, squeezing until the Hellion arched its back and roared. Black smoke poured out of its gaping mouth and then the Hellion imploded.

Roth went after Paimon, while Zayne had an obvious bone to pick with Naberius after the whole knifing-of-the-throat incident. Which sucked, because I would've really liked to knock that jerk around instead of picking off Rack demons.

"You have been such a pain in my ass," Roth said, circling Paimon. "The Boss is going to have so much fun shoving hot pokers where the sun never shines."

"Well, if it isn't the harmless puppy of the family," Paimon seethed. "The favorite Prince and the Boss's little pet."

"Don't be a hater." Roth lowered himself to the floor. It trembled under his weight. "You're just jealous because you haven't been granted permission to return topside since the Inquisition. You always make such a mess of things."

"While you're just a good little boy." Paimon shook out his shoulders. Material ripped. Dark, gnarled wings protruded from his back. The fire spread over Paimon's skin until he was nothing more than a flame in an Armani suit. "I'm going to enjoy breaking her. Burn her from the inside out. You'll hear her screams from the bowels of Hell."

Roth roared, charging Paimon. He met Roth halfway, their collision a burst of flames and then darkness. I scrambled back as Paimon launched Roth through the air and slammed him into a row of Hellions. Roth flew back, reaching into the flames and grabbing ahold of Paimon. Roth spun around, tossing the King at a cluster of Rack demons.

The doors to the gymnasium burst open.

Wardens swarmed the room, tearing through Rack demons like they were nothing more than paper. I recognized Abbot and Nicolai leading the attack. They headed straight to where Bambi had a Hellion cornered. The massive monster lurched forward, grabbing Bambi before she could wrap her powerful body around the beast.

Bambi was flung back into the bleachers, crashing through them.

Concern for the snake powered through me as I punted a Rack into the basketball pole and started forward.

"Layla?" Abbot's voice rang loudly through the room.

I stopped and turned to him. The shock in his voice, mirrored in his expression, would've been funny any other time. "I guess I'm not a mule—not really."

He might've responded but there were tons of demons to kill, and for the first time in my life, I threw myself into battle. The strength of a Warden coursed through me, as heady and powerful as tasting a soul was. The Rack demon's claws didn't even break my skin. I was stronger and faster than I could ever have imagined.

I caught up with Zayne, grabbing Naberius from behind. The demon fought wildly, but I held him in place as Zayne swung out, taking the head right off the demon.

There was no time to celebrate the victory. Roth struggled with Paimon, who no doubt had seen his dreams crash and burn by now and was trying to make an escape. I started toward them, but Zayne stopped me.

"No. I owe him this."

It went against my instincts but I held myself back as Zayne dipped under Paimon's arm and grabbed him from behind. The three of them staggered backward. I realized they were dragging him back toward the pentagram.

"Father," Zayne shouted, and Abbot spun.

They were going to trap Paimon!

As the Wardens finished off the rest of the demons, Zayne and Roth pinned Paimon in the pentagram, holding him down face-first. Together, they tied Paimon down just as I'd been minutes before.

"Tell the Boss I said hi," Roth said, forcing his knee into Paimon's back as he tightened the last of the rope. "Oh, wait. You won't be doing much talking. More like a whole lot of screaming."

Roth stood and both he and Zayne turned to leave the trap as Abbot neared the pentagram. It was over, I realized. It was all finally over. My eyes moved from Zayne to Roth. Both of them in their real forms, which were as frightening as they were oddly beautiful.

In his demon form, Roth winked.

My lips twitched into a smile. I let out a breath and it was like shedding a skin. Muscles unclenched and shrunk. A few seconds later, I was me again, standing in shredded, stretched-out clothing and barefoot.

And then everything went to Hell.

Paimon let out an inhuman roar and his body contracted. Ropes burst and whipped out. The demon rose high and grabbed the closest target, dragging Zayne back into the circle. My heart plummeted and a scream got stuck in my throat.

"Do it," Zayne yelled, his eyes widening on his father. "Do it now!"

Ice drenched my veins. Anything in the devil's trap was *trapped*—human, Warden or demon. Zayne would go to the pits along with Paimon.

Horror seized me. "No!"

Roth whirled around, and in a flurry of motion, he grabbed Zayne and tore him free from Paimon's clutches. Pushing him outside the circle, Roth then wrapped his arms around Paimon.

A new understanding sank in. There was no way Paimon would just sit docilely and stay in the trap. Ropes wouldn't hold him. Someone had to, and Roth had just made that choice.

"Get her down!" Roth yelled, holding Paimon in the trap. "Zayne, do it!"

"No! No!" I raced forward, bare feet slipping across blood and gunk, just as Abbot tossed the black salt toward the trap. "Roth! No!"

In that tiny moment of time, just a flicker of a second, his golden eyes met mine. "Free will, huh? Damn. It *is* a bitch." And then he smiled—*he smiled*—at me, a real smile, revealing those deep dimples. "I lost myself the moment I found you."

My voice broke, and my heart...

Zayne's arms wrapped around me and he turned, forcing me down onto my knees. His wings stretched out and then curled around me as his body bent, sheltering me.

Red light flashed, so brilliant and intense that it blinded me from underneath Zayne. A howling wind roared through the gymnasium. I screamed. *I screamed* because I knew Roth would make no sound as the fiery pits welcomed him. And I didn't stop screaming. Not when the smell of sulfur choked me. Not when the blistering heat hit us, causing tiny dots of sweat to break out across my skin. Not until the wind, the heat and the smell of sulfur receded.

Then there was silence.

"I'm sorry," Zayne whispered, and then he loosened his grip.

I tore free, taking a few steps toward the burned-out circle before my legs gave out. I fell to my knees. The space where Roth had stood with Paimon was scorched, the floor charred through.

Someone said something to me. Maybe Abbot or Nicolai. It didn't matter. There was nothing they could say right now. Roth had sacrificed himself for me—for Zayne. A demon had chosen an eternity of suffering for someone else.

I couldn't bear it.

Tears tracked down my cheeks, mixing with blood and soot. I lowered my head until my forehead rested against the floor and I did something I hadn't done in forever.

I prayed.

I prayed for Roth. I prayed for the Alphas to step in. What he had done should've earned him a divine intervention. I prayed that the angels would descend into Hell and lift him up. I prayed until I wanted to scream again.

But prayers like this weren't answered.

Something cool and slick nudged my hand, and I slowly

lifted my head. Blinked once and then twice before I believed what I was seeing. "Bambi?"

The large snake coiled around my arm, raising her head until she rested it on my shoulder. A fresh wave of tears clouded my eyes, but not enough to prevent me from seeing a Warden coming toward us with a murderous look in his eyes as they landed on Bambi.

"Do it and it'll be the last thing you do," I warned in a voice I barely recognized.

The Warden stopped and then backed off. No one else came near us.

My gaze swiveled back to the circle. Near the stake on the right, a tiny hole had burned through the floor. Most likely a blowback from Hell and nothing like that charred spot in the center, on which Astaroth, the Crown Prince of Hell, had made a very un-demonlike stand.

I lost myself the moment I found you.

I stared at that spot.

Roth was gone.

TUCKING THE ICY BLOND STRANDS of hair back into a messy bun at the nape of my neck, I picked up my tank top. The material felt weightless in my fingers. Sometimes I felt weightless.

In a few days I'd be going back to school, making a miraculous recovery from mono, much to Stacey and Sam's delight. Classes had been canceled for three days after a little piece of Hell had visited the school. Abbot and the police commissioner had convinced school officials that they'd thwarted some kind of domestic terrorist attempt.

The general populace remained unaware that demons walked among them and of the Wardens' true purpose. The threat of the Lilin was over—sort of. At least as long as there weren't any more demons who were in love with Lilith or wanted to kick-start the end of the world. Things were about to go back to normal. As if October and November never happened. So all was good, at least for the Alphas and the Wardens.

I hadn't shifted since that night not too long ago.

Maybe I'd never do it again, and Abbot hadn't pushed the issue. I wasn't a mule anymore, but I wasn't like other Wardens, either. If anything, now that I knew what I looked like, I felt more different than I had before.

I also tried not to think of Petr and my father, knowing that Elijah was still out there and most likely plotting my untimely demise. None of that really mattered right now. I'd deal with him when the day came.

But for the time being, there were more important things to deal with.

My eyes moved to the mirror, and like every day since the showdown in the old gymnasium, I was surprised. Years would probably pass before I got used to what I saw.

I twisted in front of the mirror, oddly relieved and comforted by what I saw in my reflection. My new and unexpected tattoo served as a bittersweet reminder.

Lowering my gaze, I let out an unsteady breath as tears pricked my eyes. Bambi had fused to the only demon left standing. Me. She was much too big for my body, but we were trying to make it work. Right now her lower body was wrapped around my torso; her thick, shiny onyx neck stretched between my breasts and sloped over my neck. The diamond-shaped head rested on the back of my shoulder. Somehow the detail still amazed me. Each scale perfectly replicated; the darker line running down the center of her body and the softer underbelly.

I ran my hand over my tummy and her tail twitched. The movement startled me, even tickled a little.

"You've got to stop that," I told her.

Bambi shifted her head and I shuddered, the feeling giving me the willies. The snake shared some of Roth's personality. In the short time she'd been with me, I truly thought Bambi lived to find new ways to torment me. Like in the middle of the night when she wanted to come off and go hunt. What she was hunting I was afraid to even find out.

I just hoped it wasn't small animals…or children.

Or when she shifted on my skin so she'd be visible when

Zayne was around, just like I imagined Roth would've done if he...

Tugging my tank top on, I cut that thought off, but the back of my throat burned. I closed my eyes and took several deep breaths, refocusing back on Bambi.

Yesterday she had made her way to the side of my face when Zayne had been watching a movie with me, and she wouldn't leave no matter what I did.

Zayne tried to ignore her, but all that did was provoke Bambi into coming off my skin and flopping her head right on his upper thigh.

So, yeah, the snake was like Roth.

There was a knock on my door, drawing my attention. "Yeah?"

Zayne came in, his hair pulled back in a low ponytail. I was expecting him today, and not just because he'd been spending a lot of time with me. We really didn't talk about what had gone down or what Roth had done for him—for us. But I knew it bothered him that he didn't know the right thing to say.

I didn't, either.

So we'd just spent a lot of time together since then, and there weren't enough words in this world that could show my gratitude. Zayne's presence had done what Roth had known it would. It kept the rougher, darker edges of the pain at bay. Our bond since childhood was like a buffer, blocking out the harsh reality that I'd lost a part of me before I'd been given a chance to realize it.

"Are you sure you want to go with me?" I asked.

"Yes." His gaze dipped along the hem of my tank top. "Man, I hate how that thing just moves all over your..."

"Body?"

A faint pink crept over the hollow of his cheeks. "Yeah, that."

I laughed softly. "Hey, Bambi's a girl."

"Doesn't make it any better," he grumbled as he picked up my hoodie and handed it to me.

I took it from him. "I think she likes you." I slipped it on and then zipped up the front. "I think that's why she messes with you."

"I think she hates me and that's why." He reached out and straightened the strings so they were even. "The snake's a—"

Bambi's tail suddenly slithered up my waist, and I jerked to the side, giggling.

Zayne lowered his hands. "What?"

"Bambi," I gasped. "She's moving—it tickles."

His eyes narrowed as his lips turned down at the corners.

"That mean face doesn't help. It provokes her." I smiled when Zayne's eyes rolled, but the smile quickly faded when I thought of what lay ahead. "You ready?"

"Are you?"

"No," I whispered and then shook my head. "Yes."

Zayne waited. "It's okay. Take whatever time you need. I'm here with you."

Just as Roth had known he'd be.

We parked several blocks from Roth's apartment, and Zayne waited at a small park a block down. I didn't think the demons would be thrilled with a Warden's presence even though Zayne wouldn't try anything today. I wasn't sure how welcome I'd be with my Warden blood, but it wasn't going to stop me.

Taking a deep breath, I pushed open the doors and stepped into the opulent lobby, looking around. Demons were pretty scarce. There was a Fiend sitting on a couch, drinking a cup of coffee while messing with his phone.

He looked up, spotted me and then went back to his screen. Okay. I prowled toward the stairs, hitting my destination without interruption. I reached the door to the stairwell, but my gaze went to the elevator nearby—the portal to Hell.

"I know what you're thinking."

I spun around. "Cayman."

The infernal ruler tilted his head in acknowledgment. "There's no way you can go down and find Roth."

I opened my mouth, but he kept going. "If you don't get eaten by the first dozen or so demons you come across and you actually make it to the pits, the Boss still isn't going to let you in."

Exhaling roughly, I glared at the elevator's doors. "I'm not stupid enough to try it."

"No. You're not. But a moment of desperation could've led you to make a very unwise decision. It's not what Roth would've wanted."

I squeezed my eyes shut. "I hate that you talk about him like he's dead."

"Isn't that how you think of him?"

The sharp slice of agony that lit up my chest told me yes. "I just want to go to his apartment. That's all. He had these kittens..."

"Oh, the three little monsters?" he asked. "They were tattoos."

My eyes widened. "They were? I never saw them on him."

Cayman stepped around me and opened the stairway door. "He rarely had them on. I don't know if he did that night. I haven't thought to check his room."

"You're going to let me?"

He gestured toward the stairwell. "After you."

In silence we headed up to the top level, the muscles in my legs burning by the time he unlocked Roth's door.

When I stepped in, Cayman remained outside. I don't know what I was expecting to feel by going in here, but nothing could prepare me for the aching void that opened in my heart at the musky scent.

Things were the way Roth had left them, I guessed. There was a book on his desk, turned facedown. I picked it up and saw that it was *Tales of Poe*. Smiling faintly, I placed it back the way I'd found it. I don't know why, but I didn't want to disturb his things.

I sat on his bed and waited for the little furballs to materialize and attach themselves to any exposed skin, but they never did. And I still sat there, my gaze tracking across the walls, the books, the TV and all the little things that made Roth real—made him more than just another Crown Prince.

Swallowing hard, I knelt down and lifted the covers. No kittens. I checked behind the piano. Nothing. The same in the bathroom. The closet was surprisingly empty. I wondered where Roth got his clothes. I checked all the nooks and crannies in the loft. The kittens were gone.

I glanced at the hallway beyond the open door.

Cayman waited. "He must have been wearing them."

I nodded. I didn't know if I should be relieved or not. At least they hadn't been left here to starve. Then again, I had no idea what they ate. Probably blood.

"I just need another second," I said.

Cayman smiled faintly, and I turned, opening the door to the roof. Up the stairs I went, one last time. The garden flourished and the knot in my throat grew. A demon that gardened? Roth… God, Roth was nothing but surprises.

Taking in the lounges and softly moving canopies, I sighed and made my way to the edge of the roof. The pain inside me felt too real, and I really couldn't imagine it going away. Logic told me it would fade one day, but—

The sweet, musky smell came out of nowhere, overwhelming the scents of the flowers surrounding me. Tiny hairs rose on my body as a shiver of awareness danced over my skin.

I spun around, heart pounding against my ribs. "Roth?"

No one was there, but his scent lingered as my gaze tracked back to the chaise lounge. Something metallic caught my eye. Moving toward it, I found a silver chain coiled on the tiny table beside the lounge. It hadn't been there seconds before. I picked it up, surprise stealing my breath.

It was my chain—the one Petr had broken. But the clasps had been repaired, the metal cleaned until it looked shiny and new. I knew it was mine because I'd never seen a chain so intricately knotted before, as if it matched the ring. In a way, I guessed it did.

Tears clogged my throat as I slowly turned around. It couldn't have been...but where had the necklace come from?

"Roth?" I whispered, my voice cracking halfway through his name. "Are you here?"

I don't know what I expected. For him to pop out of nowhere in front of me like he normally did? He didn't. I glanced down at the necklace. It *hadn't* been there.

A warm breeze, more like a soft breath of air, caressed my cheek, causing my heart to jump, and then...then the musky scent faded away, as if it had never been.

Closing my fingers around the chain, I pressed it against my chest and squeezed my eyes shut. The ache increased until I thought it would surely pull me under.

God, as much as I hated to cry, I respected the tears that sneaked out of my tightly closed lids. They meant something. They meant everything. They were the only way I could repay Roth for what he'd sacrificed.

Cayman was still waiting in the hall when I returned. "I'll take care of the garden."

I blinked slowly. "Thank you."

We didn't speak as we went back downstairs and I started toward the door, my heart and thoughts irrevocably heavy. I didn't know what the necklace really meant, if I had just not seen it at first or if his scent was simply a product of my hope-fueled imagination. I wasn't sure, but the hand that held the necklace shook.

"Layla?"

I turned back to Cayman. "Yeah?"

He smiled a little. More of a grimace, but I guess for a demon, it counted. "You know, demons don't die when they go to the pits. Roth did his job, Layla. He came here to stop the Lilin from rising." His gaze locked with mine. "The fiery pits are kind of one-way only, but the Boss is old-school, and Roth has been the Boss's favorite Crown Prince yet."

I sucked in a breath, too close to everything to let that little spark of hope grow. "What are you saying?" Hand still trembling, I held out the necklace for him to see. "I found this on the roof. It wasn't there when I first went up, and then it was."

Cayman's smile stretched a little and then he shrugged as he slipped his hands into his pockets. He turned, heading across the lobby. Halfway between the couches and chairs, he glanced over his shoulder at me and winked. Then he blinked out of existence.

Hope and disbelief warred inside me. I wanted—needed—to believe that Roth wasn't in those pits. That he was okay, that it was he who'd left the necklace for me. It made facing tomorrow a little easier, thinking there might be a chance I'd see him again. One day.

I'm not sure how long I stood there, but finally I forced myself to move. Zayne had to be getting itchy out there.

Stepping out of the apartment building, I inhaled the brisk air. Zayne waited where I'd left him, like he had said he would. Sensing me, he lifted his golden head. He didn't smile. Whether or not he gave voice to what he suspected my feelings for Roth were and whether or not he agreed with them, he still knew how I felt.

On the spur of the moment, I felt for my ring. It came off easily, the cracked surface catching the light. Without Lilith's blood, the ring looked more like a normal stone. There really wasn't any need for me to keep it, but I couldn't get rid of it. Not yet.

When I handed the chain and ring to Zayne, he seemed to

know what to do with them. The spot where Bambi had tattooed herself on my arm itched like crazy. I resisted the urge to scratch myself raw while Zayne slipped the chain through the ring.

"Did…did you take care of what you needed to?" he asked, brushing at a strand of blond hair that had escaped his ponytail.

I cleared my throat, but the lump was still there. "I think so."

Zayne wiggled his fingers and I turned around, forcing myself to take another deep breath. While he clasped the chain behind my neck, my gaze traveled up to Roth's loft. The windows were too dark to see in. Not that anyone would be there, but I'd never be able to tell.

"You ready?" Zayne asked.

The pain in my chest eased a tiny bit when I looked into Zayne's blue eyes. I tried to smile for him, and I think the little effort relieved him. He knew I wasn't going to curl up and wither away because I'd lost Roth. However, there were moments when that was the only thing I wanted to do.

I dropped the necklace under my sweater, patting where it rested between my breasts.

He offered me his hand.

And I took it, threading my fingers through his. We started down the street quietly. My heart raced with each step that took me farther away from everything that reminded me of Roth. I couldn't stop even though I wanted to turn around and race back to his apartment, camp out until…until forever passed. Every so often, I looked over my shoulder, searching for a headful of dark hair and a smile that infuriated and excited me. I strained to hear the humming of "Paradise City." Out of all the faces crowding the street, I didn't see the one I was looking for.

But I thought of the necklace and of Cayman's wink and I wondered if one day I would find it again.

★ ★ ★ ★ ★

*Turn the page to get a sneak peek at the next book in
Jennifer L. Armentrout's Dark Elements series:*
Stone Cold Touch

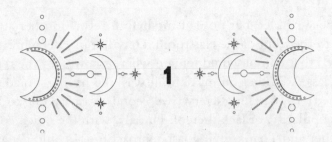

1

TEN SECONDS AFTER MRS. CLEO moseyed on into biology class, flipped on the projector, and turned off the lights, Bambi decided she was no longer comfortable where she was currently curled around my waist.

Sliding along my stomach, the very active demonic snake tattoo was not a fan of sitting still for any length of time, especially not during a boring lecture on the food chain. I stiffened, resisting the urge to giggle like a hyena as she cruised up between my breasts and rested her diamond-shaped head on my shoulder.

Five more seconds passed while Stacey stared at me, her brows raised. I forced a tight smile, knowing Bambi wasn't done yet. Nope. Her tongue flicked out, tickling the side of my neck.

I clamped my hand over my mouth, stifling a giggle as I squirmed in my seat.

"Are you on drugs?" Stacey asked in a low voice as she brushed thick bangs out of her dark eyes. "Or is my left boob hanging out and saying hello to the world? Because as my best friend, you're obligated to tell me."

Even though I knew her boob was in her shirt, or at least I hoped so since her V-neck sweater was pretty low-cut, my gaze dipped as I lowered my hand. "Your boob is fine. I'm just… antsy."

She wrinkled her nose at me before returning her attention to the front of the classroom. Drawing in a deep breath, I prayed that Bambi would remain where she was for the rest of the class. With her on my skin, it was like having a mad case of the tics. Twitching every five seconds wasn't going to help my popularity, or lack thereof. Luckily, with the much cooler weather and Thanksgiving fast approaching, I could get away with wearing turtlenecks and long sleeves, which hid Bambi from sight.

Well, as long as she didn't decide to crawl up on my face. Something she liked to do whenever Zayne was around. He was an absolutely gorgeous Warden—a member of the race of creatures who could look human at will, but whose true form was what humans called gargoyles. Wardens were tasked with protecting mankind, hunting what went bump in the night— and during the day. I'd grown up with Zayne and had nursed one heck of a puppy dog crush on him for years.

I had no idea how Roth had dealt with Bambi crawling all over him.

My breath caught as a deep, unforgiving pang hit me in the chest. Without thinking, I reached for the ring with the cracked stone—the ring that had once held the blood of my mother, *the* Lilith—dangling from my necklace. Feeling the cool metal between my fingers was calming. Not because of the familial bond, since I really didn't claim a relationship with my mother, but because along with Bambi, it was my last and only link to Astaroth, the crown prince of Hell, who had done the most un-demonic thing.

I lost myself the moment I found you.

Roth had sacrificed himself by being the one to hold Paimon, the bastard responsible for wanting to unleash an especially nasty race of demons, in a devil's trap meant to send its captive to Hell. Zayne had been doing the honors of keeping Paimon from escaping, but Roth...he'd taken Zayne's place.

And now he was in the fiery pits.

Leaning forward, I propped my elbows on the cool table, completely unaware of what Mrs. Cleo was droning on about. Tears burned the back of my throat as I stared at the empty chair in front of me that used to belong to Roth. I closed my eyes.

Two weeks. Three hundred and thirty six hours, give or take a few, had passed since that night in the old gymnasium and not a second had gotten easier. It hurt like it had happened an hour ago and I wasn't sure if a month or even a year from now would be any different.

One of the hardest parts was all the lies. When Roth hadn't returned after the night we'd located the *Lesser Key of Solomon*, the ancient book that had the answers to everything we'd needed to know about my mother, and had been caught by Abbot, the leader of the Warden clan in D.C. that had adopted me as a young girl, Stacey and Sam had asked a hundred questions. They'd stopped eventually, but it was still another secret I was keeping from them, two of my closest friends.

Despite our friendship, neither of them knew what I was—half Warden, half demon. And neither of them realized that Roth hadn't just been out with mono or changed schools. But sometimes it was easier to think of him that way—to tell myself he was just at another school instead of where he was.

The burn moved into my chest, much like the low simmer in my veins that was always present. The need to take a soul, the curse my mother had passed onto me, hadn't diminished one bit over the two weeks. If anything, it had seemed to increase. The ability to draw souls out of any creature that had one was why I hadn't ever gotten close to a boy before.

Not until Roth had come along.

Being that he was a demon, the pesky soul problem was a moot point. He didn't have one. And unlike Abbot and almost all of the Warden clan, even Zayne, Roth hadn't cared that I was a mixed breed. He had...he'd accepted me as I was.

Scrubbing my palms over my eyes, I bit the inside of my cheek. When I'd found my repaired and cleaned up necklace—the one Petr, a Warden who turned out to be my half-brother, had broken during his attack on me—at Roth's apartment, I'd clung to the hope that Roth wasn't in the pits after all. That he'd somehow escaped, but with each passing day, that hope flickered out like a candle in the middle of a hurricane.

I believed more than anything in this world that if Roth could've come back to me, he would have by now, and that meant...

When my chest squeezed painfully, I opened my eyes and slowly let out the breath I'd been holding. The room was a little blurry through the haze of unshed tears. I blinked a couple of times as I slumped back in my seat. Whatever was on the slide projector made no sense to me. Something to do with the circle of life? No, that was *The Lion King*. I was so going to fail this class. Figuring I should at least attempt to take notes, I picked up my pen and—

At the front of the class, the metal legs from a chair scrapped across the floor, screeching loudly. A boy exploded out of his chair as if someone had lit a fire under his butt. A faint yellow glow surrounded him—his aura. I was the only one who could see it, but it sputtered erratically, blinking in and out. Seeing people's auras—a reflection of their souls—was nothing new for me. They were all kinds of colors, sometimes a mixture of more than two, but I'd never seen one waver like that before. I glanced around the room and the mixture of auras glimmered faintly.

What the hell?

Mrs. Cleo's hand was frozen above the projector as she frowned. "Dean McDaniel, what in the world are you—"

Dean spun on his heel, facing the two guys sitting behind him. They were leaning back in their seats, their arms crossed and lips curved up in identical smirks. Dean's mouth was pressed into a thin line and his face was flushed. My mouth dropped open as he planted one hand on the white tabletop and slammed his other fist into the jaw of the kid behind him. The fleshy smack echoed through the classroom, followed by several surprised gasps.

Holy granola bar!

I sat up straight as Stacey slapped her hands on our table. "Holy shit balls for Sunday dinner," she whispered, gaping as the boy Dean had punched slumped to the left and hit the floor like a bag of potatoes.

I didn't know Dean very well. Hell, I wasn't sure if I'd spoken more than a handful of words to him during my four years in high school, but he was quiet and average, tall and slender, much like Sam.

Totally not the kind of kid who'd be voted most likely to knock another guy—a much bigger guy—into next week.

"Dean!" shouted Mrs. Cleo, her ample chest rising as she rushed to the wall, flipping the overhead lights on. "What are—?"

The other guy shot up like an arrow, hands clenching into meaty fists at his sides. "What the hell is wrong with you?" He rounded the table, shrugging out of his zipped hoodie. "You want some of this?"

Stuff always got real when the clothes started to come off.

Dean snickered as he stalked to the aisle. Chairs screeched as students moved out of the way. "Oh, I'm about to get me some of that."

"Boy fight!" Stacey exclaimed as she dug around in her bag,

pulling out her cell phone. Several other students were doing the same thing. "I so have to get this on camera."

"Boys! Stop it right now." Mrs. Cleo smacked her hand against the wall, hitting the intercom wired directly to the front office. A beep sounded and she turned to it frantically. "I need the security guard in room two-oh-four immediately!"

Dean launched himself at his opponent, tackling him to the floor. Arms flew as they rolled into the legs of a nearby table. In the back of the classroom, we were safe, but Stacey and I stood. A shiver coursed over my skin as Bambi shifted without warning, flicking her tail across my stomach.

Stacey stretched up on the tips of her boots, apparently needing a better angle for her phone. "This is…"

"Bizarre?" I supplied, flinching as the boy got a good hit in, knocking Dean's head back.

She arched a brow at me. "I was going to go with *awesome*."

"But they're—" I jumped as the classroom door swung open and banged into the wall.

Security officers swarmed the class, heading straight for the melee. One beefy guy wrapped his arms around Dean, dragging him off the other student as Mrs. Cleo buzzed around the room like a nervous hummingbird, clutching her tacky, beaded necklace with both hands.

A middle-aged security guard knelt beside the boy Dean had first punched. Only then did I realize the boy hadn't stirred once since hitting the floor. A trickle of unease formed in my belly, having nothing to do with the way Bambi was moving again, as the guard leaned over the prone boy, placing his head near his chest.

The guard jerked back, reaching for the microphone on his shoulder. His face was white as the paper in my notebook. "I need an EMT immediately dispatched. I have a teenage male, approximately seventeen or eighteen years of age. Visible bruising along the skull. He's not breathing."

"Oh my God," I whispered, clutching Stacey's arm.

A hush descended over the room, quelling the excited chatter. Mrs. Cleo stopped by her desk, her jowls jiggling silently. Stacey sucked in a breath as she lowered her phone.

The silence following the urgent call was broken when Dean threw back his head and laughed as the other security guard dragged him from the classroom.

Stacey tucked her shoulder length black hair back behind her ears. She hadn't touched the slice of pizza on her plate or her can of soda. Neither had I. She was probably thinking along the same lines that I was. Principal Blunt and the guidance counselor I'd never really paid attention to had given all the students in the class the option to go home.

I didn't have a ride. Morris, the clan's chauffeur, handy man and all around awesome guy, was still on the no-ride list with me since the last time we'd been in a car together, a possessed cab driver had tried to play chicken with our vehicles. And I didn't want to wake up Zayne or Nicolai—for the most part, full-blooded Wardens slept deeply during the day, entombed in their hard shells. And Stacey didn't want to be home with her baby brother. So here we were, in the cafeteria.

But neither of us had an appetite.

"I'm officially traumatized," she said, taking a deep breath. "Seriously."

"It's not like the guy is dead," Sam replied around a mouthful of pizza. His wire frame glasses slipped to the tip of his nose. Curly brown hair flopped over his forehead. His soul, a faint mixture of yellow and blue, flickered just like everyone else's had since this morning, winking in and out like it was playing peekaboo with me. "I heard he was revived in the ambulance."

"That still doesn't change the fact that we saw someone get punched in the face so hard that they *died* right in front of us," she insisted, eyes wide. "Or are you missing the point?"

Sam swallowed the bite of pizza. "How do you know he really died? Just because a wannabe police officer says that someone's not breathing doesn't mean that's true." He glanced over at my plate. "You gonna eat that?"

I shook my head at him, sort of dumbfounded. "It's all yours." A second later, he snatched the pizza with the little pepperoni cubes off my plate. His gaze flickered up to mine. "Are you okay?" I asked.

He nodded as he munched away. "Sorry. I know I don't sound very sympathetic."

"Ya think?" Stacey muttered dryly.

A dull ache flared behind my eyes as I reached for my soda. I needed caffeine. I also needed to figure out what the hell was up with everyone's auras doing the wonky thing. The colorful shading around a human represented what kind of soul they were rocking: white for an utterly pure soul, pastels were the most common and usually indicated a good soul, and the darker the colors got, the more questionable the status of one's soul became. And if a human didn't have that tell-tale halo around him, that meant he was on Team No Soul.

AKA he was a demon.

I wasn't doing much tagging anymore—another nifty ability I had thanks to my mixed heritage. If I touched a demon, it was equivalent to sticking a neon sign on their body, which made it easier for Wardens to search them out.

Well, it didn't work on Upper Level demons. Not much did.

I didn't stop because of what had happened with Paimon and being forbidden to tag. Abbot had un-grounded me for life after the night in the gymnasium, but it felt wrong to randomly tag demons, especially now that I knew many of them might be harmless. When I did tag, I went for the Posers, since they were dangerous and had a habit of biting people, and left the Fiends alone.

And truthfully, the change in my tagging routine was all thanks to Roth.

"It's just that those two idiots were probably messing with Dean," Sam continued as he finished off the pizza in a nanosecond. "People snap."

"People usually don't have fists that could be considered lethal weapons," Stacey retorted.

My phone chirped, drawing my attention. Bending, I pulled it out of my bag. The corners of my lips tipped up when I saw it was from Zayne even though the pain behind my eyes steadily increased.

Nic is picking u up. Meet me in the training room when u get home.

Ah, training. My stomach did a funny little twist, a familiar reaction when it came to training with Zayne. Because at some point during the grappling and evasive techniques, he'd get sweaty and inevitably, his shirt would come off. And well, even though I was hurting something fierce over the loss of Roth, seeing Zayne shirtless was something to look forward to.

And Zayne…he'd always meant the world and then some to me. That hadn't changed. It never would. When I'd first been brought into the clan, I had been terrified and had promptly hidden in a closet. It had been Zayne who'd coaxed me out, holding a no longer pristine teddy bear in his hands that I had dubbed Mr. Snotty. I'd been attached to his hip since then. Well, until Roth had come along, but Zayne had been my only ally—the only person who knew what I was, and… God, he'd been there for me, my rock these last couple of weeks.

"So…" Sam drew the word out as I sent Zayne a quick "ok" and dropped the phone back in my bag. "Did you know that when snakes are born with two heads, they fight each other for food?"

"What?" Stacey asked, brows furrowing together like two angry little lines.

He nodded, grinning a little. "Yep. Kind of like a death match...with yourself."

For some reason, a bit of stiffness went out of my posture when Stacey choked out a laugh and said, "Your capacity for useless knowledge never ceases to amaze me."

"It's why you love me."

Stacey blinked and heat infused her cheeks. She glanced over at me, like I was somehow supposed to help her with her recently discovered crush on Sam. I was the last person on the face of the earth to help when it came to the opposite sex.

I'd only kissed one boy in my entire life.

And he'd been a demon.

So...

She laughed loudly and brightly as she picked up her soda. "Whatever. I'm too cool for love."

"Actually..." Sam looked like he was about to explain some kind of random fact about love and temperatures when the pain in my head flared.

Sucking in a short breath, I pressed my palm above my eyes and squeezed them shut against the red-hot stabbing sensation. It was fierce and quick, over as soon as it started.

"Layla? Are you okay?" Sam asked.

I nodded slowly as I lowered my hand and opened my eyes. Sam stared back at me, but...

He cocked his head to the side. "You're looking a little pale."

Dizziness rose over me as I continued to stare at him. "You..."

"Me? Huh?" Frowning, he glanced at Stacey quickly. "I what?"

There was nothing surrounding Sam—not a single trace of robin's egg blue or the soft buttery yellow. My heart tripped as I twisted toward Stacey. The faint pink of her aura was also gone. That meant that either Sam or Stacey had—no, they had souls. I *knew* they did.

"Layla?" Stacey said softly, touching my arm.

I twisted around, scanning the packed cafeteria. Everyone

looked normal except there was no halo around any of them. No soft shade of color. My pulse picked up and I felt sweat dotting my brow. What was going on?

Searching out Eva Hasher, whose aura I was all too familiar with, I found her sitting a few tables back from ours, surrounded by what Stacey lovingly referred to as the "Bitch Pack." Beside her was Gareth, her on and off again boyfriend. He was leaning forward, arms folded on the table. Staring off at nothing, his eyes were red and glazed over. He liked to party, but I couldn't remember a time when I saw him high at school. There was nothing around him.

I shifted my gaze back to Eva. Normally there was a halo of purple surrounding the uber-hot brunette, meaning she'd been slipping into questionable soul status for quite some time. The need to taste her soul was always great.

But the space around her was also empty.

"Oh my God," I whispered.

Stacey's hand tightened on my arm. "What's going on?"

My gaze flitted back to her. Still no aura. And then to Sam. Nothing. I couldn't see a single soul.